THE NEW PENGUIN BOOK OF

Welsh Short Stories

EDITED BY ALUN RICHARDS

VIKING

VIKING

Published by the Penguin Group
Penguin Books Ltd, 27 Wrights Lane, London W8 5TZ, England
Penguin Books USA Inc., 375 Hudson Street, New York, New York 10014, USA
Penguin Books Australia Ltd, Ringwood, Victoria, Australia
Penguin Books Canada Ltd, 10 Alcorn Avenue, Toronto, Ontario, Canada M4V 3B2
Penguin Books (NZ) Ltd, 182–190 Wairau Road, Auckland 10, New Zealand

Penguin Books Ltd, Registered Offices: Harmondsworth, Middlesex, England

First published 1993
10 9 8 7 6 5 4 3 2 1
First edition

This collection copyright © Alun Richards
The Acknowledgements on pp. xiii–xv constitute an extension of this copyright page
The moral right of the authors has been asserted

Typeset by Datix International Limited, Bungay, Suffolk
Set in 11/13¼ pt Monophoto Sabon
Printed in England by Clays Ltd, St Ives plc

A CIP catalogue record for this book is available from the British Library

ISBN 0–670–84530–2

Contents

Introduction

Of all the remarks made about the short story, the one that most appeals to me was written in a letter to a friend by Robert Louis Stevenson. He had just completed *The Beach at Falesá*. 'You will know more about the South Seas after you have read my little tale than if you had read a library.'

His boast in a moment of triumph – I like to think he had barely laid down his pen after the last full stop – tells us everything about the nature of a short story since it implies, not just the distillation of an essence which is what many fine stories are, but also that a good deal has been left out, implying volumes we do not have to read, since here, encapsulated in perfect form, is all we need to know.

This, at any rate, is an ideal, although there are other criteria equally apt. What interests me most in a story is being in at the core of another life, seeing new light through the mind and world of central characters. It is not so much that a story must be exceptional enough to justify its telling, but at the end I must have had a crucial insight, or been awakened by another's discovery in the course of events which a writer's skill has revealed. It is essential that I am so involved at the outset that my attention does not wander, my sympathies are immediately engaged, and ultimately I must have the satisfaction of a completed statement. Now and again I can certainly do with a smile, but not without a revelation, and while it might not accord with my own perceptions, at least I have the satisfaction, sometimes the horror, of another's view. In either event, I have shared the experience.

These may seem obvious generalizations but stories are not written according to manuals of literary engineering, to be marked at the end of the day; consequently the stories which follow have been chosen in accord with these criteria where they can be met, and they are, in addition, of a place and time. The place is Wales, and the time is this century. They reflect Wales as it is, or has been, and collectively form part of the Welsh experience as it belongs to these writers. However, the success of the previous *Penguin Book of Welsh Short Stories* lies, I suspect, in the variety of stories as much as the badge of nationality. An anthology that bears the slightest taint of being a public relations exercise is rightfully cast aside. Perhaps the weaknesses of men and women matter to the writer as well as their virtues, be they real or imagined. There is another point. To identify the universal in the particular is the writer's primary task, and at the heart of a good story there is often a reminder that our presumed knowledge of each other is quite wrong. For this reason, and a sense of discovery, we continue to read stories. When we are entertained as well, we have a bargain.

Wales, it should be said, is a diverse and small country which can easily be crossed by car in any direction in the course of a day. It has two languages, every variety of scenery and, historically, it has been the victim of cyclical economic processes which have been accompanied by both emigration and immigration. Wales also contains areas so remote as to seem untouched by the present, and one or two places which appear almost indistinguishable from England. The collective experience of its writers reflects this diversity and in selecting the stories which follow, I have tried to represent all Welsh writers, including those whose work belies the idea of Wales as a homogeneous society. I have not sought to make any distinction between those who write in Welsh or English, although I have been mindful of an oral tradition in Welsh life implicit in a number of translated stories.

To the outsider, it should also be pointed out that several stories may seem to have no obvious Welsh connection, save that they are written by Welsh men or women, but I have included them since subject matter was not a barrier. Again, writers in the Welsh language when translated sometimes seem much the same as their English counterparts, unlike some of their contemporaries who, for a time, attempted to emphasize their difference by a forced use of language which led in some quarters to the false image of 'a Welsh short story' depending more on an artificially induced flavour than substance. I have tried to avoid these with the single exception of Caradoc Evans whose invented language may try the ear of the modern reader but who nevertheless deserves his place as the first Welsh writer in English to scorn the sentimental view of Wales. Like D. H. Lawrence, who once said to a young Rhys Davies, 'All you young writers have me to thank for the freedom you enjoy in your writing. I smashed the taboos for you,' Caradoc Evans was the first to assault what he saw as a closed and hypocritical section of society. I have broadened the selection to introduce new writers while retaining one story from the previous volume, since it best represents its author. I have also had in mind a balance between past and present, subject matter, and the varied backgrounds against which the stories are set, and have arranged them accordingly rather than in any chronological order.

Once again I am indebted to the Welsh Arts Council for their generosity in making funds available so that new translations could be considered, to the many translators, and to Professor Hywel Teifi Edwards of Swansea University for his advice and help in making available stories in the Welsh language.

Alun Richards

Acknowledgements

Thanks are due to the copyright holders of the following stories for permission to reprint them in this volume:

Dannie Abse: to Sheil Land Associates for 'Sorry, Miss Crouch' from *There was a Young Man from Cardiff* (Hutchinson, 1991)

Glenda Beagan: to the author and Seren Books for 'The Last Thrush' from *The Medlar Tree* (Seren Books, 1992)

Ron Berry: to the author for 'November Kill' (originally published in *The New Welsh Review*)

Duncan Bush: to Curtis Brown and John Farquharson Ltd for 'Hopkins'

B. L. Coombes: to Mr Vivian Davies for 'Twenty Tons of Coal' (originally published in *Penguin New Writing*)

Rhys Davies: to Mr Lewis Davies for 'Blodwen' from *The Collected Stories* (Heinemann, 1955)

Jane Edwards: to the author for 'Waiting for the Rain to Break' (first published in *Blind Dêt*, 1989)

Islwyn Ffowc Elis: to the author for 'Self-pity' (first published in Welsh as 'Hunandosturi' in *Marwydos*, Gwasg Gomer, 1974)

Caradoc Evans: to Seran Books for 'A Father in Sion' (first published in *My People*, 1915; reprinted 1985)

Emyr Humphreys: to Richard Scott Simon Ltd for 'The Suspect' from *Natives* (Secker & Warburg, 1968)

Glyn Jones: to Laurence Pollinger Ltd for 'Wat Pantathro' from *The Water Music* (Routledge, 1944)

Gwyn Jones: to the author for 'A White Birthday' from *The Still Waters* (Peter Davies, 1948)

Harri Pritchard Jones: to the author for 'Fool's Paradise' (first published in *Corner People*, in both Welsh and English, by Gwasg Gomer, 1991)

Alun Lewis: to Harper Collins Publishers for 'The Orange Grove' from *In the Green Tree* (George Allen & Unwin, 1948)

Alun T. Lewis: to Gwasg Gomer for 'Relatives' (first published by Hughes & Son, 1932; reprinted in *Y Dull Deg*, Gwasg Gomer, 1973)

Catherine Merriman: to the author for 'Barbecue' (originally published in *The New Welsh Review*)

Clare Morgan: to the author for 'Losing' (first published in *Planet*)

Leslie Norris: to the author for 'A House Divided' from *Sliding* (Dent, 1978)

Alun Richards: to Aitken & Stone Ltd for 'The Former Miss Merthyr Tydfil' from *The Former Miss Merthyr Tydfil and Other Stories* (Michael Joseph, 1976)

Eigra Lewis Roberts: to the author for 'Do You Remember Jamie?'

Kate Roberts: to Temple University Press for 'The Condemned' from *The World of Kate Roberts*, translated by Joseph Clancy (1991)

Dylan Thomas: to David Higham Associates Ltd for 'A Story' from *A Prospect of the Sea* (Dent)

Gwyn Thomas: to Felix de Wolfe for 'Oscar' (first published by Progress Publishing Co., 1946; reprinted by Hutchinson, 1972)

Dic Tryfan: to Hughes & Son for 'Good for Nothing' from *Tair Stori Fer* (1915)

D. J. Williams: to Gwasg Gomer for 'The Mecca of the Nation' from *Storiau'r Tir*, translated by R. Gerallt Jones (1949)

Raymond Williams: to Merryn Williams for 'A Fine Room to be Ill In' (first published in *English Story* (8th Series), edited by Woodrow Wyatt, 1948)

Penny Windsor: to the author for 'Jennifer's Baby' originally broadcast by BBC Radio 4

Every effort has been made to contact all the copyright holders. The publishers will be glad to make good any errors or inaccuracies in future editions.

GERAINT GOODWIN

The White Farm

He walked on to the little veranda and sniffed the morning breeze. It had become a rite now – on these days of holiday – the clear air off the sea, off the mountains, always seemed better in the early morning. But this morning it really was good, he thought. Inland, there was the clear-cut freshness of the mountainside, the fields all marked out and clear in their colours, and just a circle of mist, like a frill of steam, around the summits.

He took two or three deep breaths and heaved audibly. He was a big man, with a heavy aggressive jaw, his face very brown, and his brow, which reached up through the thin hair, blistered with sun and the salt water. His eyes were blue and sure and faintly contemptuous, and his hands large and clumsy.

He stood there on the little veranda, leaning against the door and watching his wife, very small and trim, shaking her dark hair back as she busied herself with the oil cooker, a white apron about her, and the little waist tied with a large bow. The small delicate movements of her, the large anxious eyes for ever fearful, always moved him.

He went over to her and put his big hands on her shoulders.

'What about today?' he said briefly.

She did not look up at him: instead, she slipped free and went on with the cooking. They were up late and she was not quite herself.

'Where?' she asked over her shoulder.

'Pant what-you-call-it,' he said, peeved. '*You* know.'

'If you like,' she said in the same matter-of-fact tone.

'If *you* like,' he went on. His heavy face went childish in his sulk. But he was going to humour her. He felt that he owed her something.

'But you've got the game!' she said, turning to him.

'That can wait,' he replied in the same peremptory way. 'They're nobody, anyhow,' he explained.

'But you promised,' she insisted.

'Did I? I said that I *might* make up a foursome.'

'Oh,' she said. 'That's different.'

'After all,' he went on magnanimously, 'I've got a wife.'

She did not answer, but turned to the stove again with a little shrug.

'It's not much fun for you . . . I know,' he said. He caught her by the shoulders again. 'My pretty one!'

She bowed her head on her breasts like a drooping bird. He felt uncomfortable, the words muddling him.

'My little one,' he said again in the same tentative way. He squeezed her shoulders until she winced.

'Oh, leave me alone!' she cried out.

He went out on the veranda again. Perhaps, after all, it was his fault. But then, he told himself, they were on holiday, and after all a man was a man. But he was worried all the same. And yet things could be different. If only he had a square deal. That was the phrase always on his lips – a square deal. He wanted to know where he was – and where the other person was. Then they could get down to things. That had been the secret of his success – and he had been successful. He was hard, as he said, but always fair. Up North, he would explain, they were made like that.

But had he had a square deal, now, in the ever-present, from his wife? He wondered – he had begun to wonder more and more. He did not like to think that he had not – but he wondered. And now, at the end of a year of marriage, they were farther apart than at the beginning. They were not drifting apart so much as they *were* apart. And was it his fault? It was not that they had ever been together – her little world was like herself, so small and tender and wisp-like: for ever proof against his loud and obvious heartiness. It was like hammering on a closed door and blustering on the step: and there, beyond, was the quiet and the mystery.

And yet she loved him – there was no doubt about that. He had swept her off her feet and she had never found them again: the heavy aggressive sense of him, the I-am-what-I-am triumphant had, at first, bewildered and then captivated her. He was not sure how it had all come about, but he guessed it. And he continued to play his trump card – his only card – in the hope that things would right themselves. But it was up to him to give the lead – he felt it would always be up to him to give the lead.

'Feeling better?' he said, when he went in. He gathered her in his arms but she turned her head away. Then he lifted up her chin. He knew how to humour her in his clumsy way.

'We'll be off in no time,' he said unctuously.

He went out into the sand-swept garden, with its line of sea thistles tossing, and tore the tarpaulin off the big saloon car. Then he began to tinker about with the engine, and then went round with a duster like an old maid dusting.

Within an hour they had started. He knew that it had to be done sometime – this journey to her father's people up in the mountains. The Welsh were funny people – they got something out of it, this journey to the old folks at home, even if the home were a hovel. And as they all had a home somewhere, they would all have to go back to it. Well – if it amused them! But the old man – he was a wealthy London-Welsh draper – was more Welsh than she was, and he seemed to care very little, for he spent his time at the bowling tournament at Eastbourne. A funny lot!

They had climbed beyond the little village but stopped once on the road to look back on it. In the summer sun it had come alight – just like a lot of broken china cups thrown on the shingle, and beyond it the blue fringe of sea running off into a haze. But that was the old village, with its one straight street and its white houses. Joined on it, like a fungus on an old bole, was the new part, with its modern red-tiled bungalows with their cream stucco sides. Beyond again was the golf links which reached right down to the sand-hills, blown up in a bulwark against the tides, the clumps of rushes white in the sun like scrubbed hair. The moist sour-green earth spread down to the *morfa* (the marsh) which lay inland. The land was all green, with the light burnt crust of sand as a ridge, and the washed smudge of sea and sky stretching into the distance – the whole stretch of Cardigan Bay cupped within its two arms, far in the south, far in the north.

'There they go,' he said, tracing his finger through the window.

She had sat huddled in the front seat, her mind gone off.

'That's them,' he said again, breaking into the quiet. 'That's old Wilkie – over there on the fifth tee. There now – he's driving.'

He looked at his wife sideways, the little core of resentment in him hardening.

'You're not going to get all het up again?' he asked.

'Why – of course not.'

'I said, that's old Wilkie.'

'Well! I saw.'

'That's about all,' he said, slipping into gear. It was not worth troubling about. But his friends were her friends.

'A bit bleak,' he said, after a while. They had left the main road and the lane went off over the gently swelling mountain, two parallel ruts sluiced with storm water which lay around in pools. Sometimes the track was half cluttered up with shale, sometimes the surface was worn through to the bare rock. Around about, the mountains rolled up in a gentle sweep with the mist lifting above them. Now and again there was a house, with the few wind-blown firs about it as a shelter, its white, wet sides shining in the sun, and the bare yard with a white-eyed dog skulking, and the waddling geese.

'Oh, John,' she begged. 'Do stop.'

He braked hard, with a faint smile of amusement at her urgency. He liked doing this for her. She got out of the car and ran off through the wet heather and stood up on a mound, her breast heaving.

'Better now,' she said, as she took her place. Her eyes were alight and dancing, and her lips wide open. He felt the load come off him. She excited him in the old way, so light and fresh in her young beauty, the poise and delight of her and the light in her face. She was something to be desired, as he first desired her – would always desire her. The rest was not there – had not happened.

He put his arm round her shoulder and crushed her to him.

'Not now,' she said, slipping free.

'Right,' he said, his mind reaching out at an infinite promise. 'A bargain!'

They had come to the brow of the last hill. Below them the road dropped into a *cwm*. A torrent tumbled over the mountain into it, swilling through the heather, leaping down into a spume of silver. And there, below them, was the house, standing out of the earth, with its upblown smoke curling up to them, and the pandemonium of barking dogs and the geese shrieking. It had all suddenly come to life.

A man was on the little trellis bridge, shouting. The dogs running up and down the track cowered down on their bellies and crawled back to him.

'*Uffern dân! Hei! Siân, Meg . . .*' he shouted.

'That's uncle,' she said, the words strung in her excitement. 'He won't know me: he won't know me. Now for fun!'

The old man came up to the car as it stopped. He had a round, full face, red with the weather, a grey fringe to it. It seemed hewn out in its angularity, and yet there was a light in it – a hardly distinguishable, distant gleam. And yet that was the face. The eyes were very blue and steadfast, and there seemed no end to them in their distance. He seemed always to be calling himself back as he spoke.

'The dogs will be barking,' he explained. 'Do not you mind them.'

He picked his words with great deliberation. But they were not sure whether he had seen them – his gently roving eyes had gone off again into the distance.

'*Dewch yma Siân!*' he shouted in a sudden roar. An old black sheepdog in the pack had gone slinking up for a furtive snap. Now she dropped on her paws and rolled her eyes up, her old head shaking in ecstasy. '*Beth sydd arno chi fach?*' he went on, sounding his voice as the old head rocked.

'She just come,' he went on. 'Her mister *wedi marw* – die, how you say? No teeth . . . see?' He opened her jaws.

'She obeys you?' said the husband.

'Oh, yess,' he explained. 'You know how? I tell you. You get a bit of cheese, see, and put it under your arm. Then after long time you give it her. Never go after! A bitch, see – a bitch like that.'

'Wants a master,' said the husband, helping him out.

'Oh – I won't say.' He put up his hands with mock horror. The laughter filled his face like a brimming jug.

'Don't tell lies,' the woman said in Welsh, laughing outright.

The old man never moved, but he turned his eyes on her, as though bringing them out of the distance.

'*Cymraes?*' (A little Welsh girl?) he said in the same even voice.

'A Japanese *really*!'

'Tut, tut!'

The young man stood and watched his wife in wonder. The tilted face, impenitent, and the laughing eyes. She went bubbling on like a spring. The two went on in their cross-talk, the old man, out of deference to him, still labouring in English.

'I'll be going,' he said. He got out his rod and flung his basket over his shoulders. 'I'll follow the brook up,' he added in parting. 'Don't worry.'

The old man watched him go, his face hardening. It was not polite. And yet his going had eased it as between them. It was as if a shadow had lifted.

'Softie! *Yr hen softie!* I'm Dilys,' she said.

'Dilys! Wili's Dilys?'

She burst out laughing.

'You are a funny one.' He caught her by the arm and led her in.

'Well, well.' He said no more, his face beaming.

Beside the old hearth he said casually: 'Take your seat.' She belonged. The hard-reached deference had gone out of his voice. He gave the peat fire a stir with the poker and moved the kettle across the spit.

'Well, well,' he said again. He spoke in Welsh now, his voice dropping to the homely familiar note.

'*Mam*,' he called. '*Mam*.'

The old woman came in, her thin spindle body bent across, an old shawl over her shoulders. Her eyes were very quick and bright in the old worn face – only her eyes, thin and bright, for ever hovering.

'Here she is,' he said.

The old woman shuffled across and peered at her. '*Fach*,' she said, putting her arms around her. 'Oh, the little dear.'

She reached her feet into the fender and leaned back into the old horsehair chair. The worn old house possessed her – the brass harness round about, the old dresser with its line on line of blue china plates, the rich earth smell of the peat. That fire had never been out for two hundred years, her father had always told her. And here it was! And all around, through the little tight shut windows, was the moist green of the mountain, reaching up like a shelf, and the distant rumble of the brook.

Pant-y-Pistyll – 'the Hollow of the Spring?' Always the drifting mist, for ever lifting, and the noise of the water, the sharp high tinkle to the deep, harsh earth-flooded roar of the winter: the green earth, the smell of peat and the high blue crust of the mountain – that was her home, her father's home, and that was where she belonged. She let it all possess her, gave herself up to it, as to a lover. She had gone away from herself, far, far away. Now she was – only now she was: never before, perhaps never again, but now she was.

'Oh, *Nain*' (grandmother), she said. She threw her arms around the old woman and bent her head in the old shawl.

'There, there,' said the old woman, brushing back her hair with her old withered hands. She pressed her to her old breasts and crooned to her as to a child, taking the deep, breaking sobs to herself.

'The old *hiraeth*' (longing), she said to her son, standing beside them. The old mother waved him away. He went out into the yard.

When she came out again, her eyes red and fresh, he was standing there, just as she had first seen him. Beyond him, across the brook, was the little chapel, small and grey and silent, and around it was the little wall of piled stones, lurching up against the weather, a tiny yellow sprinkle of stonecrop spilt across it. Tied on the gate was a little tin offertory box that rattled in the wind. Beyond, the grey stone slabs stood up on end among the lank grass. That and the farm were the only buildings for miles: beyond the land ran off into the mountain.

'It's time your father came back,' he said.

She bowed her head.

'Never mind,' he said gaily. 'Plenty of time. You tell him we are still here.'

They had walked beyond the little graveyard to the lush hayfield. At the bottom was the river running down the valley in a brown fresh: the little brook leapt to meet it.

'Where is Morlais?' she asked.

He pointed over the sheep-walk on the mountain. 'He can't go far now.' He pointed to his hip. 'A horse kick him. Pity – ay, indeed. A strong chap too.'

He shook his head, destroying the memory of his son's hurt.

'You were only little things – last time,' he said. 'Hair down your back.'

'Fifteen years,' she said.

'Sure to be.' He looked into the distance and nodded.

'You made a house to play,' he said, 'out of the old wall.

'Down there,' he went on, pointing.

She followed his finger. The old stones were still trailed about the field.

'Awful mess that house,' he said, wagging his head. 'So *serious*, you two.'

'Fun!' she said savagely. She could not see through the cloud of tears. She twisted and untwisted her glove and turned her head away.

'You'll be waiting for Morlais?' he asked.

'No!' she cried out.

'Pity. He'll be that sorry.'

'We must get back,' she said, a note of terror in her voice. She ran into the field in her anguish, the wet grass to her waist. The old man followed her.

'Take time: take time,' he called gently. 'No *great* hurry.'

He went on up the river calling, leaving her alone. She stood there beside the water. Years ago she and Morlais had gone off to look for its source. They never found it: they never would find it. It had no beginning as it had no end. She remembered and yet she could not remember. It was so long ago.

The water went by in a fresh, lightless and gleaming, and then beyond her through the gorge which led out to the sea; it went by her, strangely dark and gleaming, with the tufts of foam swilling down its centre in a long white line. And all above it were the hills, heavy and brooding, the little sheep clamped on to them, bleating forlornly, and the sky with no light to it. The ancient heavy sense of it possessed her again, the timeless glimpse of it. She stood there in the wonder of it, unmoving.

'Gone to sleep?' It was her husband behind her. She had not heard them return.

'Isn't she a funny one?' he said to her uncle, in a way of explanation. He was hot and excited with his sport by the brookside.

'You *must* go?' asked her uncle, dropping his eyes to her, strangely still and steady.

'I must,' she said.

'Yes,' he said. 'Perhaps so. Tell your dad. Plenty of time . . .' He waved his hand upwards. He nodded in the old ancient way of his.

As they roared up the hill from the house, she saw him standing there, his dogs about him, his wide open face lifted.

KATE ROBERTS

The Condemned

(TRANSLATED BY JOSEPH P. CLANCY)

He had asked the doctor, and by now he was sorry. He didn't
know what had made him ask and insist on knowing. It wasn't
courage, certainly, because he loved life and feared dying. He was
afraid of the nothingness of dying. When the doctor said he could
leave the hospital ten days after coming there, through some
perverse instinct, because he was afraid of knowing the worst,
Dafydd Parri pressed him to know why. When he heard that his
case was hopeless, that the growth inside him had become too
bad – if only the doctor could have caught it two years earlier –
an empty feeling crept down his body from head to foot. When
he came to his senses, he regretted that he hadn't died in that
feeling.

   The first longing that came to him afterwards was to go home
to Laura. The surprise was that he could think at all. How was
he able to breathe? How was he able to walk or anything after
hearing such news? How could he sleep that night? And yet, he
slept. His journey home the next day was worse than a nightmare;
it was closer to madness. How different from the journey to
Liverpool ten days before! He'd had hope then, despite being
afraid. There was one element of pleasure in his journey back. It
was towards home he was going, and not away from home. It
was the craving to reach home that drove him almost mad when
the train would wait for a long time at a station. He supposed his
brain was muddled, but he'd be all right again after he got home
to Laura. Yes, he'd almost say that everything would be as before,

that he himself would be exactly the same, without the knowledge he'd had from the doctor. That was entirely the feeling he'd had when he heard the news, of something filling him and smothering him. He'd feel free, fine, after he reached home, and had the same hope he'd had before, with the visit to Liverpool and the doctor's verdict nothing but a dream.

In the meantime, Laura had been seeing their own doctor. He'd had the verdict of the doctor from Liverpool, and to show Laura his cleverness, he told her straight out that her husband would not recover, and that the specialist's opinion was completely the same as his own. The news had a different effect on Laura than on her husband. She became stubborn, and she was infuriated, and she told herself there was very little doctors could do, and once she had Dafydd in her hands *she* would make him better.

When she saw Dafydd, she was not as certain. She supposed that the doctor could be right. But that feeling soon went away. By the next morning, either Dafydd looked a little better to her, or his wife was deluded into thinking that that was how he was before going away. She still had, in any case, the belief that doctors are fallible beings, and that turned into hope for herself, the only thing that kept her going on as before and accepting life in its uncertainty.

Dafydd came home like a guilty man coming from prison. He didn't want to see anyone, and he didn't want anyone to see him. The kitchen of Bron Eithin was looking as it sometimes did on Sunday, or on the day of someone's funeral, when strangers were expected to tea, the best dishes on the table, and a Sabbath tidiness on everything, though it was Wednesday; and Laura in her best blouse and her white apron as if she were serving at the head of the table at Monthly Meeting. It wasn't to a Wednesday night Bron Eithin Dafydd Parri came, but to a strange Bron Eithin.

Next morning, it was the sound of his two sons talking quietly to their mother as they ate their breakfast that woke him. He couldn't define his feelings. This was something very unnatural, because he would be closer to the quarry than to his house at the time his boys were eating their breakfast. Still it was nice to be at home and wake up at leisure, rather than be in hospital, where a person was awakened suddenly from a nice sleep at half-past five. After the boys set off, and the scurrying sound of the last laggards among the quarrymen died out on the road, Laura poked her head in at the bedroom door.

'Are you awake?' she said. 'I was here before, but you were sleeping then. Did you sleep pretty well?'

'Yes, quite well,' he said, and glad to be able to say that to Laura and not to the nurse.

'I'll bring you a cup of tea now,' she said cheerfully; and in no time she was back with a cup of tea and a slice of toast on a tray. She stayed there while he ate.

'Does it taste all right?' she said.

'It's very good,' he said, looking out through the window to the field. And he greatly enjoyed his breakfast.

This first day after coming home, he felt all day long that nothing special had happened, and that he was home as on Sunday, but that everybody else was working. He was glad to be at home with Laura, instead of being in the confinement of the hospital. This day, he was like a prisoner the first day after coming out of prison, glad of his freedom, and unable to look into the future because of the joy of being free. The doctor in Liverpool and his verdict were far off and insubstantial things. Everything was fine now that he'd come to Bron Eithin and to Laura.

But after a day or two Dafydd Parri returned to being himself, the Dafydd Parri he was when he'd work every day at the quarry, before leaving it for the hospital, and he began to fidget, if a sick man's discontent could be called fidgeting. Before going to Liverpool he'd felt fairly strong in spite of having pains. He was weaker by now, and his discontent was more yearning than fidgeting.

It was hard on him to be forced to stay in bed, and listen to his friends going to the quarry. He'd hear them climbing the hillside past the gable-end of his house, with their slow, heavy gait, and the low sounds of early morning. He'd hear them again at nightfall with their quick, steady pace and their loud, cheerful voices. On quarry days, the discussion would often be unfinished when he'd turn in at his gate from his fellow workers, but it was a hard thing to find yourself left out of the discussion altogether. He was longing for a chat with the lads in the hut at dinner time. Jac Bach talking about his dogs, and Dafydd Bengwar about his canaries. Dafydd found it most entertaining to hear Wil Elis, who dealt in cattle a bit, telling stories, half of which you could venture to say were lies. But no matter, some people's lies were more interesting than other people's truth. And it was at the quarry he'd get all the news, true and false, about people. One could get more 'tales' about the people in the quarry than in the house.

Now Dafydd Parri had to spend his time in the house and not the quarry. His world became narrow and new. A house to him before was a house after finishing a day's work, a house warm with the events of the day. He knew it only, except on Saturday afternoon and Sunday, as a place you returned to after a day of work to sit down and eat in and read a newspaper by the fire. And that sort of house was different from the house he must get to know now – a house going through the different states a house goes through from five in the morning till ten at night.

He would most often wake in the morning with a bad taste in his mouth. He'd hear Laura blowing the fire, and as usual in the morning, the gasps of the bellows, long and deep. He'd smell the scent of the heather faggot that was used to light the fire, and he could imagine the soft white smoke going thickly up through the chimney. Presently, he'd hear Laura moving the kettle, and he'd hear it begin singing shortly after, and she'd bring him a cup of tea and a piece of bread and butter. She'd move back the window curtains, and then she'd be on the go early. She'd leave the bedroom door open, and he could hear the boys talking as they ate their breakfast. He could see a little of the kitchen too, and as he looked at it over the bedside it looked unnatural, as if he were seeing it in a mirror. Around nine, after finishing with the cows and the pigs, Laura would bring him a little Scotch broth, and she'd have time to sit down and relax with him then. He'd get up a little before dinner, and the hearthstone would be just washed, and the edge of the slate could be seen drying in streaks. Laura took care to have a comfortable hearth for him every day by the time he got up.

Dafydd would wash himself deliberately and carefully on getting up. He had a habit of rubbing the towel between his fingers, and he noticed that his hands became cleaner day by day, and that the seam of grey from the quarry dust was disappearing from between his fingers.

Some days Laura would be busy baking when he got up, and he liked to see the bread rising for the second time in the iron pans by the oven bakehole, and the firelight as it came from the hole striking the dough and making a semicircle of light on it, with a few hot cinders sometimes falling on it and giving it savour.

The atmosphere would change by the afternoon. The whole house would be clean, and more activity could be felt in the air. The tranquillity of the morning was gone, and though the tranquillity of the country was there, yet one could sense more sound even there in the afternoon. Laura would beg him to go for a walk around the fields or along the road. He never wanted to go.

'Go, it'll do you good,' Laura said, and she believed it.

And he'd go, little by little, after throwing an old coat around his neck, as he'd sometimes done on coming from the quarry, and fastening it with a sack-pin. Laura would look after him, and see one of his shoulders rising higher than the other because of the coat, and she'd go into the house sighing. He didn't have much pleasure in going for a walk. He'd sit on a pile of stones in the corner of a field under a thorn to shelter from the thin breeze of April, and he'd let the sun fall on his face. On the other side of the dyke he'd hear the cow grazing, by turns munching the hay and snorting, and the smell of its wet nostrils would come through the dyke.

Different corners of fields gave him different feelings. They always had. Without any particular reason some fields made him melancholy, and others cheered him up. He didn't know why. Indeed, there was no reason why, only his state of mind, but that state was always just the same in the same field. He avoided those fields now. The earth was hard and colourless. Stones mixed with lumps of dry dung all over it. Someone would have to gather up the stones, but not him. Though it was such a disagreeable task, he'd have been happy to be able to do it this year. He'd never go to the road for a walk if he could help it. There were people there, and people ask questions that a sick man doesn't want to answer.

In the house with Laura, that's where he liked to be. After a while the house and Laura became an essential part of him, as the quarry was before. He gave up asking his sons how things went at the quarry. When his friends would come there to visit him, mentioning the quarry gave him too much pain at the beginning. But gradually his interest in it lessened, and he stopped asking. He became used to being home.

He began thinking more about Laura. He wondered, did she know the doctor's verdict? He didn't want to ask her, for fear that by some sign she'd betray the fact that she knew. Hearing the verdict for the second time, and in his own home, would have been too much for him. He'd be forced to go through the same feelings as he'd gone through the first time he heard, and he was too cowardly for that. He didn't have any feeling at all about the doctor's verdict by now. The disturbance of that moment had worn off, and he didn't feel sick enough at this time to relive that moment or to think about his end. There was pleasure in life as it was now. Having a cup of tea with Laura around three o'clock, and on baking day a dough cake with currants in it, hot. The doctor had said that he could eat anything.

He wondered, how much did Laura know? She looked as if she didn't know a thing. She went about her work cheerfully, as usual, and she talked to him about things on the farm and things in the district. Sometimes he'd catch her looking at his face and at his eyes in the light, as if she were examining his colour. Laura became closer to him and came to mean more to him than she had since their courting days. She was a pretty little lass, then, with her curly auburn hair, and indeed, she carried her age very well now, though she was fifty-five, the same age as himself. He remembered the time he first saw her, the day of May Fair, when she was changing her situation, and when he was in town with his father selling a cow. He remembered how he made a fool of himself over her till she promised to marry him. He'd go to see her every chance he'd get, and he'd see her before his eyes everywhere all day long. After they were married, the small-holding and putting their lives in order had taken up their time altogether, and as is often customary with country people, they supposed there was no need to show love after marrying. Live was what people did after marrying, not love. She, and he too, would sometimes quarrel, and since they weren't passionate people they'd become friends again in a calm unruffled way, by talking about the pigs or the cows, and there'd be no going back to the cause of their quarrel. There'd never be the place or the time, somehow, to talk affectionately. There was work in the fields after coming from the quarry in spring and summer, and there were endless meetings in chapel in winter, and there was no time for anything but to read a newspaper.

Now, Dafydd was sorry that he hadn't given more time to talking with Laura. How much better it would have been by now; that tenderness would have stayed with her after he'd gone, something to be remembered. In looking back at their life, what had they had? Only a cold unruffled life, reaching the highpoint of pleasure when the end of the month was pretty good. They didn't come closer together when the wages were small. Indeed, a poor month would make them silent and indifferent. He wanted to set the past right now. He wanted to enjoy life at home like this with Laura, to go for a spin around Anglesey by car, the two of them. They'd never got about much after marrying. Always waiting for a better time, and letting life go by without seeing the world. Yes, it was nice in the house with Laura. He loved to look at her; he knew now, what he hadn't known before, how many buttons were on her bodice, what the pattern of her homespun kerchief was, the number of pleats in her apron. A pity it couldn't be like this for ever. But he just began to realize this, when his pains began to increase. He couldn't enjoy his food as much; there wasn't as much pleasure in looking at the bread rising by the fire, or in smelling its aroma as it baked. When he was on the brink of losing something, he'd begun to enjoy it. He saw the Indian Summer of his illness slipping away from him. He was unable to get up for dinner, and a longing for the hearthstone came on him. He'd get up sometimes at nightfall so that he could sleep better. The pains increased. He couldn't take notice of things around him. The doctor came there more often, and gave him medicines to ease his pains. He'd go to sleep, and he'd be sick and depressed after waking up. He'd go into a trance sometimes. He'd forget things around him. What did he care about the doctor from Liverpool by now? It was his sickness was important, not the doctor's verdict. The verdict had nothing to do with his sickness. He had enough to do to think about his sickness without thinking about what the doctor had told him in the hospital. What he wanted was to be rid of a little bit of the pains so he could talk to Laura. She was by his bed every chance she had. Sometimes he'd have a better day, and he'd get up in the afternoon, but he didn't enjoy his tea. But in a little while he became so that he couldn't get up at all, and Laura would leave him only when he slept.

And on that hay harvest day in July he was very ill. Outside, neighbours were carrying his hay, with him too ill to take any interest in that. He didn't care this year whether he had a big rick or a small rick, whether the hay was good or poor. He was conscious of the coming and going of people back and forth to the house to have food. He was more awake than usual, and he had more need of Laura. She was there as often as she could be, continually running back and forth from the dinner-table to the bed. He wanted to speak to her, wanted to talk about their courting days, when they'd go for a walk along the White Road, and see lapwings' nests in the crannies of the mountain. He wanted to talk about the time he first saw her at the fair, when she was so downhearted about changing her place. How happy those days had been when they could hug each other tightly in returning from the Literary Meeting of the Graig! What a good time they'd had in returning from Preaching Meeting, when he'd been on fire from wanting the preacher to finish, and found himself looking more often at Laura than at the preacher! He wanted to tell her all those things. Why hadn't he told them to her those afternoons when they'd have tea together? Why was his shyness lessening as his body weakened? The next time that Laura came to the bedroom he'd insist on telling her.

When she came, the last meal was over, and there was tranquillity in the house. They couldn't hear any of the noise in the rickyard behind the house. The smell of hay was coming into the bedroom through the window. There was the smell of sickness on the bed, and an unpleasant taste in Dafydd's mouth. He was lying back, with pillows behind him. Laura came in.

'Will you have a little bit of something to eat?' she said. 'Everybody's cleared out of the house now.'

'No,' he said, 'I can't eat now.' And he added, 'I'm getting weak, you see.'

But after saying that, he observed Laura, and he saw the trace of much crying on her tired face. He looked at her.

'Laura,' he said, 'what is it?'

'Nothing,' she said, turning her face aside.

He took hold of her, and he turned her towards him, and in her look he saw the knowledge the doctor had given him. He couldn't put a sentence together. He couldn't remember what he wanted to tell her, but he held her, and he hugged her to him and she felt his hot tears running down her cheek.

Blodwen

'Pugh Jibbons is at the back door,' cried Blodwen's mother from upstairs. 'Go and get four pounds of peas.'

A sulky look came to Blodwen's face for a moment. She hated going out to Pugh Jibbons to buy vegetables, she couldn't bear his insolent looks. Nevertheless, after glancing in the kitchen mirror, she walked down the little back garden and opened the door that led into the waste land behind the row of houses.

A small cart, with a donkey in the shafts, stood there piled high with vegetables. Pugh Jibbons – the son of old Pugh Jibbons, so called because he always declared that jibbons (that being the local name for spring onions) cured every common ailment in man – leaned against the cart waiting for her. This was almost a daily occurrence.

He did not greet her. He looked at her steadily, as she stood under the lintel of the door, a slight flush in her cheeks, and ordered, in a harsh voice of contempt:

'Four pounds of peas!'

Pugh Jibbons grinned. He was a funny-looking fellow. A funny fellow. Perhaps there was a gipsy strain in him. He was of the Welsh who have not submitted to industrialism, Nonconformity or imitation of the English. He looked as though he had issued from a cave in the mountains. He was swarthy and thickset, with rounded, powerful limbs and strong dark tufts of hair everywhere. Winter and summer he bathed in the river and lived in a tiny house away up on the mountainside, near to the lower slope where his allotment of vegetables was. His father, with whom he lived, was now old and vague and useless; the jibbons had not kept him his senses; and his mother was dead. They had always lived a semi-wild life on the mountainside, earning a bit of money selling their vegetables, which were good and healthy, in the Valley below.

'Fourpence a pound they are today,' he informed Blodwen. And all his browny-red face went on grinning. He looked right down into her eyes. His were dark and clear and mocking, hers were dark blue and inflamed with anger.

She shrugged her shoulders, though she was indignant at the doubling of the price since yesterday.

'Coming to an end they are now,' he said, weighing the peas, but keeping his eye on her, which he winked whenever her disdainful glance came round to him. But she would look into the distance beyond him.

There was usually a box of flowers on the cart. Today there were bunches of pinks in it. He took one out. She held out her apron for the peas and he shovelled them into it, placing the bunch of pinks on the top.

'But I'll chuck those in for the price,' he said.

Though nearly always he would thrust a bunch of flowers on her. Usually she took them. But today she didn't want to. She wanted to tell him something. She said:

'Take those flowers back.' Her colour came up, she arched her beautiful thick neck, her eyes blazed out on him. 'And if you keep on following me about the streets at night I'll set the police on you, I warn you. Where's your decency, man?' And then she wanted to slam the door in his face and hurry away. But she waited, looking at him menacingly.

His mouth remained open for a moment or two after her outburst, comically, his eyes looking at her with startled examination. Then he pushed his cap to the back of his head, thrust out his head aggressively, and demanded:

'Is that bloke that goes about with you your fellow, then?'

Her disdainful face lifted, she rapped out, 'Something unpleasant to say to you that fellow will have if you don't watch out,
you rude lout.'

Then he became mocking and teasing again, his eyes sharp
with wickedness. 'He's not a bloke for you, well you know that,'
he said daringly. 'Toff as he is and tall and elegant, he's not a
bloke for you. I know him and I know the family out of what he
comes. There's no guts to any of his lot. Haw-haw and behave
politely and freeze yourself all up. There's no juice and no seed
and no marrow and no bones to him. Oswald Vaughan! Haw-
haw.' And screwing up his face to a caricature of a toff's expression, he stood before her undismayed and mocking, his short
thick legs apart and almost bandy.

'You . . .' she muttered, raging, '. . . You wait. You'll be sorry
for this.' She slammed the door and hurried to the kitchen.

The unspeakable ruffian! What right had he to talk of Oswald
like that. And 'He's not a bloke for you, well you know that!'
Impudence. Pugh Jibbons, someone they bought vegetables from!
Why, however had it happened? To have a ruffian of a stranger
talk of her affairs like that.

She threw the peas out of her apron on to the table. The bunch
of pinks was among them. She trembled with anger. She had
intended throwing them back at him. She ought never to have
accepted flowers in her hands or sticking them among the
vegetables. Never again. She'd throw his flowers back at him.
These pinks she had a good mind to put in the fire.

But they smelled so sweet and they were so delicate, she
couldn't throw them away. She lifted her arm for a vase. Her
shape was splendid. She was a fine, handsome young woman of
twenty-five, all her body graceful and well-jointed, with fine
movements, unconsciously proud and vehement. Her face, when
she was silent and alone, was often sullen. But always it had a
glow. She was a virgin. Her sister was married, her father was
checkweight man in the colliery, her mother was always urging
her to wed.

Oswald Vaughan, the son of the local solicitor, had been courting her for some months now. He was in his father's office. His
family was one of the most respected in the place, big chapel
people. Mrs Vaughan had been put away in an asylum at one
time. Even now there was a strange dead look about her. But
Oswald was quite normal, he was all right and all there. He was
the smartest man in the Valley, with his London clothes and little
knick-knacks. Both father and son read big books, and indeed
they were very clever, in their minds. Very brainy.

Oswald courted Blodwen with great devotion. He came to her
as though to a meal. He himself said he was hungry for women.
He would sit with her in the parlour of her home and hold her
hands tightly or hug her shoulders with a lingering pressure. He
respected her and, believing her to be intelligent, he brought
books on verse and read her Wordsworth and Tennyson, especially the latter's *In Memoriam*, of which he had a profound
admiration. When he left her he was refreshed and walked home
in an ecstasy. Blodwen would go to the kitchen for supper and,
oddly enough, something would be sure to irritate her, always,
either something wrong with the food or she took offence at some
observation of her mother or father. She was a difficult girl,
really.

Her anger against Pugh Jibbons persisted as she went about
the duties of the day, fuming continually not only in her mind
but in her blood. If there had been a stick near as he had mocked
at her that morning she would have laid it about him. It was the
only way to treat a man of his kind. She was quite capable of
giving him a good sound beating with a strong stick. The low-
down ruffian. And her anger had not abated even by the time
Oswald called that evening. She went into the parlour, her eyes
glittering with bad temper.

Oswald sat opposite her and laid his clean yellow gloves on his
knee. His face was pale and narrow, with a frugal nose and pale,
steady eyes. Dull his face was, Blodwen suddenly decided, looking
at him with a new gaze, dull and unredeemed by any exceptional

expression. And what he said, as he neatly pulled up his fine creased trousers at the knees and then sat back with his hands clasped in an attitude of prayer, made her want to slap him.

'You're looking very wicked and naughty this evening, my dear. That's no way to receive your young man.'

Her face became inscrutable: she stared through the window. He went on:

'You know, I always think a woman should never be anything but bright and happy when her menfolk are about. That's her duty in life.' He leant towards her and took her hand. 'When you're my wife, my dear –'

'Let's go out,' Blodwen suddenly interjected. 'I feel I must have some fresh air this evening. I've been in all day.' Her voice had become even and calm.

He drew back, a bit stiffly. He sighed. But he was submissive, much as he wanted to stay in the parlour and caress her. He began to draw on his gloves.

'We'll go to the pictures if you like,' he said. He was very fond of going to the cinema with her. Nothing he liked better than sitting in the warm, florid atmosphere of the cinema, pressing Blodwen's hand and watching a love film.

'I'd rather go for a walk,' she answered, turning her sparkling eyes on him fully.

'There's so few walks about here,' he sighed.

'There's the mountains,' she said.

She liked going up the mountains. He didn't. Not many people climbed the mountains: they had been there all their lives and seemed not of much account, and dull to walk on. Great bare flanks of hills.

'All right,' he said, getting up and looking in the mirror over the mantel to put his tie straight. Blodwen went out to put on her hat.

As they went down the street the neighbours looked at them appraisingly. Everybody said what a picture they looked, the picture of a happy couple. He with his tall, slim elegance and she with her healthy, wholesome-looking body, her well-coloured face, they seemed so suitably matched to wed. His fine superiority and breeding wed to her wild fecund strength. They looked such a picture walking down the street, it did the heart good to see it.

They crossed the brook that ran, black with coal-dust, beneath some grubby unkempt alders, and climbed a straggling path at the rocky base of the hills. Presently Oswald remarked:

'You're very quiet this evening.'

Then there came to her eyes a little malicious gleam. He had taken her arm and was gazing down at her fondly – even though, as the path became steeper, he began to breathe heavily, almost in a snort. She said:

'I've been upset today.'

'Oh! What was it?'

'You know that man called Pugh Jibbons, the son of old Jibbons, who sells vegetables in a donkey-cart?'

'Yes, of course. Everybody knows him. They're a fine rough lot, that family. Half wild.'

'Well, he molests me.'

'Molests you!' Oswald exclaimed. 'He has attacked you, you mean?' His mouth remained open in astonishment and horror.

'Oh no. Not attacked me. But he bothers me and follows me about. And this morning I was buying vegetables from him at our back door and he said – oh, he said some rude things.'

'Does he follow you about in the streets, make himself a nuisance to you?' Oswald demanded alertly, the young solicitor.

'Yes, he does,' she said angrily.

'Then,' said Oswald, 'we'll send him a warning letter. I can't have you being bothered like this. The rapscallion. I'll put a stop to him. I'll have a letter sent him tomorrow.'

'Will you?' she said mechanically, looking up to the hills.

'Of course. That's where I come in useful for you. A solicitor's letter will frighten him, you'll see.'

'Perhaps,' she said after a moment or two, 'you'd better leave it for a time. Nothing serious is there to complain of. And I told him myself this morning, I warned him. So we'll wait perhaps.'

She persuaded him, after some debate, that it would be better to postpone the sending of the letter: but as he argued she became angrier and nearly lost her temper. Then he became very gentle with her, endeavouring to soothe her, realizing she had had a trying day. But her eyes remained hard.

Not until they got to the mountain-top did she seem to regain her good spirits. She loved the swift open spaces of the mountain-tops. They sat beneath a huge grey stone that crouched like an elephant in a dip of the uplands, which billowed out beneath them in long, lithe declivities. They could see all the far-flung valley between the massive different hills. Some of those hills were tall and suave and immaculate, having escaped the desecration of the coal-mines, others were rounded and squat like the wind-blown skirt of a gigantic woman, some were shapeless with great excrescences of the mines, heaps of waste matter piled up black and forbidding, others were small and young and helpless, crouching between their bulked brothers. Blodwen felt eased, gazing at the massed hills stretched along the fourteen miles of the Valley. She felt eased and almost at peace again. Oswald glanced at her and saw she wanted to be quiet, though the storm had left her brow. He sat back against the rock and musingly fingered his heavy gold ring. He did not care for the mountain-tops himself. It was dull up there: and he seemed to be lost in the ample space.

He couldn't bear the silence for very long. He had to say something. He couldn't bear her looking away so entranced in some world of her own.

'A penny for them,' he said, touching her shoulder lightly.

She gave a sudden start and turned wondering eyes to him. And her eyes were strange to him, as though she did not know him. They were blue and deep as the sea, and old and heavy, as though with the memory of lost countries. She did not speak, only looked at him in startled wonder. One would have thought a stranger had touched her and spoken.

'Why d'you look at me like that?' he said at last, uneasy and hating her staring.

Her expression changed. She almost became his familiar Blodwen again. She smiled a little.

'You're a funny little woman,' he said, sliding his arm round her waist.

'It's fine up here,' she said.

But still she was different and not the human Blodwen that he knew in the parlour or the cinema. He couldn't warm himself with her at all. Her body seemed rigid and unyielding in his caress. She was hard and profitless as these mountain-tops. Almost he began to dislike her, and something inside him stirred in dark anger against her. But all the time his manner and tactics became gentler and more coaxing and more submissive to her whim. His face was appealing and submissive. But she persisted in her odd aloof withdrawal, and at last he decided she couldn't be well, that she was suffering from some esoteric feminine complaint that he must not intrude upon. So he abandoned his lovemaking and sat back against the rock and became deliberately meditative himself. He did not see the shade of impatience that crossed her face.

He considered the evening wasted and a failure as they descended the mountain in the grey-blue light. And something had happened to Blodwen, something curious and beyond his understanding. Yet for all his secret dissatisfaction he became more anxious in his behaviour towards her, more gentle and tremulous in his approaches. But she spoke to him and treated him as though she were another man: they might have been men together instead of lovers. He was hungry to hold her, to feel the strong living substance of her body. But somehow he could not penetrate the subtle atmosphere of aloofness that she wrapped herself in. He kept on sighing, in the hope that she would notice it. Women were very funny.

She did not ask him into the house, but lifted her lips to him, her eyes shut, inside the gateway of the garden. In a sudden spurt of anger he pecked quickly at her mouth and withdrew. She opened her eyes and they seemed unfathomable as the night sky.

They both waited in silence for a few moments and then, lowering her head, she said calmly:

'Good night, Oswald.'

'Good night, Blodwen.'

He lifted his bowler hat and turned resolutely away.

She went in, slowly and meditatively. Her face was calm and thoughtful now. But she was aware of Oswald and his dissatisfaction. She couldn't help it. There were times now and again when his limp and clumsy lovemaking affronted her, as there were times when it amused her and when it roused her to gentle tenderness. After all, he was young: only twenty-five. Married, she would soon change him and mould him, surely she would? She wondered. Married, things would be different. She'd have to settle down. Surely Oswald was the ideal husband to settle down with. She would have a well-ordered life with no worries of money or work. Oswald would have his father's practice and become a moderately wealthy man: and his family had position. Had always been of the best class in the place. Different from her family, for her grandfather had been an ordinary collier and even now they were neither working- nor upper-class. Her mother was so proud of the step up marriage to Oswald would mean: she had already bought several things on the strength of it – a new parlour set of furniture, a fur coat and odd things like a coffee-set and silver napkin-rings and encyclopedias and leather books of poetry. It would be a lovely showy wedding too.

But she wished she didn't have that curious empty feeling in her when she thought of it all, sometimes. Not always. Sometimes she realized Oswald's virtues and deeply respected him for them: good manners, breeding, smartness, a knowledge of international affairs and languages, a liking for verse. Yet she knew and feared that void of emptiness in her when she thought of all that marriage with him implied.

When she went to bed a little perplexed frown had gathered on her brow. She rose early in the morning feeling very discontented and melancholy. She had a cold bath. In a kind of anguish of bliss she shuddered in the water, sluicing it between her pink-white breasts so that it rippled down her fine length like a quick, cool hand. Her wild fair hair glistening as though with dew, her limbs tautened by the cold bath, she strode downstairs and ate a good breakfast of bacon and eggs, stewed apples, toast and tea. Then she felt somewhat better, though she was far from being content.

She remembered Pugh Jibbons and how angry she had been with him yesterday. What he wanted now was a good rude snub and she'd give it him that morning. And thinking of him, her blood began to run faster again. She'd never heard of such impudence. Anybody would think she had encouraged him at some time or other. That riff-raff!

When she heard his shout in the back lane she asked her mother what vegetables they wanted and sauntered up the garden to the door.

'Morning,' said Pugh, looking at her with just a suspicion of mockery in his face. 'And how's the world using you today, then?'

Statuesque, with that insulting ignoring of a person that a woman can assume, she did not hear his greeting and ordered peremptorily:

'Three pounds of beans and six of potatoes.'

'Proud we are this morning,' he observed.

He stood before her and looked at her directly, unmoving. She began to flush and arch her neck; she looked beyond him, to the right, to the left, and then her glance came back to him. His smile was subtle and profound, the light in his gleaming dark eyes was shrewd. She wanted to turn and hurry away, slam the door on him. But she didn't. His swarthy face, with its dark gipsy strain, was full of a knowledge that she sensed rather than saw. His head rested deliberately and aggressively on his powerful neck.

Suddenly she ejaculated furiously:

'Don't stare at me like that! D'you hear! Where's your manners? What right have you to stand there staring at me!'

'You know what right I have,' he answered slowly. And the smile had left his face and given way completely to the hard determination of desire.

She hadn't expected all this, she had meant to coldly snub him and depart. And how strange she had gone, how still and waiting her body, as though absorbed in expectant fear for what would happen next. And she was amazed, when she answered, unable to bear the silence, that her voice faltered in her beating throat:

'I know, do I? I warn you, Pugh Jibbons, not to molest me.'

'Suppose,' he answered, a thin, wiry grin coming to his face, 'that Oswald Vaughan would have something to say and do about it?'

Her anger flowed up again. 'What right have you,' she demanded again, 'to interfere with me? Never have I encouraged you. Haven't you any decency, man? You're nothing to me.' And then she was angry with herself for submitting to his advances to the point of discussion, instead of maintaining a haughty aloofness. She couldn't understand why she had given way to him so easily.

He looked at her. All his body and face seemed tense, gathered up to impose themselves on her.

'I figure it out,' he said, 'that I've got a right to *try* and have you. Because I want you. You're a woman for me. And I think I'm a man for you. That's what I think. I could do for you what you want and I want. That's what I feel.'

She stared at him. She had got control of herself. But she couldn't snub him in the harsh final way she had intended. She said haughtily:

'I don't want to hear any more about this. Give me the beans and potatoes, please.'

Pugh Jibbons came a step nearer to her, and she became acutely conscious of his body and face.

'You come to me one evening,' he said. 'You come to me one evening and a talk we'll have over this. I promise to respect you. I've got more to tell you about yourself than you think.'

She drew back. 'Ha,' she exclaimed with fine derision, 'what a hope you've got! Are you going to give me the beans and potatoes or not?'

He looked her over and then immediately became the vegetable man. He weighed out the beans and potatoes. Aloofly she watched him, her face stern. Today there were bunches of wide flat marguerites in the flower-box at the front of the cart. He took out a bunch.

'I don't want the flowers, thank you,' she said coldly.

'Nay,' he said, 'you must take them. You're one of my best regular customers.'

'I don't want the flowers,' she repeated, looking at him stonily.

He tossed the bunch back into the box.

'Silly wench,' he said.

'Don't you call me names!' she turtled up again.

'You deserve them,' he said. Then he looked her over with desiring appreciation. 'But a handsome beauty you are, by God, a handsome beauty. Different from the chits of today. Pah, but your mind is stupid, because you won't be what you want to be.'

She quivered: and her anger had become strange in her blood, rather like fear. She could find nothing to say to him; she turned, slammed the door and hurried with the vegetables to the kitchen. All her blood seemed to run cold, fear seemed to sink down in her body, and suddenly she felt desperately anxious. Desperately because something was withering within her being, some living thing she should have cherished. Beyond the anger and irritation of her mind she knew a fear and anxiety like a touch of icy death in her being.

The day became cold and drab to her. She went about the house shut in a sullen resentful silence. Her mother looked at her with ill temper. The mother was a tall, vigorous woman. But her face had gone tart and charmless with the disillusion frequent in working women whose lives have been nothing but a process of mechanical toil and efforts to go one better than their neighbours. She, too, in her day had had her violences. But her strength had gone to sinew and hard muscle. Even now she cracked brazil nuts with her teeth, heaved a hundredweight of coal from cellar to kitchen and could tramp twenty miles over the hills on bank holidays. And now she distrusted the world and wanted security for herself and her daughters.

'What's the matter with you, girl?' she demanded irritably, as Blodwen sat silent over the midday meal. 'Shift that sulky look off your face.'

Blodwen did not answer. But her mouth sneered unpleasantly.

'You look at me like that, you shifty slut,' the mother exclaimed angrily, 'you'll leave this table.'

The daughter got up and swept out of the room. Her head was turtled up fearless as an enraged turkey.

'Ha,' shouted the mother after her, 'don't you dare show that ugly face to me again, or, grown-up or not, you'll feel the weight of my hand. Out with you.'

But Blodwen had dignity, sweeping out of the room, and her silence was powerful with contempt.

'Bringing a girl up,' muttered the mother to herself, 'to snarl and insult one, as though she's what-not or the Queen of England. Ach, that she was ten years younger. I'd give her what for on that b.t.m. of hers. The stuck-up insulting girl that she is.'

Blodwen stayed in her bedroom for the rest of the day, knitting. At six-thirty Oswald called. She came down to the parlour, still a little sulky. There was anxiety on Oswald's face as he greeted her. She had frightened him last night. And now he couldn't live without her: she was the sole reality in his life.

'My dear,' he murmured, pressing her hand, 'my own dear.'

She actually smiled up at him.

'Are you better?' he asked gently.

'I haven't been ill,' she said.

'Nothing physical, perhaps,' he said, primly, 'but out-of-sorts mentally, I should think.'

She sat beside him on the sofa.

'Oswald,' she said, 'when shall we get married?'

He started excitedly. Before, he had never been able to make her decide anything definite about their marriage. She had always dismissed the subject, declaring there was plenty of time yet. He wanted to get married quickly, so that he could proceed to entire happiness with this fine woman: he wanted it quickly.

'My darling,' he cried gratefully, 'my sweet, as soon as you like. I could be ready in a month. There's a house going on Salem Hill and I've got the money for furniture. We could begin buying at once. I saw a lovely walnut bedroom suite in a shop in Cardiff last week; I wanted to reserve it there and then. I'll phone for it tomorrow. And all the other things we could choose together. We'll go down to Cardiff tomorrow. I'll get the day off.' His face began to shine excitedly.

She looked at him.

'Not a month though,' she said slowly; 'perhaps we want more than a month to prepare.'

'Six weeks, then,' he said.

'Soon,' she said, in a curious kind of surging voice, 'soon. Let it be soon. Six weeks, then. That will be soon enough.' Her hand crept up his arm. 'That will give us time to prepare and not too much time to change our minds. Six weeks. Oh, you do want to marry, don't you, Oswald?'

'My dear,' he cried in pain. 'How strange you are!'

But she put her face to his to be kissed. Their mouths met. She clung to him desperately.

She would not go out to buy vegetables off Pugh Jibbons again. She told her mother how he molested her. The mother went to the back door and roundly denounced the young hawker. Pugh had laughed at her. And Oswald again offered to have a letter sent him.

The weeks went by: autumn came on. There were endless preparations for the wedding. Blodwen, it was true, took little interest in them. She allowed Oswald to arrange and buy everything. She was very calm; and her manner and behaviour changed. She lost her high-flown demeanour, she never lost her temper, and her face went a little wan. Now her dark blue eyes seemed deeper and more remote beneath her long brows, and her mouth was flower-soft, red as geranium, but drooped.

The week before the wedding there was a touch of winter in the air. Blodwen liked the winter. She was as strong as a bear amid the harsh winds and the wild snow and the whips of rain that winter brings to the vales of the hills. She took on added strength in the winter, like a bear.

One early evening as the wind lashed down through the serried rows of houses huddled in the vale she stood looking out at the hills from an upstairs window of her home. The grey sky was moving and violent over the brown mountains, and the light of evening was flung out. Her face was lifted like an eager white bird to the hills. She would have to go, she could not stay in the house any longer. She entirely forgot that Oswald was due in a few minutes.

She wound a heavy woollen scarf round her neck and, unknown to her mother and father, who were in the kitchen, she let herself out. And blindly, seeing no one and nothing in the streets, she went on towards the base of the lonely mountains. Slowly the light died into the early wintry evening, the heavens were misted and darkened, moved slower, though in the west a dim exultance of coppery light still loitered.

Her nostrils dilated in the sharp air, but her limbs thrilled with warmth. Her feet sank in the withering mignonette-coloured grass of the lower slopes, and she climbed lithely and easily the steep pathless little first hill. She was conscious of Pugh Jibbons' allotments surrounding his ramshackle stone house to the left, but she did not look at them. He, however, saw her, rising from his hoeing of potatoes.

The night would soon come. She cared nothing. She wanted to be on the dominant mountain tops, she wanted to see the distant hills ride like great horses through the darkening misty air. She quickened her steps and her breasts began to heave with exertion. She had crossed the smaller first hill and was ascending the mountain behind it. She was quite alone on the hills.

The black jagged rocks jutting out on the brow of the mountains were like a menace. She began to laugh, shaking out her wild hair; she unwound her scarf and bared her throat to the sharp slap of the wind. She would like to dance on the mountain-top, she would like to shake her limbs and breasts until they were hard and lusty as the wintry earth. She forgot her destination in the world below.

She had reached the top. Night was not yet; and out of the grey seas of mist the distant hills rode like horses. She saw thick, massive limbs, gigantic flanks and long ribbed sides of hills. She saw plunging heads with foam at their mouths. She saw the great bodies of the hills, and in her own body she knew them.

Oswald sat in the parlour with Blodwen's mother. The gas had been lit and a tiny fire burned in the paltry grate. Oswald looked distracted. He had been waiting for over an hour already. It was most strange. It had been a definite arrangement for him to see Blodwen that evening. There were important things to discuss for the wedding on Saturday. Her mother could offer no explanation but kept on repeating angrily:

'Why didn't she say she was going out! The provoking girl.'

'Can't you think where she has gone to?' Oswald asked more than once.

'No. Most secretive she's been lately. Secretive and funny. I've put it down to the fuss of preparing. A serious job it is for a girl to prepare for marriage. Some it makes hysterical, some silly and others secretive and funny, like Blodwen.' She tried her best to keep the conversation going with the distracted young man. Inside, she was fuming. She suspected that Blodwen had gone out with the deliberate intention of escaping Oswald. What madness! She'd give the girl a good talking-to when she returned.

'Have you noticed it too?' exclaimed Oswald. 'I've wondered what's the matter with her. But, as you say, it's such a big change for a girl to get married, she must lose her balance now and again.'

'Especially a highly strung girl like Blodwen,' said the mother. 'For highly strung she is, though in health as strong as a horse. No trouble of ailments have I had with her. From a baby she has trotted about frisky as can be.' And to try and soothe him she added gravely, 'Do you well she will, Oswald, a big satisfaction you'll have out of her. And in house matters she can work like a black and cook like a Frenchie, she can make quilts and eiderdowns and wine, and she can cure boils and gripe and other things by herbs as I have cured them in my own husband. Taught her all my knowledge I have. A girl she is such as you don't see often nowadays. Highly strung she might be, but, handled properly, docile enough she'll be.'

'I think we'll get on all right,' said Oswald nervously, 'though no doubt we'll have our ups and downs.'

'Aye,' said the mother.

The clock ticked away. Oswald kept on glancing at it mournfully, then at his watch, to make sure that *was* the time. The mother looked at him with a sort of admiring bliss in her eyes. He was such a toff and belonged to such a family. Fancy her Blodwen marrying into the Vaughan family! No wonder she was an envied mother and people were deferential to her now. She had been a cook at one time.

'Wherever can she be?' he repeated, sighing.

'I can't think at all,' said Blodwen's mother, sharpening her voice to sympathize with his agitation. 'But I'll tell her of this tonight, I'll tell her, never fear.'

'Oh, don't, please,' he begged. 'We must be gentle with her the next few days, we must put up with her whims.' He looked at her appealingly and added, 'No doubt she'll have a reasonable explanation when she arrives back.'

But Pugh Jibbons, in his old stony house on the hillside, was laying a flower on the white hillock of her belly, with tender exquisite touch a wide, flat, white marguerite flower, its stalk bitten off, his mouth pressing it into her rose-white belly, laughing.

GWYN JONES

A White Birthday

With their next stride towards the cliff edge they would lose sight
of the hills behind. These, under snow, rose in long soft surges,
blued with shadow, their loaded crests seeming at that last
moment of balance when they must slide into the troughs of the
valleys. Westward the sea was stiffened to a board, and lay
brown and flat to the indrawn horizon. Everywhere a leaden sky
weighed upon land and water.

They were an oldish man and a young, squat under dark cloth
caps, with sacks worn shawl-like over their shoulders, and other
sacks roped about their legs. They carried long poles, and the
neck of a medicine-bottle with a teat-end stood up from the
younger man's pocket. Floundering down between humps and
pillows of the buried gorse bushes, they were now in a wide bay
of snow, with white headlands enclosing their vision to left and
right. A gull went wailing over their heads, its black feet retracted
under the shining tail feathers. A raven croaked from the cliff
face.

'That'll be her,' said the younger man excitedly. 'If that
raven –'

'Damn all sheep!' said the other morosely, thinking of the
maddeningly stupid creatures they had dug out that day, thinking
too of the cracking muscles of his thighs and calves, thinking not
less of the folly of looking for lambs on the cliff face.

'I got to,' said the younger, his jaw tensing. 'I got reasons.'

'To look after yourself,' grumbled the other. He had pushed

his way to the front, probing cautiously with his pole, and grunting as much with satisfaction as annoyance as its end struck hard ground. The cliffs were beginning to come into view, and they were surprised, almost shocked, to find them black and brown as ever, with long sashes of snow along the ledges. They had not believed that anything save the sea could be other than white in so white a world. A path down the cliff was discernible by its deeper line of snow, but after a few yards it bent to the left, to where they felt sure the ewe was. The raven croaked again. 'She's in trouble,' said the younger man. 'P'raps she's cast or lambing.'

'P'raps she's dead and they are picking her,' said the older. His tone suggested that would be no bad solution of their problem. He pulled at the peak of his cap, bit up with blue and hollow scags of teeth into the straggle of his moustache. 'If I thought it was worth it, I'd go down myself.'

'You're too old, anyway.' A grimace robbed the words of their brutality. 'And it's my ewe.'

'And it's your kid's being born up at the house, p'raps this minute.'

'I'll bring it him back for a present. Give me the sack.'

The older man loosed a knot unwillingly. 'It's too much to risk.' He groped for words to express what was for him a thought unknown. 'I reckon we ought to leave her.'

Tying the sack over his shoulders the other shook his head. 'You leave a lambing ewe? When was that? Besides, she's mine, isn't she?'

Thereafter they said nothing. The oldish man stayed on the cliff top, his weight against his pole, and up to his boot tops in snow. The younger went slowly down, prodding ahead at the path. It was not as though there were any choice for him. For one thing, it was his sheep, this was his first winter on his own holding, and it was no time to be losing lambs when you were starting a family. He had learned thrift the hard way. For another, his fathers had tended sheep for hundreds, perhaps thousands of years; the sheep was not only his, it was part of him. All day long he had been fighting the unmalignant but unslacking hostility of nature, and was in no mood to be beaten. And last, the lying-in of his wife with her first child was part of the compulsion that sent him down the cliff. The least part, as he recognized; he would be doing this in any case, as the old man above had always done it. He went very carefully, jabbing at the rock, testing each foothold before giving it his full weight. Only a fool, he told himself, had the right never to be afraid.

Where the path bent left the snow was little more than ankle deep. It was there he heard the ewe bleat. He went slowly forward to the next narrow turn and found the snow wool-smooth and waist high. 'I don't like it,' he whispered, and sat down and slit the one sack in two and tied the halves firmly over his boots. The ewe bleated again, suddenly frantic, and the raven croaked a little nearer him. 'Ga-art there!' he called, but quietly. He had the feeling he would be himself the one most frightened by an uproar on the cliff face.

Slowly he drove and tested with the pole. When he had made each short stride he crunched down firmly to a balance before thrusting again. His left side was tight on the striated black rock, there was an overhang of soft snow just above his head, it seemed to him that his right shoulder was in line with the eighty-foot drop to the scum of foam at the water's edge. 'You dull daft fool,' he muttered forward at the platform where he would find the ewe. 'In the whole world you had to come here!' The words dismayed him with awareness of the space and silence around him. If I fall, he thought, if I fall now . . . He shut his eyes, gripped at the rock.

Then he was on the platform. Thirty feet ahead the ewe was lying on her back in snow scarlet and yellow from blood and her waters. She jerked her head and was making frightened kicks with her four legs. A couple of yards away two ravens had torn out the eyes and paunch of her new-dropped lamb. They looked at the man with a horrid waggishness, dribbling their beaks through the purple guts. When the ewe grew too weak to shake her head they would start on her too, ripping at the eyes and mouth, the defenceless soft belly. 'You sods,' he snarled, 'you filthy sods!' fumbling on the ground for a missile, but before he could throw anything they flapped lazily and insolently away. He kicked what was left of the lamb from the platform and turned to the ewe, to feel her over. 'Just to make it easy!' he said angrily. There was a second lamb to be born.

'Get over,' he mumbled, 'damn you, get over!' and pulled her gently on to her side. She at once restarted labour, and he sat back out of her sight, hoping she would deliver quickly despite her fright and exhaustion. After a while she came to her feet, trembling, but seemed rather to fall down again than re-settle to work. Her eyes were set in a yellow glare, she cried out piteously, and he went back to feel along the belly, pressing for the lamb's head. 'I don't know,' he complained, 'I'm damned if I know where it is with you. Come on, you dull soft stupid sow of a thing – what are you keeping it for?' He could see the shudders begin in her throat and throb back the whole length of her, her agony flowed into his leg in ripples. All her muscles were tightening and then slipping loose, but the lamb refused to present. He saw half a dozen black-backed gulls swing down to the twin's corpse beneath him. 'Look,' he said to the ewe, 'd'you want them to get you too? Then for Christ's sake, get on with it!' At once her straining began anew; he saw her flex and buckle with pain; then she went slack, there was a dreadful sigh from her, her head rested, and for a moment he thought she had died.

He straightened his back, frowning, and felt snowflakes on his face. He was certain the ewe had ceased to work and, unless he interfered, would die with the lamb inside her. Well, he would try for it. If only the old man were here – he would know what to do. If I kill her, he thought – and then: what odds? She'll die anyway. He rolled back his sleeves, felt for a small black bottle in his waistcoat pocket, and the air reeked as he rubbed lysol into his hand. But he was still dissatisfied, and after a guilty glance upwards reached for his vaseline tin and worked gouts of the grease between his fingers and backwards to his wrist. Then with his right knee hard to the crunching snow he groped gently but purposefully into her after the lamb. The primal heat and wet startled him after the cold of the air, he felt her walls expand and contract with tides of life and pain; for a moment his hand slithered helplessly, then his middle fingers were over the breech and his thumb seemed sucked in against the legs. Slowly he started to push the breech back and coax the hind legs down. He felt suddenly sick with worry whether he should not rather have tried to turn the lamb's head and front legs towards the passage. The ewe groaned and strained as she felt the movement inside her, power came back into her muscles, and she began to work with him. The hind legs began to present, and swiftly but cautiously he pulled against the ewe's heaving. Now, he thought, now! His hand moved in an arc, and the tiny body moved with it, so that the lamb's backbone was rolling underneath and the belly came uppermost. For a moment only he had need to fear it was pressing on its own life-cord, and then it was clear of the mother and lying, red and sticky on the snow. He picked it up, marvelling as never before at the beauty of the tight-rolled gummy curls of fine wool patterning its sides and back. It appeared not to be breathing, so he scooped the mucus out of its mouth and nostrils, rubbed it with a piece of sacking, smacked it sharply on the buttocks, blew into the throat to start respiration, and with that the nostrils fluttered and the lungs dilated. 'Go on,' he said triumphantly to the prostrate ewe, 'see to him yourself. I'm no damned nursemaid for you, am I?' He licked the cold flecks of snow from around his mouth as the ewe began to lick her lamb, cleaned his hand and wrist, spat and spat again to rid himself of the hot foetal smell in nose and throat.

Bending down to tidy her up, he marvelled at the strength and resilience of the ewe. 'Good girl,' he said approvingly, 'good girl then.' He would have spent more time over her but for the thickening snow. Soon he took the lamb from her and wrapped it in the sack which had been over his shoulders. She bleated anxiously when he offered her the sack to smell and started off along the ledge. He could hear her scraping along behind him and had time at the first bad corner to wonder what would happen if she nosed him in the back of the knees. Then he was at the second corner and could see the old man resting on his pole above him. He had been joined by an unshaven young labourer in a khaki overcoat. This was his brother-in-law. 'I near killed the ewe,' he told them, apologetic under the old man's inquiring eye. 'You better have a look at her.'

'It's a son,' said the brother-in-law. 'Just as I come home from work. I hurried over. And Jinny's fine.'

'A son. And Jinny!' His face contorted, and he turned hurriedly away from them. 'Hell,' he groaned, reliving the birth of the lamb; 'hell, oh hell!' The other two, embarrassed, knelt over the sheep, the old man feeling and muttering. 'Give me the titty-bottle,' he grunted presently. 'We'll catch you up.' The husband handed it over without speaking, and began to scuffle up the slope. Near the skyline they saw him turn and wave shamefacedly.

'He was crying,' said the brother-in-law.

'Better cry when they are born than when they are hung,' said the old man grumpily. The faintest whiff of sugared whisky came from the medicine bottle. 'Not if it was to wet your wicked lips in hell!' he snapped upwards. He knew sheep: there was little he would need telling about what had happened on the rock platform. 'This pair'll do fine. But you'll have to carry the ewe when we come to the drifts.' He scowled into the descending snow, and eased the lamb into the crook of his arm, sack and all. 'You here for the night?'

Their tracks were well marked by this time. The man in khaki went ahead, flattening them further. The old man followed, wiry and deft. Two out of three, he was thinking; it might have been worse. His lips moved good-humouredly as he heard the black-backed gulls launch outwards from the scavenged cliff with angry, greedy cries. Unexpectedly, he chuckled.

Behind him the ewe, sniffing and baa-ing, her nose pointed at the sack, climbed wearily but determinedly up to the crest.

GWYN THOMAS

Oscar

Rainwater streamed down the walls of the Harp. It had rained for a week. There was nothing of the many things I could feel around me in the dark that was not soaked. I wore a waterproof jacket. That jacket was thick and good. It had belonged to an uncle of mine. I took it from his house without telling anybody, just after he died. The rain did not bother him any more. It bothered me. I leaned with the full weight of my shoulders against the walls of the Harp. I was standing in the yard of that pub. The rain bounced down from the chutes about six inches from where I stood. Beside me was a lighted window, small. The light from that window was very yellow and had a taste. Behind that window were about a dozen drunks, singing. Among those drunks was Oscar. I could tell that Oscar's voice if I was deaf. There was a feel about it, a slow, greasy feel. Oscar was a hog. I knew him well. I worked for Oscar. I was Oscar's boy. It was for Oscar I was waiting in that streaming, smelling yard of the Harp, pressing my shoulders against those walls that were as wet and cold as the soil of the churchyard that stood across the road. The wind blew a kite's tail of the falling water from the chute across my mouth. I licked in the water and cursed Oscar, called him a hog seven times. I did not speak under my breath but out loud. No one could hear me in that empty yard. If anyone had heard me and if he did not know Oscar he would have said I was mad, shouting in that fashion. If he knew Oscar he would have said I was quite right. Everybody in the valley knew Oscar was a very dirty element.

I stared at the tall railings that the Council had planted on the wall of the churchyard opposite. I tried to count the number of spikes in those railings and gave up the job with the thought that they were many. I wondered whether those tall railings were to keep the dead voters in or the live voters out. There were many things done by the Council that I did not understand. But I was young. That I was working for a hog who spent less than one day in a hundred sober meant that I must have been very dense as well. The only bright thing I ever remember doing was to take that waterproof jacket from the house of my uncle who had just died.

I sang a bit of the song the drunks were singing. It was a song called 'Roll Me Home', and the voters behind the curtain were singing it to some words that were coated with dirt that they had no doubt made up for themselves to work up a heat. There were maidens' voices too behind the curtain and I thought it was funny that maidens should have the chance or the time to do any such thing as sing with such a great, busy ram as Oscar in the same room. I sang in a light tenor voice that sounded very well in that enclosed yard. I used to be a boy soprano. I used to sing very sweetly and on a sad song I could make as many people cry as death. If it had not broken so soon I would have taken that soprano voice around the place singing for money and perhaps I would have made so much out of it I would not have had to take that job with Oscar when I found there were no jobs in pits or shops for youths like me.

I glanced at the hills around. The hills of the valley were close together around the Harp. The houses of the valley were thickest at this point. They were built around a colliery and the Harp. The local voters did a lot of work in the colliery, and some of them did a lot of drinking at the Harp, not as much as Oscar did, but there was nothing ordinary about him. Behind the Harp to the north was the broad mountain that Oscar owned. It was his. I always thought it queer that a man could point to a thing like a mountain and say 'That's mine,' just as you would with a shirt or a woman or a pot. But that is what Oscar could do with this mountain. He got it from his father. I never knew his father and I never knew where he got this mountain from. Stole it as like as not from sheep or from some people who were dafter than sheep. And on top of this mountain a colliery company had built its tip, its dump, the stuff that had to be got out from underground to let the elements that work there get at the coal. Oscar owned that tip too. He owned the mountain and the huge cake of black refuse that the pit people had tossed on to it. So Oscar owned a lot of dirt. He owned me too, I suppose, or I would not have been such a dense crap as to stand there in pouring rain waiting for him to fill his guts to a point where I would have to undo his buttons for him. So, for a hog, Oscar did very well out of being a man. Nobody liked him in the valley. The elements who went to chapel thought he was on a par with the god Pan who was half a goat. The elements who did not go to chapel thought he was all Pan or all goat, or they were red revolutionary elements who thought that all such subjects as Oscar who got fat out of stolen land should have a layer of this land fixed over them in such a way as to stop their breathing. And a lot of this dislike for Oscar which was felt by the local voters was felt for me too. I worked for him and was, as they saw it, part of him. Lads who in the old days would always say, 'Hullo, Lewis,' when I passed, in a very friendly way, grew either to saying just 'Hullo,' or nothing at all, and these habits came to hurt me in a deep sensitive part of me. All because Oscar was a hog and owned a mountain. All I said in answer to the voters who claimed I ought to be hanging my head in shame for getting pay from such an element was that I spent much time looking for jobs that there were not there or ran to cover whenever I was around and when a youth has spent much time in such a search he will get desperate and unparticular and will take a job even from Satan if he finds Satan. I did not find him but I found Oscar who was the next worse thing. And there we are. In Clay Street, a dark thoroughfare, where the feet get in deeper and stickier with every forward step we take.

A small cart came rolling down the road. It stopped outside
the entrance to the yard where I stood. I could hear the driver of
the cart clicking his tongue at the horse. He kept clicking his
tongue for a whole minute after the horse had stopped and that
made me think that the horse had a lot more sense than the
driver. I knew this driver well. He was a small man by the name
of Waldo Williamson who sold vegetables from a cart about the
streets and made some sort of a living in this way because his
horse was nearly as daft as Waldo and allowed itself to be driven
up steep slopes that no other carter would touch to serve voters
who liked living in high places. Waldo's wife and kids did not see
much of this living that he made, for this element Waldo Williamson was a man who greatly feared rheumatism and went
around all the year wearing heavy oilskins and went into every
pub he passed to get cool from all the heat he worked up from
wearing such a load of leggings and capes. So this Waldo was
nearly always drunk and broke and only his wife who had to
sleep with him off and on knew what he looked like without all
this waterproof. She would not tell because she was not interested
enough in this Waldo to talk about him and I always felt she was
right in that because this Waldo could not have been much of a
man to live with or sleep with and his wife, no doubt, would have
slept elsewhere if she could have found another bed, which was
difficult in a crowded, poor place like that valley.

Waldo came into the yard eating a piece of swede and I could
hear him groaning softly because he was getting on in age and his
teeth could not have been strong, not strong enough to cope with
so hard an item as a swede. He stopped in front of me, right
beneath the shower from the chutes. It shows what sort of a man
this Waldo was to stand there still as a mummy and get a drenching.

'You're getting wet,' I said.

'Who are you?' he asked, his voice indistinct and distant with
swede eating.

'You know me, Waldo. I'm Lewis. You're drunk as a wheel.'

'Always drunk, boy. You're Lewis. Hullo, Lew. You're Oscar's boy.' He started to laugh, rocking about in his oilskins and making a rustle like wind in a wood and his breath was right in my face. 'He got sick of women, did he, Lewis boy, and now he's got you instead.'

I drove my open hand into his face and he went down into a puddle. He laughed at that, too. Dressed like that, Waldo could have lived in puddles like a duck and not seen much difference. He looked altogether like a duck as he sat there, his lips stuck outwards like the beginnings of a beak and wondering how the hell he got down there so near the ground with waves all around him. I jerked him to his feet, swiftly, proud of my strength which could have jerked twelve Waldos, oilskins and all, to their feet. He waddled into the side door of the Harp. He was a well-known drinker at the Harp and he never went in by the front way. His father, who was still alive and very old, was a Rechabite and did not like the notion of his son Waldo entering pubs the front way. So Waldo used the side doors of as many as fourteen pubs in one day to please his old man. It baffled me to know how an element as old as Waldo's old man could have wit enough left to be a Rechabite or anything else; also, how it could have escaped the attention of Waldo's old man that the best and shortest cut to solving such a problem as Waldo's drinking was to get rid of Waldo, who was of no use that I could see.

At the side door through which Waldo had gone appeared Clarisse, one of the girls who worked at the Harp. Clarisse was wearing a red blouse and the strong light from the passageway shone hard upon this blouse, and it was smooth red and had an effect on me. Clarisse was a stoutish girl with black hair, black as mine, which was very black, and her lips were thick and red like good chops of meat. Most of the young elements in the valley had chased Clarisse at some time or the other and when they got tired Clarisse chased them, because she lived well at the Harp, slept soundly and had plenty of strength left over from serving up the malt and dusting around the furniture for such activities as love. I always kept away from Clarisse, although I knew she could never have kept ahead of me if I started chasing. I did not want to give the local voters any idea that I was as mad for the maidens as Oscar was, and if I fooled around with Clarisse I knew I would be mad. I was always like a kettle on the boil with nobody to take it off or turn the gas down whenever that Clarisse came within a yard of me. So I kept away from her and lived a life that was cleaner than my linen.

'Come on in here,' said Clarisse.

I made no answer. I pressed closer to the wall.

'Don't be so daft, Lewis. Come on in here. I got tea made. You'll like that. There's nobody in here.'

When she said that about nobody being in there my body twitched a little and I had the old spots in front of my eyes. My eyes rested on the smooth, scarlet shine of her blouse and I thought of what my father had told me once, after he had had a few pots, not long before he passed over with the lung trouble he got in the pits.

'You're like me, Lewis. Just like me, boyo. You're a good-for-nothing bloody nuisance. It's stamped all over your face like it's stamped all over the inside of me. You won't do yourself any good by trying to be any different.' A nice man, my father, but given to saying dark, moody things like the one you have just heard. I did not agree with him. An element does not have to be like his old man. An element does not have to be like the element he works for. He grows up the way the world lets him and if he does not want to be like any element whatever, he can always pass over and be like nobody. I wanted to show people that I could be clean and good like these elements who go to chapels and boast a lot about being good and clean, without, very often, being so, except when they are actually inside the chapels where a voter is very limited in his choice of what he would like to do. So I made no answer to this Clarisse who stood there in the lighted passageway asking me to come inside and drink tea and so on. I drank in the smooth redness of her blouse as if it were a glass of hot cordial you get at a penny a glass in the Italian refreshment shops.

'There's nobody in here,' said Clarisse again.

'I'm waiting for Oscar. I got to wait here for Oscar. Got to take him home.'

'Don't worry about him. He's well away. He's got one of those Macnaffy girls from Brimstone Terrace and he'll be a long time with her.'

'Got to wait for him. So long, Clarisse.'

She put her hands over her head and ran out into the rain towards me. She stood by my side. I stuck my lips hard into hers. I could not help doing that, as you could not help sticking your head into a soft pillow if you were in a bed and very tired. Her whole body came at me in a rush and burned mine. The steam was whistling through my ears.

'You're big and dark and strong,' she glugged, and it was this glugging sound which Clarisse seemed to have picked up from the pictures or the chickens that gave me the strength to remain like my linen, clean. What she told me was nothing new. I knew I was big and dark and strong. I was big because my father had been like that. I was dark because my mother's hair is raven and her skin the softest brown you ever saw. I was strong because all the work I had done as a kid, such as carrying loads of coal, furniture and God knows what for voters who could not afford to pay somebody grown-up to do this carrying, could not have been done by anybody weak.

'You talk a lot of nonsense,' I said to Clarisse.

'You're dark and strong, Lewis, like a man in the book I'm reading.'

I did not know that Clarisse could read. We had been at school together and I remembered she had worn out three teachers because these three elements had vanished after a few months of trying to put some knowledge into Clarisse. I supposed she must have picked up a bit of culture from the softer spoken customers at the Harp who were clerks. I was very pleased to find that she could read books as well as spend her time bringing young, sensitive elements like me to the boil at a speed that nearly drove us forward like engines.

'What is the name of this book you are reading, Clarisse?' I asked, thinking a serious question of this type would cool her down straightaway.

'It's called *Four Green Eyes*.'

'Who's the element who's got four green eyes?'

'Two. With two green eyes each. Green with being jealous, see?'

'That's fair enough.'

'I'm jealous about you, Lewis. I'm green for you, like that book says. Why don't you ever go with girls, Lew?'

'I've got enough to do with Oscar. I haven't got the time. I haven't got the fancy.'

'Nor the strength,' she snapped, a bit angry, but I only laughed when she said that, because I knew I had the strength to lift her over the building. 'That Oscar is a hog,' she said, and I thought that if a girl like Clarisse, who was not bright at anything except making shapes at men and giving off waves of heat like a furnace, could reel off this slogan pat like that, it must be a very well-established slogan.

'He is that, twice over,' I said. 'And tell him when you get back in that I'm getting wet and cold out here. Tell him to hurry up with that element from Brimstone Terrace, Mactaffy or Macnaffy or whatever the hell her name is. Tell him I'll be too stiff to lead him and his bloody horse home over the mountain if he keeps me hanging about this yard much longer.'

'It'll be dark on that mountain, Lewis.'

'Like pitch. But me and that horse could do the journey blindfold and Oscar does it blind. So the dark doesn't matter much.'

'Why don't you get a decent job, Lewis?'

'I got one.'

'You don't call being with Oscar a decent job. I mean a good, useful job where you could get married or something.'

'Because,' I said, and my voice was deep and steady and grown up, 'because Oscar gave me a job when no one else would give me one, and as for being married, I keep my mother.'

'Oh . . . well, so long, Lewis. See you again. I'll tell Oscar to put a move on.'

Her lips pushed on mine again. As she went from me my mind went along in large circles, slowly, sadly, as I thought there was not much shape on my life at all. That did not hurt me as badly as it might have, for I could not guess what alternative shape it might have had. But I felt it to be ugly and unpleasant, overweighed with as large a cake of black refuse as Oscar's mountain, but not bringing in the same kind of income. It struck me that Clarisse's mind might have come into a good patch when she had told me to get away from Oscar. I noticed that the elements behind the lighted window had now stopped singing 'Roll Me Home'. They were belting up great volume of the hymn 'Bring Forth the Royal Diadem' and singing the words right out as if they had the diadem right there. This was a strange item to be hearing from such elements, but I joined in all the same because it is a hymn that goes with a great swing and I wanted something to keep my mouth busy.

Another voice hailed me from the side door. This time it was Mrs Wilson, the landlady of the Harp. She was a woman about fifty, dressed in brown; seeing her in that doorway after Clarisse was like looking at a grate from which the fire has been scraped out. But she was a clean, healthy woman, like the woman you see on the self-raising flour advertisement, and better to look at than a lot of the women in the valley who were short of food and reasons for living.

'Come and get him,' said Mrs Wilson. 'He's in the little room down there on the left.'

I knew the room. I had fished Oscar out of it more than once. It was where he went when he was with a woman, or when he wanted to talk to himself and when Oscar was not with a woman he always felt so odd he did a lot of talking to himself, so he spent a good deal of his time in the small room on the left-hand side of the main passageway of the Harp.

I pushed open the door. The Macnaffy element, from Brimstone Terrace, was sitting on a chair, her legs in dark brown stockings, stuck on the low mantelshelf above the gas fire which was full on. The air was warm, dry, nasty, a mixture of heat and maiden and landowner. The girl was sucking at a cigarette. She was pushing it far into her mouth and there was wet halfway up the barrel. The fingertips of her left hand were caressing the bulging calf of her right leg, hot from the gas fire, as if this bulging calf were a good friend. Her face was tired, thin and savage. I could imagine her coming from a place called Brimstone Terrace. I had never heard of a street of that name in the valley. She might have made Clarisse think of brimstone, scorching stuff which catches at the nostrils, and I did not blame Clarisse for that. She was the sort of element who has been steadily preached against ever since preaching started, which was a long time ago, but the preaching does not seem to have done much in the way of cooling elements like Macnaffy.

Oscar was sitting by the table, his head right down on the table boards. His huge, fat body poured over the sides of the chair on which he sat. His very weight gave him some kind of balance or he would have been on the floor, or under the floor where he deserved to be, a long way under the floor, a thick stone floor. I took hold of his head by the hair and the ear. I lifted it a foot. The table boards beneath were dull and steamy from the heat of him. His jacket and waistcoat hung open and there were dark finger-marks all the way up his white shirt, pulled up, crumpled. If these finger-marks were the marks of the savage looking Macnaffy, I thought she must have been playing on Oscar like a piano. I wondered what kind of music would come out of a hog. Brief, dirty, snorting little tunes. I dropped his head back on to the table and even the sharp bang he got from that did not make him any wider awake.

The girl sitting by the fire grinned at me, as if she were trying to be friendly. I was strong and lean and must have been a great and pleasant change for her eyes after a session with Oscar in so close a room. I looked back at her, without smiling. She was no change for my eyes.

'What a bloody weight,' she said, jerking her head at Oscar. Her voice was soft and dark, which was a great feature of most women in the valley, even women who looked as if they were going to rip you open like this Macnaffy. Voices like cats' backs, the velvet of skin and purr.

'He's big,' I said, sticking my knee into the blue-serged overflow of Oscar's flesh to give a leverage.

'How the hell do you feed him up to that size?' The girl's face was angrier and more savage as she asked that as if she herself had never had anywhere near enough food and disliked the idea of Oscar wolfing more in a day than she had to get through a lifetime on in Brimstone Terrace, or wherever it was she lived. 'What do you feed him on?'

'Acorns. And twice a year I bathe him in swill.'

'Looks like it. How do you get him home?'

'First I drag him. Then I get him on a horse.'

'That doesn't sound like much of a job to me. Why don't you get fixed up as a waiter or a welder or something?'

'Dragging Oscar was a hard enough job to get.'

I put my hands beneath Oscar's armpits and tried to lift him. He budged only a little, only such a little as caused him nearly to tip off his chair. The eyes of the Macnaffy girl were fiercer as they glared at the still, sodden Oscar. Her face was like chalk writing something on the air. She did not have the body to cope with a man like Oscar. She flicked a burning chunk of tobacco from her cigarette which had started to burn unevenly.

'What gives him the right to think he can go around expecting girls to lie at his feet like mats to be jumped on?'

'Did he jump on you?' I dropped Oscar to ask the question clearly. I was interested in Oscar's antics.

'Near as hell to jumping. First he got me a bit drunk. Then he got me in here. Next thing I know I think the whole bloody roof has come down on me. What gives him the right? That's what I'd like to know.'

'He owns a mountain. He can jump on that and he thinks there's nobody as important as a mountain.'

'Owns a mountain? What sort of god does that make him?'

'Anybody who owns a mountain can jump anywhere. There is also a big coal tip on top of Oscar's mountain and he owns that, too. And there are twenty or thirty people who work on that tip picking up bits of coal and putting them into sacks for Oscar. He sells those sacks of coal. So he's got a lot of money as well as a lot of mountain. As far as Oscar goes, there's nobody bigger than Oscar.'

'You know a lot, for a kid. How old are you?'

'Past nineteen.'

'You know all about life?'

'I know all about Oscar.'

'He's most of it. What a bloody weight.'

'What a bloody life.'

'It strikes me like that, too. So long, boyo. What's your name?'

'Lewis.'

'So long, Lewis.' And this Macnaffy element pushed her hat down on to her hair, which was black and flat and glossy, and looked as hard and full of thoughts as the skull underneath. She walked slowly out of the room into the passageway. She heeled over on a sliding mat outside the door and rubbed her face against the rough plaster work of the wall. She cursed in a streaming fashion that made me certain Clarisse was right about the name of the street this element lived in. Mr Wilson, the landlord, came out from a back room and said there were plenty of words in the language to draw on without needing to stray into the black pastures where the Macnaffy girl seemed to do most of her talking. She opened the front door and banged it behind her. From outside I could hear her talking still. She was probably telling Wilson to go to hell. Wilson, up the corridor, went on with his speech against strong language, using a throaty, solemn voice as if he were some kind of apostle who had got himself landed in a pub by some mistake about buses. I decided that Wilson would be giving everybody a lot more pleasure if he shut up and came to give me a hand with Oscar. I shouted on him.

Wilson came into the room where I stood alongside Oscar wondering whether to kick the chair from under him or wait for a crane. Wilson was eager to help. He wanted to get Oscar out of the building. It was getting late, and, in any case, no building with decent stone in the walls and clean wood in the beams would want Oscar in it for long.

'He's all right as long as he keeps on singing,' said Wilson.

'Then why don't you keep on singing?'

'About quarter to ten the boys always start on hymns. Then Oscar loses interest and comes in here. Is he a pagan?'

'God knows what he is. Never asked him and he never tells me. Jack him up there, Mr Wilson. We can carry him between us.'

And between us we got Oscar to the side door.

'You prop him up there, Mr Wilson, while I go and get the horse.'

Wilson tilted his body hard against Oscar and kept him upright that way. He was a stout man, Wilson, but nowhere near Oscar's class. He was clean looking, too, but nowhere near his wife's class.

I got Oscar's horse from the outhouse in the yard where we stabled it. There were chinks in the roof of that outhouse. The horse was wet and miserable and whinnied when I touched it. It was a brown mare, strong, and never had a thought. It always did as it was told and, just because it did that, would die, before its time, of weakness, like most of the voters who lived in that valley. This horse did not even have savage thoughts about Oscar to warm the inside of its head when living made it icy, so I felt very sorry for that horse.

The rain had slackened, sick of itself. The water still came down in stutters from the chute. Wilson helped me to get Oscar out into the yard and we stood him under the falling water. After two minutes of that Oscar was soaked and half awake. Wilson said Oscar would probably get pneumonia after that treatment.

'If he gets that,' I said, 'it'll keep him off the booze for a spell and I'll get some peace. But if the pneumonia feels like me, it'll keep away from him and he won't get it.'

'You're very fierce.'

I made no answer to that, because I knew Wilson for a man who would get you stuck in an argument about human nature the second you showed an interest in the subject. I wiped Oscar's mouth and eyes with my sleeve, which was thick and rough and made him grunt.

'Your father was a very fierce man, too,' said Wilson. 'I remember him. He was a great man for strikes.'

'He spent most of his time not working. Get the horse against the wall. Then we'll get Oscar up. Lot to be said for my old man's views on work.'

It took us five minutes to get Oscar settled in the saddle. The struggle winded Wilson and for a while he was in no way to talk about human nature or anything else. I told Oscar to hang on to the saddle with both hands, and, mumbling some words which I did not understand, except two, gas and fire, he did that.

I wheeled the horse around. I said 'So long' to Wilson. He was asking himself aloud how long Oscar could keep up this pace.

'He'll never fill,' I said. 'If it was water that Oscar drank, he'd be full of fish.'

I led the horse out of the yard. I bawled to Oscar the whole time that if his hands slipped off the saddle and he fell off he could stay off as far as I and the horse were concerned. The horse was whinnying again. It must have felt as if somebody had just dumped the earth on to its back and I was sorrier for it than ever. I heard Wilson say that horses were just like human beings, after all, and I thought to myself that keeping the Harp had not done much in the way of gingering up Wilson's wits. Clarisse came to the side door, too, and said she would be seeing me again soon. I looked back as we got on to the main road. I could see Clarisse against the strong, white light of the passageway. She was rubbing her head against Wilson's shoulder. That is how Clarisse was. If she saw anything, she would rub some part of herself against it. Ready, eager, kind, too much and too often to be wise.

The main road took us upward for ten minutes. I kept one hand on Oscar and the other on the bridle. The houses on either side of us were low, grey, poor, alike. They were different from the churchyard we had passed only in that rents on the houses were steadier and the rain more of a nuisance. We came to a corner where two large chapels faced each other from opposite sides of the street. They were ugly, flat-faced buildings and even in all that dark they seemed to be scowling at each other. They had that mean, grey look and the windows were thin, peeping slits. One was Baptist and what the other was I never did know. It must have been something different or they would not have been so near. Or would they? We continued upwards. We came to a pair of iron gates. They had been torn half off their hinges and had sagged heavily into the earth. They did not move any more. On both sides of the gates extended a tall wall, built to last. Inside the enclosure was what the wall had been built to protect, a disused air-fan, a knocked-in building, from which most of the machinery had been stolen or sold as scrap. The fan had once driven air into a surface colliery working, a level, as it was called, from which soft coal was swiftly and easily dug. It had made a lot of money and been bad to work in. It had killed many men, so many they had to close it up at last and then needed no more air from that fan which stood alongside those gates that were rusting and unmoving, needed no more air than the men it had put away.

Through the gates we passed to approach the base of the mountain that Oscar owned. Up the mountain, with its vast black cap of coal tip, we followed a broad, winding path. We skirted a wood that had been made thin by the axes of voters who had chopped down many of these trees for firewood during strikes. Oscar had brought up policemen to defend these trees, which he said were his. But those voters, who were savage in their ways of thinking and doing, even when they had firewood and no axes, were even more savage when they had axes and no firewood. So the policemen had had to leave them alone and they told Oscar that if he had any sense he would leave them alone, too, or the axe-bearing voters might get him mixed up with a tree and start lopping bits off him.

The tip stretched up to a sharp peak and to the left of that peak was a grassy plateau they had not yet thought of covering with tip. The path across the plateau took us close to the lip of a deep quarry. The wind was blowing in strongly from the direction of the sea. I had to watch the horse carefully at this point to see that it did not stumble on the sodden path. There was always a wind blowing across the plateau. Perhaps it was always there, did not come from anywhere, did not go anywhere, and that would belong to Oscar, too. The cold of it caught Oscar on the face and he rolled his head and made noises in his throat to show that he was now taking more notice of things. He took up a part of that song they had been singing in the Harp, 'Roll Me Home to Where the Good Old Wife is Waiting', a song especially made for weak-headed elements who have been warned off thinking. Oscar always woke up at that point of the ride home. I was always glad to hear the sound of his singing. His mumbling kept me company and it meant, too, that he was getting sober enough to keep himself on the mare and that saved me all the bother of having to jerk him back on when he started to slip in his sleep. The lip of the quarry we were skirting was jagged and bitten in at parts and was dangerous to all those who did not know the path and had no wish to leave the path by way of the quarry. Oscar had tried stringing a wire fence across the lip, but some voters had kicked the fence down because they did not like the idea of Oscar covering the mountain with wire as well as owning it. A few sheep had walked over this quarry and got themselves killed. One man, too, had thrown himself over and broken his neck. But this man had been walking around the mountain for months before preaching on a high note to molehills and ferns and other such things that cannot hear and do not take to preaching; so everybody thought that it was not exactly the quarry's fault if this element had broken his neck at the bottom of it.

The plateau ended and we passed down into a shallow ravine where the path was stony and flanked a fierce, yellow little stream. On our right was the northern slope of the tip. This was the place where all the tipping was done and the only place where the tip continued to grow. This was the place where those people, poor elements from some streets called the Terraces, picked coal for Oscar at fivepence a bag and Oscar sold each bag for one and sevenpence. Those elements must have been very poor indeed, lower down even than the dole, I supposed, to be spending their time bending down, skipping out of the way of big lumps of stone that came hurtling out of the trams which were emptied at the top of the tip and picking coal for Oscar at so little profit to themselves and at so great a profit to him.

We came to a clump of trees. Behind this clump was Oscar's house. It was a bigger house than most in all that valley. It was not much to look at, but it was quite big, with a stone yard in front and a lot of windows. If jails were built smaller this house would have looked just like a jail. As I helped Oscar from his horse, I could hear from beneath us the swish of buses making their way along the main road of the valley. Using one of those buses Oscar could have got more quickly to and from the Harp. But he did not like using the buses. He liked crossing the mountain. It was his.

We entered the kitchen of the house. It was a big room, half stone-flagged, half lino-covered, with about six square feet in front of the hearth, covered by three odd coloured mats which I had bought without Oscar knowing because the place was so cold. There was a light showing from beneath the pantry door and I could hear the sound of a saw-knife going through the crust of a loaf. I lit the gas and led Oscar to sit in a further corner, far away from the fire, a corner cold enough to keep him awake so that he could have his supper and not keep me waiting. Oscar sat quietly in his chair, his huge face hanging low, staring at the odd coloured mats in front of the hearth as if he were wondering how they could have grown there. When his eyes grew weary of the mats he stared at the piled-up fire as if wondering what it was for. He looked more tired, dafter than I had ever seen him before. I thought his brain might be starting to dissolve or swim about in his head as a result of all the stuff he drank. I reminded myself to explain about the mats to Oscar one night to save him the bother of going crazy through trying to puzzle how they had come to be there.

Out of the pantry came Meg. Meg was about thirty and big in the body, with a face that was dark and solemn, that had lost most of its shape and all its laughter. Alone, Meg and I would talk all night together, talk about pictures we had seen and sometimes sing songs we had learned from the gramophone or picked up as kids from the chapel, sing in harmony, nicely, too, for Meg had a low contralto to put a soft frame around my tenor. But if Oscar was with us that dark, solemn look, that was like the butt-end of a long funeral, stayed on Meg's face as if it were nailed there. At one time Meg had been one of the elements who had picked coal for Oscar on his tip. She and a brother of hers had been together as pickers. Oscar had fancied the look of her and taken her into his house to get meals ready. Then the brother found that Meg was preparing meals in Oscar's bed and even years of stooping down for Oscar had not made this brother so simple as to believe that there was any cooking to be done in that quarter of Oscar's house. So he made a dive at Oscar one day when Oscar was riding around the tip helping me to keep the pickers up to the mark. Oscar beat Meg's brother with his whip and his boots and got him put in jail for assault. Meg always said that her brother deserved to go to jail for being silly enough to think that being a home comfort to Oscar was any worse than picking coal at fivepence a bag on that bloody tip. So she had stayed on with Oscar, his cook, his cleaner and his stand-by in the nights and around her face the time was nearly always night-time.

Meg laid the food on the table and made our tea in a six-pint teapot on the deep polished hob.

'It's ready,' she said.

'Don't want any,' said Oscar, and he shook his great, fat head stupidly from side to side.

'He doesn't want any,' I said, surprised, because one of the notable things about this Oscar was that he hardly ever stopped eating. He ate like a goat.

'What's the matter with him?' asked Meg. 'He must be going to die if he won't eat.'

'He's tired.'

'Who's he been with?'

'Somebody from Brimstone Terrace, Macnaffy. Funny name like that. Looked like a bag. She didn't like Oscar much.'

Meg said 'Oh', as if she could read right into the mind of that Macnaffy element and thought it was a good mind to have had those thoughts about Oscar. Then, after she had said 'Oh', Meg took a good long stare at Oscar, uttered a short little groan and began slowly to strip off the clothes from the top part of her body. She stood half naked about a yard away from me, and, to take my mind off this exhibition, I lit a cigarette and watched her. Her breasts were big and feeble looking, but her waist still seemed slender and firm, although I knew not much of such items. She dragged a hard, wooden chair from against one of the walls and placed it with its back to the fire. She sat down on it facing Oscar. That was part of Meg's job. It might sound funny, but that is what Meg had to do whenever Oscar came home at nights weary and stupid and listless after a long session of drinking and chasing. She would half strip in that fashion and sit there facing him. Oscar would look at her and before very long, he being a hog and a bit crazy from owning that mountain, the sight of her flesh, which was very white and soft, would coax all his snoring desires from their rat-holes and he would come lunging to his feet like some element who has just been brought back from the dead, a solid sheet of flame with all his appetites barking like dogs from him, hungry for food and Meg and Christ knows what. But that night he just kept staring at Meg as if she were no more than a dead person wearing a double layer of clothes than usual to celebrate the coming of the final frost. Meg fidgeted a bit on the hard seat of her chair. Not an eyelid of Oscar's batted. Meg's head drooped suddenly until she was bent almost double. She pushed her fingers through her hair. A thick belt of redness showed on her neck and the top part of her back. I thought she was going to cry. My mind was reddish, too, and I tried to match up the shade of it with the flush on Meg's back. I was sorry for her, in a raw, hesitating way, as I had felt sorry for Oscar's horse. 'Get your clothes on, Meg,' I said. 'Nothing will stir him much before Christmas. Go to bed.'

Meg pulled her clothes on and stood against the fire. I handed her what was left of my cigarette. She liked smoking my stumps. She nodded her head at Oscar.

'You can do away with cats, dogs,' she said, 'and nobody bothers you. But you can't do away with him. If you did that, there'd be a hell of a howl.'

'Don't you try doing it, Meg,' I said. 'It's not worth getting into trouble for something you do to Oscar.'

'You're right, Lewis. I think you're right.'

Oscar's eyes brightened a shade. He flung his right arm out towards us.

'You two,' he said. 'Get out of my house. Get right out of my bloody sight.'

Meg went through the door that led to the stairs. Most often I slept in Oscar's house, too. But that night I wanted more than anything to sleep somewhere else. So I made my way towards the house in the Terraces, those rows of houses that stretched along the mountain side, where my mother lived. I shouted to Oscar as I went through the front door that I would be back up at his house at eight o'clock the next morning. I got no answer back from him. I did not want an answer, Oscar could not see into the future as far as eight o'clock the next day. It would have pleased me if he had not been able to see at all. He was a hog.

Outside, the night had become still and clear. Somewhere in the sky the moon must have come out, but I could not see it and had no wish to jerk my neck around looking for it. Above the tops of the trees that surrounded Oscar's house, I could see the tall tipping equipment standing out against the sky on the peak of Oscar's tip. I stood quite still for a minute in that stone-flagged yard. I thought of the faces of Meg and the Macnaffy element. I cursed that tipping equipment because it was ugly and noisy and dangerous and because the stuff it shot down the tip's side often hurt the limbs of the people who stood waiting to pick up the scraps of coal that went to fill Oscar's bags and Oscar's pockets. It struck me as odd that I should think one second about Meg and Macnaffy and the next about elements who had picked the coal on Oscar's tip. It was because, some time or another, I had seen the same look on all their faces, the look of people who are being fed in parts through a mangle. And at the handle of the mangle, turning away like blue hell in case anybody should have a little less pain than he paid rent on, stood Oscar. Every way I looked, down, up, sidewards, I could see Oscar. He was a big figure, planted there on his mountain.

I followed the course of the small, yellow stream that cut into the ravine's bed and soon I reached the top Terrace where my mother lived. My mother's house was one of a hundred in a row and it was just like the other ninety-nine. Even the smells were the same, a mixture of cabbage and onion which came from the damp and another smell that arose from rent that had gone high. Oscar owned a lot of these houses and I loved him no more deeply for that. I did not bother to go around the front way to the house. That would have added minutes to my journey and it was getting late. The back wall looked out on to the mountain. There was a door let into this wall. It was bolted from the inside. I climbed the wall. I knew exactly where to put my hands and feet. I had done the climb a thousand times in dark and light. A cat could have done it no better. As I straddled the top of the wall, a policeman passed, flashed his lamp and asked me what I was up to. I said it was my house and what of it. He recognized me as Oscar's boy and passed on. The policemen never bothered you in the Terraces if they knew you were connected with some such character as Oscar.

My mother was in bed and the fire out. I never saw much of her. She had greyed off into a fixed quietness since my father died. She said my job with Oscar was not respectable and she had not liked me for taking it. So, even when I saw her, she just looked at me, offered me what bit of food happened to be going, never said very much, looked as if she were very far away in some place where the air was sweeter and the rates were lower, as if she thought everything around was cruel and dirty, which, no doubt, it was.

There was a light shining in the kitchen of the house next door. This was the house where my friend, Danny, and his wife, Hannah, lived. Danny was older than I. He would have been about thirty-five, but he was a nice element, as was his wife, Hannah. He had been a friend of my father and he was my friend, too. I decided to go in and have a chat with them before going to bed. I told myself that it was a good thing to talk once in a while with people like Danny, who did not own mountains, and to people like Hannah, who were not whores. I told myself that I would discover boils breaking out all over my brain if I spent my time talking only to elements like Oscar, Meg, Clarisse and that girl from Brimstone Terrace who looked savage and sucked at a wet cigarette.

The wall between my mother's house and Danny's was so low I could step over it. The voters in the Terraces had nothing of such value as to make it worth their while to build high walls to keep other voters away from it. From the small back-paving of Danny's house, I could look through the uncurtained window of his kitchen. Through the window I could see Danny and Hannah sitting in silence by the fireplace.

I went in. They were glad to see me, as if they had been sitting for too long in silence. They smiled as they dragged a third chair up to the fire for me to sit on. There were only three chairs in the room. Danny was a short, frail, unhealthy-looking man with a gentle, musical voice that went up and down, as if it were searching for something, as it might have been, for there were a lot of things that Danny did not have. He wore a flannel shirt, open at the neck, and having that shirt hanging loose over his chest only made him look frailer. Hannah was stronger-looking, dark, with the loveliest face that was ever seen in all the valley. I, as I sat between them, knowing little about such things, thought that if it was Oscar who was married to Hannah and the deep loveliness she had he would not have been sitting up as late as Danny crouching over an almost dead hearth. But Danny had not worked for nine years and his body was weak, so that must have made a great difference.

'I'll go and get a bit of coal for this fire,' said Danny. 'I'm not sure I'll be able to find any, but I'll try. There's been a spell on that fire ever since I tried burning that old boot mixed up with the cokes. God, we got to have some brightness now and then.'

'Brightness is all right,' I said. It was not much of a remark to make. But there was a sad sound in Danny's voice that had started pumping up the old sorrow in me again and you cannot think of anything very smart to say when you are being pumped like that.

Danny went outside. Hannah turned in her chair and looked full into my face. What I felt when she did that was what I cannot describe. It was something I could never have felt even after a hundred years of being chained up and stared at by Meg or Clarisse. It went to my roots and stuck there, tingling. Her face was sad, like a mountain under long-falling rain. She glanced at the door through which Danny had gone and I could sense a whole river of words inside her, dyked-up, wanting to come out to where somebody but her could hear them.

'Oh, Christ, Lewis,' she said, suddenly, and in a whisper: 'I get fed up sometimes, fed up so I can't stand it.'

'You wait, Hannah,' I said. 'You wait until Danny gets work and then things will be fine.' I never remembered Danny working and never thought he would work again, but I had always heard people in the Terraces saying that when so-and-so was working again, everything would be fine. So I passed it on to Hannah and hoped it made some sense to her. She looked no happier. Rather did she look as if the rain was belting a little harder on the wet mountain that she looked like. Her features came closer together in a central clump of sadness.

'He had work,' she said. 'Last week he had a job delivering coal for Simons, the coalman. He wasn't on that job for a day. The sacks were too heavy for Danny and he finished up on the pavement, so Simons told him to go home and work up some strength.'

'You just wait till he works up some strength.'

'Where the hell from?' asked Hannah. She kicked her black, dull shoe-tip into the lowest bar of the grate where the powdered ash had formed into a tight, airless drift. The ash loosened and the dust came up into the air around us, making for our heads as if it were wanting to answer our questions for us and I do not suppose the dust would have made any messier a job of that than we did. Hannah wiped her shoe on her stocking. 'When'll that be, Lewis?' she asked. 'Where'll it come from, that strength?'

'I don't know. There's a lot of things I don't know. Every day there's more and more things I don't know, Hannah. I must be dimp.'

'But you got strength,' she said.

I said 'Aye' and was glad I had strength, because from what I could see life was very hard in those Terraces if you did not have

it, and from what I heard the whole world was just like the
Terraces, only worse in parts and colder. Danny came back in
with a single piece of coal on a shovel. He nodded at it.

'That's the last of it and that took some finding.' He threw it
on the fire. 'There was a cat sitting on it. If I thought the cat
could have hatched another lump out of it I'd have let it stay. It's
dear stuff to buy when you're not working, this coal. I've had to
buy every lump we've burned since Oscar got the policemen to
stand guard over his tip and stop us helping ourselves to a bagful.
If it gets any dearer to buy we'll have to burn it first and eat
what's left to save a bit on the groceries.'

'Oscar's doing well out of that tip,' I said.

'It wasn't so bad when we could pick an odd bag off that tip,
but now he's got those poor bloody halfwits picking the coal for
him to sell.'

'They're very backward. They'll do anything for a few bob.
They don't know any different.'

'You ought to know different. You got some sort of brain. But
you work for Oscar.'

'Oh, it's a job, Danny.'

'But that Oscar's a hog. You've said that yourself, God knows
how many times. Your old man would have kicked you over the
roof for taking money off such a crap. Somebody'd be doing the
world a kindness to put him out of the way. But you help to keep
him in the way.'

'As long as he gives me pay, he can be any sort of hog he likes.'

'That's not the point,' said Danny in a high, excited voice, and
I could see that something was worrying him and that he would
like a long argument with me or even a quarrel to relieve his own
feelings.

Hannah jumped to her feet and her lips were small and bitter
as she looked down at Danny.

'That is the point,' she said. 'Let's be glad somebody can have
a job and keep it. So long, Lewis.' She pushed her chair out of the
way. 'I'm going to bed.'

She left the room. Danny's mouth, which had been hanging open, closed tight and his grey skin flushed as if a brush were being drawn over it, hard.

'She meant that for me, Lewis. Last week I got a job. I waited a long time for it. There should have been an eclipse to celebrate, but there wasn't and that was just as well. It was a job carrying sacks of coal. I found after a couple of hours that I couldn't even carry a sack of coal and they had to pick me off a pavement. Jesus, Lewis, I felt bad. Not just because the only job I've had in nine years finished almost before it started. I felt bad inside, too. I went and saw the doctor. He said my heart is bad. By the look of him as he said that it must be very bad. But he couldn't have looked any worse than I felt. So what are the chances of me working again? Not much now, with people knowing how I finished up on the ground after carrying one sack for Simons the coalman. I didn't tell Hannah what's supposed to be wrong with me. She'll guess that. Oh, hell, Lew, just think what kind of life she's had. That's what makes me sick. I lost my work seven months after we got married. I was healthy enough then, strong enough. I could have dug a whole mountain away if it would have helped Hannah and if there had been a mountain that did not belong to some bastard like Oscar. The doctor said strain was my trouble. He's talking nonsense. It was plain, simple bloody worry that ate the strength out of my heart. But now, I'm not worrying. What if I die. I won't lose anything by getting rid of myself, and Hannah might gain something. That's a hell of a thing for a man to be saying who's still pretty young, but I'm saying it and I mean it.'

'A hell of a thing,' I said.

'And I'm not going to be so daft as I've been.'

'What you mean, Danny?'

'I've been afraid. Afraid of Oscar, afraid of policemen, afraid of offending anybody in case I made things bad for myself. Now nobody can make things worse for me. Funny how good knowing that makes you feel. There's nothing worse than dying, is there?

They never can do anything worse than that to you, never mind which of their ten million bloody laws you break. The pity is that I've waited and worried myself into a state where I haven't got the strength to make any kind of trouble that would warm all the coldness of me. But I suppose they'll beat me in the end, all those people who helped to push me and Hannah down into the drain. They've broken most of the spirit I ever had. You can't be afraid for years and years and then say: "To hell with fear." It's not as simple, boy. It stays, like blood or bone, part of what makes you live. So even if I studied the problems hard and fought for what I wanted like a bloody beast, I could never get back a millionth of what they've taken from me. They are cruel bastards, Lewis, these people who stand above us and kick our lives into any shape that pleases them, cruel and bad and blind. They've beaten me. They'll never have any more trouble with me than they'd have with a louse. I wouldn't have the nerve to take a bite at anybody's flesh if there was no other food around. I'd be afraid of the copper who'd call around in the morning. They've sucked me dry as a cork. They can be proud of what they've done to me and pass on to the next life they want to make a little meatball out of. But one thing I will do, just one thing. I'm not going to pay for any more coal. That's a wonderful bloody triumph. They tell me I'm going to die years too soon and years too late, depending on who's talking. So I stand up and defy the world. How do I defy it? I say I'm not going to pay for any more coal. That's life at its highest, that was.'

I kept my eyes on the fireplace. A lot of what Danny had said had slipped past my ears, but I had the feeling that all his words were bunches of nettles being drawn up and down the bare sides of my body.

'Where you going to get your coal then, Danny?'

'From Oscar's tip.'

'Oscar'll get you put in jail.'

'What's the difference? I'll be up there tomorrow morning.'

'Why don't you pick for Oscar, Danny? You'd get some free bags then.'

'I'd rather pick the stuff that covers my own bones.'

'You don't like Oscar.'

'I could choke him.'

'But look, Danny, how you going to carry sacks of coal down a steep mountain if you couldn't carry one along a flat pavement for Simons?'

'Well,' and Danny smiled a bit for the first time that night, 'Hannah might think I've gone beyond the stage of wanting to try. I'll show Hannah.'

After that, there was not much that either Danny or I could say. I asked him if he was sleepy. He opened his eyes wide and said he did not mind if he never slept again. We went outside on to the small back-paving. We looked up at the stars, not because there was anything we wanted to find out about them, but because stars are good things to look at when you feel fierce enough to put your boot through somebody and I was sorry for Danny in a way that made me want to do that to somebody. Then we crossed over into the kitchen of my mother's house. I made us some tea. As we drank it, we stared in silence for a while at the fireless grate. Then we hummed together. Singing, for people who live in the Terraces, is good. It puts the brain to sleep at times when it is neither wise nor useful to have the brain awake. When they sing the edges of things are not as sharp as they are usually.

'See you tomorrow morning then,' said Danny as he got up to go.

'All right, Danny,' I said, and hoped I would not see him, because I knew that Oscar was savage in his ways with trespassers and all other voters whom Oscar thought were laying hands on anything that Oscar thought belonged to him. As I watched the small, stooped body of Danny make its way over the wall that separated his house from mine, it came into my head that Oscar could never be as savage as the life of this Danny had been, and, knowing Oscar, that was not saying much for the life.

*

The sun woke me the next morning. I could hear no stir from below or from my mother's bedroom. I got up and dressed. Downstairs I scraped the cinders from the grate and kindled a fire. I threw some sugar on the fire to make the sticks catch more quickly. My mother would have told me not to do that. She would have said sugar was to be eaten, not tossed on fires. I did not like eating sugar, so I always thought it was nice to see the fire jumping into flame after getting a handful of stuff I did not like. I made some tea. I poured out a strong cup for my mother and took it upstairs. I knocked on her bedroom door. There was no answer. She slept well. I remembered that there was nothing in my mother's world worth getting up at a quarter to seven for. The distant look she wore showed that. She was elsewhere all the time. I could not blame her for being like that in the Terraces. That was a hard place to be in whatever kind of look you wore on your face. I did not knock a second time on my mother's door or I might have heard her asking me what kind of new world had come into being that I should be rousing people so soon after the dawn. I drank the tea myself as I tiptoed down the stairs. A section of the wallpaper swung loose from the damp wall that led from the bottom of the stairs to the front door. I fixed that back with a nail I had in my pocket. I knew that the nail, unhammered, would soon work itself loose, but I felt pleased at having done it, because it showed that being with Oscar had not yet made a hog out of me or I would not have been doing all these kind and thoughtful things at a quarter to seven in the morning. Anybody who will go to the trouble of fixing wallpaper back to the wall in a house in the Terraces, where whole houses are liable to fall down on your head if you kick too hard against the wainscoting in passing, must be a very pure and noble kind of element. From the pavement outside I could hear the nailed boots of workers scraping along home from work and that made me think of Danny. I swallowed some more tea and with it a chunk of bread pudding, ice-cold and smooth to the tongue, which I found in the pantry. I chewed and drank and made as great a noise in my head as I could with these activities, because I did not want to think of Danny, and any noise in the head kept up long enough is a great cure for thought. There was nothing I could do about Danny or for him. The sun could have been twice as strong and warm and heavy, the hills twice as high and green, and Danny would still be in a mess. I thought that was funny, so funny it took about half the taste from my bread pudding.

As I left the house, I called out: 'So long.' I did not think anyone would be awake to hear it, but it makes me uneasy to leave any place in silence. But as I stood by the back door throwing back the rusted bolts, another voice said: 'So long.' I turned around. Hannah was standing by her bedroom window which was a quarter open, staring across the valley in a fixed way as if she were looking for someone there. The black of her hair made a wide margin for her face. Her face was white, a kind of over-washed, lily-valley whiteness. She looked to me as if she might still be asleep, drawn to that window by a dream, but I did not think any dream, even after a cask of cheese, would be so odd as to draw an element to a bedroom window to look down over the Terraces, or to make them say 'So long' to someone like me. I did not open the back door. I swung myself with a strong, easy upswing of arms and body and got on top of the wall for a few seconds. I was showing off before Hannah. But Hannah was not looking and that made me decide that I would never again go over a door instead of through. It was a great waste of time and skill unless you made sure there was somebody looking.

'So long, Lewis,' said Hannah again, and her low voice, matching the smooth thickness of the sunlight, made me feel better as I jumped from the wall on to the grass of the mountain side. I made my way to the path that would lead me to Oscar's house.

On that path, I came across a small voter of about fifty, very grey about the head and wearing a large, rainproof fisherman's hat which he wore pulled down towards his neck and this hat, looking strange on a voter who had nothing to do with fish, gave him the look of something growing out of the earth, something you would think twice, and more than twice, about picking. I knew this voter. Everybody called him No Doubt. That was because he nearly always said 'No doubt' in answer to whatever it was you said to him. This meant that conversation did not get along very fast with this element, but I did not blame him for going in for these brief answers like 'No doubt.' In the Terraces many an element has been fined or put in jail for what is called free speech, so it is useful to keep your talk limited to such phrases as nobody can put two meanings on or put you in jail for, such a phrase as 'No doubt', for example, which is quite harmless to governments and kings and bishops and so on. I was surprised to see this voter marching up the mountain at seven o'clock in the morning. He was one of the pickers on Oscar's tip and they were not supposed to start picking until eight o'clock. True, it was a fine morning and healthier than bed, but I thought he would have seen enough of the mountain during his work without queueing up on it an hour before time. He was still limping from a crack on the leg from a rolling stone he had got on Oscar's tip a month before.

'God, it's a lovely morning,' I said.

'No doubt,' said No Doubt, taken aback a bit, because he must have thought I was addressing him as God, which he was not, being little, grey, overworked, and limping.

'What are you doing up here so early?' I asked.

'No doubt,' said No Doubt, cautiously.

'That isn't an answer.'

'My leg, it hurts in the morning. So I like to come up here.'

'I'm sorry to hear about your leg, No Doubt. You'll have to take care of it. You won't get any compensation from that Oscar if it goes bad.'

'Don't want any.'

'I don't follow you there, No Doubt.'

'I'm grateful to Oscar.'

'What are you grateful to him for?'

'For giving me the chance to come up here on the mountain to work.'

'You joking?'

'I love the mountain. I don't like being down there in the houses. I don't like the houses much at all. If I didn't have this picking to do for Oscar people would say I was funny to come up here so early in the morning and spend most of my day up here. I feel more at home on the mountains.'

'You got any kids, No Doubt?'

'I've got four kids. They've gone away now. They went away to work. The house has gone very quiet since they went. They made a lot of noise, those kids. But when I'm up here, on the mountain, I don't think about them or the house. Always very nice and peaceful up here.'

'You ought to have been a sheep, No Doubt. No offence, mind, when I say that, but I really think you ought to have been a sheep.'

'No doubt,' said No Doubt.

The path divided. To the right it went to Oscar's house. To the left it went to Oscar's tip. No Doubt went to the left and as I watched him limp away between the ferns, it seemed as if the loneliness of this little element came out from him and stuck in the air like a smell. He was like Meg and Danny and Hannah, because they, too, seemed to be going around with a rope at their necks jerking them to a halt every time they tried moving forward and a load of old iron where their hearts should have been. This is a great waste of iron, besides being the cause of great pain to those elements who carry it about. So I felt sorry for No Doubt and thought I was doing well enough in this line of being sorry to get some pay for it, like a preacher.

In Oscar's house I found Meg in a clean, blue apron standing over a breakfast table that had not been touched. Oscar's porridge basin, which always looked to me bigger than the contraption I had had to bath in when I was a kid, stood on its usual plate, full of porridge that had gone cold.

'Where's Oscar, Meg?'

'He says he's not coming down. He's sitting up in bed. He's

grey and he's trembling and he's going crazy, I think. He told me
to send you up when you came in. I think he's going off his head
this time and I hope he goes the whole way and chucks himself
through the bloody window on to those stone slabs.' Meg was
talking out loud in a wild, singing voice and in her excitement
she had let her fingers clasp the edge of Oscar's porridge bowl
and her fingertips were sliding down fast into the porridge. I
nodded my head at her hand and she drew up her fingers and
wiped them on her blue apron. 'He's queer. All he does is sit
there and stare at himself in the mirror on the wall and mumbles
a bit. The big mirror, you know, the big one with the brown
frame that has the heads carved at the top, the one he looks at
himself in when he walks about naked in the nights.'

'I know that mirror, Meg. I know very well the one you mean.'
I was a bit annoyed by the way Meg was carrying on about this
mirror as if it were more important than the fact that Oscar was
sitting up in his bed, going grey and gibbering and clean off his
head for all I knew. Women do that. They see two things, one
big, one little. If they want to take their minds or your mind off
the big one they will chatter like hell about the little one. I told
Meg to sit down and drink tea and not worry.

I walked up the stairs, very slowly and letting my fingers slide
and jolt over the joints in the wood with which the walls of the
stairway had been encased by Oscar's father, who had got hold
of more wood by chopping down trees than he had known
rightly what to do with. I walked slowly, because I wanted to
give Oscar time to come back to normal. Once he got hungry he
would be all right again. The only trouble with that man as I saw
it was that he never saw beer without drinking it, never saw a
woman without wanting her, never wanted a woman without
getting her, and, most important, never wanted to get away from
that big slab of earth he owned and got his wealth from.

I pushed open the bedroom door without knocking: I had
become a kind of shadow to this Oscar and shadows do not
knock. I found him just as Meg had described. He was sitting in

the bed with his legs drawn up and between his vast gut and his legs looked as if he had taken another bed into bed with him to start some new fashion that only landowners could afford. The colour had drained from his face. It might have gone lower down his body for a change, being sick of Oscar's face as I sometimes got, but his face was like the fine ash when the cinders have been riddled away. His lower lip was hanging down over his chin like a pale red sunshade. He looked daft and dazed about the mouth, but in his eyes there was still the old, bright cunning. I did not suppose there would be enough good air in the heart and mind of this Oscar to keep alive for long that part of man's sadness which causes the eyes to become for ever dark and dead looking.

I stood by the side of the bed and looked right down at him. He did not stop gazing at himself in the huge mirror on the wall opposite. He seemed afraid that his reflection would vanish and never return if he turned his eyes away from it for a second.

'What's the matter with you, Oscar?' I asked. I called him Oscar because a shadow can be as free as it pleases in its ways of talking and, anyway, I did not give a split damn whether or not I was polite to an element like Oscar. To me he was just part of a mountain.

'I feel queer, Lewis.' He upturned his head sharply to look at me.

'You look queer. You look as if you were stunned. Who stunned you?'

'No, not stunned. My head's clear, clear enough. I want a change.'

'You live all right, Oscar. You live better than most; like a prince, seems to me. What you want a change for?'

'Don't know exactly. Just want it.' He waved his hand as if he were fanning his chest, as if his hand were his tongue trying to light on some words that would make some sense to him and to me. 'I don't want to do any more drinking. Like a bloody tank. Going to give it up.'

'That'll save me a lot of trouble. That'll save me and the mare nights of trouble.'

'And women. I could be sick at the thought of them. So many, my God. Every damned one of them the same. Always the same. From now on, to hell with them.'

'That'll save the women a lot of trouble. That'll save them a lot of time and weight and trouble.'

'You're a cheeky young bastard,' said Oscar, but quite quietly. He gave me a stare with both his eyes, forgetting his reflection in the mirror now and I could see as clearly as I could see him that he had no love for me, because I was lean and young and strong, because I did not give a damn for anything he was or anything he had, because I would never draw my tongue in adoration across his toes as a lot of other elements were willing to do, elements that misery had squeezed the guts and goodness and hope out of, like No Doubt.

'I'm only telling you, Oscar, what the women tell me. I'm just passing it on.'

'What women?'

'Macnaffy, for one. The lolly you had in the Harp last night. She looked as if she had been walked over by a horse. She said she felt like that too. And Meg could do with a rest. You are a great burden on Meg.'

'Meg? Who the hell is she to . . . I'll show that Meg.'

'You can't show her. She's seen everything.' I had gingered up my tone a little and it was hard. Oscar gave me another glance.

'That's right, boy,' he said. 'I want a change.'

'Why not go away for a spell? You've got nothing much to do here.'

'I'm all right here. Never been away from here. I'm all right just where I am. I want to do something different, something I've never done before.'

'Try some work. A lot of the voters go in for that.'

'I own a mountain. I own fifty houses. And that's work.'

'Nice work.'

'I want to feel something different.'

'Try being poor. You've never tried that. A lot of voters go in for that too.'

'Less of your bloody lip. I got money. There must be something I could do to get a new feeling. All the other feelings are old and they stink. I been drunk so often. And women, I've had them under me so often they're like part of the earth. Sit down there on the side of the bed. Don't feel quite so bloody now talking to you. Sit down for Christ's sake when I tell you to. You're standing there like a bloody judge and I know you're only a kid. I want to talk. I feel queer and when I talk I get better. You know those people that pick for me on that tip. They're mine. If it wasn't for me saying they can come and pick my coal they wouldn't be there picking. When I wanted to I cleared them off the tip. That's what I can do. If I told them to get off this mountain, off they'd have to get. They'd be rotting about on their beds having more bastards like themselves. I ought to be able to do as I like to people like that. Don't know what they live for, anyway. Sometimes I've watched them. Sometimes when a stone has come rolling down the tip I've watched them run and duck and lie on their guts full stretch to get out of the stone's way as if they had as much to live for as a bloody king or me or somebody like that, and sometimes I've prayed, I've watched the stone and prayed that the stone would be smarter than them and smack their bloody brains out, just to teach them a lesson. I ought to be able to do as I like to them. I've often felt like that. I'd like to kill somebody, Lewis. That's the thing to make you tingle, I bet. To smash somebody into hell and to shout as you're smashing, "There you are, you poor blundering bastard. There go your dreams and your eyes and your hopes and your arms, all the bloody things you got that make you feel so grand, so proud . . ."'

Then Oscar twitched his legs down flat and threw his head back with a crack against the back of the bed. I jumped to my feet, thinking he was going to pass into a fit. I moved back a little from the bed and looked at the door. I did not wish to be in that room if Oscar was going to be taken in such a fashion. I did not know how I would handle a man with a body shaped so much like a whale and a mind shaped so much like another man's rear.

But all Oscar did was to press his knuckles with violent force into his eyes and start to shake as if he were freezing. The room, to me, was heavily, stickily warm, and the sight of Oscar shaking as if he had long icicles sticking into him was very surprising indeed. But I told myself that if a man was going to make such speeches as the one Oscar had just made, no icicle could be made too long to be jerked into him and he deserved to tremble. I thought that if I were in Oscar's place I would have cracked my head against that bed back with such vigour I would have put an end to all temptation to make further speeches of that kind, for such speeches seemed to be opening up a pathway that would lead Oscar at great speed to wherever it is they take people who have dumped their wits into the early morning ash bucket.

He uncovered his eyes and gazed at me as if he were trying to put me under a spell. His eyes were red and painful and weak, and their stare would not have affected a woodlouse.

'Even you,' he said.

'What about me?'

'Even you would come in handy if I wanted to try out my hand with that new feeling. You wouldn't be living if it wasn't for me. You're as much mine as those people who stand about on the tip up there waiting around with their sacks to pick my coal. I could try it out even on you. That would stop your bloody lip, you . . .' And he rolled like a flash on to his side and shot his hand beneath the bed. His hand swung wildly back and fore in search for the chamber. For a second I could not see what was meant by all this activity. Then I saw he had a notion of swinging this article up from under the bed and breaking it over my head. I kicked his hand as hard as I could. The vessel shot from his grasp and landed with cracking force against a farther wall.

'You'd better not try any of those tricks with me, Oscar.' I pushed him back into the bed. He was weak as a baby now and crying and sucking his hand where I had kicked it, sucking it slowly as if he liked it, as if it were a toffee apple. 'So you'd like to kill people, would you, because your mouth's a bit stale after the beer and you're a bit worn out by the women. That's a very nice thing for you, Oscar. Owning a mountain's driving you off your head, boy. One day you'll be ordering all the people who pick your coal and pay your rent to come filing one by one into this bedroom while you brain them with the bloody jerry, like you wanted to do to me. Just to give you a few new thrills. Be careful, Oscar. You are not the only voter in these parts who feels he'd like to put somebody away. It's a very widespread feeling. I know a lot of people who feel like that. And it's just you they'd like to put away. Not anybody. Just you. And they wouldn't do it to give themselves a fresher outlook after Christ knows how many years on the booze and the batter on money they never worked for. They'd do it because they think you are a dirty nuisance who goes around having the same effect as an eclipse or a disease. You get a lot too much to live on, Oscar, and you get it too easy, and you live among too many people who don't get enough to live on and never get it easy, like my pal Danny. That's mad. Anybody can see that's mad. So you follow suit. You go mad too. Nothing surprising in that, Oscar.' I do not think he heard much of what I had said. If he had, he would probably have leaped out of bed and made a fresh start with the chamber swinging. I marched from the bedroom, leaving him to his trembling, sucking and owning.

When I got down to the kitchen, Meg cut me a slice of cold, fat pork and sandwiched it for me. I was fond of that and I ate it with a cup of tea. We looked at each other and we said all we wanted to say in that way without opening our mouths. Even if I had wanted to talk, my mouth was too full with all the pork and bread and Meg would have had to lay her ear on my face to follow what I was saying. But there was no need for that. We both knew how the other felt to the last shiver of the last nerve.

I was glad when I left the house. The air was sweet on the face and the brush of grass and fern was fresh on my legs. I got to the tip early that morning. I walked up the tip's steep side and cursed every time my feet slipped on its crumbling surface. I cursed too the elements who had been daft enough to dump all those tons of black dirt on to the head of so lovely a mountain. It struck me that a character like that No Doubt, with all his talk of love for mountains, must hate that tip deeply, but the hates of a voter like No Doubt must be so deep and silent, he being poor and queer in his ways, they had probably got all tangled and did not mean anything more, bumping into one another and being battered instead of shooting outwards and battering the things he hated.

When I got to the top of the tip, I started to do my job. It was a very simple job. An idiot could have done it, only an idiot would have been too honest to put up with Oscar. All I had to do was to stand there, far enough away from the tipping machine to be out of the dust, and count the number of elements who turned up to do the picking and count the number of sacks picked. Then I had to see that these sacks were piled up in the proper order to be taken away by the cart that came for them at the end of the afternoon. Any job connected with counting I consider to be very easy, especially when you are doing this job within hearing and seeing distance of other elements whose jobs cause them to be scratching about bent up like monkeys for bits of coal, getting their guts turned half solid with coal dust and their limbs occasionally knocked inside out by those small rocks that came flying down from the trams emptied by the tipping machine. I would not blame any voter who told his parents that he would rather stay permanently under the bed or on the Insurance if he could not find some job connected with counting.

I liked being on the top of that tip. It was high. Even the wind in winter when it was high and seemed in a mood to toss me about two miles, I did not dislike it, for I dislike only those people and things that harm me and know they harm. From this summit I could see for great distances. To the south ran the fat green plain, full of plants and farmers and other voters I knew little of and that plain finished with the sea. The sea did not interest me because the urge to fish was never in my family, and there were plenty of places to drown in inside the hills. To the north ran ranges of hills till the eye lost them. On each new hill there would most likely be some element like Oscar owning it, and between the hills, on the valley sides, elements like Danny getting it in the neck and going black in the face because of it. It all seemed very endless and unsweet and I never felt that I would like to leave the mountain on which I stood and travel over the mountains I could see to the farthest distance. There was no mystery in them. I knew and did not love the life that crawled between the cracks.

About two hours after the picking started, the tipping machine broke down. This machine was often breaking down and it made such a lot of dirt and noise when it was not, you liked it much better when this breaking down took place. Job Hicks, a fair-haired voter, who was in charge of this contraption, and whose hair was never fair for much longer than ten minutes after jerking the thing into life, came up to me and said there was a very serious break this time. A crankshaft had gone, said Job, and from the solemn tone in which he said that, I understood that this crankshaft was as important to this tipping contraption as rent to a landlord or breath to an ordinary voter or God to some element at prayer.

'All right, Job,' I said, 'it's not our loss. It doesn't grieve me at all. I'll go and ask Oscar if he wants to send the pickers home.'

I raced down the tip. I could go down that tip fast as the wind, picking out places for my feet to land where they would not double up under me and never once did I choose a wrong place. The speed I gathered carried me at a gallop about fifty feet from the base of the tip.

I found Oscar sitting in front of the kitchen fire, stroking the barrel of a heavy sporting gun which he had laid across his knees. All his trembling and greyness had gone. He was merry again and chewing great slices of meat from a plate which Meg had arranged for him on the hob. He looked as if he might have just used the gun to kill the very animal he was eating.

'Hullo, Lewis,' he said, smiling, as if he had never even dreamed of opening the top of my skull with the bedroom vessel. It was getting difficult to follow the changes in this man.

'The machine's broken down,' I said, when I saw that his jaws were quiet enough to let him hear something. 'There'll be no more picking today. What about the pickers? Shall I send them home?'

'Send them home, boy. When the tipper's not sending any fresh stuff down there's so little coal there to pick they start fighting about who's to have it. And they haven't got so much strength they can afford to throw it away on fighting.' And he started to laugh, stuffing his mouth with meat at the same time, as if he had just let off the joke of the month and was refuelling to work up steam for the next one.

'All right. I'll tell them that.' I took the top thick slice of buttered toast that Meg was bringing from the table to the fireplace. My eyes must have brightened as my teeth sank into it because Meg smiled at me as she passed. She probably saw something clean about the great hunger of an element like me as compared with Oscar.

Back at the tip, I gathered the pickers together, about twenty of them, and told them there would be no more picking that day; they could go home. Most of them laughed. All the younger ones did and I was glad to see that because it is a very strange thing to see voters who are too earnest about their work, especially such work as brings in little more than sunburn and backache. They arranged their full, half-full or empty sacks in a tidy heap on the side and in the little red note book I used to note down the results of my counting, I made a record of how much each had done. As I wrote small knots of the pickers took turns at peering over my shoulder to make sure that I was not doing my duty to Oscar by cheating them. The old man called No Doubt lingered behind after the others and asked me if he could stay on and do some quiet picking on his own. The old man looked very weary and was more stooped than he had been when I met him on the mountain path earlier that morning. His hand kept wandering down to his hurt leg and stroking it as if the pain kept calling to his fingers.

'You go home, No Doubt,' I said. 'Go home and lie down and rest.'

'Don't want to go home. It's quiet there. Too quiet.'

'That's all the better for sleep. That's what you want, boy, sleep. Go on down now and for Christ's sake don't be so anxious about making profit for Oscar.'

He went off, muttering something about that not being what he was anxious about. As I watched him go, I hoped he would go home and sleep, sleep for a long time and have a whole procession of dreams, good dreams that would make him laugh and pass on the time for him more quickly than waking, dreams of some place where no tips crowned the mountains, where all the kids a man had were not obliged to leave their homes and go to work elsewhere. I thought maybe that the brain of this No Doubt might have shrunk with sadness to a size so small there was no room left in it any more for such items as dreams and that when he lay down the only thing he felt were ancient aches that stamped across his body like voters on the march, and that when he woke again he would count, by his bruises, the hours he had slept. I wondered how the kids of this No Doubt could have felt when they left him like that, in a body, to walk about in an empty house where the joy went out of the window as the rain came through the roof, driven to find his minutes of peace in the trade of his feet on a mountain that for him was not much more than a bulging grave . . . No Doubt vanished from sight over the breast.

I wandered to the farther side of the mountain, away from Oscar's house, away from the tip. I did not want to see Oscar again for a spell. On the mountain's lip were two small crags, and between them, a natural seat, a flat slab of rock. I liked sitting there, on the sun-warmed rock, staring down into the narrow valley, at the untidy straggle of houses that mounted it. I picked out the cream-washed house standing apart from the others on the edge of an allotment in which Clarisse lived. It was nice to sit there with the sun passing from the rock into my body, warming it, and thinking of Clarisse, who seemed to have plenty of warmth, whether the sun was about or not. There was a man digging in the allotment that bordered Clarisse's dwelling. I wondered if that element had enough interest left over from digging and growing things to take any interest in the shapes that Clarisse made or to have the same kind of thoughts about Clarisse as I had.

I got tired of looking at those houses in their formless journey to the summit of the hill that divided the valley from the plain. I got tired of looking at the cream-washed walls of the house where Clarisse lived. Looking at walls was not the same as looking at Clarisse. They were of different colours, and after a while said different things to my senses. So I slewed my body away from the valley and looked back over the mountain. I saw a man's figure walking up from the direction of the Terraces towards the tip. It looked like Danny because the figure had a small, stooped way of walking and there was something that looked like an empty sack thrown over its shoulder. As the man came to the foot of the tip I saw that it was Danny. He walked up the tip about six feet and bent down as he started to pick. There would be but little there for him to pick, but I could not expect Danny to know that.

My eyes moved towards Oscar's house. Oscar was riding his horse at walking pace towards the tip. Even from that distance I could see the slight sway of his body always as he rode. He was such a big element, that Oscar. You could have seen him half a world away. I knew he would play hell with Danny if he found him picking coal on his tip. I did not want Danny played hell with. He was my friend and my father's friend, and he had plenty on his plate without being chivvied around by Oscar. So I stood up and started signalling to Danny to get away. I shouted too to help out the signalling. Danny turned his head to face the spot from which I was shouting, but he made no sense of the words that came from me or of the tricks I was doing with my waving arms. I started to run, hoping I could reach Danny before Oscar and strife did. But Oscar had already seen Danny and was bawling in a way that even I, far off, could hear.

'Get off that tip, you dirty bastard.' He must have shouted that a dozen times, shouted it up in a huge voice from a stomach that had the size and quality of a big drum, so that the grass and ferns and Danny and me could not help having a clear idea of what Oscar thought of Danny and what he expected Danny to do.

I stopped running. There was no point in running any more. I walked as slowly as I could, my eyes fixed, not on Oscar, but on Danny. Danny was not moving, just standing there, his sack dangling in his hand, the other hand keeping the mouth of the sack open to admit the ribblings of coal he picked up. Oscar had dug his horse into a gallop now, and, almost in the time it took me to get a mouthful of spittle and swallow it, he had brought his horse to a halt about ten yards from where Danny stood, his face brownish with his rage, a colour not much different from the horse's. Oscar had his sporting gun slipped into two clips he had fixed on to his saddle. I was quite close to them now, but neither of them seemed to notice me. Danny had his head lowered and his face was fuller of anger even than Oscar's. And it was white, white as lime against the surface of that tip. He looked as if he were so frozen and quiet inside, all his fear had gone asleep or died.

'Who's a dirty bastard?' asked Danny, not loudly or defiantly, but as if he were asking the time.

'You are,' said Oscar, and he smacked his little whip against the side of his brown riding boot. 'Get off this mountain before I kick you off.'

'Look, brother,' said Danny. 'Last night I had a dream. In this dream I saw God. And God said, "I've washed my hands of those landowners. They're a worse plague than frogs or boils and I wash my hands of them." So you can go to hell, Oscar.'

Oscar spurred his horse at him, leaned forward as he lunged out at Danny. The tip of the whip skimmed Danny's forehead.

Danny crouched and sprang forward like a bullet. He got his fingers fastened tight into Oscar's shirt-front, and, at first, I thought he was going to choke Oscar and I was very interested. Danny gave a great tug and it was his whole mind and heart that seemed to be tugging and not just the muscles and strength part, which could not have been very great in Danny. Oscar came tumbling down from his horse and if he had landed upon Danny, Danny would have died. But Danny had skipped out of the way and was standing over Oscar with the sole of his boot planted on Oscar's mouth. Oscar had landed on his back on the softish gravel of the tip, the breath knocked out of him, but not hurt.

Danny picked up a stone the size of his own head. He held this above Oscar's eyes.

'If I had any sense,' he said, 'I'd bring this down over your head and if I did that, I'd have the feeling I'd done one useful thing on earth. But I don't like giving pain. People of my sort don't as a rule. We just get it, get it, get it till we can't hold any more and we pass over with the feeling how the hell we stood it for so long. It's boys of your stripe who like giving out the pain, and, holy Christ, you always get away with it. We've put up with enough from the people we can't see, who live far away, who make a mess of our lives without ever clapping their eyes on us. But you live on our doorsteps and we're going to deal with you. If I want free coal from this tip, I'll get it.'

And Danny turned away from him, climbed back up the tip to a point farther than where he had been standing before. Oscar jacked himself up from the ground, twitching and groaning and moving slowly, so slowly you would have said he had made a bet to move more slowly than anybody else. It seemed like a year before he got himself up straight. His stomach sagged down, because all the breath had not come back into his body, and he seemed to need this breath to keep it up. He wiped his sleeve hard across his mouth to wipe away the black scraps of earth Danny's boots had left there. He had the expression on his face of one who had just had an experience which he finds very new, very bad. He did not look at me. Nor did he turn around to look at Danny. His hand found the bridle of his horse and he led it away. Danny was bent low over the side of the tip, searching for the scraps left over by Oscar's pickers. Once I saw his hand tremble as it touched the tip's surface and a thin, black dust rose around his arm. I watched Danny, I followed with my ears the clomp of Oscar and his mare through the tall, dry grass. Then the clomping stopped. I turned my head towards Oscar. He was standing beside his horse, his gun levelled at Danny.

'Watch out, Danny,' I shouted and I did not feel I could do any more than that. I fixed my eyes on the ground, expecting a great noise when the gun went off. It went off. The noise was not as great as my promise of it. The zip of its passing dragged my eyes to the tip. I saw the earth a yard to the right of Danny shoot up. Startled, Danny swung around, his arms above him in the air, off balance. His legs shot from beneath him and he came plunging down, somersaulting. He slithered the last two feet and his head came to a stop against one of the large stones that littered the tip at its extreme edge. The stone moved with the force of Danny's body against it. But Danny did not move. I began shouting at Oscar, but he was on his horse and galloping away by the time I had got ten words from my mouth.

I sat down beside Danny. I did not touch him. His face seemed to be all on a slant. I knew little about such things as death, but I knew that Danny was dead, because I could not feel that he was anything else but that. I sat by his side, not wanting to move, because he moved not at all. I wondered at that slant of his head and the wide, senseless openness of his mouth. I sat there for fifteen minutes and never have I done less thinking than I did then. I was blank, part of the mountain, part of Danny, and both those things, as I saw it, were dead. I sat on a stone, quite near him, crouched over him, like a kid, as if I wanted to stand between him and the cold I knew would soon be coming. My body got cramped, cramped as my brain, sitting in that position. I got to my feet with a jump and walked quickly back to Oscar's house.

Oscar was sitting by the fire when I went in. As I pushed the door open, he turned around quickly and he seemed glad to see that it was me.

'All right, Oscar,' I said. 'You got your new feeling. He's dead. How does it feel?'

'Say you didn't see me, Lewis. Say you didn't see me,' like a song, with a soft, blubbering, sliding tune. 'Say you didn't see me, Lewis.'

'All right, I'll say what you want me to say. I got a job with you. The truth is nothing up against that. Anything you want, I'll say. But all the same, he's dead.'

'Oh, Christ.'

'He died of fright.'

'Fright?'

'Your bullet didn't hit him. He wasn't hit by that at all. He was frightened and he fell. He thought he'd got away from his fear. He thought he'd be brave for a change. But in the end the fear caught up with him again. It must travel very fast and stick like hell, this fear.'

'What you talking about? Speak clear, for God's sake. I don't know what you're talking about. So I didn't hit him? So I . . .'

'But you fired at him.' I threw that at Oscar, because I could see he was getting less pale, less afraid.

'Say you didn't see me, Lewis.' He got up and searched in one of the drawers of the big chest against the wall. He found a wallet and from one of the inner flaps he took some notes, about ten. He handed them to me. 'I don't want them,' I said. 'But I'll take them and I'll say anything you want.'

He sat down again and I could see he was very frightened, as frightened as Danny had been when he started somersaulting down that tip. But I knew Oscar. I knew his fright would pass as soon as he had had some food to eat, some drink and time to feel that he was in no danger. And he would be glad, too, glad he had killed somebody, somebody who had been on his mountain without the right to be there, somebody poorer than he was, somebody who had been on the same earth as Oscar without the right to be there either. And I felt my hatred of Oscar boiling down into a solid lump with a hard, biting point. He shouted on Meg to bring him something to eat. I knew as I looked at him that I could say anything to him and he would not answer back.

'In any case,' I said, 'nobody'd believe me. If you were to say you'd seen forty bullets put into the bloke and they couldn't find either the bullets or the bloke, they'd still believe you. You're a great figure in these parts, Oscar, what with owning a mountain and about a hundred bloody houses. I live in one of those houses. I help my mother to pay the rent on it. So that would make me out to be a liar from the beginning. That fellow who's dead out there, name's Danny, friend of mine. He lived in one of your houses, too. Never thought much of it. Damp, draughty, bloody hole he said it was. Always reckoned he'd have done better in the shelter line if he'd been born a rabbit. His life was just like his house. Damp and draughty. Not sorry to get out of it, from what he was telling me. Nice chap, very quiet, and, Christ, he's got a pretty wife, Oscar. You ought to see her, Oscar. She's the prettiest woman I ever saw, but you've never seen her because she wouldn't be seen dead in the knocking shops you call at. But if you had seen her, you'd have killed Danny just for the sake of getting her. Honest to God.'

He looked at me, his eyes made small by the task of trying to eat too much at once and his look said that he could not make up his mind whether to smile at me or kick me in the chin. But he said nothing and just watched Meg bringing in more food.

'And now,' I said, 'I'd better go down into the valley and tell whoever ought to be told that somebody's dropped dead on Oscar's top.'

It was early afternoon two days later when an inquest was held on Danny. This event took place in a vestry, the vestry of one of those two chapels that snarled at each other across a road on the hill that led up to the disused air-fan at the foot of the mountain.

I thought as I took my place on one of the benches in this small room that Danny would not have liked having his business discussed in such a place, for he had never been a great friend of vestries and chapels. He had told me often that his only notion of a sound religion was a tank to be used as protection for the skull from the many elements who seemed eager to take a whack at it. He had surprised me that day on the tip when he spoke to Oscar of having heard God in a dream delivering a very sensible statement on landowners. I had never heard Danny mention God before and either he had eaten an odd supper to have such mixed company in his dreams or he had been making the whole thing up like a story for the benefit of Oscar. But there was not much that Danny could do now to protest against being talked about in a vestry. He was even more under people's thumbs now than he had been before and it made me sad to consider that not even dying seemed to make any improvement for the voters in this respect.

The vestry started to fill up with various elements. Most of them were very important-looking and were not known to me at all. They seemed to have something to do with the law which seems to breed many elements who have a knack of dressing up to look a lot more important than they are. As I waited for these voters to stop shaking hands and settle down I remembered that I had done some singing in that vestry a long time before. It was as one of a choir in a cantata called 'Rainbow Tints'. In this cantata the young elements who did the singing were dressed up in a lot of coloured stuff like chintz and the aim of all these colours was to show how joyful they were about being Christians. There was not much plot to that cantata and the most I remember of it was crouching down behind a big alto called Wilkinson James and wearing a kind of red shirt made from a bedspread, my tint being scarlet. I told myself that that vestry must be leading a very interesting life to house two such events as that cantata and an inquest on Danny. I wondered what the composer of 'Rainbow Tints', a happy man, no doubt, would have thought of the darkly dressed collection of voters who had gathered in the vestry that afternoon to decide why a man should die while picking a bag of coal on a tip where he had no business to be, according to what they took to be the law. If he looked closely enough, it would certainly broaden his rainbow.

Oscar came and sat beside me. He had taken off his brown riding-boots for once and was wearing a blue serge suit, very tight on him, because Oscar put on weight as easily as other people take on breath. Hannah took a seat on a bench opposite ours. She looked dazed, like a person would look listening to a lot of nonsense in foreign tongues. It was not that the idea of Danny being dead had not sunk into her yet. It had probably sunk in too far. There is a region beyond understanding that contains a lot of pain. Hannah was wearing a grey topcoat that hung loosely from her shoulders. She could not have had the money to get fitted up with black yet. The insurance elements were most likely waiting the usual three days before being sure that Danny would not go in for miracles and start rubbing his eyes. As soon as Hannah sat down, Oscar began staring at her and after a while I noticed that he was rubbing his left kneecap with his right hand, which is what he always did when he got excited. I knew he would do that as soon as he saw Hannah. I had never seen anybody quite like Hannah. Nor, for that matter, had I seen anybody quite like that Oscar. The grief in Hannah's face was the purest, whitest midwinter and would have moved most men to a bitter prayer for the past and future of our race. But not Oscar. The animals learned from him. From the promise of him, a long time ago, the apes came, must have come. I reminded myself to give Hannah a half of the money I had got from Oscar.

Silence fell as the coroner took his seat, and this man looked like a part of silence. He had lost a lot of hair and I supposed that was only right, because it must be very difficult to keep a check on death and your hair at the same time. He had a mumbling way of speaking, as if he were throwing his voice and it never quite landed, and I did not catch much of what he was saying. The next man to talk was a lot clearer, too clear. His tongue seemed to go bouncing about the room. He wore a come-to-Jesus collar, which is a collar that has two wings sticking out of it instead of going down flat. I have noticed that something is always bouncing about the room when an element wearing a collar of this type is present. The sharp wings must stab them into making a stir. This element was a solicitor and strongly in favour of Oscar. If he had not been so young and thin I would have said he was Oscar's father, so highly did he think of Oscar. He made sure that everyone knew that Danny had had a seizure on a tip that was private property on which he had been trespassing and picking coal which amounted to thieving and he repeated this rigmarole so often I got to the point of thinking that this element was such a firm believer in the law he even believed that anybody who took to trespassing and thieving on a tip that did not belong to him just got a seizure as a matter of course, the law keeping a stock of these seizures in reserve to be bolted out every time the police got a notion there was trespassing going on. Then a doctor who looked sleepy got up and said things about Danny's heart, in a peevish way, as if it was thinking about his heart that had made him sleepy. He sounded altogether as if he found the subject very dull and not likely to ginger him up at all. The element with the wings on his collar kept smiling at Oscar and shaking his head in agreement with every word the doctor said and he got such a great roll into this head-shaking it would not have surprised me to see the wings suddenly outspreading and this element whirring his way through the ceiling. Following the doctor was Simons, the coal merchant. He wore a bow-tie and a long, new, black overcoat, in which he looked very impressive and all this splendour of Simons's outfit seemed to mean that either Simons considered this inquest to be a very high-class event or that Simons was doing very well out of the coal trade. At first I could not understand why Simons should be there at all unless he had applied for the chance of showing himself off. Then I remembered he had employed Danny for about two hours of work in about nine years, that made Simons a great figure in Danny's life, so great that if Danny had had kids instead of his other troubles, some of these kids would have been called after this Simons. He was nervous and I had noticed him bobbing to his feet several times, thinking it was his turn before his turn actually came around. No doubt, Simons had never before seen so much law in one room in one afternoon in all his life. He described how he had engaged Danny and he said he had done this largely because Danny was such a poor and haggard-looking element. Then he spoke of finding Danny flat on a pavement with a sack of coal across his back. Some of the coal, said Simons, had spilled out of the sack and had rolled off into a gutter where kids had picked it up, showing how careful you had to be to engage only elements who could stand up straight when carrying sacks of coal. Simons got sort of fixed in his description of Danny lying on that pavement with the sack above him as if Danny had got into that position right at the beginning of the day and had waited for somebody to place the sack across him. Then they called me and I spoke up steadily and without nerves, because I had a strong feeling that I was the daftest person present, not in competition with Simons, who was too dressed-up to think; Oscar, who was too dirty about the mind to think; Hannah, who was too beaten about by grief to think ... Compared with those elements, I felt very bright indeed. I told them I had been standing about a hundred yards from the tip when I saw Danny picking above on the tip. I said I had heard him shout as if in pain, had seen him spin around and come tumbling down until his head came to rest against one of those large stones. The coroner asked me if there was any sign of life in him when I reached him. I was silent for a while. I was thinking of those long, blank, peculiar minutes I had spent at Danny's side. I said no, there was no sign of any life.

After that, they seemed to have had enough and I was not sorry. The sight of Oscar there fixing his hot little eyes on Hannah

and squirting his desire from them like a hose was making me
wild. I knew that all I had to do to slap his face into the yellowest
colour of clay and to make his fat body tremble in a way that
would make the vestry rock was to mention that I had seen him
point his gun at Danny, that he would have put a bullet clean
through Danny if he could have kept his aim steady enough. But
I said nothing about that. I felt no sense of shame or dirtiness at
keeping my tongue silent about such things. Living in a place like
the Terraces gives you very peculiar feelings about items like
truth and honesty and on top of that my spell with Oscar had
done something to my conscience, covered it with ice or corns.
Anyway, there was very little feeling in it. Maybe I had never had
much. Maybe my mother was never able to afford the kind of
food that makes for conscience. All I know is that if I have one it
might well have been dead for all movement I got out of it as I
stood up and spoke my piece for those voters in the vestry, and I
have always thought that as long as men keep on behaving so
much like monkeys off the lead, that was just as well.

The air in the vestry became warm. The windows in such
places as vestries are not opened any too often. And listening to
the slowly told tale of how death came to a man you have known
well, with no great pity shown by the tellers, is like sitting in a
room in which a damp fire burns with much smoke and no flame.
Most of the elements present began to stir about in their seats. We
heard the coroner give out that Danny's death was natural. We
were glad to hear that, although there were some of us who would
have liked to hear the coroner pass a verdict on nature as well.

Hannah was the first to leave the room at the finish. Oscar and
I followed her out. We stood on the kerb and watched her mount
a bus. Oscar craned his body to be able to watch her as she made
her way down the aisle of the bus. He said nothing. His lust, I
suppose, was right beneath his tongue, swelling, fierce, jamming
it hard against his palate, making him dumb.

'We'll go to the Harp,' said Oscar. 'We'll go there now and
have something to eat and I could do with a drink.'

'On Tuesday, you said you weren't going to drink any more.'

'What Tuesday? I couldn't have said anything like that. I must have been daft to say anything like that.'

'You said it. You were in bed. I heard you saying it.'

'Must have been joking.'

'Nobody laughed.'

I looked at him. His face was red, eager, thoughtful. It did not seem as if he remembered anything about the spasm on the bed. I thought Oscar was lucky indeed to be able to clear out of his head things he had said and done no more than two days before. If you have the courage that comes from never being slapped down, cheated or made hungry, you can perform this cleaning-out process and think nothing of it. Only those whose poverty seems to have existed from the earth's beginning have to put up with being dragged below the surface by the dead chains of past years, past days. The poor hug to their hearts all the yesterdays they know have not been lived and the burden is a heavy one. But Oscar was free. He could cut afresh the tape of each new morning and the day he marched through was a road in itself, whole and complete, attached to no navel string of before or after. Yesterday meant no more to Oscar than the past life of the farthest star to me. It was all right, for Oscar.

The Harp had not opened its doors for the evening session when we got there. We went around the side and knocked. Wilson came to the door with his waistcoat open and a newspaper in his hand. He looked twice at Oscar to make sure that Oscar was not riding a horse, then asked why Oscar was not riding a horse. He could not get over this and seemed surprised at Oscar's blue serge suit and buttoned up his own waistcoat as if in tribute to this new neatness that he saw in Oscar.

'A chap died on my tip,' said Oscar. 'So I had to dress up for the inquest. A bloody nuisance, some of these chaps.'

'Same as I think,' said Wilson, letting us in and shaking his paper in our faces as if we were a pair of wasps. 'And this paper says the same. It says the world is losing its moral sense.'

'Its what?'

'Its moral sense. You know that thing.'

Oscar did not know at all what it was, judging by the blank look he wore, but he told Wilson in a low voice that it was a pity the world was losing it, just to be on the safe side.

'I don't know where the world is going to be without a moral sense,' said Wilson, upon whom this item had obviously made a deep impression and who seemed to be worrying about it as if the moral sense were the tail of his only shirt and he were standing in a draught. I did not see why Wilson should worry his guts out in this fashion about the moral sense. From what I knew of the Harp and the capers of such customers as Oscar, the cellar and attic of the place must have been full of moral sense that had gone mouldy and been pushed out of the way because nobody could find any use for it except to stuff chairs.

'Bring us something to eat in the little room, Wilson,' said Oscar.

'The usual? Bacon, sausage, kidneys, liver?'

'That'll do. And three pints.'

Wilson led us into the small room where Oscar had taken the Macnaffy girl. He lit the gas fire and handed his newspaper to Oscar. Oscar looked at it for just over a minute, took in the pictures, giggled a bit over a photograph of two old chimpanzees scratching a young chimpanzee, then gave the paper to me. He closed his eyes and leaned back on his chair. He had no interest in print. As far as he was concerned, reading had no point. There was nothing in life he wanted to read about. He was doing all right. There was nothing to be said about that. He was all the comment that was needed. Mountains and tips and houses are very solid things and not likely to be washed away by words. So words contained not even the attraction of terror for Oscar. I read an article about God in the middle of the paper and the element who wrote this article was making it his business to bring back to the world that moral sense which, according to Wilson, had got itself lost. After reading the article I did not see that it made much difference to the situation at all.

Clarisse brought in the food and drink. Seeing me in a clean collar and tie made her treat me with more respect than usual. She did not often see me in a tie and the one I wore then was green with red stripes and was very prominent, like a flag. At the sight of that tie Clarisse must have felt like saluting as well as showing me respect which took the form of keeping quiet instead of praising the shape of my body, her usual approach. But all she did was rub her leg against mine. She did that with Oscar's leg, too, which made me think that if there had been eighty or so legs in that room instead of just four Clarisse would have rubbed part of her own leg right away before she got out into the fresh air again. In all that valley Clarisse was the fullest answer to a cold climate I ever came across.

Oscar cleaned his plate minutes ahead of me. I was keeping my bacon and kidneys until the last, because I considered these items very tasty and not to be rushed. Before I could get to them Oscar took hold of my plate and ate them for me. I asked him whether I had kept them in just the right condition for him and whether he would not like all his food served by way of my plate, but he was too busy eating to pay any attention to all this wit.

'And you can take the beer you bought for me, too,' I said. 'You know I don't like it.'

'More for me. More for me. More for me,' he started to shout in a high, childish voice, which sounded odd coming from an element with so tremendous a body as Oscar, an element whose own childhood was so deeply buried beneath the thick hogdirt of sodden lusting. He was very excited about something. I had seen that from the way his hands kept playing about in the vestry and this high, childish voice caper was running in the same lines. His eyes, peeping over the rim of his third pot, caught me making a disgusted grimace.

'I ought to shove your face into the gas fire,' he said, dropping his voice back to normal.

'I wouldn't do that.'

'Why shouldn't I do it?' He leaned forward and surveyed me

solemnly, as if his whole future was now bound up with this question of shoving my face into the gas fire.

'Because,' I said, 'if you did that, you would get yourself mixed up with Wilson in an argument about moral sense which has already been posted as missing.'

And funnily the prospect of arguing with Wilson about the moral sense seemed to scare Oscar a bit and his temper simmered down right away. He started to beam at me as happily as could be, as if I were wearing a lining of haloes and he were the element who had given me these haloes as a gift out of his own large stock. He called for the same amount of beer again. Halfway through the second load I helped him hoist his legs on to that low mantelshelf above the gas fire on which the Macnaffy girl had rested hers a few nights before.

'Oh, Christ, Lewis,' he said, blowing the words out suddenly like coughs, 'she's lovely. Boy, she's a pippin.'

'Who? The Macnaffy girl?' I was thinking of her and I assumed Oscar's mind might be on the same target.

'Hell, no. That woman we saw today.'

'Oh, Hannah. She's all right, Hannah.'

'I'd give a lot to have her, Lewis. I've learned a lot about women, Lewis. I'd take that sad look off her face.' He dropped his feet to the carpeted floor with a bang and his hot, bulging face bent close to mine. 'I'd give a lot to have her and by the time I'd had her a bit, Jesus, I'd make her glad I'd frightened the guts out of her old man and made him drop down dead.' He paused to gulp powerfully at his pot. He was running to a high tide. Breathless, he started to talk again. 'If I had known there was a woman like that living in those bloody Terraces, one of my houses, too, I'd have shot that husband of hers a long time ago. Fancy a dirty, penniless little bastard like that keeping a woman like her from a man like me.' He looked honestly shocked and disgusted that Danny could have done any such thing. 'But he can't keep her from me now, can he, Lewis? He's dead now, isn't he, Lewis? It was my gun that did it, wasn't it, Lewis? Did you see him jump? Did you see him jump and roll and then lie still, Lewis? Oh, Jesus, that was something worth watching. Did you see him, Lewis?'

He was laughing now, but the merriment of it was lost somewhere in the vast, swollen redness of his face. He only stopped laughing to take another pot and half drain it.

'I saw him, Oscar,' I said. 'And if I was you, I'd stop bawling about it at the top of my voice or somebody might hear.'

He started fidgeting on his seat and crinkling his eyes as if he were in pain. The fear came up in spouts from that man whenever he became afraid.

'But I want her. I got to have that woman, Lew. How the hell'm I going to get her? That's what I want to know. How am I going to get her?'

'I'll get her for you, Oscar.'

'You'll get her? You're joking with me. That's what you're doing. Don't joke with me or I'll do what I said I'd do with your face and the gas fire.'

'No need for you to get nasty with me, Oscar. Mine isn't the only face that could do with some pushing and you're not the only one with jobs to offer either. Not these days. Things are picking up. Of course I can get her for you. She'd be keen as hell to get a man like you. There isn't a woman in the Terraces who wouldn't pawn her husband to get a man like you. They're so bloody poor they got no option. Take this Hannah. You own the house she lives in. You own all the tip her old man passed out on. And now he's passed all she'll get is the pension which is sweet Billy Adams to live on if you don't want to live on acorns. You'd be like God to her, just like God. You leave it to me, Oscar. I'll get her for you.'

'Honest?' He was very pleased and a little doubting.

'You see. I'll get her for you. Bring her to you on a lead. Eat out of your hand. She got to eat. May as well be out of your hand as anybody else's.' I stood up, glad to get my face from off the same level as his.

'Where are you going?' he asked.

'You don't want me, do you?'

'I'll be here till stop.'

'I'll go then. You don't need me to help you swallow. So long.'

So I left Oscar to his drinking and made my way, full of thought, towards the top terrace where Hannah lived.

I took my time over the steep road that led to Hannah's house. I stared at the many voters who were moving about on the pavements, making their way to cinema shows, chapels and courting. It was interesting trying to guess which of these characters were going to which activities. And it was often hard to get this guessing right, because life in the Terraces is a large, black item that has been kicked clean out of shape by years of being a lot poorer than even life has a right to be. So you had very often to be a seer, a prophet or, perhaps, a Means Test investigator to get anything like a correct bead on any particular element you happened to be observing. I would pass, perhaps, some voter with a bowler and a black suit who looked as if he were going to be the central figure in some chapel gathering, but the odds were that this voter would have for his programme for the evening nothing holier than a few hours of rolling about on the grass of the mountainside with a maiden, also in black, in mourning for whatever it was she was going to lose as a result of all this rolling. Then some other voter with his shirt hanging open at the neck and with a generally pagan look about him might well be on his way to give a rousing sermon to one of the many sects that thrive in the Terraces. Most of the front doors I passed were wide open. From these open doors came either bits of gentle singing or bits of talk that were clear enough to listen to and this talk was often of such a sudden, savage and impatient character that one could understand why the front doors were kept open. It was to allow any of the talkers who got a sudden wallop to roll right into the road without danger of being bruised by any immovable woodwork that might be in the way.

When I got to Hannah's, three men and a woman were coming out of the front door. These people had the same short, dark, worried look as Danny and I thought they were his relatives, although this look I have mentioned was very widespread in the Terraces. I was glad these relatives were going and not coming. The worry was much too thick upon their faces for them to be bright company. They all tilted their hats at me for no reason I could see. It might have been my tie or they probably thought it would mean some fresh trouble if they did not.

With Hannah in the kitchen was an old man, an uncle of hers, an aged element who was called Hopkin the Rasp because in the days when his fingers had been less stiff he had been able to make some very pretty things from bits of wood with the help of no more than a rasp or two. He had a very high, sleepy voice and no teeth and it was difficult to listen for more than about five minutes without getting the feeling that life was heading for a great lull. He was talking away at Hannah as if she were a concert and he a reciter. Hannah looked steadily into the fire with just the same expression as she had worn at the Vestry. I sat down and she did not turn to say hullo or smile at me. I thought it was a good idea to have this Hopkin the Rasp to talk to people who were feeling grief. The sound of him was like the drip of dope on the face. After a spell with him, one could feel nothing very much. Hopkin turned his head my way when he found I had my eyes fixed on him interestedly, trying to listen. I supposed he would be talking about Danny and I would not have minded listening to that. I remembered then that although I had known Danny ever since I could walk, there was still not much I knew about him.

'You remember Iolo,' said Hopkin to me.

'Iolo who?'

'Iolo the sheepdog.'

'What are you talking about sheepdogs for, Hopkin? This is no time to be talking about sheepdogs.'

'Because I had one once. They're smarter than men. This one I had died before I could give him a trial. Died, just like Danny.'

'I'm sorry to hear about that,' I said, very kindly, but thinking all the same that voters who go around putting dogs on a par with men ought to be treated like bones and fed to a couple of dogs.

'That was a long time ago,' said Hopkin. 'It never grew to be more than a pup. But Waldo Williamson the Fruit who knows dogs – he's got his failings, mind, Waldo, but he knows dogs – he said that Iolo would have been a winner. That was years ago.'

I gave no answer for a minute. I thought that a conversation between Hopkin the Rasp and that Waldo Williamson, who could hardly think with drink and waterproofs, must have been very interesting. I looked around for some way of getting this Hopkin out of the house short of setting him alight or hitting him over the head. He would have sat there for a month by the look of him, wanting to talk of nothing else but Iolo the sheepdog. There did not seem to be any subject closer to the heart of Hopkin. I did not suppose that there had ever been in all his life any event or person as great as that Iolo. But I had no interest in sheepdogs. Nor in elements whose minds wept over their passing. Nor was I fond of the way in which this Hopkin the Rasp sang instead of talked.

'There was a woman looking for you, Hopkin,' I said.

'What woman?'

'Didn't catch her name. Sort of plump woman. Nice-looking woman.' His head jerked up as I said that and it struck me that I had been wrong in putting him down as having no other interest than sheepdogs. 'She said she was very keen to see you.'

'That would be Agnes, no doubt,' said Hopkin, proudly, as if this Agnes was no more than one of a whole parade of women who went about the place inquiring after him. 'I'll go and see her.'

'She'll be glad of that, Hopkin. She was very keen.'

'I suppose she was, boy, I suppose she was.' And he left the house saying in a very high key that he would be back.

'Hope he breaks his neck,' said Hannah, without shifting her eyes from the fireplace. The dark skin of her face was glazed with the fire's heat and that made her seem prettier to look at.

'He's old and daft,' I said. 'He can't help being like that.'

'He's old and daft. He walks around. People can talk to him. But Danny, he's up there.' She swung her head up towards the bedroom where Danny was.

'Sorry about Danny. Nice fellow, Danny. We'll miss him.'

'You won't. Not as much as me.'

'No. Not as much as you, Hannah. He was a nice fellow. Used to go for walks with him. Over the mountain, when I was a kid. But he was different then. He changed a lot.'

She looked straight at me, surprised, as if I had given her some bit of news. Her face changed slowly, like the sky will change when the sun gives over to rain and you see the black cloud ridges moving without sound into place. She swivelled around on her chair and she brought her face down on to the edge of the table. She slipped and landed kneeling on the canvas mat. I put my arms beneath her shoulders and lifted her back on the chair. Her face was ugly and flattened out with weeping and fast as the tears came from her eyes the words came from her mouth.

'He never did any harm at all. He just got harm like he always said. He was so patient, so patient and kind it withered him away being so patient and getting nothing out of it. All his strength went out of him, see, Lewis? For years I could see the strength going out of him. He wouldn't even give me love in the nights, because he said he wasn't fit to love any woman. He said when things were better it would be different. God, how we used to pray that things would be different. I wanted him to love me like he did at the beginning, so much, for so long. But always he said not till things are better. We waited too long, Lewis. We waited too long and this is all we get. He goes up on a tip and they bring him down like that. It isn't right, is it, Lewis? A thing like that isn't right, is it? Why should anybody be treated like me and Danny been treated? Oh, Christ, I'm sick, Lewis. I'm sick of being alive like this. I'd rather be like Danny is than sick like this . . .'

'Don't talk like that, Hannah. You're just hurting yourself. Be quiet now, Hannah.' I pressed my fingers into her armpits. I thought she was going to scream, but she quietened and wiped her eyes.

'I'll be quiet,' she said. 'I was tired, listening to that Hopkin. The bloody rasp. I'll be all right. You're kind, boy. Thank you, Lewis.'

'Where do you keep the teapot and the tea?'

She showed me. I made the tea strong and she smiled a little as she drank it. I drank nothing, said nothing and smiled not at all. There were a lot of fists inside me beating to a hard, bitter tune.

'We put up with a lot,' I said after a while.

'Too much,' said Hannah.

'We are stepped on.'

'All the time we are stepped on.'

'They stepped on Danny good and proper.'

'He never harmed anybody.'

'They harmed him like hell.'

The pale agony crawled back into her cheeks, into the stiffening red of her lips.

'Seen him, Lewis? Seen him since he's dead?'

'I found him, Hannah. Don't forget that. I found him. I helped to bring him down. Jesus, he was quiet.'

'That was his seat there, where you are sitting. Always he sat there. And in the nights when he came in, he'd sit there and talk. I liked to hear him talking . . . He was . . .'

I could see she was on the point of starting off on that crying again. I could not have stood that.

'For a change,' I said, 'it's time we stepped on somebody.'

'We ought to do that. We ought to get something out of all the trouble we put into getting nothing.'

'Danny never had the chance to get his own back.'

'No. No chance.'

'We ought to step on that bloody Oscar.'

'Who could get up high enough to step on him?'

'You ought to. Listen, Hannah, Oscar killed Danny.'

'Don't be daft, Lewis. Things are bad enough. Don't make them worse by talking daft.'

'I was there. I was on the tip when he shot his gun at Danny. It frightened Danny when the bullet came right close to him and he fell.'

The silence then seemed to come right out from the walls, to form in a thick column around the spot where Hannah and I were sitting. The little alarm clock on the mantelshelf ticked with a hard, unwilling, underpaid tick and I rubbed my wetted fingers up and down my thumb, cleaning it. A beetle moved around on a ball of brown paper that had been tossed into a corner.

'You stood up in that vestry,' said Hannah. 'You told them there how you saw Danny dying. But you didn't say anything about Oscar. You didn't say anything about a gun. What kept your mouth shut, Lewis?'

'Oscar'd have said I was lying. They'd have believed Oscar. Why should I have told anybody else, anyway? Danny's gone. Talking won't bring him back this way again. This is your business and mine, Hannah. That Oscar's not fit to be alive. It isn't only that he stands on that mountain and calls it his and boots the people off it. It isn't only that he gets a crowd of poor bastards to pick coal for him off that tip and makes a pile of dough out of it. It isn't only that he fired his bloody gun at Danny and made him fall. Hell, Hannah, he's dirty, that Oscar. He's dirtier than anything. He's got no pity for anybody, and if he sees anybody who's kind and clean like Danny was, he hates them worse than poison. That morning, the day Danny died, he was lying on his bed talking to me. Said he was feeling a bit stale, wanted something new to amuse him. Said he ought to be allowed to kill a few people, people who were poor, of no account, like Danny, who wouldn't be missed. Said that would give him a new feeling. That's why he shot his gun at Danny. He thinks he's a bloody god sitting up there on a mountain his old man stole, getting policemen to boot the backsides of people who set their feet on it.'

'He said those things?'

'All those things.'

'He said he'd like to kill somebody, somebody like Danny?'

'Like Danny, that's it.'

'Somebody poor, of no account, who wouldn't be missed?'

'That's right.'

'Who wouldn't be missed, by Christ. He said that, did he? When I finish, nobody'll miss him.'

'What are you going to do, Hannah?'

'I'm going to kill that bastard of an Oscar. Don't know how, but I'm going to do that.'

'You got a right to do it, Hannah. Somebody should have done it a long time ago. But nobody ever had as much right to do it as you. You . . . you got to do it.'

'And I won't do it to get any new feeling. I'll do it just to get clean again. All the things I went through with Danny, the cold and the hunger we put up with as we waited and the way it finished, those things make me feel dirty. Doing something to that Oscar will make me feel clean again. That'll be good, to be clean again.'

'How will you do it, Hannah?'

'Get him near me. That's all. Just get him near me.'

'I can do that. He comes when I whistle.'

'The last thing Danny ever gave me was a hammer. Funny thing, a hammer. He said he wanted to give me something. So he stole a hammer from a woodwork class he was going to down in the Settlement, you know, the Social Settlement. He stole it because he wanted to give me something. But he was sorry he did it as soon as he brought it home. That's how Danny was. He hid it away, never used it at all, in case somebody would see it. It's in a drawer over there. It's new and big.'

'Danny was good to get that for you.' I did not fancy the notion of Hannah working on Oscar with a hammer, but I gave no thought to difficulties of that sort and took things as they came. There is a rhythm about things when you are angry and I could feel the rhythm strong about me. 'I'll get him here for you, Hannah.'

'When?'

'Tomorrow night.'

'That's soon.'

'Oscar didn't ask Danny if he'd like to wait a while. Oh, you're just talking. You don't mean what you say. I can see by your look that you're just talking. Nobody'll ever touch that Oscar.'

'No, I'm not just talking. I could do it now even as I'm standing here. Bring him here tomorrow night. Bring him when you please. Tomorrow night. The day after that is the funeral. So Danny'll know he's quits with Oscar before he leaves here. Danny'd like to know that.'

'That'll cheer him up. He needs some cheering up, God knows. Get that sofa from behind the table. You and Oscar sit there when he comes. He'll like it sitting next to you. He's fancied you, Hannah. You're pretty. And if you can make an eye at him he'll roll all over you. He's like that, is Oscar.'

'I'll give him roll. I'll have the hammer on the sofa, behind a cushion.'

'Keep it close to you, Hannah. Keep it close.'

'. . . And then I'll stop him rolling.'

'That'll be a new feeling for him.' I was happy, excited, almost shouting. 'That'll be a new feeling for you, Oscar, you sod.'

Hannah rubbed her hands together, hard. I looked down at her. She was biting her lips as if she were sorry for some of the things she had said. I could almost see the old, white fears seeping back into her brain. A lot of the temper seemed to have drained out of her and once more she began to look as she had looked before I had said anything about Oscar – a sad woman, short of food and hope.

'You'll be afraid,' I said. 'You'll never be able to do that to Oscar.'

'I'll do it. Honest, Lewis.' Her voice was trailing off into dumbness with every other word. 'The way I feel . . . I could do anything.'

'I'll get you something to drink. Something to warm your blood, see? I'll buy you whisky. You drink that. Then you'll feel nobody's too big or too small any more. You'll just see yourself and that dirty nuisance who took Danny away from you and you'll know what to do.'

'Get some for me.'

'Tomorrow. And here's some money for you. It's a half of what Oscar gave me.'

'It's a lot.'

'It's not much. Looks a lot to you and me. But it's not much. And when Oscar comes in here you better keep the doors locked. You don't want people walking in. But it'll be late when he comes so there won't be many people about to bother you.'

'God, it's quiet in this house.'

'It is, too.'

'What's that noise in the corner?'

'That's a beetle. Only a beetle. What are you so pale for, Hannah?'

'It was so quiet then. Step on that beetle, Lewis.'

I did that. I could see Hannah was afraid, just as afraid as that beetle had probably been when it first felt the graze of my boot on its back. Hannah's fingers opened and shut on the money I had given her. There was no more for me to say or do.

'See you tomorrow evening, early. So long, Hannah.'

I left the house and made my way up the mountain path to Oscar's house. I had to get the horse to get him home. The evening was cool. The air was nice around my head and made me thoughtful. One of my thoughts brought my legs to a halt.

'Jesus,' I told myself, 'I've got Hannah to say she'll kill Oscar. To kill him with some bloody hammer. That's a hell of a thing.' And as I looked at it the idea seemed daft, mad. Then I thought of Hannah's face as she had slipped by the table, ugly and flattened out with tears. I thought of the mess her life was in, poorer than she had ever been and not even Danny now to give the business an occasional streak of light and I knew that these things would not be if it were not for hogs of Oscar's stripe making the world their sty. Then I thought it was good and fair and just that Hannah should take a hand in pushing Oscar from the world which he had helped to make a little dirtier than it needed to be. And if men there were who would blame her or punish her for so doing, then, I told the mountain, God help men. Hannah could not be in a worse mess, anyway. If she could, then God help Hannah and I could not help thinking that that kind of phrase did not help much.

'In any case,' I muttered, 'I don't give a damn. Mountains, tips, Oscar, Danny, Hannah, work and pain, living and dying, it all looks terribly bloody odd to me.'

Next day I asked Oscar for an afternoon off. He gave it me, because he was pleased when I told him I had seen Hannah and got her to agree to seeing him late that night. I told him the session should be easy and joyful, because Hannah had brightened up no end when told that a man like Oscar was interested in her.

'You can always depend on me, Oscar.'

'You're a good boy, Lewis. What did she say when you told her?'

'Not much. That sort never say much. But I could see she was pleased. Her old man couldn't have been much use to her anyway. Too weak and they're always cold in those Terraces. This is a kind of promotion for her.'

'Where's he now, the husband?'

'Oh, he's still there, in the house.'

'In the house?'

I could see that Oscar was not much taken with this idea of being in the same house as a dead man.

'But you don't need to mind that, Oscar. You had something to do with him being dead so it won't be so bad. You'll soon forget about him.'

'That's right, boy. Who the hell was he, anyway?'

'Nobody. He's better out of the way.'

'Absolutely.' And he wagged his huge, red face from side to side, solemnly, as if he were having a talk about the hymns at last Sunday's service.

'I'll call for you at the Harp,' I said.

I went down into the valley. I was nervous, even though I walked fast to keep myself from thinking. Now and then I went cold from head to foot. I buttoned up all the buttons of my leather jacket to see if that would put a stop to these cold spells, but they kept on just the same. I suppose people who have lived in places like those Terraces and who have been kicked around for the sole benefit of others, have been afraid of things for so many years and for such good cause that they get into the habit of being afraid even when their brains are screaming at them that there is no sense in their fear. I thought of what Danny had told me on that subject. There was a man whose brains had done a lot of screaming. But the fear had still kept a jump ahead of him. I felt I wanted to be doing something that would take my mind off Oscar.

I called at the Harp for the whisky I wanted Hannah to drink. Clarisse was there, having a slack time and ready to talk bits off my ears if I had let her.

'This bottle's for my mother,' I said. 'She's got the chills and a birthday today so I'm taking her this. I've got to go now, but I'll be back later. Can I see you tonight, Clarisse?'

'I'll be looking forward. Gee, you're so dark, Lewis.'

'What the hell's so great about being dark?'

'I don't know. I just like looking at you because you're so dark.'

'I can't understand that.'

I slipped the bottle into my jacket and walked, without hurry, to Hannah's. There were some more relatives in the kitchen when I got there. One of them, a woman, was detached from the rest of the group and was crying away in the corner where I had stepped on the beetle. She was crying strongly as if she were celebrating some kind of plague. She would have drowned that beetle even if I had not stepped on it. Hannah had drawn the sofa from behind the table and it stood now in front of the fireplace. It was a red, wooden contraption, old, but still firm enough. There were two cushions on it. I could not take my eyes off that sofa. There were two voters sitting on it, two men, sitting up very stiffly, holding their bowlers in their hands, saying nothing and just waiting by the look of them for the woman in the corner to get dry enough to start moving. They must have thought I was staring at them and not at the sofa. They started fumbling at their bowlers and coughing in the direction of the weeping woman. She calmed down when she saw there was a stranger present. She came and shook hands with me and her fingers were wet with the tears she had wiped from her face.

'It passeth all understanding,' she said.

I wanted to ask what passeth, but all I said was: 'There's no doubt about that. It doth.' I remembered that word 'doth' from the chapel and I thought it sounded all right. I passed my hand over one of the arms of the sofa.

'Nice bit of wood,' I said to the nearest of the two voters who sat on it.

'Nothing like it to be had today,' he said.

'There's no doubt about that.'

When they saw that I was just going around agreeing with everybody, they prepared to go. I was glad of that. The whisky bottle was hard and heavy beneath my jacket, on my chest. They shouted 'So long' to Hannah, who was in some other part of the house.

When they had left, Hannah came in. She was paler than I had seen her before.

'I couldn't stand to talk to them,' she said. 'I kept out of the way. They drive anybody crazy. Twice today I felt like taking that money you gave me and getting away, right away from these Terraces and never come back.'

'Danny wouldn't like you to do that.'

'Oh, what the hell does it matter what Danny . . .'

But she was sorry right away for that thought and her mouth closed up on the rest of the sentence. But she was right all the same. What the hell did it matter what Danny might think. He was dead. Still pretty near, but dead.

I took out the bottle and put it on one of the pantry shelves. The shelf had oilcloth of a pretty pattern on it. I could have stood there for a spell looking at that pattern, because I did not know what to say when I went back into the kitchen. When I went back in Hannah was sitting on the sofa, a handful of her red apron upraised to her mouth nibbling at it and looking as if the last thing she wanted was to hear anything from me.

'It's in there,' I said. 'In the pantry. Just take sips of it. Slow sips, till you get to the right pitch, the pitch where the only thing you feel is your anger and that boiling all the time. You listening, Hannah?'

'All right, Lewis. I'll do that. So long.'

'About nine to half-past, I'll bring Oscar.'

'All right, bring him.'

That evening, I sat with Clarisse in the kitchen of the Harp. She had built a big fire. Life was easy, full and warm, sitting there with Clarisse. As I lay back in the deep fireside chair with her sprawled above me, I would dearly have liked to cut every thread that bound me to any other man or woman outside that room. I had my mouth pressed into the small of her back. I was doing that on orders. Clarisse said she liked it, and, in any case, I had not much choice because the way she sprawled covered my mouth with the small of her back. I was as near bliss, as I saw it, as I would ever come. But the threads that led outward could not be cut; they were thicker than I was. From down the corridor came the bawling voice of Oscar, singing.

'What's the time, Clarisse?'

'About nine. No hurry. Plenty time yet.'

'Got to go.' I stirred.

'Stay there, for God's sake. You're a fidget, Lewis. You always got to go. It's early. Stay there.' She slapped at my leg like a mother arguing with a kid. 'It's nice here.'

I lifted her from above me and stood up.

'I know it's nice in here, Clarisse. Nicer than I've known anything before. I'd like to stay in here with you for always, because it's a very queer place outside. Queer men. Queer women. All putting up with queer kinds of trouble.' I talked like that because I was content for a brief spell and so tired I ached. 'But I got business to do and I got to do it.'

'What business?'

'Got to get Oscar and go.'

'There'll be other evenings.'

'Plenty more. I'm very warm for you, Clarisse.'

'I knew you'd be like that one day, Lewis.'

'Time I had some warmth. Never had much. Got to go now.'

It took me five minutes to get Oscar from the room where he was doing his singing. The Macnaffy element was in the same room. He was concentrating on her. He was singing right at her. She was swinging her thin, strong arms in front of his face, conducting the bawl of singing that splurched out of his mouth. She looked merry and glad to have Oscar ramming his tonsils on to her face. She seemed to have forgotten the night when she was so savage about him and called him a bloody weight. Elements like that Macnaffy cannot afford to remember things for very long. I grabbed Oscar by the arm and kicked him in the leg, always a good way of attracting attention, especially if that somebody is a hog who has just drunk about eighteen pints and is too far gone to pay much heed to whispered messages.

'Come on, Oscar,' I said. 'You know where we are going. Hannah. You remember. The Terraces.'

Oscar let his mouth drop and stood there swaying. As he stood there I thought by the look of him that, given about twenty years, he might have remembered his name and that would be all. The

Macnaffy element took one of his arms and began dragging him towards her. I caught hold of his coat-tail and the thin Macnaffy, while strong in her lean, Brimstone Terrace sort of way, was no match for me. I got Oscar out of the room in a rush.

We got into the yard outside.

'Start up towards the Terraces,' I said. 'I'll tell Wilson we're leaving the mare.'

'The mare. The mare,' muttered Oscar. 'I want to stroke that bloody mare.'

'I'll stroke you in a minute, Oscar. Start walking and try to keep upright.'

He steered his way by instinct towards the Terraces. I caught up with him quickly and armed him to keep him steady. It was a long, hard walk I had with him. The weight of his body against mine wearied me and its warmth sickened.

I pushed him up the steps that fronted Hannah's. He chuckled a little as he glimpsed at the drawn blinds of the house. The blinds were too short and left gaps. We walked softly up the cemented gully that flanked the house. A yard from the end of the gully, I gave him a last push.

'She'll be there, waiting. Go on, Oscar.'

I stayed where I was, not moving at all. I heard him shuffle across the paving. I heard him knock upon the door. The door opened. I heard Hannah's voice. It was high, lively, piercing, not low as I had heard it before. The door closed. I waited and did not move. It began to grow dark quickly, as if the dark were racing down that night from the height of the hills to celebrate something.

I moved to the top of the gully and on to the paving. The gas had been lit in Hannah's kitchen. Through the window which had no curtain the inside of the kitchen could clearly be seen. With the lower part of my eyes I could see the forms of Hannah and Oscar on the sofa. Most of my vision was taken up with a picture on the wall opposite, a big picture showing Moses bringing a sackful of frogs down on the head of some Egyptian. It was a whole minute before I could bring my eyes downward from Moses and those frogs to the two on the sofa.

Hannah was lying back on the sofa, further away. Her eyes were closed and strange white thrills seemed to be surging through her face causing her eyelids and her chin to twitch from moment to moment. Oscar was bent above her. His body was motionless save for a heaving of the shoulders that kept time with the twitching of Hannah's eyelids and chin. Hannah's arm was outstretched behind Oscar and rested on the fringe of the cushion. She is reaching for the hammer, I said to myself. The hammer is behind that cushion and she is reaching for it. And soon the hammer would be put upon Oscar, just like a hog being auctioned, Oscar in all his heat and dirt and then Oscar, cold and getting colder and cut off from all the things that make men dirty, would be clean too. In my eagerness I pressed my body against the window-sill and felt the lime with which the stonework had been washed crush and flake against my clothes.

Hannah's hand dropped, dropped out of sight. But not behind the cushion. It dropped to somewhere my eyes could not follow, not even my aching, open eyes in a head slanted excitedly on a stretching neck. Hannah's head dropped back. I could see the muscles around her eyes contract as she closed her eyes tighter, as if to lose the sight of herself and the conscience of her from sight. Her mouth hung open. And then, with the unhurried silence of falling snow, she gave herself to Oscar. There was nothing I could not see now. She gave herself and Oscar, with his huge body flat-tened in skilled and solemn ecstasy, took her with a rapture and a joy that could almost be seen rising from him like a mist. I had to stand there, watching them. It was long and the pain of watching them sucked the strength from me as if the pain were a forceps. My sight became clouded. I had been pressing my eyes hard against the window-pane and that had made my eyes water. Sickness passed like a light-flash through my stomach. It had gone before I could think much about it, leaving only my stomach, wonderingly hungry, in me, wonderingly alone. I walked softly backwards and sat on the low wall that divided the house of Danny from my mother's house. I was full of wailing songs that passed through zones of light and dark inside me and went from very high to very low in their sad, sickening passage.

I sat on that wall for two or three minutes. Then I walked back to the window, calmer, inwardly silent now. Hannah was helping Oscar to his feet now. He looked vacant, dumb and sweaty. When she had got him off the sofa, she turned sharply on her side and sunk her head in the cushion that had been beneath her shoulder. I made my way back into the gully. A bat had been caught between the narrow walls and the sound of its flight was the only sound in all the night.

The kitchen door opened. I heard Oscar take two or three steps along the paving. Then he stopped. That would be the night air poking into his brain. He started off again, unsteadier, I thought, than when I had brought him up to the Terraces an hour before. He had gone past the stage of knowing who I was when I came out of the dark gully to take his arm.

I took him along the pavement of the Terrace. Then up right through a stony alley on to the mountain and towards the path that would lead us to his house.

'Where's the horse?' he mumbled, his head nearly down on his chest with fatigue. 'Where's the horse, Lewis?'

'At the Harp.' I pushed his head up sharply or he would have fallen asleep on top of me. 'A walk will be a nice change for you, Oscar. You did very well tonight. You ought to give thanks by giving the horse a rest.'

We mounted. The old wind met us as we passed the breast. The old wind that made its ancient sobbing home on that mountain with Oscar, and, Christ, it had reason to sob, living on that mountain. It awakened Oscar, and, as ever, he became merrier, started to chuckle and blabber.

'Hell, Lewis. She's lovely, that Hannah. Don't want anybody but her. Said she'd come with me and live in my house. That's what she said, Lewis, boy. Said she was sick as hell where she is and she wants to be with me. Oh, hell, Lewis, she's lovely. Never known anybody like her, Lewis.'

'That's right, Oscar. There's not much you want you can't have. It's a big thing, having a mountain. When you get a mountain, there's nothing you can't have.'

The moon, which had shone briefly, now vanished. I did not blame it for vanishing. It had not much to look at. Only me and Oscar pushing his face into mine, breathing into my eyes, scalding them with the heat of his breath.

We came to the point where the path forked. I led Oscar along the path that would lead him away from his house. We entered the ravine that skirted his tip. We ascended the path that led us on to the broad plateau, on the lip of which I used to sit in the sun and stare down into the narrow valley where Clarisse lived. I had no thought for Clarisse. Oscar slipped on the loose stones of the path. When I yanked him to his feet I noticed that I did so without effort. I was at full strength, because I had never felt as fully wise as I felt then. I had never before known when all the old stupidities, all the old doubts, have been laid to rest. And I knew, too, that thousands of people who slept in their cramped, terraced houses on the sides of that mountain would nod their brave, tired, friendly faces in agreement with what I wanted to do.

Along the path across the plateau, we walked without haste.

'It's long,' said Oscar. 'Where we goin', Lewis?'

'Home, Oscar. There's the lights of the house. Can't you see them?' I pointed my fingers into a great distance. Far away, the tiny lights of lighthouses came and went. Oscar must have glimpsed them, because he started to chuckle again.

'An' we'll get rid of Meg,' he said. 'We don't want Meg any more.'

'I'll tell Meg that.'

'Where's Meg, Lewis?'

'In the house. Where d'you think?'

'You tell her, boy.'

'All right, Oscar. I'll tell her.'

Then he started to sing as he always did when he came near the edge of that deep quarry which lay on the southern side of the mountain. His voice seemed to be louder than it had ever been, drenching the world with it. I made a buzzing sound in my head to make the noise of his singing less. Now and then he would wave his right arm in my face and shout:

'She's lovely, Lewis. Honest to Christ, she's lovely. That Hannah.'

'Yes,' I would say. Hannah was lovely, I knew that.

We came to the fence that had been put up to keep people away from the quarry, the fence that various voters had made it their business to kick down. I told Oscar to lift his legs to keep them free of the tangled tracks of wood and wire which were all that was left of the fence. He did that. He lifted his legs up a lot higher than was necessary and he screamed that that movement made him feel like a bloody woman.

'That's right, Oscar,' I said. 'Like a woman. Go on, boy.'

And on he went, right over the quarry. As his body landed on the jagged shelves and boulders beneath I thought the earth shook, but it was I who shook. The earth was quite still. I stepped back and sat down on a dew-wet knoll and my mind was full again of those strange, blank minutes I had spent sitting alongside Danny at the base of the tip.

From the quarry no sound came. I stood up and the air that circled on the mountain, all the air in the world, maybe, seemed fresher, cleaner, blowing to better purpose. I ran my knuckles up from my temples until they met in the middle of my forehead and I ground them together with the puckered flesh between. It was a waste. All the blood and bone and sight and sense that had been Oscar. A waste that it had been the way it had been. That notion coming from God knows where cooled me with its odd note of pity and I felt less giddy.

I turned and ran along the path I had come by. Passing Oscar's house, I thought I would go in and tell Meg she need not bother about waiting up for Oscar, that she could go to bed in peace for once. But I did not fancy talking to her. There was something in her face that thickened the layers of silence in me. And anyway, I thought Meg had gone past the stage where peace meant anything any more. I ran faster towards the house where Hannah was.

The kitchen door of Hannah's house was on the latch when I got there. I walked right in. Hannah was still on the sofa, lying on her side, her head stuck into the cushion as I had seen her last. I touched her softly on the shoulder. Her sleep was hard and she did not awaken. I touched her hard, pressing the flesh of her shoulder with my fingers. She stirred, turned her head and saw me. Her eyes were dull, misty. Then the mist blew up into a storm. She slung her arms around my legs and cried like mad.

'I was going to do it, honest,' she said.

'You're a bright, bloody beauty, Hannah.'

'I was going to do it.' She flung aside one of the cushions and behind it was the hammer. 'I didn't know exactly who he was. That's what it was. I didn't know . . . exactly. When he came and sat there I thought he was Danny. Oh, hell, I couldn't see. I didn't want to see. I thought he was Danny and all I wanted was for him to do what I always wanted Danny to do, but Danny never did. I thought he was Danny and I didn't know anything except I wanted him to do what he was doing. I been so cold, Lewis, so cold, so long. And I wanted to be warm again or I'd have died being cold. Oh, Jesus, Jesus, Jesus.'

Her crying went up like a bird that has had its wings torn off and flies for a few more moments through sheer pain. I kicked my legs from the embrace of her arms. She did the rest of her crying into the mat on the floor. I had never heard such sounds. It was as if the whole world was crying and she was just a part of it.

'You'll wake the dead, Hannah.' I walked into the pantry and filled a cup from the whisky bottle. I took it to her. 'Drink that, Hannah. Or you'll go mad. And me, too.'

She drank it and she did not seem to notice it was not water.

Her crying was no more than soft, hiccuped echoes in her throat now. She sat on the sofa. Her head rested back on the wooden support. Her face smiled and her arms came out on to my shoulders and the look she gave me would have been burning bright had the room been dark. She was lovely, just like that Oscar had said. She was lovely, that Hannah. I shook her arms away and pushed her head to rest. 'In a minute,' I said, 'you'd be thinking I was Danny. For Christ's sake.'

I wanted to move and keep moving. I found myself pushing open the door that led to the stairway. I walked up the stairs. On the small landing, my hands groped for the door of the front bedroom where I knew Danny was. I opened it. The room was lit dimly by a lamp-post across the street. Danny lay on the bed, boxed, unpuzzled. 'You're lucky, boy.' I yelled hard to keep myself from crying, crying in the pained and wingless bird style I had heard from Hannah. 'You're lucky, Danny. There's a very peculiar bunch of sods performing around here.' Then I jumped back down the stairs, crossed through the kitchen without a glance at Hannah and made my way into my mother's house. I bit deeply, savagely at my thumbnail and I wanted to talk. I wanted to talk in the dark with that quiet, distant woman who was my mother and who was no doubt wise about why there was so little peace in the strange, tormented area that separated me from Oscar and Danny, the shrinking ditch between the stirring and the resting.

DYLAN THOMAS

A Story

If you can call it a story. There's no real beginning or end and there's very little in the middle. It is all about a day's outing, by charabanc, to Porthcawl, which, of course, the charabanc never reached, and it happened when I was so high and much nicer.

I was staying at the time with my uncle and his wife. Although she was my aunt, I never thought of her as anything but the wife of my uncle, partly because he was so big and trumpeting and red-hairy and used to fill every inch of the hot little house like an old buffalo squeezed into an airing cupboard, and partly because she was so small and silk and quick and made no noise at all as she whisked about on padded paws, dusting the china dogs, feeding the buffalo, setting the mousetraps that never caught her; and once she sleaked out of the room, to squeak in a nook or nibble in the hayloft, you forgot she had ever been there.

But there he was, always, a steaming hulk of an uncle, his braces straining like hawsers, crammed behind the counter of the tiny shop at the front of the house, and breathing like a brass band; or guzzling and blustery in the kitchen over his gutsy supper, too big for everything except the great black boats of his boots. As he ate, the house grew smaller; he billowed out over the furniture, the loud check meadow of his waistcoat littered, as though after a picnic, with cigarette ends, peelings, cabbage stalks, birds' bones, gravy; and the forest fire of his hair crackled among the hooked hams from the ceiling. She was so small she could hit him only if she stood on a chair, and every Saturday night at half-past ten he would lift her up, under his arm, on to a chair in the kitchen so that she could hit him on the head with whatever was handy, which was always a china dog. On Sundays, and when pickled, he sang high tenor, and had won many cups.

The first I heard of the annual outing was when I was sitting one evening on a bag of rice behind the counter, under one of my uncle's stomachs, reading an advertisement for sheep-dip, which was all there was to read. The shop was full of my uncle, and when Mr Benjamin Franklyn, Mr Weazley, Noah Bowen, and Will Sentry came in, I thought it would burst. It was like all being together in a drawer that smelt of cheese and turps, and twist tobacco and sweet biscuits and snuff and waistcoat. Mr Benjamin Franklyn said that he had collected enough money for the charabanc and twenty cases of pale ale and a pound apiece over that he would distribute among the members of the outing when they first stopped for refreshment, and he was about sick and tired, he said, of being followed by Will Sentry.

'All day long, wherever I go,' he said, 'he's after me like a collie with one eye. I got a shadow of my own *and* a dog. I don't need no Tom, Dick, or Harry pursuing me with his dirty muffler on.'

Will Sentry blushed, and said: 'It's only oily. I got a bicycle.'

'A man has no privacy at all,' Mr Franklyn went on. 'I tell you he sticks so close I'm afraid to go out the back in case I sit in his lap. It's a wonder to me,' he said, 'he don't follow me into bed at night.'

'Wife won't let,' Will Sentry said.

And that started Mr Franklyn off again, and they tried to soothe him down by saying: 'Don't you mind Will Sentry' ... 'No harm in old Will' ... 'He's only keeping an eye on the money, Benjie.'

'Aren't I honest?' asked Mr Franklyn in surprise. There was no answer for some time, then Noah Bowen said: 'You know what the committee is. Ever since Bob the Fiddle they don't feel safe with a new treasurer.'

'Do you think *I*'m going to drink the outing funds, like Bob the Fiddle did?' said Mr Franklyn.

'You *might*,' said my uncle slowly.

'I resign,' said Mr Franklyn.

'Not with our money you won't,' Will Sentry said.

'Who put dynamite in the salmon pool?' said Mr Weazley, but nobody took any notice of him. And, after a time, they all began to play cards in the thickening dusk of the hot, cheesy shop, and my uncle blew and bugled whenever he won, and Mr Weazley grumbled like a dredger, and I fell to sleep on the gravy-scented mountain meadow of uncle's waistcoat.

On Sunday evening, after Bethesda, Mr Franklyn walked into the kitchen where my uncle and I were eating sardines with spoons from the tin because it was Sunday and his wife would not let us play draughts. She was somewhere in the kitchen, too. Perhaps she was inside the grandmother clock, hanging from the weights and breathing. Then, a second later, the door opened again and Will Sentry edged into the room, twiddling his hard, round hat. He and Mr Franklyn sat down on the settee, stiff and moth-balled and black in their chapel and funeral suits.

'I brought the list,' said Mr Franklyn. 'Every member fully paid. You ask Will Sentry.'

My uncle put on his spectacles, wiped his whiskery mouth with a handkerchief big as a Union Jack, laid down his spoon of sardines, took Mr Franklyn's list of names, removed the spectacles so that he could read, then ticked the names off one by one.

'Enoch Davies. Aye. He's good with his fists. You never know. Little Gerwain. Very melodious bass. Mr Cadwalladwr. That's right. He can tell opening time better than my watch. Mr Weazley. Of course. He's been to Paris. Pity he suffers so much in the charabanc. Stopped us nine times last year between the Beehive and the Red Dragon. Noah Bowen, ah, very peaceable. He's got a tongue like a turtle-dove. Never an argument with Noah Bowen. Jenkins Loughor. Keep him off economics. It cost us a plate-glass window. And ten pints for the Sergeant. Mr Jervis. Very tidy.'

'He tried to put a pig in the chara,' Will Sentry said.

'Live and let live,' said my uncle.

Will Sentry blushed.

'Sinbad the Sailor's Arms. Got to keep in with him. Old O. Jones.'

'Why old O. Jones?' said Will Sentry.

'Old O. Jones always goes,' said my uncle.

I looked down at the kitchen table. The tin of sardines was gone. By Gee, I said to myself, Uncle's wife is quick as a flash.

'Cuthbert Johnny Fortnight. Now there's a card,' said my uncle.

'He whistles after women,' Will Sentry said.

'So do you,' said Mr Benjamin Franklyn, 'in your mind.'

My uncle at last approved the whole list, pausing only to say, when he came across one name: 'If we weren't a Christian community, we'd chuck that Bob the Fiddle in the sea.'

'We can do that in Porthcawl,' said Mr Franklyn, and soon after that he went, Will Sentry no more than an inch behind him, their Sunday-bright boots squeaking on the kitchen cobbles.

And then, suddenly, there was my uncle's wife standing in front of the dresser, with a china dog in one hand. By Gee, I said to myself again, did you ever see such a woman, if that's what she is. The lamps were not lit yet in the kitchen and she stood in a wood of shadows, with the plates on the dresser behind her shining – like pink-and-white eyes.

'If you go on that outing on Saturday, Mr Thomas,' she said to my uncle in her small, silk voice, 'I'm going home to my mother's.'

Holy Mo, I thought, she's got a mother. Now that's one old bald mouse of a hundred and five I won't be wanting to meet in a dark lane.

'It's me or the outing, Mr Thomas.'

I would have made my choice at once, but it was almost half a minute before my uncle said: 'Well, then, Sarah, it's the outing, my love.' He lifted her up, under his arm, on to a chair in the kitchen, and she hit him on the head with the china dog. Then he lifted her down again, and then I said good-night.

For the rest of the week my uncle's wife whisked quiet and quick round the house with her darting duster, my uncle blew and bugled and swole, and I kept myself busy all the time being up to no good. And then at breakfast time on Saturday morning, the morning of the outing, I found a note on the kitchen table. It said: 'There's some eggs in the pantry. Take your boots off before you go to bed.' My uncle's wife had gone, as quick as a flash.

When my uncle saw the note, he tugged out the flag of his handkerchief and blew such a hubbub of trumpets that the plates on the dresser shook. 'It's the same every year,' he said. And then he looked at me. 'But this year it's different. *You*'ll have to come on the outing, too, and what the members will say I dare not think.'

The charabanc drew up outside, and when the members of the outing saw my uncle and me squeeze out of the shop together, both of us cat-licked and brushed in our Sunday best, they snarled like a zoo.

'Are you bringing a *boy*?' asked Mr Benjamin Franklyn as we climbed into the charabanc. He looked at me with horror.

'Boys is nasty,' said Mr Weazley.

'He hasn't paid his contributions,' Will Sentry said.

'No room for boys. Boys get sick in charabancs.'

'So do you, Enoch Davies,' said my uncle.

'Might as well bring *women*.'

The way they said it, women were worse than boys.

'Better than bringing grandfathers.'

'Grandfathers is nasty too,' said Mr Weazley.

'What can we do with him when we stop for refreshments?'

'I'm a grandfather,' said Mr Weazley.

'Twenty-six minutes to opening time,' shouted an old man in a panama hat, not looking at a watch. They forgot me at once.

'Good old Mr Cadwalladwr,' they cried, and the charabanc started off down the village street.

A few cold women stood at their doorways, grimly watching us go. A very small boy waved goodbye, and his mother boxed his ears. It was a beautiful August morning.

We were out of the village, and over the bridge, and up the hill towards Steeplehat Wood when Mr Franklyn, with his list of names in his hand, called out loud: 'Where's old O. Jones?'

'Where's old O?'

'We've left old O behind.'

'Can't go without old O.'

And though Mr Weazley hissed all the way, we turned and drove back to the village, where, outside the Prince of Wales, old O. Jones was waiting patiently and alone with a canvas bag.

'I didn't want to come at all,' old O. Jones said as they hoisted him into the charabanc and clapped him on the back and pushed him on a seat and stuck a bottle in his hand, 'but I always go.' And over the bridge and up the hill and under the deep green wood and along the dusty road we wove, slow cows and ducks flying by, until 'Stop the bus!' Mr Weazley cried. 'I left my teeth on the mantelpiece.'

'Never you mind,' they said, 'you're not going to bite nobody,' and they gave him a bottle with a straw.

'I might want to smile,' he said.

'Not you,' they said.

'What's the time, Mr Cadwalladwr?'

'Twelve minutes to go,' shouted back the old man in the panama, and they all began to curse him.

The charabanc pulled up outside The Mountain Sheep, a small, unhappy public house with a thatched roof like a wig with ringworm. From a flagpole by the Gents fluttered the flag of Siam. I knew it was the flag of Siam because of cigarette cards. The landlord stood over the door to welcome us, simpering like a wolf. He was a long, lean, black-fanged man with a greased love-curl and pouncing eyes.

'What a beautiful August day!' he said, and touched his love-curl with a claw. That was the way he must have welcomed the

Mountain Sheep before he ate it, I said to myself. The members rushed out, bleating, and into the bar.

'You keep an eye on the chara,' my uncle said; 'see nobody steals it now.'

'There's nobody to steal it,' I said, 'except some cows,' but my uncle was gustily blowing his bugle in the bar. I looked at the cows opposite, and they looked at me. There was nothing else for us to do. Forty-five minutes passed, like a very slow cloud. The sun shone down on the lonely road, the lost, unwanted boy, and the lake-eyed cows. In the dark bar they were so happy they were breaking glasses. A Shoni-Onion Breton man, with a beret and a necklace of onions, bicycled down the road and stopped at the door.

'*Quelle un grand matin, monsieur,*' I said.

'There's French, boy *bach*!' he said.

I followed him down the passage, and peered into the bar. I could hardly recognize the members of the outing. They had all changed colour. Beetroot, rhubarb, and puce, they hollered and rollicked in that dark, damp hole like enormous ancient bad boys, and my uncle surged in the middle, all red whiskers and bellies. On the floor was broken glass and Mr Weazley.

'Drinks all round,' cried Bob the Fiddle, a small absconding man with bright blue eyes and a plump smile.

'Who's been robbing the orphans?'

'Who sold his little babby to the gyppoes?'

'Trust old Bob, he'll let you down.'

'You will have your little joke,' said Bob the Fiddle, smiling like a razor, 'but I forgive you, boys.'

Out of the fug and babel I heard: 'Come out and fight.'

'No, not now, later.'

'No, now when I'm in a temper.'

'Look at Will Sentry, he's proper snobbled.'

'Look at his wilful feet.'

'Look at Mr Weazley lording it on the floor.'

Mr Weazley got up, hissing like a gander. 'That boy pushed

me down deliberate,' he said, pointing to me at the door, and I slunk away down the passage and out to the mild, good cows. Time clouded over, the cows wondered, I threw a stone at them and they wandered, wondering, away. Then out blew my uncle, ballooning, and one by one the members lumbered after him in a grizzle. They had drunk the Mountain Sheep dry. Mr Weazley had won a string of onions that the Shoni-Onion man raffled in the bar. 'What's the good of onions if you left your teeth on the mantelpiece?' he said. And when I looked through the back window of the thundering charabanc, I saw the pub grow smaller in the distance. And the flag of Siam, from the flagpole by the Gents, fluttered now at half-mast.

The Blue Bull, the Dragon, the Star of Wales, the Twll in the Wall, the Sour Grapes, the Shepherd's Arms, the Bells of Aberdovey. I had nothing to do in the whole, wild August world but remember the names where the outing stopped and keep an eye on the charabanc. And whenever it passed a public house, Mr Weazley would cough like a billygoat and cry: 'Stop the bus, I'm dying of breath!' And back we would all have to go.

Closing time meant nothing to the members of that outing. Behind locked doors, they hymned and rumpused all the beautiful afternoon. And, when a policeman entered the Druid's Tap by the back door, and found them all choral with beer, 'Ssh!' said Noah Bowen, 'the pub is shut.'

'Where do you come from?' he said in his buttoned, blue voice.

They told him.

'I got a auntie there,' the policeman said. And very soon he was singing 'Asleep in the Deep'.

Off we drove again at last, the charabanc bouncing with tenors and flagons, and came to a river that rushed along among willows.

'Water!' they shouted.

'Porthcawl!' sang my uncle.

'Where's the donkeys?' said Mr Weazley.

And out they lurched, to paddle and whoop in the cool, white, winding water. Mr Franklyn, trying to polka on the slippery stones, fell in twice. 'Nothing is simple,' he said with dignity as he oozed up the bank.

'It's cold!' they cried.

'It's lovely!'

'It's smooth as a moth's nose!'

'It's *better* than Porthcawl!'

And dusk came down warm and gentle on the thirty wild, wet, pickled, splashing men without a care in the world at the end of the world in the west of Wales. And, 'Who goes there?' called Will Sentry to a wild duck flying.

They stopped at the Hermit's Nest for a rum to keep out the cold. 'I played for Aberavon in 1898,' said a stranger to Enoch Davies.

'Liar,' said Enoch Davies.

'I can show you photos,' said the stranger.

'Forged,' said Enoch Davies.

'And I'll show you my cap at home.'

'Stolen.'

'I got friends to prove it,' the stranger said in a fury.

'Bribed,' said Enoch Davies.

On the way home, through the simmering moon-splashed dark, old O. Jones began to cook his supper on a primus stove in the middle of the charabanc. Mr Weazley coughed himself blue in the smoke. 'Stop the bus,' he cried, 'I'm dying of breath!' We all climbed down into the moonlight. There was not a public house in sight. So they carried out the remaining cases, and the primus stove, and old O. Jones himself, and took them into a field, and sat down in a circle in the field and drank and sang while old O. Jones cooked sausage and mash and the moon flew above us. And there I drifted to sleep against my uncle's mountainous waistcoat, and, as I slept, 'Who goes there?' called out Will Sentry to the flying moon.

ALUN LEWIS

The Orange Grove

The grey truck slowed down at the crossroads and the army officer leaned out to read the signpost. 'Indians Only', the sign pointing to the native town read. 'Dak Bungalow' straight on. 'Thank God,' said Staff-Captain Beale. 'Go ahead, driver.' They were lucky, hitting a dak bungalow at dusk. They'd bivouacked the last two nights, and in the monsoon a bivouac is bad business. Tonight they'd be able to strip and sleep dry under a roof, and heat up some bully on the Tommy cooker. Bloody good.

These bungalows are scattered all over India on the endless roads and travellers may sleep there, cook their food, and pass on. The rooms are bare and whitewashed, the veranda has room for a camp bed, they are quiet and remote, tended for the government only by some old *khansama* or *chowkey*, usually a slippered and silent old Moslem. The driver pulled in and began unpacking the kit, the dry rations, the cooker, the camp bed, his blanket roll, the tin of kerosene. Beale went off to find the caretaker, whom he discovered squatting amongst the flies by the well. He was a wizened yellow-skinned old man in a soiled dhoti. Across his left breast was a plaster, loose and dripping with pus, a permanent discharge it seemed. He wheezed as he replied to the brusque request and raised himself with pain, searching slowly for his keys.

Beale came to give the driver a hand while the old man fumbled with the crockery indoors.

'The old crow is only sparking on one cylinder,' he said.

'Looks like TB,' he added with the faint overtone of disgust which the young and healthy feel for all incurable diseases. He looked out at the falling evening, the fulgurous inflammation among the grey anchorages of cloud, the hot creeping prescience of the monsoon.

'I don't like it tonight,' he said. 'It's eerie; I can't breathe or think. This journey's getting on my nerves. What day is it? I've lost count.'

'Thursday, sir,' the driver said, 'August 25th.'

'How d'you know all that?' Beale asked, curious.

'I have been thinking it out, for to write a letter tonight,' the driver said. 'Shall I get the cooker going, sir? Your bed is all ready now.'

'OK,' Beale said, sitting on his camp bed and opening his grip. He took out a leather writing-pad in which he kept the notes he was making for Divisional HQ, and all the letters he'd received from home. He began looking among the letters for one he wanted. The little dusty driver tinkered with the cooker. Sometimes Beale looked up and watched him, sometimes he looked away at the night.

This place seemed quiet enough. The old man had warned him there was unrest and rioting in the town. The lines had been cut, the oil tanks unsuccessfully attacked, the court house burnt down, the police had made lathi charges, the district magistrate was afraid to leave his bungalow. The old man had relished the violence of others. Of course, you couldn't expect the 11th to go by without some riots, some deaths. Even in this remote part of central India where the native princes ruled from their crumbling Moghul forts through their garrisons of smiling crop-headed little Gurkhas. But it seemed quiet enough here, a mile out of the town. The only chance was that someone might have seen them at the crossroads – it was so sultry, so swollen and angry, the sky, the hour. He felt for his revolver.

He threw the driver a dry box of matches from his grip. Everything they carried was fungoid with damp, the driver had been striking match after match on his wet box with a curious depressive impassivity. Funny little chap, seemed to have no initiative, as if some part of his will were paralysed. Maybe it was that wife of his he'd talked about the night before last when they had the wood fire going in the hollow. Funny. Beale had been dazed with sleep, half listening, comprehending only the surface of the slow, clumsy words. Hate. Hate. Beale couldn't understand hate. War hadn't taught it to him, war was to him only fitness, discomfort, feats of endurance, proud muscles, a career, irresponsible dissipations, months of austerity broken by 'blinds' in Cairo, or Durban, Calcutta or Bangalore or Bombay. But this little rough-head with his soiled hands and bitten nails, his odd blue eyes looking away, his mean bearing, squatting on the floor with kerosene and grease over his denims – he had plenty of hate.

'. . . tried to emigrate first of all, didn't want to stay anywhere. I was fourteen, finished with reformatory schools for keeps . . . New Zealand I wanted to go. There was a school in Bristol for emigrants . . . I ran away from home but they didn't bother with me in Bristol, nacherly . . . Police sent me back. So then I become a boy in the army, in the drums, and then I signed on. I'm a time-serving man, sir; better put another couple of branches on the fire; so I went to Palestine, against the Arabs, seen them collective farms the Jews got there, sir? Oranges . . . then I come home, so I goes on leave . . . We got a pub in our family and since my father died my mother been keeping it . . . for the colliers it is . . . never touch beer myself, my father boozed himself to death be'ind the counter. Well, my mother 'ad a barmaid, a flash dame she was, she was good for trade, fit for an answer any time, and showing a bit of her breasts every time she drew a pint. Red hair she had, well, not exactly red, I don't know the word, not so *coarse* as red. My mother said for me to keep off her, my mother is a big Bible woman, though nacherly she couldn't go to chapel down our way being she kept a pub . . . Well, Monica, this barmaid she slept in the attic, it's a big 'ouse, the Bute's Arms. And I was nineteen. You can't always answer for yourself, can you? It was

my pub by rights, *mine*. She was *my* barmaid. That's how my
father'd have said if he wasn't dead. My mother wouldn't have
no barmaids when he was alive. Monica knew what she was
doing all right. She wanted the pub and the big double bed; she
couldn't wait . . . It didn't seem much to pay for sleeping with a
woman like that . . . Well, then I went back to barracks, and it
wasn't till I told my mate and he called me a sucker that I knew I
couldn't . . . Nothing went right after that. She took good care to
get pregnant, Monica did, and my mother threw her out. But it
was my baby, and I married her without telling my mother. It
was *my* affair, wasn't it? *Mine.*'

How long he had been in telling all this Beale couldn't
remember. There was nothing to pin that evening upon; the fire
and the logs drying beside the fire, the circle of crickets, the
sudden blundering of moths into the warm zone of the fire and
thoughtful faces, the myopic sleepy stare of fatigue, and those
bitter distasteful words within intervals of thought and waiting.
Not until now did Beale realize that there had been no hard luck
story told, no gambit for sympathy or compassionate leave or a
poor person's divorce. But a man talking into a wood fire in the
remote asylums of distance, and slowly explaining the twisted
and evil curvature of his being.

'She told me she'd get her own back on me for my mother turning
her out . . . And she did . . . I know a man in my own regiment that
slept with her on leave. But the kid is mine. My mother got the kid
for me. She shan't spoil the kid. Nobody'll spoil the kid, neither
Monica nor me . . . I can't make it out, how is it a woman is so
wonderful, I mean in a bedroom? I should 'a' murdered her, it would
be better than this, this hating her all the time. Wouldn't it . . .?'

'The Tommy cooker's OK now, sir,' the driver said. 'The
wind was blowing the flame back all the time. OK now with this
screen. What's it to be? There's only bully left.'

'Eh? What?' Beale said. 'Oh, supper? Bully? I can't eat any
more bully. Can't we get some eggs or something? Ten days with
bully twice a day is plenty. Can you eat bully?'

'Can't say I fancy it,' the driver said. 'I'll go down the road and see if I can get some eggs.'

'I shouldn't bother,' Beale said. 'The storm will get you if you go far. Besides, it's dangerous down the town road. They've been rioting since Gandhi and Nehru were arrested last week. Better brew up and forget about the food.'

Beale was by nature and by his job as a staff-officer one who is always doing things and forgetting about them. It was convenient as well as necessary to him. His 'pending' basket was always empty. He never had a load on his mind.

'I'll take a walk just the same,' the driver said. 'Maybe I'll find a chicken laying on the road. I won't be long.'

He was a good scrounger, it was a matter of pride with him to get anything that was wanted, mosquito poles, or water or anything. And every night, whether they were in the forest or the desert plains that encompass Indore, he had announced his intention of walking down the road.

Some impulse caused Beale to delay him a moment.

'Remember,' Beale said, 'the other night, you said you saw the collective farms in Palestine?'

'Aye,' said the driver, standing in the huge deformity of the hunchbacked shadow that the lamp projected from his slovenly head.

'They were good places, those farms?' Beale asked.

'Aye, they were,' the driver said, steadying his childish gaze. 'They didn't have money, they didn't buy and sell. They shared what they had and the doctor and the schoolteacher the same as the labourer or the children, all the same, all living together. Orange groves they lived in, and I would like to go back there.'

He stepped down from the porch and the enormous shadows vanished from the roof and from the wall. Beale sat on, the biscuit tin of water warming slowly on the cooker, the flying ants casting their wings upon the glass of the lamp and the sheets of his bed. An orange grove in Palestine . . . He was experiencing one of those enlargements of the imagination that come once or perhaps twice to a man, and re-create him subtly and profoundly. And he was thinking simply this – that some things are possible and other things are impossible to us. Beyond the mass of vivid and sensuous impressions which he had allowed the war to impose upon him were the quiet categories of the possible and the quieter frozen infinities of the impossible. And he must get back to those certainties . . . The night falls, and the dance bands turn on the heat. The indolent arrive in their taxis, the popsies and the good-timers, the lonely good-looking boys and the indifferent erotic women. Swing music sways across the bay from the urbane permissive ballrooms of the Taj and Green's. 'In the Mood', 'It's Foolish but it's Fun', some doughboys cracking whips in the coffee room, among apprehensive glances, the taxi-drivers buy a betel leaf and spit red saliva over the running-board, the panders touch the sleeves of soldiers, the crowd huddles beneath the Gateway, turning up collars and umbrellas everywhere against the thin sane arrows of the rain. And who is she whose song is the world spinning, whose lambent streams cast their curved ways about you and about whose languors are the infinite desires of the unknowing? Is she the girl behind the grille, in the side street where they play gramophone records and you pay ten chips for a whisky and you suddenly feel a godalmighty yen for whoever it is in your arms? But beyond that, beyond that? Why had he failed with this woman, why had it been impossible with that woman? He collected the swirl of thought and knew that he could not generalize as the driver had done in the glow of the wood fire. Woman. The gardener at the boarding-school he went to used to say things about women. Turvey his name was. Turvey, the headmaster called him, but the boys had to say *Mr* Turvey. Mr Turvey didn't hold with mixed bathing, not at any price, because woman wasn't clean like man, he said. And when the boys demurred, thinking of soft pledges and firm stars and the moon, Mr Turvey would wrinkle his saturnine face and say: 'Course you young gentlemen knows better than me. I only been married fifteen years. I don't know nothing of course.' And maybe this conversation would be while he was emptying the ordure from the latrines into the oil drum on iron wheels which he trundled each morning down to his sewage pits in the school gardens.

But in an intenser lucidity Beale knew he must not generalize. There would be perhaps one woman out of many, one life out of many, two things possible – if life itself were possible, and if he had not debased himself among the impossibilities by then. The orange grove in Palestine . . .

And then he realized that the water in the biscuit tin was boiling and he knelt to put the tea and tinned milk into the two enamel mugs. As he knelt a drop of rain the size of a coin pitted his back. And another. And a third. He shuddered. Ten days they'd been on the road, making this reconnaissance for a projected army exercise, and each day had been nothing but speed and distance hollow in the head, the milometer ticking up the daily two hundred, the dust of a hundred villages justifying their weariness with its ashes, and tomorrow also only speed and distance and the steadiness of the six cylinders. And he'd been dreaming of a Bombay whore whose red kiss he still had not washed from his arm, allowing her to enter where she would and push into oblivion the few things that were possible to him in the war and the peace. And now the rain made him shudder and he felt all the loneliness of India about him and he knew he had never been more alone. So he was content to watch the storm gather, operating against him from a heavy fulcrum in the east, lashing the bungalow and the trees, infuriating the night. The cooker spluttered and went out. He made no move to use the boiling water upon the tea. The moths flew in from the rain, and the grasshoppers and the bees. The frogs grunted and creaked in the swirling mud and grass, the night was animate and violent. He waited without moving until the violence of the storm was spent. Then he looked at his watch. It was as he thought. The driver had been gone an hour and twenty minutes. He knew he must go and look for him.

He loaded his revolver carefully and buckled on his holster over his bush shirt. He called for the old caretaker, but there was no reply. The bungalow was empty. He turned down the wick of the lamp and putting on his cap, stepped softly into the night. It was easy to get lost. It would be difficult to find anything tonight, unless it was plumb in the main road.

His feet felt under the streaming water for the stones of the road. The banyan tree he remembered, it was just beyond the pull-in. Its mass was over him now, he could feel it over his head. It was going to be difficult. The nearest cantonment was four hundred miles away; in any case the roads were too flooded now for him to retrace his way to Mhow. If he went on to Baroda, Ahmedabad – but the Mahi river would be in spate also. The lines down everywhere, too. They would have to go on, that he felt sure about. Before daybreak, too. It wasn't safe here. If only he could find the driver. He was irritated with the driver, irritated in a huge cloudy way, for bungling yet one more thing, for leaving him alone with so much on his hands, for insisting on looking for eggs. He'd known something would happen.

He felt the driver with his foot and knelt down over him in the swirling road and felt for his heart under his sodden shirt and cursed him in irritation and concern. Dead as a duck board, knifed. The rain came on again and he tried to lift up the corpse the way he'd been taught, turning it first on to its back and standing firmly astride it. But the driver was obstinate and heavy and for a long time he refused to be lifted up.

He carried the dead-weight back up the road, sweating and bitched by the awkward corpse, stumbling and trying in vain to straighten himself. What a bloody mess, he kept saying; I told him not to go and get eggs; did he have to have eggs for supper? It became a struggle between himself and the corpse, who was trying to slide down off his back and stay lying on the road. He had half a mind to let it have its way.

He got back eventually and backed himself against the veranda like a lorry, letting the body slide off his back; the head fell crack against the side wall and he said 'Sorry', and put a sack between the cheek and the ground. The kid was soaking wet and wet red mud in his hair; he wiped his face up a bit with cotton waste and put a blanket over him while he packed the kit up and stowed it in the truck. He noticed the tea and sugar in the mugs and tried the temper of the water. It was too cold. He regretted it. He had the truck packed by the end of half an hour, his own bedding roll stretched on top of the baggage ready for the passenger. He hoped he'd be agreeable this time. He resisted a bit but he had stiffened a little and was more manageable. He backed him into the truck and then climbed in, pulling him on to the blanket by his armpits. Not until he'd put up the tailboard and got him all ready did he feel any ease. He sighed. They were away. He got into the driving seat to switch on the ignition. Then he realized there was no key. He felt a momentary panic. But surely the driver had it. He slipped out and, in the darkness and the drive of the rain, searched in the man's pockets. Paybook, matches, identity discs (must remember that, didn't even know his name), at last the keys.

He started the engine and let her warm up, slipped her into second and drove slowly out. The old caretaker never appeared, and Beale wondered whether he should say anything of his suspicions regarding the old man when he made his report. Unfortunately, there was no evidence. Still, they were away from there; he sighed with relief as the compulsion under which he had been acting relaxed. He had this extra sense, of which he was proud, of being able to feel the imminence of danger as others feel a change in the weather; it didn't help him in Libya, perhaps it hindered him there; but in a pub in Durban it had got him out in the nick of time; he'd edged for the door before a shot was fired. He knew tonight all right. The moment he saw that dull red lever of storm raised over his head, and the old caretaker had shrugged his shoulders after his warning had been laughed off. You had to bluff them; only sometimes bluff wasn't enough and then you had to get away, face or no face. Now he tried to remember the route on the map: driving blind, the best thing was to go slow and pull in somewhere a few miles on. Maybe the sun would rise sometime and he could dry out the map and work out the best route; no more native towns for him; he wanted to get to a cantonment if possible. Otherwise he'd look for the police lines at Dohad or Jabhua or wherever the next place was. But every time he thought of pulling in, a disinclination to stop the engine made him keep his drenched ammunition boot on the accelerator pedal. When he came to a road junction he followed his fancy; there is such a thing as letting the car do the guiding.

He drove for six hours before the night stirred at all. Then his red-veined eyes felt the slight lessening in the effectiveness of the headlights that presaged the day. When he could see the red berm of the road and the flooded paddy-fields lapping the bank, he at last pulled up under a tree and composed himself over the wheel, placing his cheek against the rim, avoiding the horn at the centre. He fell at once into a stiff rigid sleep.

A tribe of straggling gipsies passed him soon after dawn. They made no sound, leading their mules and camels along the soft berm on the other side of the road, mixing their own ways with no other's. The sun lay back of the blue rain-clouds, making the earth steam. The toads hopped out of the mud and rested under the stationary truck. Land-crabs came out of the earth and sat on the edge of their holes. Otherwise no one passed. The earth seemed content to let him have his sleep out. He woke about noon, touched by the sun as it passed.

He felt guilty. Guilty of neglect of duty, having slept at his post? Then he got a grip on himself and rationalized the dreadful guilt away. What could he have done about it? The driver had been murdered. What did they expect him to do? Stay there and give them a second treat? Stay there and investigate? Or get on and report it? Why hadn't he reported it earlier? How could he? The lines were down, the roads flooded behind him, he was trying his best; he couldn't help sleeping for a couple of hours. Yet the guilt complex persisted. It was a bad dream and he had some evil in him, a soft lump of evil in his brain. But why? If he'd told the man to go for eggs it would be different. He was bound to be all right as long as he had his facts right. Was there an accident report to be filled in immediately, in duplicate, Army Form B- something-or-other? He took out his notebook, but the paper was too wet to take his hard pencil. 2300 hrs on 23 August 1942 deceased stated his desire to get some eggs. I warned him that disturbances of a political character had occurred in the area ... He shook himself, bleary and sore-throated, in his musty overalls, and thought a shave and some food would put him right. He went round to the back of the truck. The body had slipped with the jolting of the road. He climbed in and looked at the ashen face. The eyes were closed, the face had sunk into an expressionless inanition, it made him feel indifferent to the whole thing. Poor sod. Where was his hate now? Was he grieving that the woman, Mona was it, would get a pension out of him now? Did he still hate her? He seemed to have let the whole matter drop. Death was something without hate in it. But he didn't want to do anything himself except shave and eat and get the whole thing buttoned up. He tore himself away from the closed soiled face and ferreted about for his shaving kit. He found it at last, and after shaving in the muddy rain water he ate a few hard biscuits and stuffed a few more into his pocket. Then he lashed the canvas down over the tailboard and got back to the wheel. The truck was slow to start. The bonnet had been leaking and the plugs were wet in the cylinder heads. She wouldn't spark for a minute or two. Anxiety swept over him. He cursed the truck viciously. Then she sparked on a couple of cylinders, stuttered for a minute as the others dried out, and settled down steadily. He ran her away carefully and again relaxed. He was dead scared of being stranded with the body. There wasn't even a shovel on the truck.

After driving for an hour he realized he didn't know where he was. He was in the centre of a vast plain of paddy-fields, lined by raised bunds and hedged with cactus along the road. White herons and tall fantastic cranes stood by the pools in the hollows. He pulled up to try and work out his position. But his map was nowhere to be found. He must have left it at the dak bungalow in his haste. He looked at his watch; it had stopped. Something caved in inside him, a sensation of panic, of an enemy against whose machinations he had failed to take the most elementary precautions. He was lost.

He moved on again at once. There was distance. The milometer still measured something. By sunset he would do so many miles. How much of the day was left? Without the sun how could he tell? He was panicky at not knowing these things; he scarcely knew more than the man in the back of the truck. So he drove on and on, passing nobody but a tribe of gipsies with their mules and camels, and dark peasants, driving their bullocks knee-deep in the alluvial mud before their simple wooden ploughs. He drove as fast as the track would allow; in some places it was flooded and narrow, descending to narrow causeways swept by brown streams which he only just managed to cross. He drove till the land was green with evening, and in the crepuscular uncertainty he halted and decided to kip down for the night. He would need petrol; it was kept in tins in the back of the truck; it meant pulling the body out, or making him sit away in a corner. He didn't want to disturb the kid. He'd been jolted all day; and now this indignity. He did all he had to do with a humility that was alien to him. Respect he knew; but this was more than respect; obedience and necessity he knew, but this was more than either of these. It was somehow an admission of the integrity of the man, a new interest in what he was and what he had left behind. He got some soap and a towel, after filling his tanks, and when he had washed himself he propped the driver up against the tailboard and sponged him clean and put PT shoes on his feet instead of the boots that had so swollen his feet. When he had laid him out on the blankets and covered him with a sheet, he rested from his exertions, and as he recovered his breath he glanced covertly at him, satisfied that he had done something for him. What would the woman have done, Monica? Would she have flirted with him? Most women did, and he didn't discourage them. But this woman, my God, he'd bloody well beat her up. It was her doing, this miserable end, this mess-up. He hadn't gone down the road to get eggs; he'd gone to get away from her. It must have been a habit of his, at nights, to compose himself. She'd bitched it all. He could just see her. And she still didn't know a thing about him, not the first thing. Yes, he hated her all right, the voluptuous bitch.

He slept at the wheel again, falling asleep with a biscuit still half chewed in his mouth. He had erotic dreams, this woman Monica drawing him a pint, and her mouth and her breasts and the shallow taunting eyes; and the lights in her attic bedroom with the door ajar, and the wooden stairs creaking. And the dawn then laid its grey fingers upon him and he awoke with the same feeling of guilt and shame, a grovelling debased mood, that had seized him the first morning. He got up, stretching himself, heady with vertigo and phlegm, and washed himself in the paddy flood. He went round to the back of the truck to get some biscuits. He got them quietly, the boy was still sleeping, and he said to himself that he would get him through today, honest he would. He had to.

The sun came out and the sky showed a young summer blue. The trees wakened and shook soft showers of rain off their leaves. Hills showed blue as lavender and when he came to the crossroads he steered northwest by the sun, reckoning to make the coast road somewhere near Baroda. There would be a cantonment not far from there, and a service dump for coffins, and someone to whom he could make a report. It would be an immense relief. His spirits rose. Driving was tricky; the worn treads of the tyres tended to skid, the road wound up and down the ghats, through tall loose scrub; but he did not miss seeing the shy jungle wanderers moving through the bush with their bows, tall lithe men like fauns with black hair over their eyes that were like grapes. They would stand a moment under a tree, and glide away back into the bush. There were villages now, and women of light olive skin beating their saris on the stones, rhythmically, and their breasts uncovered.

And then, just when he felt he was out of the lost zones, in the late afternoon, he came down a long sandy track through cactus to a deep and wide river at which the road ended. A gipsy tribe was fording it and he watched them to gauge the depth of the river. The little mules, demure as mice, kicked up against the current, nostrils too near the water to neigh; the camels followed the halter, stately as bishops, picking their calm way. The babies sat on their parents' heads, the women unwound their saris and put them in a bundle on their crowns, the water touched their breasts. And Beale pushed his truck into bottom gear and nosed her cautiously into the stream. Midway across the brown tides swept up to his sparking plugs and the engine stopped. He knew at once that he was done for. The river came up in waves and over the sideboards and his whole concern was that the boy inside would be getting wet. A gipsy waded past impersonally, leading two bright-eyed grey mules. Beale hailed him. He nodded and went on. Beale called out 'Help!' The gipsies gathered on the far bank and discussed it. He waved and eventually three of them came wading out to him. He knew he must abandon the truck till a recovery section could be sent out to salvage it, but he must take his companion with him, naturally. When the gipsies reached him he pointed to the back of the truck, unlaced the tarpaulin and showed them the corpse. They nodded their heads gravely. Their faces were serious and hard. He contrived to show them what he wanted and when he climbed in they helped him intelligently to hoist the body out. They contrived to get it on to their heads, ducking down under the tailboard till their faces were submerged in the scum of the flood.

They carried him ashore that way, Beale following with his revolver and webbing. They held a conclave on the sand while the women wrung out their saris and the children crowded about the body. Beale stood in the centre of these lean outlandish men, not understanding a word. They talked excitedly, abruptly, looking at him and at the corpse. He fished his wallet out of his pocket and showed them a five-rupee note. He pointed to the track and to the mules. They nodded and came to some domestic agreement. One of them led a little mule down to the stream and they strapped a board across its bony moulting back, covering the board with sacking. Four of them lifted the body up and lashed it along the spar. Then they smiled at Beale, obviously asking for his approval of their skill. He nodded back and said, 'That's fine.' The gipsies laid their panniers on the mules, the women wound their saris about their swarthy bodies, called their children, formed behind their men. The muleteer grinned and nodded his head to Beale. The caravanserai went forward across the sands. Beale turned back once to look at the truck, but he was too bloody tired and fed up to mind. It would stay there; it was settled in; if the floods rose it would disappear; if they fell so much the better. He couldn't help making a balls of it all. He had the body, that was one proof; they could find the truck if they came to look for it, that was the second proof. If they wanted an accident report they could wait. If they thought he was puddled they could sack him when they liked. What was it all about, anyway?

Stumbling up the track in the half-light among the ragged garish gipsies he gradually lost the stiff self-consciousness with which he had first approached them. He was thinking of a page near the beginning of a history book he had studied in the Sixth at school in 1939. About the barbarian migrations in prehistory; the Celts and Iberians, Goths and Vandals and Huns. Once Life had been nothing worth recording beyond the movements of people like these, camels and asses piled with the poor property of their days, panniers, rags, rope, *gramm* and dhal, lambs and kids too new to walk, barefooted, long-haired people rank with sweat, animals shivering with ticks, old women striving to keep up with the rest of the family. He kept away from the labouring old women, preferring the tall girls who walked under the primitive smooth heads of the camels. He kept his eyes on the corpse, but he seemed comfortable enough. Except he was beginning to corrupt. There was a faint whiff of badness about him . . . What did the gipsies do? They would burn him, perhaps, if the journey took too long. How many days to Baroda? The muleteer nodded his head and grinned.

Well, as long as he had the man's identity discs and paybook, he would be covered. He must have those . . . He slipped the identity discs over the wet blue head and matted hair and put them in his overall pocket. He would be all right now, even if they burned him . . . It would be a bigger fire than the one they had sat by and fed with twigs and talked about women together that night, how many nights ago?

He wished, though, that he knew where they were going. They only smiled and nodded when he asked. Maybe they weren't going anywhere much, except perhaps to some pasture, to some well.

Wat Pantathro

I got the crockery and the bloater out of the cupboard for my father before going to bed. He would often cook a fish when he came in at night, using the kitchen poker to balance it on because we didn't have a gridiron. Then I lit my candle in the tin stick, and when I had blown out the oil-lamp I went upstairs to bed. My father was a horse-trainer, and on the handrail at the top of the stairs he kept three riding saddles, one of them very old with leather handles in front curved upwards like the horns of a cow. We slept in the same bedroom which was low and large, containing a big bed made of black iron tubes with brass knobs on the corner posts. Behind our thin plank door we had a cow-horn coat-hook on which hung a trainer's bridle, one with a massive bit and a heavy cluster of metal fingers like a bunch of keys, to daunt the young horses. There were no pictures or ornaments in our bedroom, only a green glass walking-stick over the fireplace and my father's gun licence pinned into the bladdery wallpaper. When I had undressed I said my prayers against the patchwork quilt which my mother had finished the winter she died. Then I climbed up into the high bed and blew the candle out.

But I couldn't sleep at first, thinking of my father taking me down to the autumn horse fair the next day. I lay awake in the rough blankets hearing the squeak of a night bird, and Flower uneasy in her stall, and the hollow dribble of the dry plaster trickling down behind the wallpaper on to the wooden floor of the bedroom. I dozed, and when I awoke in the pitch darkness I could see narrow slits of light like scattered straws shining up through the floorboards from the oil-lamp in the kitchen beneath me, and by that I knew my father was home. And soon I was glad to see the light go out and to hear him groping his way up the bare stairs, muttering his prayers to himself and at last lifting the latch of our bedroom door. I didn't want him to think he had wakened me because that would worry him, so I pretended to be asleep. He came in softly, lit the candle at the bedside and then finished the undressing and praying he had started on his way upstairs.

My father was very tall and slender, his hard bony body was straight and pole-like. At home he always wore a long check riding jacket, fawn breeches and buttoned corduroy gaiters. He had an upright rubber collar which he used to wash with his red pocket handkerchief under the pump, but because he had not been to town there was no necktie round it. His face was long and bony, dull red or rather purplish all over, the same colour in the candle flame as the underside of your tongue, and covered with a mass of tiny little wormy veins. He had thick grey hair and rich brown eyebrows that were curved upwards and as bushy as a pair of silkworms. And when he pushed back his plum-coloured lips, baring his gums to get rid of the bits of food, his long brown teeth with the wide spaces between them showed in his mouth like a row of flat and upright bars.

He stood beside the bed for a moment wiping the greasy marks off his face with his scarlet handkerchief. He did this because when he balanced his fish over the fire it often tumbled off into the flames and became, by the time it was cooked, as black and burnt as a cinder. Then when he had done he blessed me with tobacco-smelling hands and laid down his warm body with care in the bed beside me. I listened, but I knew he had not been drinking because I could not smell him or hear the argument of the beer rolling round in his belly.

The next morning we went down to the fair in the spring body.

This was a high black bouncy cart with very tall thin wheels painted a glittering daffodil yellow. It had a seat with a back to it across the middle and a tiger rug for our knees. Flower, my father's beautiful black riding mare, was between the shafts in her new brown harness, her glossy coat shining in the sun with grooming until she looked as though she had been polished all over with hair-oil. As I sat high above her in the springy cart I could see her carrying her small head in its brown bridle a little on one side as she trotted sweetly along. I loved her, she was quiet and pretty, and I could manage her, but I was afraid my father would sell her in the fair and buy a younger horse for training.

The hedges that morning were full of birds and berries. The autumn sun was strong after the rain and the long tree shadows in the fields were so dark that the grass seemed burnt black with fire. The wheels of the light cart gritted loudly on the road and the steel tyre came turning up under my elbow as it rested on the narrow wooden mudguard. We sat with the tiger-skin rug over us, my father beside me holding the brown reins loosely and resting the whip across them, his hands yellow with nicotine almost to his wrists. He looked fresh and handsome in the bright morning, wearing his new black riding coat and his best whipcord breeches and his soft black hat with the little blue jay's feather in it tilted on the side of his head. And round his upright collar he had a thick scarlet scarf-tie smelling of camphor, with small white horseshoes sprinkled all over it.

I said to him, 'We are not going to sell Flower are we, my father?'

'No, little one,' he answered, teasing me, 'not unless we get a bargain, a biter or a kicker, something light in the behind that no one can manage.' And then with his tusky grin on his face he asked me to take the reins while he struck a match on the palm of his hand and lit another cigarette.

It was six miles down to town and all the way my father waved his whip to people or drew rein to talk to them. Harri

Parcglas taking his snow-white nanny for a walk on the end of a thirty-foot chain stopped to ask my father a cure for the warts spreading on the belly of his entire; the vicar under his black sunshade put his hand from which two fingers were missing on Flower's new collar of plaited straw and reminded my father he was due to toll the funeral bell the next day; and Lewsin Penylan the poacher coming from his shed brought a ferret whose mouth he had sewn up out of his inside pocket and offered us a rabbit that night if my father would throw him a coin for the shot. It was on the hill outside Lewsin's shed a month or two ago that I had been sheltering from the pelting storm after school when I had seen my father, soaking wet from head to foot, passing on his way home to Pantathro. He was riding a brisk little bay pony up from town, his long legs hanging straight down and nearly touching the road. He had no overcoat on and the heavy summer rain was sheeting over him from the cloudburst and running off his clothes as though from little spouts and gutters on to the streaming road. But although he was drenched to the skin and there wasn't a dry hair on the little brown pony, he was singing a hymn about the blood of Jesus Christ loudly to himself as the rain deluged over him. When he saw me he didn't stop the pony, he only grinned and shouted that it looked devilish like rain. The boys who were with me laughed and pointed at him and I blushed with shame because they knew he was drunk again.

We came down into the town at a sharp trot and I could see the long narrow street before us crowded with people and animals. There were horses of every size and colour packed there, most of them unharnessed and with tar shining in the sun on their black hoofs, and yellow, red and blue braids plaited into their manes and tails. And there was a lot of noise there too, men shouting and horses neighing and clattering about. The horses were all over the roads of the town and over the pavements as well, standing about in bunches or being led by rope halters up and down the street, or disappearing through the front doors of the public houses behind their masters. I hardly ever came to town and I loved it. From the high position in the cart where we sat the crowd of bare backs before us seemed packed together as close as cobblestones, so that I thought we should never be able to get through. But my father governed our mare with his clever hands. He kept her going, waving his whip gaily to people he knew, even sometimes urging her into a little trot, easily steering his zigzag way among the mixed crowds of men and horses around us. And as we passed along he had often to shout 'No,' with a grin on his face to the dealer who asked him if Flower was for sale, or called out naming a price for her. Because our mare was pretty and as black as jet and many people wanted her.

But just when we were taking the sharp turn out of Heol Ebrill at the White Hart corner, breaking into a trot again, suddenly, without any warning, we came upon Trehuddion's big grey mare, a hulking hairy cart-horse standing out at right angles from the pavement, with her thick hind legs well forward into the narrow street. Without hesitating for a moment my father leaned over and took the turn, and the axle-hub of the cart struck the big mare a stinger across her massive haunches as we passed, sending her bounding forward and then in a twist up into the air on her hind legs with pain and fright. The Trehuddion brothers, two short black little men, ran out at once cursing and swearing into the road to get hold of her head which she had torn loose from them. I was shocked and excited and I clung to the mudguard board because the light trap with all the leathers wheezing rocked over on its springs as though it was going to capsize with the suddenness of the blow. And Flower, frightened by the shouting and by the unexpected jerk and shudder of the cart behind her, threw back her head and tried to swerve away across the road. I looked up anxiously at my father. He was grinning happily, showing the big boards of his teeth in his reddish face. He didn't stop at all when Trehuddion swore and shouted at him, he only whipped the mare up instead.

My father sold Flower after all to a man he met in the bar of the

Three Salmons, the inn where we put up. Then, after the business was over, we went across to the large flat field which the farmers used for the horse fair. We wandered about for a time talking to many people and listening to the jokes of the auctioneers but I was downhearted because I wouldn't see Flower any more. And in the end my father bought a lovely slender mare with a pale golden coat to her shining like the wing-gloss of a bird and a thick flaky cream-coloured tail reaching almost to the ground. She was shod but she seemed wild, only half-broken, with wide-open black nostrils, and a thick-haired creamy mane and large dark eyes curving and shining like the black marble nobs of a gravestone. In a nearby field a fun fair was opening and each time the loud roundabout siren hooted the tall filly started as though she had received a slash with a cutting whip, her large black nostrils opened wide with fear at the sound, and she began dancing up her long slender legs off the grass as though a current of terror were shooting through her fetlocks. She edged warily out of my father's reach too as long as she could, keeping at the far end of the halter rope, and when he put out his hand towards her dark muzzle she shied away in a panic, peeling open the terrified whites of her eyes as they stood out black and solid from her golden head. But he wouldn't have that from any horse and after a time she became quiet and docile, fawning upon him and allowing him to smooth, with hands that were almost the same colour, the glossy amber of her flanks. Then telling me to fetch her over to the Three Salmons he handed me the halter rope and walked off laughing with the man who had owned her before.

It was hot and sunny in the open field then, so bright that if a man threw up his hand it glowed like a burning torch in the sunlight. The great golden mare trod heavily behind me, a thick forelock of creamy mane hanging tangled over her eyes and her frightened ears pricked up sharply on her high head like rigid moonpoints. I didn't want to lead her, perhaps she was an animal nobody could manage, but I was ashamed to show my father I was afraid. I was almost in a panic going in the heat among the tall and awkward horses that crowded the field, I was afraid of being crushed or trampled down, or of having a kick in the face from the hoof of a frightened horse. And most of all I dreaded that the fairground hooter would begin its howling again and scare this wild creature up on to her hind legs once more with terror and surprise. It became more and more frightening leading her across the crowded field with the hot blast of her breath upon my flesh. I was in a sweating agony expecting her to shy at any moment or to rear without warning and begin a sudden stampede among the horses that crowded around us. My panic and helplessness as the tall blonde mare came marching behind me, large and ominous and with heavy breath, were like the remembered terror rippling hotly over my flesh one night as I sat alone in our kitchen through a thunderstorm, waiting for the endless tension of the storm to break.

But all the time my father, using long and eager strides, went ahead with the other man, waving his cigarette about, enjoying himself among the crowds and slapping the horses recklessly across the haunches with his yellow hand if they were in his way. 'Indeed to God, Dafydd,' he shouted to a sallow man with a fresh black eye, 'you're getting handsomer every day.'

At last the gate came in sight, my hopes began to rise that I should get out of the field before the siren blared into the sky again. To leave the fairground we had to cross a shallow ditch which had a little stream in it because of the rain, and over which someone had dropped a disused oaken house-door to act as a footbridge. As soon as the young mare heard her front hoofs resounding on the wood panels she recoiled powerfully with fright and flung herself back against the rope; she began plunging and shying away from the ditch with great violence, her nostrils huge in her rigid head with surprise and terror and the fiery metals of her shining hoofs flashing their menace in the sun above my upturned face. I was taken unawares, but I didn't think of letting go. The halter rope became rigid as a bar of iron in my hand but in spite of the dismay I felt at her maddened plunging and the sight of her lathered mouth I didn't give in to her. I clutched hard with both hands at the rod-like rope, using all my weight against her as she jerked and tugged back wildly from the terror of the ditch, her flashing forefeet pawing the air and her butter-coloured belly swelling huge above me. My father hearing the noise and seeing the furious startled way she was still bucking and rearing on the halter rope ran back shouting across the wooden door, and quickly managed to soothe her again. Meanwhile I stood ashamed and frightened on the edge of the ditch. I was trembling and I knew by the chill of my flesh that my face was as white as the sun on a pot. But although I was so shaken, almost in tears with shame and humiliation at failing to bring the mare in by myself, my father only laughed, he made nothing of it. He put his hand down in his breeches pocket and promised me sixpence to spend in the shows after dinner. But I didn't want to go to the shows, I wanted to stay with my father all the time.

After the meal I had the money I had been promised and I spent the afternoon by myself wandering about in the fairground eating peppermints and ginger snaps. I was unhappy because my father had been getting noisier during dinner, and when I asked him if I could go with him for the afternoon he said, 'No, don't wait for me, I've got to let my tailboard down first.' I was ashamed, I felt miserable because he never spoke to me that way or told me a falsehood. In the fair field the farm servants were beginning to come in, trying the hooplas and the shooting standings and squirting water over the maids from their ladies' teasers. I stood about watching them and when it was teatime I went back to the inn to meet my father as we had arranged. My heart sank with foreboding when they told me he wasn't there. I waited in the Commercial for a time, hungry and homesick, pretending to read the cattle-cake calendar, but he didn't come. I went out and searched the darkening streets and the muddy fairground, heavy-hearted and almost in tears, but I couldn't find him anywhere. And at last, after many hours, I heard with dismay a tune spreading its notes above the buildings and I saw it was ten by the moon-faced market clock. The public houses were emptying, so that the badly lighted town was becoming packed with people, the fair-night streets were filled with uproar now, and drunken men were lurching past, being sick and quarrelling loudly. I stood aside from them near the fishes of the monumental lamp, weary with loneliness and hunger, glimpsing dimly through my tears the heedless faces of the strangers who crossed swearing and singing through the green gaslight. And then, suddenly I realized I could hear someone singing a hymn aloud in the distance above the uproar of the town. I knew it was my father and all my fears dropped from me like a heavy load as I hurried away because at last I had found him.

I ran along the dark and crowded street until I came to the open square outside the market entrance where the two lamps on the gate pillars had IN painted on them, and there I saw a lot of people gathering into a thick circle. I failed to get through the crowd of men, so I climbed on to the bars of the market wall at the back where the children had chalked and looked over the bowlers and the cloth caps of the people. There was my father, his black hat sitting on the back of his head, standing upright beneath the bright gas lamps in an open space in the middle of the crowd, singing '*Gwaed y Groes*' loudly and beautifully and conducting himself with his two outspread arms. But although he was singing so well all the people were laughing and making fun of him, and that puzzled me and made me angry with them. They stood around in their best clothes or with axle grease on their boots, laughing and pointing, and telling one another that Pantathro had had a bellyful again. By the clear green light of the pillar globes above the market gates I could see that my father had fallen, because his breeches and his black riding coat were soiled with street dirt and horse dung, and when he turned his head round a large raw graze was to be seen bleeding on his cheekbone. I felt myself hot with love and thankfulness when I saw him, my throat seemed as though it were tightly barred up, but I couldn't cry any more. He soon finished his hymn and the people began cheering and laughing as he bowed and wiped the sweat off his glistening head with his red handkerchief. And soon the serving men were shouting, 'Come on Wat, the "Loss of the Gwladys", Watcyn,' but I could see now they only wanted to make fun of him while he was saying that sad poem. I couldn't understand them because my father was so clever, a better actor and reciter than any of them. He cleared away one or two spaniels from the open space with his hat and held up his arms for silence until all the shouting had died down; he stood dark and upright in the centre of the circle, taller than anyone around him, his double shadow thrown on the cobbles by the market lamps pointing out towards the ring of people like the black hands of a large clock. Then he spat on the road and started slowly in his rich voice to recite one of the long poems he used to make up, while I muttered the verses from the wall to help his memory. As he recited in his chanting way he acted as well, gliding to and fro in the bright light of the ring to describe the pretty schooner shooting over the water. Or he held his tall, pole-like body rigid and erect until something came sailing at him from the mocking crowd, a paper bag or a handful of orange peel, and at that he cursed the people and threatened not to go on. When I saw them do that I went hot with shame and anger, because my father was reciting so well and doing his best for them. Then suddenly he stood bent in a tense position, shading his eyes, still as a fastened image with a peg under its foot, his eyes glittering under their thick brows and the big bars of his teeth making the gape of his mouth like a cage as he stared through the storm at the rocks ahead. Rousing himself he shouted an order they use at sea, mimicking a captain, and began steering the schooner this way and that among the dangerous crags, pointing his brown finger to the thunderous heavens, burying his face in his hands, embracing himself and wiping away his tears with his coat sleeves. Every time he did something dramatic like this, although he imitated it so well that

I could see the mothers kissing the little children for the last time, all the people listening laughed and made fun of him. I didn't know why they couldn't leave him alone, they were not giving him fair play, shouting out and jeering all the time at his good acting. When the ship struck in the imitated howling of the wind he shrieked in a way that made my blood run cold, and began chasing about the open space with his arms outspread and a frightening look of terror and despair on his face. He was acting better than ever he had done for me in our kitchen, the sweat was pouring from him now because he was doing all the parts and yet the people were still mocking at him. Sinking his head resignedly into his hands and dropping on one knee in the middle of the circle he sang a few bars of the pitiful death hymn '*Daeth yr Awr im' Ddianc Adre*', in his beautiful bass voice. It was so sweet and sad I was almost breaking my heart to hear him. Some of the farm boys took up the tune, but he stopped them with an angry wave of his hand, which made them laugh again. And then suddenly he gave up singing and as the sinking decks of the ship slid under the water and the mothers and the little children began drowning in the tempest he crouched down low on the cobbles with his hands clenched in agony before him, asking with the sweat boiling out of his face that the great eternal hand should be under him and under us all now and for ever. He forgot he was a drunken actor reciting before a jeering ring of people, he ignored the laughs of the crowd and behaved like a man drowning in the deep waters. He wept and prayed aloud to the King of Heaven for forgiveness, sobbing out his words of love and repentance, and when the ship with her little flags disappeared under the waves he dropped forward and rolled helplessly over with a stunning sound, his face flat downwards on the cobbled road and his limp arms outspread in exhaustion and despair. Just then, as he sprawled still and insensible on the cobbles li! a flimsy scarecrow the wind had blown over, one of the spaniels ran up again with his tail wagging and lifted his leg against the black hat which had fallen off and lay on the road beside my father's head.

The crowd laughed and cheered more than ever when they saw that and I could feel the scalding tears trickling down my face. I jumped down from the market wall and started to hurry the six miles home with angry sobs burning in my throat, because the people had laughed at my father's poem and made him a gazing-stock and the fool of the fair.

All the afternoon I had dreaded this, and in the dark street before finding my father I had wept with alarm and foreboding at the thought of it. I knew I should never be able to manage the golden mare alone and bring her in the night all the way up to Pantathro. And now I was doing it, holding the whip across the reins like my father, and the tall indignant creature with her high-arched neck was before me in the shafts walking along as quietly as our Flower and obeying the rein as though my father himself were driving her. I had prayed to God, who always smelt of tobacco when I knelt to him, and I was comforted with strength and happiness and a quiet horse. The men at the Three Salmons who had altered the brown harness for the mare said when I went back that if I was Wat Pantathro's son I ought to be able to drive anything. I had felt happy at that and ever since I had been warm and full of light inside as though someone had hung a lantern in the middle of my belly. At first I wished for the heavy bridle from the horn hanger behind our bedroom door for the mare's head, but now I didn't care, I felt sure I could manage her and bring her home alone. There was no one else on the road, it was too late, and no dogs would bark or guns go off to frighten her. And beside, it was uphill nearly all the way. Only, about a hundred yards from the railway I pulled up to listen if there was a train on the line, because I didn't want to be on the bridge when the engine was going under, but there was not a sound spreading anywhere in the silent night.

And what made me all the happier was that my father was with me, he was lying fast asleep under the tiger rug on the floorboards of the spring body. His pretty horseshoe tie was like a gun rag and the blue jay's feather was hanging torn from his wet hat beside me on the seat, but he was safe and sleeping soundly. When the men at the Three Salmons lifted him still unconscious into the spring body they examined him first, holding his head up near the light of the cart lamp. I saw then the whole side of his face like beef, and when they pushed back his eyelids with their thumbs the whites showed thick and yellow as though they were covered with matter. And on the inside of his best breeches too there was a dark stain where he had wet himself, but I didn't care about that, I was driving him home myself with the young mare between the shafts and I was safe on the hill outside Lewsin Penylan's already.

The night was warm, the moon up behind me and the stars burning in front bright and clear like little flames with their wicks newly trimmed. And in the quietness of the country the yellow trap-wheels made a pleasant gritty noise on the lonely road and from time to time the mare struck out bright red sparks with her hoofs. We passed the vicarage where one light was still lit, walking sharply all the way, and came to Parcglas where Harri's snow-white nanny pegged on her chain chuckled at us like a seagull from the bank. I thought the mare would be frightened, so I spoke soothingly to her to distract her attention. She just pointed her sharp ears round anxiously in passing, and then took no more notice, she went on smoothly, nodding her high-crested head, her golden toffee-coloured haunches working in the candle flame thrown from the two cart lamps stuck in the front of the spring body.

The sloping hedges slipped by me on both sides of the white road. I wanted more than anything else to please my father after what they had done to him, shouting he had done dirt on the breeching again and was as helpless as a load of peas, I wanted to bring him home safely by myself with the golden mare, and I knew now I should do it. Because at last I saw a star shining over our valley, a keyholeful of light, telling me I was home, and I turned into the drive of Pantathro without touching the gateposts with the hubs on either side.

DIC TRYFAN

Good-for-Nothing

TRANSLATED BY DAFYDD ROWLANDS

How he'd been able to go down into the dark quarry hole in such a drunken state is difficult to comprehend; but that's where he was, at the level which he'd been working for some months past.

'I'm a rotten good-for-nothing,' he said dolefully, as he held his parched mouth under the flow of water that issued from a crack in the rock face.

It was only five o'clock in the morning, and there was no one in the quarry except him. He shouldn't have been there either, but when a man wakes from a drunken stupor at the roadside, before the world has roused itself, he naturally goes to the place he loves best. And Harri Huws's idea of heaven was the level at the bottom of Coed Quarry.

Having painfully bumped his head in his attempt to cool his mouth, he lay down on a heap of rubble. 'I'm a good-for-nothing scoundrel,' he said again, more earnestly this time, and the next moment he was fast asleep.

He was more or less sober when a fifteen-year-old lad arrived at the level carrying a candle. He was singing at the top of his voice, as young lads do in the morning; but when he saw his 'partner' on the pile of rubble in his best clothes, his happy-go-lucky expression darkened.

'You've been at it again, haven't you?' said the lad reproach-fully.

'Yes, Dic *bach*,' answered Harri, with a touch of remorse in his voice.

'Aren't you ashamed of yourself?'

'Yes, I am, boy.'

'You're worse than a pig.'

'Yes, I am, aren't I?'

'Yes, I'll say you are. Go home and change your clothes. You've torn your jacket. Your mam will be angry.'

'Yes, she will, won't she?'

'You bet she will. Now, go on, and come back as soon as you can.'

Harri went, focusing his eye on a gleam of light that showed him the mouth of the level. But he hadn't gone ten yards when he heard a sound like the sound of an earthquake from another world, and the level shuddered as though it was about to come crashing down all around him. His brain cleared in a flash, and his eyes shone like fire. But he couldn't see the glimmer of light which had been shining so clearly a moment ago. The fall had extinguished it, leaving Harri and Dic trapped in the black level.

Whistling, Harri returned to where he'd left Dic, and relit the candle which the boy had dropped in his fright. Then, he went towards the mouth of the level, with Dic close on his heels sobbing audibly.

An experienced quarryman can assess the magnitude of a fall from the noise it makes, and Harri realized that there was at least five thousand tons between himself and daylight. But dying never entered his mind. Wasn't he as healthy as the rock that was now slowly settling at the mouth of the level?

He struck it once, twice, with his hammer. It was as sound as a bell – the best rock he'd seen for a long time. But he would have to shatter it. He would make a hole in its centre in order to blast it when his fellow quarrymen arrived to rescue him and Dic.

But would they come in time? He cut off a piece of twist, and placed it very carefully in the corner of his mouth. Yes, would they arrive in time, that was the question. How many days would it take them to clear five thousand tons – no, six, the sound hadn't stopped yet? Could they shift it in a week? If they worked night and day – and they would for Dic's sake – they could do it.

'Harri!'

'Yes, Dic *bach*?'

'Let's get out of here.'

'Get out, lad?'

'Yes. Can't we get out, Harri?'

'Yes, pretty soon, when they clear this lot.'

'But I want to go now, Harri. Can't you clear it? Come on, push.'

'No use, Dic.'

'I'll help you. Come on, do your best. One, two, three. Why don't you shove, Harri?'

'I am shoving. There you are. We've moved it a little bit. It'll be easier for them to shift it tomorrow now.'

'Tomorrow, Harri?'

'No, what I meant was tonight.'

'But it didn't budge an inch, Harri. I'll swear it didn't. D'you think we'll be out tonight?'

'Yes, sure of it.'

'Harri!'

'Yes, Dic *bach*?'

'Shouldn't we pray?'

'I don't know what good it would do, to be honest.'

'But they're bound to find us. Dad won't let me die. Tell me that I won't die, Harri. Perhaps it would be better for us to pray. They will come, won't they? Where are you, Harri? Don't go away. Listen! Somebody's coming!'

'Yes they'll be here soon. We'll go back to work. Come on. Slowly now. Where are you? On the floor?

'Yes, Harri.'

'Do you feel funny?'

'Funny?'

'Yes, kind of drowsy?'

'A little bit.'

'Do you feel sleepy?'

'A little.'

'Sit down, then. There you are. I'll look for another candle. Where's your food?'

'Under my jacket.'

'You're a big eater, boy. Six rounds of bread and butter, a hefty chunk of cheese, and an egg! You live like a gentleman, Dic.'

'Mam packed it. Says I'm not strong enough, growing too fast. I won't die, will I, Harri?'

'No, you'll be all right.'

'Can I eat now?'

'No, not a morsel.'

'Why not?'

'We've got to work all night to make up for the time we've wasted here doing nothing . . . Thank God I've got enough twist . . . Where's your tea?'

'I don't have any tea, Harri, only milk. Mam says I don't . . .'

'So you said. Hand me your flask. It'll be safer on this ledge. Can you reach it?'

'No, Harri, I can't.'

'The rats won't be able to get at it now. They prefer milk to cheese.'

'But they can't gnaw through the tin, Harri.'

'Don't talk rot! They could eat this rock here if they were hungry enough.'

Dic shuddered at the thought.

'Perhaps they'll eat us, Harri.'

'And perhaps we'll eat them. They know that right enough and they'll keep away. You needn't worry about them.'

'Harri!'

'Yes, boy?'

'I want to sleep. Can I sleep here?'

'Sleep? Yes, as if you were at home.'

'But will I wake then?'

'Of course you will.'

'Are you sure we can't go out? You didn't really shove very

hard, Harri. I'm sure you didn't. I think I'll go to sleep. Do you feel like sleeping?'

'No, not just yet. Too early, Dic, too early. Are you cold?'

'Just a little.'

'I thought so. You lie down and I'll put my jacket over you . . . No! I don't need it. There you are, all right now?'

'Yes, fine, Harri.'

Five minutes later, young Dic was sleeping soundly. And as his slumber deepened the look of fear on his pale face seemed to disappear. Harri looked at him closely, and chewed his twist of tobacco as fast as he could.

'I'd be a lot happier if the lad were on the other side of that old fall,' he said. 'Hello! You're here already, are you, you old bitch? Go back to your hole, or by damn I'll crush your bones . . . There you are, I warned you . . . Don't worry, I'll break the news to your family soon enough.'

He grabbed his hammer, and with the candle in the other hand, he went to look for the other rats. In the dim candlelight he saw another one frantically hurling itself against the side of the level in an attempt to escape from the light. The silence was broken by a sudden squeal. More rats appeared in the light, and within half an hour a row of corpses lay on the floor of the level.

'There you are,' said Harri. 'You're better off than the boy and me. No pain, nothing. Now for the mourners.'

He took a piece of cheese from Dic's lunch-box, and put it on a stone in a prominent place where the rats couldn't fail to see it. He was determined to destroy them all, for Dic's sake.

One rat after another emerged from the darkness, and stood within a few inches of the bait. Harri watched them intently, and he couldn't understand why their bodies shivered when their eyes displayed such ferocity. But a man cannot understand a rat. He has to kill every one of them. The hammer fell on one rat after the other, and the blazing eyes suddenly went misty and dull. So effectively did the hammer do its work that there was no squeak to warn the living that this was nothing more than a new death-trap.

And soon, the last rat appeared. Harri knew that it was the last one because it was a lame rat. And a lame rat always has to stand back. It dragged itself over the rubble, and for one fleeting moment Harri felt pity for the poor creature. But even a lame rat can inflict a lot of damage, and the hammer fell once again.

Three days had gone by. Harri roused himself from an uneasy sleep. He'd been dreaming that dead rats were tearing his face apart. The pain was terrible. He put his fingers to his face, and it was wet. He couldn't understand it at all. He lit the candle. Yes, it was blood. His hands were covered with it, and it ran down his jaw. Had they attacked young Dic as well? He crept on his hands and knees again. He didn't try to get up, because something told him that he wouldn't be able to, that he was too weak. But he couldn't understand the weakness. No, Dic was asleep, and there was no blood on his face. Strange! He dragged himself back to his corner, and put his hand in a pool of blood. He pondered. Could it be his blood? Yes, and he felt weak because he'd lost so much. But how? He couldn't fathom it, and for a while he just stared at the congealed blood. It had trickled down the side of a rock. Now he understood. He'd fallen asleep with his head against the rock, and the sharp edge had pierced his flesh.

Gradually, his senses revived, and his legs regained some of their strength. The pain left his face and settled in his stomach. He remembered that he'd not eaten – since when? The day before the fall he hadn't been able to eat. He'd been on the booze for a whole week; and until now, when his stomach was crying out for food, he'd forgotten that his tin, which was behind the rock that had so painfully torn his face, was packed with food. He grabbed it excitedly.

'Dic *bach*!'

He shook the young lad tenderly.

Dic rubbed his drowsy eyes, and looked around in wonder.

'You'd better have something to eat.'

Dic's eyes lost their look of wonder, and he began to sob.

'Haven't they come, Harri?'

'No, boy.'

'But they will come?'

'Yes, of course they will. Here, take this.'

'This isn't my bread and butter, Harri. Have you eaten?'

'Yes, a bellyful.'

'Honestly?'

'On my word of honour.'

'They'll be here soon, won't they?'

'I'm expecting them any minute.'

'Shouldn't you eat something, then?'

'Not a crumb. If you've finished, we'll keep what's left here. Now, you have a lie down. I'll wake you when they come.'

He placed the tin near Dic's right hand, so that the boy could find it should God see fit for him to wake up again. The candle was burning low and dim, only an inch or so remained. Harri lit another one. Dic was again fast asleep, but his breathing was becoming more laboured all the time.

Harri tried to get up. Something was bothering him. It was the sound of the water falling from the top of the level. Up to now, he'd not noticed it, but now it sounded like a waterfall, and it affected him strangely. He felt he would go mad if it didn't stop, but he didn't make a move to stop it. Why didn't it stop? It was stopping. It was growing fainter, fainter, and then it stopped completely and Harri slept.

On the fifth day, a ray of light penetrated the darkness; and when the mouth of the level was clear, four quarrymen entered slowly. They knew they were entering a tomb, and there was no need to hurry. It was a sad sight that they beheld. In one corner, stripped to the waist, lay Harri, a dead rat in his hand. In another corner, wrapped from head to toe in Harri's clothes, Dic lay weeping, with two empty food tins beside him.

'Harri's gone,' said one of the men, shaking the good-for-nothing scoundrel. 'Strange that he should have died before young Dic.'

But he looked at the half-naked body and the two boxes, and he understood. It wasn't strange, after all, but it was strange that the biggest waster in the quarry had sacrificed his life to save someone else.

But everyone agreed that, his drinking apart, that was just like Harri.

A *Father in Sion*

On the banks of Avon Bern there lived a man who was a Father in Sion. His name was Sadrach, and the name of the farmhouse in which he dwelt was Danyrefail. He was a man whose thoughts were continually employed upon sacred subjects. He began the day and ended the day with the words of a chapter from the Book and a prayer on his lips. The Sabbath he observed from first to last; he neither laboured himself nor allowed any in his household to labour. If in the Seiet, the solemn, soul-searching assembly that gathers in Capel Sion on the nights of Wednesdays after Communion Sundays, he was entreated to deliver a message to the congregation, he often prefaced his remarks with, 'Dear people, on my way to Sion I asked God what He meant.'

This episode in the life of Sadrach Danyrefail covers a long period; it has its beginning on a March night with Sadrach closing the Bible and giving utterance to these words:

'May the blessing of the Big Man be upon the reading of His Word.' Then, 'Let us pray.'

Sadrach fell on his knees, the open palms of his hands together, his elbows resting on the table; his eight children – Sadrach the Small, Esau, Simon, Rachel, Sarah, Daniel, Samuel, and Miriam – followed his example.

Usually Sadrach prayed fluently, in phrases not unworthy of the minister, so universal, so intimate his pleading: tonight he stumbled and halted, and the working of his spiritful mind lacked the heavenly symmetry of the mind of the godly; usually the note of abundant faith and childlike resignation rang grandly throughout his supplications: tonight the note was one of despair and gloom. With Job he compared himself, for was not the Lord trying His servant to the uttermost? Would the all-powerful Big Man, the Big Man who delivered the Children of Israel from the hold of the Egyptians, give him a morsel of strength to bear his cross? Sadrach reminded God of his loneliness. Man was born to be mated, even as the animals in the fields. Without mate man was like an estate without an overseer, or a field of ripe corn rotting for the reaping-hook.

Sadrach rose from his knees. Sadrach the Small lit the lantern which was to light him and Esau to their bed over the stable.

'My children,' said Sadrach, 'do you gather round me now, for have I not something to tell you?'

Rachel, the eldest daughter, a girl of twelve, with reddish cheeks and bright eyes, interposed with:

'Indeed, indeed, now, little father; you are not going to preach to us this time of night!'

Sadrach stretched forth his hand and motioned his children be seated.

'Put out your lantern, Sadrach the Small,' he said. 'No, Rachel, don't you light the candle. Dear ones, it is not the light of this earth we need, but the light that comes from above.'

'Iss, iss,' Sadrach the Small said. 'The true light. The light the Big Man puts in the hearts of those who believe, dear me.'

'Well spoken, Sadrach the Small. Now be you all silent awhile, for I have things of great import to tell you. Heard you all my prayer?'

'Iss, iss,' said Sadrach the Small.

'Sadrach the Small only answers. My children, heard you all my prayer? Don't you be blockheads now – speak out.'

'There's lovely it was,' said Sadrach the Small.

'My children?' said Sadrach.

'Iss, iss,' they answered.

'Well, well, then. How can I tell you?' Sadrach put his fingers through the thin beard which covered the opening of his waistcoat, closed his eyes, and murmured a prayer. 'Your mother Achsah is not what she should be. Indeed to goodness, now, what disgrace this is! Is it not breaking my heart? You did hear how I said to the nice Big Man that I was like Job? Achsah is mad.'

Rachel sobbed.

'Weep you not, Rachel. It is not for us to question the all-wise ways of the Big Man. Do you dry your eyes on your apron now, my daughter. You, too, have your mother's eyes. Let me weep in my solitude. Oh, what sin have I committed, that God should visit this affliction on me?'

Rachel went to the foot of the stairs.

'Mam!' she called.

'She will not hear you,' Sadrach interrupted. 'Dear me, have I not put her in the harness loft? It is not respectable to let her out. Twm Tybach would have sent his wife to the madhouse of Carmarthen. But that is not Christian. Rachel, Rachel, dry your eyes. It is not your fault that Achsah is mad. Nor do I blame Sadrach the Small, nor Esau, nor Simon, nor Sarah, nor Daniel, nor Samuel, nor Miriam. Goodly names have I given you all. Live you up to them. Still, my sons and daughters, are you not all responsible for Achsah's condition? With the birth of each of you she has got worse and worse. Child-bearing has made her foolish. Yet it is un-Christian to blame you.'

Sadrach placed his head in his arms.

Sadrach the Small took the lantern and he and Esau departed for their bed over the stable; one by one the remaining six put off their clogs and crept up the narrow staircase to their beds.

Wherefore to her husband Achsah became as a cross, to her children as one forgotten, to everyone living in Manteg and in the several houses scattered on the banks of Avon Bern as Achsah the madwoman.

The next day Sadrach removed the harness to the room in the

dwelling-house in which slept the four youngest children; and he put a straw mattress and a straw pillow on the floor, and on the mattress he spread three sacks; and these were the furnishings of the loft where Achsah spent her time. The frame of the small window in the roof he nailed down, after fixing on the outside of it three solid bars of iron of uniform thickness; the trapdoor he padlocked, and the key of the lock never left his possession. Achsah's food he himself carried to her twice a day, a procedure which until the coming of Martha some time later he did not entrust to other hands.

Once a week when the household was asleep he placed a ladder from the floor to the loft, and cried:

'Achsah, come you down now.'

Meekly the woman obeyed, and as her feet touched the last rung Sadrach threw a cow's halter over her shoulders, and drove her out into the fields for an airing.

Once, when the moon was full, the pair were met by Lloyd the Schoolin', and the sight caused Mishtir Lloyd to run like a frightened dog, telling one of the women of his household that Achsah, the madwoman, had eyes like a cow's.

At the time of her marriage Achsah was ten years older than her husband. She was rich, too: Danyrefail, with its stock of good cattle and a hundred acres of fair land, was her gift to the bridegroom. Six months after the wedding Sadrach the Small was born. Tongues wagged that the boy was a child of sin. Sadrach answered neither yea nor nay. He answered neither yea nor nay until the first Communion Sabbath, when he seized the bread and wine from Old Shemmi and walked to the Big Seat. He stood under the pulpit, the fringe of the minister's Bible-marker curling on the bald patch on his head.

'Dear people,' he proclaimed, the silver-plated wine cup in one hand, the bread plate in the other, 'it has been said to me that some of you think Sadrach the Small was born out of sin. You do not speak truly. Achsah, dear me, was frightened by the old bull. The bull I bought in the September fair. You, Shemmi, you know the animal. The red and white bull. Well, well, dear people,

Achsah was shocked by him. She was running away from him, and as she crossed the threshold of Danyrefail, did she not give birth to Sadrach the Small? Do you believe me now, dear people. As the Lord liveth, this is the truth. Achsah, Achsah, stand you up now, and say you to the congregation if this is not right.'

Achsah, the babe suckling at her breast, rose and murmured:

'Sadrach speaks the truth.'

Sadrach ate of the bread and drank of the wine.

Three months after Achsah had been put in the loft Sadrach set out at daybreak on a journey to Aberystwyth. He returned late at night, and, behold, a strange woman sat beside him in the horse car; and the coming of this strange woman made life different in Danyrefail. Early in the day she was astir, bustling up the children, bidding them fetch the cows, assist with the milking, feed the pigs, or do whatever work was in season.

Rachel rebuked Sadrach, saying, 'Little father, why for cannot I manage the house for you? Indeed now, you have given to Martha the position that belongs to me, your eldest daughter.'

'What mean you, my dear child?' returned Sadrach. 'Cast you evil at your father? Turn you against him? Go you and read your Commandments.'

'People are whispering,' said Rachel. 'They do even say that you will not be among the First Men of the Big Seat.'

'Martha is a gift from the Big Man,' answered Sadrach. 'She has been sent to comfort me in my tribulation, and to mother you, my children.'

'Mother!'

'Tut, tut, Rachel,' said Sadrach, 'Martha is only a servant in my house.'

Rachel knew that Martha was more than a servant. Had not her transfer letter been accepted by Capel Sion, and did she not occupy Achsah's seat in the family pew? Did she not, when it was Sadrach's turn to keep the minister's month, herself on each of the four Saturdays take a basket laden with a chicken, two white-hearted cabbages, a peek of potatoes, a loaf of bread, and half a pound of butter to the chapel house of Capel Sion? Did she not drive with Sadrach to market and fair and barter for his butter and cheese and cattle and what not? Did she not tell Ellen the Weaver's Widow what cloth to weave for the garments of the children of Achsah?

These things Martha did; and Danyrefail prospered exceedingly: its possessions spread even to the other side of Avon Bern. Sadrach declared in the Seiet that the Lord was heaping blessings on the head of His servant. Of all who worshipped in Sion none was stronger than the male of Danyrefail; none more respected. The congregation elected him to the Big Seat. Sadrach was a tower of strength unto Sion.

But in the wake of his prosperity lay vexation. Rachel developed fits; while hoeing turnips in the twilight of an afternoon she shivered and fell, her head resting in the water ditch that is alongside the hedge. In the morning Sadrach came that way with a load of manure.

'Rachel *fach*,' he said, 'wake you up now. What will Martha say if you get ill?'

He passed on.

When he came back Rachel had not moved, and Sadrach drove away, without noticing the small pool of water which had gathered over the girl's head. Within an hour he came again, and said:

'Rachel, Rachel, wake you up. There's lazy you are.'

Rachel was silent. Death had come before the milking of the cows. Sadrach went to the end of the field and emptied his cart of the manure. Then he turned and cast Rachel's body into the cart, and covered it with a sack, and drove home, singing the hymn which begins:

> Safely, safely gather'd in,
> Far from sorrow, far from sin,
> No more childish griefs or fears,
> No more sadness, no more tears;
> For the life so young and fair
> Now hath passed from earthly care;

God Himself the soul will keep,
Giving His beloved – sleep.

Esau was kicked by a horse, and was hurt to his death; six weeks later Simon gashed his thumb while slicing mangolds, and he died. Two years went by, by the end of which period Old Ianto, the gravedigger of Capel Sion, dug three more graves for the children of Sadrach and Achsah; and over these graves Sadrach and Martha lamented.

But Sadrach the Small brought gladness and cheer to Danyrefail with the announcement of his desire to wed Sara Ann, the daughter of Old Shemmi. Martha and Sadrach agreed to the union provided Old Shemmi gave to his daughter a stack of hay, a cow in calf, a heifer, a quantity of bedclothes, and four cheeses. Old Shemmi, on his part, demanded with Sadrach the Small ten sovereigns, a horse and a cart, and a bedstead.

The night before the wedding Sadrach drove Achsah into the fields, and he told her how the Big Man had looked with goodwill upon Sadrach the Small, and was giving him Sara Ann to wife.

What occurred in the loft over the cowshed before dawn crept in through the window with the iron bars I cannot tell you. God can. But the rising sun found Achsah crouching behind one of the hedges of the lane that brings you from Danyrefail to the tramping road, and there she stayed, her eyes peering through the foliage, until the procession came by: first Old Shemmi and Sadrach, with Sadrach the Small between them; then the minister of Capel Sion and his wife; then the men and the women of the congregation; and last came Martha and Sara Ann.

The party disappeared round the bend: Achsah remained.

'Goodness me,' she said to herself. 'There's a large mistake now. Indeed, indeed, mad am I.'

She hurried to the gateway, crossed the road and entered another field, through which she ran as hard as she could. She came to a hedge, and waited.

The procession was passing.

Sadrach and Sadrach the Small.

Achsah doubled a finger.

Among those who followed on the heels of the minister was Miriam.

Achsah doubled another finger.

The party moved out of sight: Achsah still waited.

'Sadrach the Small and Miriam!' she said, spreading out her doubled-up fingers. 'Two. Others? Esau. Simon. Rachel. Sarah. Daniel. Samuel. Dear me, where shall I say they are? Six. Six of my children. Mad, mad am I?' . . . She laughed. 'They are grown, and I didn't know them.'

Achsah waited the third time for the wedding procession. This time she scanned each face, but only in the faces of Sadrach the Small and Miriam did she recognize her own children. She threw herself on the grass. Esau and Simon and Rachel, and Sarah and Daniel and Samuel. She remembered the circumstances attending the birth of each . . . And she had been a good wife. Never once did she deny Sadrach his rights. So long as she lasted she was a woman to him.

'Sadrach the Small and Miriam,' she said.

She rose and went to the graveyard. She came to the earth under which are Essec and Shan, Sadrach's father and mother, and at a distance of the space of one grave from theirs were the graves of six of the children born of Sadrach and Achsah. She parted the hair that had fallen over her face, and traced with her fingers the letters which formed the names of each of her six children.

As Sara Ann crossed the threshold of Danyrefail, and as she set her feet on the flagstone on which Sadrach the Small is said to have been born, the door of the parlour was opened and a lunatic embraced her.

ALUN T. LEWIS

Relatives

(TRANSLATED BY HYWEL TEIFI EDWARDS)

My uncle Edward was a bank manager in Deganwy, that histori-
cal spot where the river Conway seems to hurry before thrusting
into the sea and subsiding. We called him Uncle Ted and his wife
Aunty Bet. She was my mother's sister. She always addressed him
as Edward and in conversation with his wife I never heard him
use any name other than Elizabeth. That's the kind of couple
they were, rather fastidious, proper and very courteous; it was
just that such unrelenting good manners inhibited a creature as
unruly as a ten-year-old country bumpkin. It took so little to
excite my aunt and when agitated she would move the china dogs
and the brass candlesticks on the mantelpiece, or the dishes on
the dresser, back and forth, needlessly, all the while breathing in
and out quickly through her nose like a sexually aroused
hedgehog.

But they were very kind and we would spend a fortnight or
more every August in the fifth house from the end after crossing
the railway bridge, where the row of houses forms an arch directly
above the river's bed.

The river flowed deep and swift on its course and the stony
beach sloped steeply from the narrow promenade. Across the
river on Conway's sea marsh were flats and sand dunes as there
were nearer the sea towards Llandudno beach where the river
now widened and coasted along.

But in this trough, opposite Glanaber, hardly anything was
ever still – although aunty expected me to be – except for a short

while when the tide turned. At that time, you could see a cluster of seaweed, or a twig or a ball swirling on its spot; but very quickly the tide would ebb, sweeping swiftly towards the sea between Anglesey and Great Orme's Head. Then, in its own good time, it would race back just as swiftly and the little boats riding at anchor would turn their noses, pointing at the estuary to sniff the breeze blowing over Conway and Llansantffraid from the uplands of Hiraethog and Aled, passing Bryn-y-Maen church as it came.

Tom Huws fled from Port Dinorwic because, as the poet put it, nothing chanced there but sun, wind and rain. Deganwy's splendour for me lay in the fact that everything happened there – in due course.

It was through watching the boatmen there that I learnt that the target isn't always reached by the direct route. With the turn of the tide, when the river's course would be brim-full from bank to bank, they would have to row energetically against the current, halfway to Conway and then turn the boat's prow and slip quickly, a little aslant, on the tide before landing directly opposite the starting-point.

I no sooner hear the doleful mewing of the seagulls as they follow the plough in the very early spring than I am transported for a moment to that little loft above the door in Glanaber, where I have got up in my nightgown to listen to the seagull on the roof and to look through the window to see the boats, all of one mind, tugging at their ropes – sometimes towards the sea and sometimes towards Conway's bridges. I wasn't enough of a scientist, neither did I have the patience, to watch closely and see the turn of the tide.

We went occasionally past the golf-course to the sandy beach where I would be allowed to build sand-castles and dig ditches and paddle – 'You're surely not going to let him go to the beach in those clothes?' said aunty. 'What if you should see someone that we know!'

But the ideal place to play was the jetty. It was a wooden

gangway, with handrails on each side, resting on hardwood piles cut and shaped for their purpose. The actual landing-stage, of the same black, hard wood, was at the far end of the jetty; it lay top-heavy and limp on the stones when the tide was low and rose gradually as it came in, the handrails levelling out, the gangway less steep and easier to traverse to the landing-stage, which came to life and heaved up and down sensuously as the tide fondled and jiggled it.

The big event of each day – except Sunday – was the arrival of the steamer from Conway to pick up passengers from Deganwy and Llandudno and carry them up the river to Trefriw. But not always to Trefriw, mind, only when the tide was high enough; failing that you had to make do with Tal-y-Cafn. They were small, jaunty ships each with a straight-backed funnel belching smoke and two big paddle-wheels on each side like huge mill-wheels, churning the water into a great froth.

We didn't venture on board one of them for some years despite many a prod and a hint from me. Sometimes, I surmised that my father was too poor to afford the trip, but thanks to that strange instinct present in both animals and children, I half comprehended that Aunt Bet was the stumbling-block. I didn't think she was afraid of drowning, she came with us once on a steamer from Llandudno round Anglesey. A wind blew up that time before we reached Holyhead and she was seasick. I'll always remember that man telling her, 'Turn your head the other way missus!' But there was little danger of that happening either on the still waters of the Conway! It remained a mystery to me until the hot summer of 1911 when my father, with my enthusiastic backing, persuaded her to go on the trip to Trefriw.

My aunt was very reluctant. 'That old man will be on the ship,' she said.

'Nonsense!' said father. 'Joshua Gruffydd is alright in his place.'

'Yes,' answered Aunty Bet in a steely voice, 'the trouble is that he doesn't know his place. And I have Edward's position to think about.'

But, as I said, she came. I was in my Sunday best, 'like a little gentleman', to quote my aunt, but prancing in a most ungentlemanly way on the beach seeing the ship pass the landing-stage, turn noisily, and pull in, the sailors yelling and two of them jumping on to the jetty to wind ropes around the bollards.

Then the gate at the far end of the jetty was opened and we went on board.

'We'll go ahead to keep us a place, Hannah,' said my father to my mother, and he said to me, 'You come along with Aunty Bet.'

My uncle, of course, was at the bank.

My aunt grasped me firmly by the hand in case I should fall in the river and I was glad that the Llangarrog boys weren't there to see me being treated like a baby just beginning to crawl.

Within two minutes we were ascending the gangway to the ship's deck, me eyeing everything eagerly, the great wheels, the bridge where the captain stood in all his glory, and under the bridge a hole leading to the depths of the ship.

As we were passing to go in search of my father and mother a sailor came up from somewhere below and stood in the hole like a picture in a frame. He wore a blue jersey and baggy trousers with a belt around his middle. His cheeks and chin were blue-black, not because he was growing a beard but because he hadn't shaved for two or three days.

Aunty Bet saw him and began to sniff and look agitated. She took hold of my hand clumsily, grasped it tightly and began to drag me after her, and the man said, 'Well blow me down! Betsy!'

My aunt stood transfixed as if confronted by a wall.

Then she turned and faced the sailor.

'How are you, Joshua Gruffydd?' she said dryly.

'I'm surviving, Betsy *fach*,' he said, 'just to avoid funeral costs. I've no money in the bank, you see.'

He extended his hand, black with coal dust, especially under the fingernails, but aunty ignored it.

'You have enough time to loaf around like this?'

The sailor smiled, showing two uneven rows of yellow teeth. 'He who made time, has made plenty of it, you see, Betsy.'

He looked at me. 'Good God,' he said, 'whose boy is this? That little man has never –'

I felt a sudden tug at my hand which made me feel that my arm was being disconnected.

'Come, Dewi,' said my aunt, 'your father and mother will be wondering where we've got to.'

And away we went, Aunty Bet with her nose in the air dragged me after her, my feet stuttering along in pursuit of my head as I turned back for another look at the strange man who had upset my aunt so much.

'Don't drag your feet,' she said, in a fiercer tone than I had ever heard her use before. 'Don't mind that old man, and don't you dare tell anyone about this ever.'

In a trice we had got to the ship's stern and had found my mother and father.

'I knew that we shouldn't have come,' snuffled my aunt. 'The day has been spoilt for me. That common old man.'

'Oh! You saw Joshua Gruffydd,' said my father. 'Don't let that spoil this glorious afternoon. Sit back and enjoy this incomparable scene.'

And it was beautiful, the water so calm and we now ready to land on the quay in Conway.

'Look,' said mother, 'there's the smallest house in the world, and there's the castle, and there's Telford's bridge with the railway bridge behind it.'

'How will we go under the bridge?' I asked.

'Questions, questions,' said mother.

'They lower the stacks on their side,' said my father. The ship reversed a short distance from the quay and then started again towards the bridges.

I was determined to see the ceremony of lowering the stack,

and I told my father that I was going to find a spot amidships where I could see everything clearly.

'Go with him, Huw David,' said my Aunt Bet. 'What if he should fall overboard?'

'Tut,' said my father, 'let him go. You mollycoddle him too much, Elizabeth. The boy must learn to stand on his own feet.'

And away I went, hardly hearing my mother say, 'Take care.'

By the time I got amidships, the bottom of the stack had been released on one side and two sailors were ready on the other side to pull on a rope to turn it on its side, and lower it, while the captain stood on the bridge awaiting the exact moment to give the command.

'Lower the stack.'

And they pulled on the rope so that the stack folded like that picture of the tower of Pisa I once saw in a book in school, and we sailed gracefully with the tide, under Telford's steel ropes and the steel box of the railway bridge, as if the little ship genuflected humbly and thankfully in recognition of the right to pass under on its way to the splendours of the Vale of Conway.

Then, another shout from the bridge, 'Raise the stack', saw them pull on another rope, and the stack stood erect after its salaam to the keepers of the vale. The ceremony was over.

All around me were sitting down again but I decided to go forward, retracing my steps past the hole that opened on the mysteries of the engines.

Would that man be there, I wondered.

Tremors of expectation ran through me. I knew that my aunt Bet wouldn't approve of this, although I didn't know why.

I wanted to see the sailor again, and yet I was also afraid of seeing him.

The sun warmed the nape of my neck and I paused awhile, leaning over the deck-rails to watch the ship's bows cleaving the water. When I got near the bridge I was in the shade, and after reaching the opening to the ship's maw, I ventured to put my head inside, and felt the hot air playing around me.

And who should be there, just about to descend some iron steps, but the man I had seen before, the man who had been so forward with Aunty Bet.

I suppose I shut out the light and he turned his head.

'Hello,' he said. 'No one is allowed down here.' He came a step or two nearer. 'Oh,' he said, 'it's you again.'

'Tell me,' he said, bending down and looking me straight in the eye, 'is that woman you were with related to you?'

What a daft question!

'Of course she is,' I said, 'she's Aunty Bet. She has to be related to me then.'

'Huh! You are clever. Whose boy are you? And don't say your mother's boy. I know that much about this old world. What's your mother's name?'

'Mrs Oliver,' I said. 'She's the wife of the Revd David Oliver, Llangarrog.'

The sailor took hold of my shoulder, gripping me like a blacksmith's tongs. 'Your mother,' he said, 'what's her name?'

I was sorry I had gone there and I turned my head to see if my father or mother or Aunty Bet were anywhere in sight, but they were not.

'Hannah,' I said.

The fingers of the tongs that seemed to want to come together in the flesh of my shoulder relaxed their grip and the rough voice softened.

'Well! Well!' he said. 'Hannah's boy is it. I'm a half-brother to your mother, you see.' Then a second or two later. 'And to her sister, Betsy,' he said, in an angry tone again.

I didn't know what a half-brother was, but I was less afraid.

'What's your name?'

'Dewi.'

'Dewi. Well, Dewi, don't you want to know what my name is? And I your half-uncle.'

I was beginning to pluck up courage by now. 'What is your name, uncle?' I asked.

'Aha! That's better. Uncle is it! My name is Joshua. Have you heard about him? He was the man who made the sun stand still. But you shall call me Josh – because we're related – Uncle Josh.'

'Thank you, Uncle Josh,' I said.

My new uncle chewed tobacco all the time, and a yellow dribble ran from the corner of his mouth, along his chin and meandered through the stubble of his beard.

'Would you like to come down to see the boilers and the engine?'

That's what you would call being a man! I knew enough English to understand the significance of the words 'No Admittance' above the door. And I was being admitted!

The steps were full of drainage holes and made of cast iron and the heat increased as I descended, step after step, behind Uncle Josh. After reaching the bottom, we walked along an iron landing again, with rails on each side, and two pistons of gleaming steel thrusting back and forth regularly were attached to the cogs of the two big wheels which churned the water outside driving the ship onward.

The engine-room was at the far end of the path; a huge stack of coal half filled it and there was a hole in the roof through which the coal was delivered.

It was insufferably hot there. I removed my jerkin.

'Yes, take your coat off,' said my uncle, 'and I'll take off my jersey. I'll have to stoke a bit of these boilers. You sit on that box there.'

I obeyed and sat on a wooden box which had been turned upside down in the middle of the room.

My uncle took hold of a huge long iron hook and clawed open the door of one of the two furnaces, the heat striking me in my forehead and the sudden burst of light from the white-hot fire blinding me for a minute. Then my uncle spat on his palms, grasped the shovel and threw shovelful after shovelful into the heart of the fire.

What a muscular man he was! Sweat poured down his face, his

vest stuck to him like a wet rag and the tufts of black hair in his
armpits glistened in the firelight as he turned to lift another shovelful.

He finished shortly, shutting the furnace doors with a clang,
but I had started sweating by this time.

Uncle Josh came and sat beside me on the box, the smell of
sweat filling my nostrils. I also noticed a black smudge of oil on
the sleeve of my white shirt.

My uncle saw me staring at it. 'Tut,' he said, 'a little dirt never
harmed anyone.'

If only every adult was that sensible!

'My Aunt Bet will scold me,' I said disconsolately.

'Oh! Betsy is it! Not your father or mother. Are you afraid of
her then?'

'Yes, I am,' I said, angry with him for forcing me to admit it,
'but her name isn't Betsy. My father and mother call her Beth,
and Uncle Ted calls her Elizabeth.'

'Huh! That little penny-counting doll! Other people's money at
that! The snob! At home in Y Lleiniau she was called Betsy, and
your mother was little Hannah. She was the last little arse in the
nest, you see.'

I didn't know what that meant, either. That was another question I would have to ask my father. I could ask him. But I wasn't
going to show Uncle Josh my ignorance.

'Another five minutes before you go back on deck,' he said,
taking a box from his trouser pocket and a two-bladed knife.
From the box he took a roll of black tobacco, not unlike liquorice
except that it was thicker, and harder, too, I guessed, judging by
the way he had to use the knife to cut a piece. He spat once more
and the yellow juice sizzled on the side of the furnace. He put a
fresh quid in his mouth and started chewing anew.

'Is it nice?' I asked.

'Nice! Yes of course! But not sweet, mind you, sweet like
London mouse shit. This is lovely and bitter and warms your
insides.'

'What's London mouse shit?' I said, hurrying over that word so as not to hear myself saying it.

'Those small, small sweets of all colours. We used to buy a fistful of them for a ha'penny in Siân Price's shop a long time ago.'

'Hundreds and thousands,' I said.

'Good Lord! A scholar too! A fluent Englishman! I wonder what Betsy calls them by now?'

'Aunty Bet says "Pw",' I said, my mind still on that prohibited word.

'Pw!' My uncle laughed so much his belly wobbled. 'That's baby talk you see, Dewi,' he said.

Calling me a baby and I nine years of age and already able to swim!

'Aunty Bet says you are common,' I said, like some David picking up a smooth pebble from the river.

My uncle sobered instantly and his face changed.

His eyes narrowed like pigs' eyes.

He stared at me, almost sullenly, his forehead furrowed.

'Does she!' he snorted. 'The old bitch.'

Then he changed again just as quickly and smiled broadly; but the eyes narrowed even more.

'Never mind, Dewi, my lad,' he said. 'Hi, would you like to try this baccy?'

I didn't dare refuse. 'Yes I would,' I said.

He cut a piece with his knife and gave it to me.

'You have to chew it mind, not swallow it. You'll have to learn to spit then. Is there a spittoon in Betsy's house?'

'Yes, a brass one, in the fireplace; and my aunt polishes it every week. Is that what it's for?'

'Yes of course. You spit in that. You'll be a proper sailor then. AB Dewi Oliver, by damn!'

'What's an AB?' I asked. I was asking more questions than any sailor or man should . . .

'Able-bodied seaman,' said my uncle.

I put the quid hesitatingly in my mouth. Its taste was worse than the wormwood mother used to give me when I was constipated, or when she wanted to prevent me having tapeworms. In a minute or two my mouth was full of the bitter juice, and I was afraid to swallow after my uncle's warning.

And afraid to spit, too!

I had to swallow some of it, and then I started to choke and beads of sweat stood out on my forehead. My uncle was somewhat startled and he leapt to his feet slapping the palm of his big hand on my back, whereupon I swallowed the whole chaw.

'I feel sick,' I said, the gorge rising in my throat.

'Come up to the fresh air. You'll feel better there.'

The place was starting to spin and I must have half-tripped because my uncle took hold of my two shoulders and pushed me before him along the iron landing, the deafening sound of the pistons in my ears, back to the hole and into the fresh air. 'You stand there for a minute,' he said, 'until you come round.'

It was so good to escape from the overpowering heat and feel the breeze on my face. I gulped the air into my lungs.

I still felt sick, however, and wanted mother; so I set out along the deck, walking carefully like a drunken man, colliding with people as I passed and they looking at me in astonishment.

I found the family at last. I don't suppose it took long but my feet were like lead and there was a strange heaving in my belly.

'Where have you been?' said father.

'Look at his shirt,' said Aunty Bet.

'What's the matter with you?' said mother.

My father got up from his straw chair. 'Sit here,' he said, 'and put your head between your knees.'

It was too late!

I saw the deck rising to meet me, the ship standing on its head and everything going dark.

When I came round I was sitting on the chair, my head between my knees and my father had his hand on the nape of my neck.

'He's surely not seasick and this river like a duckpond,' said father.

'It must be something he's eaten,' said Aunty Bet.

'Are you better, my darling?' asked mother.

Then I vomited over everything and over my father's shoes and Aunty Bet shouted 'Oh!' and pushed back her chair.

I was better after throwing up, a sailor brought me a glass of water and a bucket and mop to clear up the mess. And everybody stared.

When my father saw me beginning to perk up the questions started.

'Where have you been?'

'What have you been doing?'

'Did you eat anything?'

'Nowhere,' I said – 'nothing – no.'

'Well something has caused this,' said my Aunt Bet.

'Tut! Leave him be,' said father after a while, 'the main thing is that he has recovered. You sit still until we reach Trefriw.'

I didn't go to see the stack being lowered for the ship to pass under Tal-y-Cafn bridge, but just looked at the fields alongside us as the river narrowed and saw an occasional cow raise its head to stare at us and the sheep scattering for the furthest hedges. A large cormorant stood on a rock by the riverside, its wings spread wide in the sunshine, motionless as if it were on a coat of arms; and the seagulls wheeled about us like a retinue, swooping now and again to catch a piece of bread or cake which someone had thrown up in the air. I could see the ship's wake like the arms of some enormous letter V reproducing itself, lapping under the banks as the river narrowed adding to the constant erosion of the tides and the floods.

We didn't stay long in Trefriw for fear of losing the tide and finding ourselves on a sandbank in the middle of the river instead of at the landing-stage in Deganwy.

But we had time to walk along the quay, and there was a café there and a place that sold ice-cream and a wooden shop; an ideal place selling all kinds of things, sweets, fruit, toys, decorative dishes with 'A Present from Trefriw' branded on them in paint, and, of course, all kinds of materials from the famous woollen mill. But I didn't want anything despite all Aunty Bet's urgings. It was mother who said the wisest thing.

'Would you like a cup of tea?' she asked.

And we went to the café and I never had as good a cup of tea, hot and sweet, scouring my gullet of the taste of tobacco.

I was warned that I was not to wander about on the return journey, and we sat in a row in the stern of the ship with nothing to do but think.

Then somewhere about Tal-y-Cafn I asked suddenly, 'What's a half-brother, father?'

I felt Aunty Bet stiffen in her seat and draw in her breath.

'That man,' she said, 'he's got hold of him – poisoned his mind.'

'Poisoned his belly more likely,' said my father.

'Now then, Dewi,' he added, with a stern look in his eye, 'the whole truth, my boy. What happened?'

'Uncle Josh said that he was your half-brother, Aunty Bet,' I said, and the stunned look on her face made me fear that she would jump over the rail into the river, 'and that you were the last little arse in the nest, mother. What does that mean?'

My father turned his head to watch a seagull that was flying with wings outspread behind us, before starting to explain.

'Your grandfather lost his first wife, you see, and Uncle Josh . . .' He paused for a second, looked at Aunty Bet, and smiled, '. . . is one of her children.'

She tossed her head angrily and raised her shoulders.

'Then he married a second time and had more children. Aunty Bet and your mother included. Your mother was the last one, you see, the last little chick. Do you understand?'

'Yes.'

'I don't. Why were you sick? What did you chew?'

'Tobacco,' I said bluntly, and was frightened when I saw how my father's face changed.

'Tell me everything,' he said, and I had to obey, I told him everything in detail.

He sat in his seat tight-lipped, his two fists bunched at his side, saying nothing.

Somewhere between Tal-y-Cafn and Conway he stood up, still

angry, and said, 'I'm going to have a word with Joshua Gruffydd.'

'Don't be hasty, David,' said mother.

'Hasty,' said my father, looking at her. I never knew before that mother, even, was afraid of him when he meant business. But I saw it in her eyes.

And my father walked with long, slow steps towards the bridge, and the hole and the 'No Admittance'.

I couldn't restrain myself for long. I leapt to my feet and ran after him, weaving through the people who were now preparing to leave the ship.

I soon saw him, one hand leaning on the 'No' in 'No Admittance', his body sickle-shaped as he leant into the hole. I crept quietly on tiptoe until I stood behind him. I had to hear what he was saying. I could tell from his lips, that he was talking to someone.

'It's an abominable thing to avenge oneself on the innocent,' said my father in his pulpit voice. It sounded like a verse. My father would circle the vestry floor during the mid-week chapel meeting and people would tell him their verses, to which he would respond occasionally with a verse of his own.

I saw my Uncle Josh in the gloom inside and unfortunately he saw me, too.

'Hello,' he said, instead of answering my father.

'Hello, Uncle Josh,' I said, 'I'm all right now.'

'The little one at least doesn't bear me any grudge, David Oliver,' said my Uncle Josh.

At that my father turned, looked at me, and smiled. 'Unless you become as little children,' he said.

That was definitely a verse. I had learnt it for the chapel meeting a few weeks before.

'Come on, Dewi, it's time for us to go ashore.'

He grasped my right hand and moved away.

I waved the other at Uncle Josh and winked at him.

'No Admittance' it said above the hole, but I had been allowed in without let or hindrance.

D. J. WILLIAMS

The Mecca of the Nation

(TRANSLATED BY R. GERALLT JONES)

Mrs Lloyd, who kept the Epynt guest-house in Llandrindod, had a pale hatchet face; and Mr Dogwell Jones, QC, whose knock on the door she went to answer, had a pink hatchet face. Apart from his perfectly respectable clothing, a matter of concern to any landlady, the only remarkable thing she noticed about the stranger was that his nose was somewhat flattened, and pushed into his face, 'as though someone had pressed his hand into it before it had properly set', as Pergrin was to say later in the story. Iron strikes iron, says the old proverb. Judging from externals alone, maybe that is what happened here.

Catherine Lloyd, who had fallen, by chance as it were, among the red suburban villas of Llandrindod from her native habitat on the slopes of Mynydd Epynt, was a lady who got up pretty early in the morning. And so, having found herself in such a place, she prospered. She had been in the town now for fifteen years, ever since she had lost her husband – first as a sort of companion and general help for Janet, her cousin, and then as sole mistress of the Epynt. Her command over the English language, however, continued to give her trouble; and much head-shaking beneath the white frilly cap and many gestures of her long, gnarled hands were often more effective means of communication than words. Something of her native Puritanism still remained with Catherine Lloyd, but in course of time, keeping a guest-house, even a dry guest-house, had been a pretty effective means of easing the pangs of that uncomfortable syndrome. She would only act the fierce Puritan now if some poor lodger came in with a suggestion on his breath that he had frequented a species of bar less pure than a milk bar, or when Anne the maid stayed out late while a pile of supper dishes awaited her. On this occasion, all the stern virtues of the past descended heavily upon the place.

Nevertheless, she would muse to herself, it was quite remarkable how modern her ideas were, considering how old-fashioned her upbringing had been. Not that, hopefully, she was one whit the less religious. But it was such a different age, especially in a modern place like Llandrindod, with landladies in cutthroat competition with each other. And then there were the prodigal, light-headed maids, so expensive to keep. No Christian woman could live honestly in such a place – and pay her way. For her part, whoever wished to could go to chapel; her religion, for years now, had been to slave away, day in, day out, so that others might have the benefit. Who could begin to appreciate a landlady's world?

It was necessary to study each guest individually in order to make him comfortable and content – and in order to get the best out of him too, come to that. Each one who spent a period in her care would bring credit, or discredit. However, it was essential that she should keep a tight hold on the whole operation. Between her own experience and that of her cousin Janet before her, Catherine Lloyd reckoned that she had by now acquired most of the necessary street-wisdom of the true landlady. The very essence of such wisdom, of course, was to conceal it; she would imitate the plover, which rolled away from its nest so that no one could see it move. It wasn't everyone who could get the better of Catherine Lloyd these days. Arising from her rural past, she had a prosperous black market at her fingertips. This extended her kingdom, as her suppliers were numerous and comparatively easy to control.

She had her own system for dealing with guests, and she kept this system secret, even from Anne. In general the principle was that each guest should be given a special welcome and meticulous attention, as far as food and comfort were concerned, during the first few days of their stay, then things would gradually be tightened so that guests would not return home from their holidays suffering from anything so unpleasant as indigestion. Then a rather special meal on the day of their departure before the account was paid. She had discovered early on that there was nothing so effective for taking away the aftertaste of a bill which contained a substantial number of 'extras' at the bottom than a good dinner. Then again, if an unusually fashionable lady were to come to stay, she would place her most expensive silk counterpane on the bed; after a few nights of luxuriating under this, it would quietly be replaced with something more hard-wearing. If there were to be any complaint, as indeed there had been once or twice, by some particularly sensitive and stiff-necked creature – well, who but the stupid maid could have done such a thing!

Mr Dogwell Jones, QC, settled into the Epynt at once. He came in like a sea breeze, with his jaunty voice and his jocular 'ha-ha-ha' playing about its portals. He could either be a man of the world or a meditative philosopher as the need arose, he admitted it; and he could speak copiously on any topic without tiring himself at all. If one couldn't actually claim that he was handsome, there was nevertheless something unmistakeable about his appearance, a useful enough characteristic for a man with an eye on the public. Anyone who had once seen him on the Eisteddfod field, or at a railway junction, didn't find it easy to forget the tall head, the long, rosy-cheeked face, the strong chin and the somewhat flattened nose; nor did anyone who saw him on the street, on Quarter Sessions day, the quick, bouncy walk signifying a man in a mortal hurry to meet all the heavy calls upon his time. And, of course, the law's safety umbrella always hooked on his arm. Furthermore, to see Mr Dogwell Jones, QC, meant to hear him as well.

Mrs Catherine Lloyd was exceptionally proud to have a man of Mr Dogwell Jones's distinction among her guests; and without realizing it, she paid three times as much attention to him as to any of her other guests – preachers rather green in worldly matters, some of them, a teacher or two with their wives and an occasional well-to-do farmer – one of them at least a County Councillor and an OBE, as she had seen last night on his luggage label as she was tidying his room – apart from that Pergrin, of course, whom she couldn't make head or tail of. All this gave her the idea that she should raise the social status of the Epynt as a guest-house; and she had been trying to work out – as she was peeling the potatoes and going about a thousand other domestic tasks – what would bring the best financial return, assuming she tailored the price to the quality of the cloth: keeping one barrister in all his splendour, two front-rank preachers, or three or four ordinary little chapel deacons, one of whom should preferably be an insurance salesman in order to ensure lively conversation. (She had come to realize that silence at table was an expensive thing for a landlady.) Perhaps the farmers' constant theme that pedigree stock paid better than the nondescript had something to do with this latest flash of vision. As far as she could, she decided, she would avoid the teachers. She found many of them to be limp, colourless creatures, all very well with children, no doubt, but lacking the presence of a man like Mr Dogwell Jones, QC, a man whose opinion could be sought on any topic. Another thing, only yesterday, as she was up to her ears in work, one of them had wasted a whole quarter of an hour of her time while she explained to him, item by item, the sundries at the foot of his bill. And even then she had had to allow him four shillings and sixpence discount. And all after he had had an excellent dinner! So much for education, as far as she was concerned, if its business was to interfere with honest people working hard to make a living.

The world of the Bar, as is well known, has its own ritual, its own patterns of behaviour in society. But for a Welsh Welshman like Mr Dogwell Jones, QC, enjoying a few days' leisure among ordinary people, where the miner and the teacher, the farmer and the quarryman, the shopkeeper and the tinman, yes and even the

minister and the parson, for a brief time were one warm egali-
tarian community, all that legal mumbo-jumbo melted away like
wax before a flame, becoming a matter of ridiculous vanity in his
eyes. He loved the common people, and it was his dream to serve
them, if only he knew how. He wished one day to make his voice
heard throughout Wales on behalf of the nation. He remembered
how he and a number of like-minded young students, towards
the end of the First World War, used to go for a week each
summer to the School of Young Prophets in Llandrindod, to talk
about the ideals and problems of Wales. Like himself, each one
of these warm-hearted young men, whether at heart a politician,
a writer, a historian or a scientist, felt that the future of Wales
depended to a considerable degree on his own personal future.
But times changed rapidly – the boys came home from war, and
from prison some of them, with their experiences burning inside
them. These saw, before long, that dilettantism, playing at politics
in Wales, did not pay. That was when the young men of
Llandrindod went their ways, and their visions with them. On
the strength of those early dreams, several of them secured
prosperous positions. And then it was that the kingdom of Britain
was secured.

Those were the lines along which Mr Dogwell Jones, QC, was
musing in the Pump House, with his glass of mineral water
before him, the morning after he arrived, remembering, not
without some envy perhaps, the successful careers of some of
those who had been with him in Llandrindod twenty-five years
before. Then he remembered the early summer schools of the
Nationalist Party, the excitement and joy of feeling that the old
country was at last stirring itself from sleep; he chose to hover
around the edges, either in or out depending on the company at
the time. Then his early marriage, and his wife's family beginning
to interfere in his affairs. They could see, much more clearly than
he could, that the paths of Nationalism were not likely to be
paths of plenty, not for a very long time.

That had always been his fate, he mourned – sometimes his

head ruling, sometimes his heart – never totally certain of himself. Although one had, of course, always to appear confident in public.

And now here he was, in middle age, a barrister who had made something of a name for himself. Nevertheless, he had gained more plaudits than profit. Last year, for example, had been a poor enough year for him. It was true that he earned a reasonable amount of money annually; but his family was becoming more and more expensive to keep. Between everything, it was a matter of catching a mouse and eating it. He wasn't at all sure by now whether his reputation wasn't more of a hindrance than a help in the matter of earning his living. Often in court he had expressed himself with more passion than wisdom when he had seen a Welshman, or the rights of Wales, receiving unjust treatment – his Celtic heart once more betraying him. He forgave himself more easily for an over-abundance of Welsh zeal at the occasional St David's Day dinner. The steam rising from the tables made matters rather hazy at some of these functions. But such little titbits were meat and drink to the press, never mind their other consequences. (For example, there was that newspaper report the other day that he had called one of the Welsh MPs 'an aborted weakling' when it was actually his measure on 'The Welsh Language in the Courts of Law' that he was referring to. The mistake was corrected immediately, but the fury of a Member who could have been of personal help to him was unabated.) His livelihood, after all, depended on being in favour with little conservative-minded solicitors, as unimaginative as their documents; fearful, colourless jurymen; and as much as anything on being in the good books of icy English judges for whom Wales was nothing more than a place to dine and a breeding ground of liars, offenders and pheasants.

In spite of all this, Mr Dogwell Jones, QC, was not a man who went through life merely following his nose. No; he had plans. But even with the best planners, things don't always work out precisely as intended. This year, for example, he had his own particular reasons for choosing Llandrindod – that little mecca of Welsh conferences, and the hatchery of innumerable irresolute resolutions – as the location of his few days' change of air. For one thing, there was an election in the air, the election which would mark the end of the war. And there were stretches of water in Llandrindod and an opportunity to fish from the river banks; an opportunity also to roll the occasional bowl skilfully past the other bowls towards the jack. Ever since youth he had had half an eye on Parliament as the pinnacle from which he would be able to perform his highest and most prominent service to his nation. And he was pretty familiar with the Welsh MPs. He knew that it was as fishers of men that most of them had reached the goal of their high calling, or – to bring the figure down to earth – because some fluke of a lucky bowl had knocked the others out of the way. And why hadn't his luck turned, long before now?

He had chosen the Epynt rather than the Grand Hotel in the first instance because it would be substantially cheaper – an important consideration this year of all years. His wife had already gone to her mother's home in the Tywi Valley for a week or two, where the children would get an opportunity to improve their patchy Welsh. But no doubt the most important reason for his choice was the type of person he would be most likely to meet in the Epynt – responsible people, not too great in number, coming from various parts of Wales – just the place for a man like him to cast his fly on the water. There were two things Mr Dogwell Jones, QC, knew like the back of his hand – the Scriptures and human nature. He surprised even himself by the ease with which he could recall scriptural quotations, thanks to his being suckled at the breast of the Sunday School. In court these were sometimes a hindrance. But then again, if only he could address his fellow Welshmen who served on juries in their own language instead of in some affected English to please the ear of the law – an English that they only half-understood, if the truth be told – he felt that nothing could have withstood his

eloquence. And he recalled that fine Welshman, Llywelyn Williams, the great hero of his youth, melting the jurymen of
Carmarthenshire into a pool of compassion on that occasion
when he defended Sam Tŷ'n Tân, the greatest scoundrel in his
native town.

Before twenty-four hours had passed, Mr Dogwell Jones, QC,
had captured the citadel of the Epynt, won the heart of its queen,
and secured for himself a place at the Knights' Table – 'The
Round Table', as he jocularly baptized the special table which
stood in the recess of the bow-window, facing the green and the
street beyond. Well done indeed, you might say, all in such a
short time. It was his voice that was now heard, his nose which
was seen, his authority felt, soft as lavender, over the white
tablecloths of the dining-room. The Epynt had been accorded a
new dignity and the inhabitants bathed in its warmth. None
more so than Mrs Catherine Lloyd, her long old head bobbing
and bowing regularly as she tried to adjust and balance the many
plans that lay within it. As for the two tall, blond, long-necked
Englishmen, and the plump, red-faced woman, and the little girl
the very spit of her father, who sat coldly together at the far end
of the room, one could almost say that they literally retreated
under the table when Mr Dogwell Jones, QC, arrived. For practically the first time in history Hengist and Horsa were silenced. As
for that Pergrin who sneaked in late and left early, he counted for
nothing. He would sit, perched on the edge of the most uncomfortable chair in the place, beak to the ground, half-listening, one
might imagine, to the conversation going on around him.

After whiling away the day, sipping the water and chatting,
playing a little bowls some of them, the residents of the Epynt
would never retire before the Knights had held their evening
parliament about the Round Table in the alcove. It was wartime,
and all manner of topics were discussed, from Adam's fall to the
rise of Hitler, through the plagues of Egypt, Caradoc Evans and
the Nationalist Party. As they went upstairs to bed, these guests
felt that they could eventually return home possessed of one or

two secrets the revelation of a mere corner of which would stir envy in their simple friends for the rest of the year. And did they not have the advantage of Mr Dogwell Jones's judgement on any dispute that might arise regarding current affairs? They were indeed fortunate to have been impelled to stay at the Epynt.

Catherine Lloyd was a durable old lady. She would be at it all day, her long, tired loins weaving among the tables, and then late at night making sure that no water-tap or electric light bulb was being wasted. And it was she who would be first up in the morning. Men wondered at her all-sufficient energy, like an eight-day clock, never missing out one tick, even on Sunday. No one but Anne the maid knew the secret miracle of her afternoon nap. If Catherine Lloyd missed out on this, having to settle a troublesome bill or something of the sort, nothing went right for the rest of the day. And these were the only times when she would occasionally speak of giving up the Epynt.

As the last of the guests were preparing to retire one night, the old lady contrived to detach Mr Dogwell Jones, QC, from the remainder; she beckoned him quietly into her private room, where she kept her greatest treasures. An easy chair had been prepared for him, a cup of good coffee, some chocolates, and one or two other titbits, equally rare in those straitened times. His heart swelled at this further sign of favour. Wasn't he after all adept at understanding human nature! After some idle talk, during which an almost youthful skittishness could be detected in Catherine Lloyd's demeanour, she drew his attention, little by little, to a number of personal matters – things that she wouldn't for the world, Mr Dogwell Jones *bach*, want anyone to know of at all other than a particularly sensitive and discreet person who she could entirely trust. Then she showed him some fairly substantial insurance policies, angling prettily for his opinion as to what she should do with them when they matured. He suggested in his turn, from his store of knowledge of financial matters, several promising investments – and went into more detail than she could readily swallow at that time of night, dogged though she was. And somewhere in Mr Dogwell Jones's being the idea was born that there might be some mutual benefit to be derived here, worth nurturing and developing. Each of them smiled internally and savoured his or her own cleverness. Is it not such who will inherit the earth?

These late-night sessions in the Epynt's small private room became common enough occurrences during the remainder of Mr Dogwell Jones's holiday. It wouldn't always be the same topic of conversation; but sooner or later it would slowly edge towards the personal and family concerns of Catherine Lloyd herself. Nor were these small in number or lacking in variety. For example, a fortnight earlier, one of the maids had broken two plates from the best set in the house; and good crockery was not to be had at any price now, in wartime. Because of the reprimand she was given for her carelessness, the maid went home without giving a moment's notice. Was she then entitled to collect her wages? And if she was – quite apart from the matter of replacing expensive plates – could Catherine Lloyd then make a counter-claim for the loss of income incurred by the house as she was now able to supply plates to two fewer guests? She could bring Anne the maid to court to bear witness to that. How did the law stand in such matters?

And then there was old Mrs Ridings from Oaklands who had told some people, according to Anne, that the best thing about the Epynt was its front window. Such loose talk could cause great harm to the business were it not that everyone in Llandrindod knew perfectly well what a fine place she kept. Could one not put a stop to Mrs Ridings and her sort? And then there was the matter of having to put down Moc the cat, than whom there had been no cleaner or more well-behaved animal in anyone's house, and that only because he had been caught, just very occasionally, scratching a little in the flowerbeds of those peculiar people next door. And so, in the steam of black, black coffee with three helpings of white, white sugar in it (old stock, of course) and two delicate biscuits on a plate, the sure and certain judgement of the law was obtained on such complex matters – and that without costing anything, except for a little courtesy from a landlady who understood her business and knew how to treat guests.

As the late-night discussions of the Round Table grew gradually later, a sudden, somewhat unexpected friendship developed between the QC and the OBE. It doesn't matter very much what the OBE was called, as it wasn't the name that was important, rather that which was attached to it. Although he was a gentleman of importance – a Methodist deacon, a County Councillor, and a Welsh Black breeder of note in one of the northern counties – yet the OBE was quite clear that this small token of His Majesty's appreciation of his not insubstantial contribution to the war effort outweighed everything else he possessed. Feeling as he did, it was not enough that his full name appeared in well-defined letters on his luggage labels. Was not the medal, the OBE medal, his identity card? Above and beyond all other distinctions – the Methodist Conference, Welsh Blacks, County Council – this was the final guarantee that he would never again be dragged back into the ranks of the unprivileged. His bosom swelled visibly and his face assumed a serious dignity every time he pulled out the thick pigskin wallet bound by a stout elastic band wherein the medal was kept. He was a man experienced in the matter of significant detail. It was a pleasure to behold the fine copper ring in the nose of his black bull in the shows. Considering the quality of the ring in the bull's nose and the OBE tailing the owner's name in the catalogue, the most stupid and prejudiced adjudicator would have difficulty passing by without pausing and thinking.

There was one remarkable thing about the OBE's appearance. Although he was a Welsh Black man, he always liked to dress like a horseman, whenever he was out of the black shadows of the Methodist Conference. He was a small man, slightly built, with a thin, sharp face and rather prominent ears. His natural feathering was a kind of light green, the colour of harvested hay, with a flash of cock pheasant in his tie. He wore breeches and leggings, or tight trousers, with a cap or a peaked hat. But rather than lifting from his knees upwards as he walked, like many horsemen do, he walked low to the ground. Perhaps it was this inborn gait that impelled him to choose a cow's rear rather than the back of a horse as his means of climbing to fame; and that his jockey's outfit was merely a reaction against nature.

Speaking figuratively, the OBE was well-enough hoofed, even if the hoof was small. He knew his own mind, and he could therefore often deal with men of rather more substance than himself. In council, he could feel the weight of his title thudding down with hammer blows to emphasize any proposal he made. He was also a great battler – on his own territory – during both wars. It was this perhaps, and his Welsh Blacks and the certainty of his opinions upon every topic, with the aid of an occasional Methodistic clearing of the throat when he wasn't particularly clear what was going on, that brought him considerable attention in the County Council and on the Liberal Party Committee.

When all this was gradually borne in upon Mr Dogwell Jones, QC, his own eloquence began to ebb away, and he bent his ear increasingly to his friend's remarks. And he awaited the opportunity, with all his skill, to cast a fly on to the surface of the water. Once or twice he thought he had a bite. But no; and he rapidly reeled in his line. He cast again; and it became evident to others that some diligent fishing was going on. It drew the attention of watchers on the shore; and Pergrin, restless, uneasy, his cap on his knee, nervously surveyed the game.

'As I was telling you,' said the OBE, after the discourse had reached a point of mutual advantage, 'I've been on the Liberal Selection Committee in our county for some years now. And although I say it myself, I suppose my word reaches as far as anybody's. And seeing as the two of us have brought the matter this far between us, Mr Dogwell Jones, I'm going to ask your personal permission here and now, in the presence of our friends, to place your name before our Selection Committee, which will be meeting in a few days' time, as our parliamentary candidate in this coming election.'

Mr Jones, QC, made as if this was all very sudden. But his heart was beating wildly. Here at last was a real bite; and perhaps, who could tell, his great opportunity had come, his opportunity to serve his people. He could barely contain himself. But he was an old hand, and he wanted to make very sure of his catch before making a move.

'Yes, well, many thanks indeed, Mr OBE, for thinking so highly of me. But I would hardly wish to give a definite answer this very minute. We have still some more time together – we have until tomorrow at least, before turning for home.'

The OBE now judged that his tactics had been somewhat hasty. But he had felt that there had been an opportunity to bring something back to his native county – a brilliant parliamentary candidate, as good a Welshman as anyone in the land, but one who was also – as far as he could judge – a firm opponent of that new, wild party which brought so much infamy upon Wales in all it did; furthermore it was an opportunity to bring his own name, complete with title, into prominence in the newspapers. Another consideration was that he certainly did not wish all these bystanders to see that he had taken a false step. And his customary decisiveness returned.

'Now or never, Mr Dogwell Jones, QC,' said the OBE, thumping his little brown fist hard on the table; and he added, more quietly, after a moment's pause, 'Of course, I can't guarantee anything beforehand; as some of you, I know, will have noticed often enough on a showground a number of good horses will be shown and trotted around the ring; in the end, four or five will be called into the middle by the adjudicators. You can't really tell which one of them will get the red card. A lot depends on the jockey . . .'

'Well, upon my life, boys, that's it,' interrupted Pergrin, in the unmistakeable accents of the Rhondda, 'the Welsh Black jockey mounting a bullock to take him all the way to Parliament!'

The thing was so sudden, and from Pergrin of all people – that disregarded mute – that not everyone realized all at once where the blow had struck. Nevertheless, its accuracy was unerring. Some couldn't resist laughing out loud, however discourteous that might have been. One or two had a fit of coughing, and others looked for an excuse to leave the room. But the harm had certainly been done; the arrow had found its mark ... And that night only two knights sat at the Round Table, two knights somewhat low in spirits, but too proud to admit, even to each other, that they had been floored that day by a pygmy camp-follower.

The pygmy himself, however, did not escape scot-free. The very minute after the damage had been done, as he turned on his heel to go out, he almost fell into the arms of the Queen of the Castle who happened to be standing immediately behind him. Catherine Lloyd insisted that she smelt drink on Pergrin's breath. This challenge to the purity of the Epynt, her instinctive antipathy towards Pergrin from the start, together with what she had already heard and seen, were sufficient to fire her primitive Puritanism at once. Oddly enough, once his tongue had been untied, the mute began to utter with remarkable freedom, as though a complex anger against something he only half under-stood had been gathering inside him; now the dam had broken, sweeping everything before it. Pergrin swore that he had never been more sober in his life, and judging from his appearance, he might well have been telling the truth. That was when Mr Dogwell Jones, QC, thrust his nose into the argument and when that organ received the mortal blow referred to at the beginning of this history – a blow that scattered the Round Table once and for all. Very early that next morning the stunted one could be seen leaving the Epynt, carrying his knapsack with him.

At the incomplete post-mortem which was held over the remains of the character of the departed, after much debate an open verdict was arrived at – that he was either a Communist or a member of the Welsh Nationalist Party; and on the further suggestion of the foreman of the jury, the OBE, after he had consulted the Law, a rider was added, to be sent to the Town Council, noting that the state of health of the Welsh Society in Llandrindod was such that every care should be taken to prevent infectious persons entering the town, thereby polluting the atmosphere. The rider was passed unanimously.

As he left the Epynt in the company of the OBE the same day as Pergrin but at a later hour, it took some time for Mrs Catherine Lloyd to persuade Mr Dogwell Jones, QC, that it was his account and not someone else's she held in her hand, with its lengthy attachment of sundries hovering at the end of it like the tail of a kite. In vain did he point out that it would have been cheaper for him after all to have stayed at the Grand; for the undeniable evidence lay visible before him as Catherine Lloyd's long finger pointed out one item after another; every biscuit, every cup of tea or coffee, that had fallen unregarded from above like evening manna upon the plains of the Round Table – all here on his bill if you please! Yes and more than all of it, perhaps, if the truth were known, added to the original agreement of five guineas a week. Then, after a moment of self-questioning, like a just man of the law he admitted to himself that it had indeed been he who had asked for these comforts at the beginning and that no one else had mentioned them subsequently. He felt that this bill, after all, was a tribute to his importance compared with the others, and the old lady's devious way of flattering him. A tribute indeed, he said to himself, but the devil's own way of paying tribute by playing on a man's weakness. But the law is the law, added the judge within him, and it must be respected.

For a few seconds, the two hatchets stood once more, the pink and the pale, steel matching steel, blade to blade. Then Mr Dogwell Jones, QC, smiled a most gracious smile and then apologized deeply for the sad fact that he had left his cheque-book at home, and went on to assure her at some length, etc., etc.

'It's quite all right, Mr Dogwell Jones *bach*,' said the old lady, seeing that the barrister's sudden geniality had overcome his dismay at the size of the bill, 'I would trust you until Kingdom Come, if it was necessary. Hi-hi-hi! Until Kingdom Come, Mr Dogwell Jones *bach*. Of course I would, of course I would.'

And the two parted the best of friends.

Some days after he had returned home from Llandrindod, as Mr Dogwell Jones, QC, was sitting in his office one morning without too much to do, glancing at various items in his newspaper that he had previously left unread, his eye fell on the short list of Liberal candidates for the OBE's county. He looked at it a second and a third time. No, his name wasn't there.

He put the paper down. He did his best to fight back a sigh. He sat for a long time, with a faraway sadness in his eyes.

'It was that idiot Pergrin who cooked my goose,' he said after a while. 'What possessed me to go to a place like the Epynt in the first place? No; I was the biggest idiot after all.' A sigh! And another period of meditation.

He got up at last and made his way slowly to the corner cupboard. He opened a door at the bottom of it where half a bottle of whisky lurked among various oddments and papers. He poured himself a generous glass.

'Goodbye, mineral water,' he said, taking a large mouthful and luxuriating in its taste on his lips. 'A fortnight almost with those spongers and lying, hypocritical cowards, not to speak of that old wizened witch, robbing a man under his nose, is more than any honest, conscientious Welshman should have to bear.'

He emptied his glass. Then he took out his pipe and filled it to the brim. He had no matches. He felt in his pocket for a scrap of paper. The Epynt account – unpaid! After peering at it once more, he poured out another glass.

'Ah! Good stuff – pre-war – present from the landlady at the Blue Boar – after that trial.'

Slowly the corners of his mouth relaxed, like a schoolboy seeing his way through a problem. He made a small, thin, compact spill with the Epynt account, and lit his pipe with it from the gas fire. Then he took a piece of paper from his desk, and wrote on it: 'Mrs Catherine Lloyd – owing to – Dogwell Jones, Barrister – for legal opinion and advice – between – this date and that date – '

Both accounts came to exactly the same total amount!

Together with this account, Mr Dogwell Jones, QC, placed ready for posting a card noting the date when it would be convenient for him to address the opening meeting of the Cardiff Cymrodorion Society that winter. He emptied his glass and went out into the open air, the horizon of his further service to Wales growing lighter and brighter with every step of his rapid, bouncing walk towards the Blue Boar, where he would obtain his lunch from the landlady at a very reasonable cost.

RAYMOND WILLIAMS

A Fine Room to be Ill In

1

The room was surprisingly large for so modest a house. It occupied three quarters of the space on the ground floor, and its
high ceiling, its series of bay and french windows, its large arched
fireplace of Spanish walnut, all served to accentuate its size.
When Mr Peters first saw it, at the time of the redecoration of
the house after six years' service as an army property, it was bare
and dusty, the floor unstained, and the one, incongruous, piece of
furniture was a full-size enamel bath, which, placed in the
mathematical centre of the room, under the oblique dusty sun-
rays, reminded Mr Peters instantly of a coffin. But it was difficult
now to remember the room as it had then been. Mr Peters had
paid great attention to the floors – they were rough-scrubbed and
splintering, for the house had served as a NAAFI institute and
the room had been the service canteen – a circumstance which
Mr Peters tried hard to forget. Then the walls had been cream-
washed, the formal floral pattern of the plastered ceiling delicately
cleaned, the window frames painted, until at last a dignity appropriate to its size had been restored. There were few blemishes;
one of the tiles of the fire grate was broken in half, and another
was loose, but Mr Peters resettled them with the tips of his long
fingers so that from most angles no disturbance could be seen.
And there was an unfortunate patch of black paint which some
careless workman had spilled near the centre of the room, and
which all the efforts of Mr Peters's careful creosoting had failed
to remove. The furniture, which was travelling by road, was

delayed by an unofficial strike – an event for which Mr Peters felt every sympathy, for he understood the conditions of the workers, but which was really very trying just at this moment. As a result, Mr Peters had several days, after the redecoration of the room had been completed, in which he could sit in the room, choosing varying points of vantage, and conjure up pictures of how his furniture would look when it was arranged, and finding frequently, as the whole problem settled through his consciousness, that previous patterns of arrangement were not satisfactory, and that rearrangements were necessary in order to accommodate new angles of vision. When the furniture at last arrived, Mr Peters was able to direct the workmen with great accuracy. He knew exactly where each piece should go. Indeed, one of the men remarked to him, 'It's a pleasure, sir, to work with a man as knows his own mind.' When it was all in, and the men had gone, Mr Peters resumed his peripatetic squatting. In general, it was all as he had foreseen. It was true that the carpet looked rather lost. It was a good, large carpet, but really, one could not expect to find a carpet large enough for a room like this outside the private property of a shah. But it just failed to cover the offensive splash of black paint. Mr Peters moved it back over this, but then it was too far from the fireplace, and it was essential to have a continuity of pattern right up to the grate, so that solitary emphasis was not placed on the tiles. It was a difficult problem. At last Mr Peters took an occasional table, and, placing it exactly over the offending patch, he draped on it a fine silk cloth, which on the side nearest the door, and so on the side from which it would be viewed when entering the room, came down to the ground and decently veiled the paint without however drawing too much attention to itself.

The rest of the furniture looked most fitting. There was the fine dark oak cupboard, with its glass doors, behind which could be seen the carefully arranged relics of Mr Peters's travels in Sicily and Mexico. Then the matching bookcase, with its titles arranged according to branches of literature, for as Mr Peters so often said to his students, there is really very little point in a kind of inclusive chronology of literature; it is the development of work in specific media which it is so important to emphasize. So there was drama, from the fine old calf-bound Greek texts, through the red texts of the Romans, on to the green collections of the miracles and moralities, the uniform saffron editions of the Elizabethans, the patterned green covers of Racine and Corneille, the blue omnibus texts of Restoration tragedy and comedy, right down to the cherry collected works of Ibsen, the poison-bottle-green of Strindberg, and the tall black and pastel volumes of the modern verse dramatists. It was the same with novels, with poetry, with essays, with biographies, and with criticism. The size of the bookcase was certainly an advantage. Fronting the bookcase stood the heavy sideboard, also in dark oak, with the rich carvings of the capon and the hare on its doors. Mr Peters was a vegetarian, and at mealtimes he found the sideboard slightly disquieting, but as a rule its solidity, the fine full flanks of the hare, for example, was most pleasing. Then there was the suite, blue-patterned; old, of course, and creaking at times if one sat down on it indelicately, but pleasant; and after all, how could one nowadays replace it, for the sake of some horrid utility rexine?

Mr Peters's occasional woman, who was cleaning for him until his wife and child should arrive from their holiday, seemed to think the room under-furnished. She never actually mentioned it, but Mr Peters was very sensitive to human atmosphere, and apprehended her disapproval. He decided to raise the question openly with her, but she shied away from every direct attempt, and he could only conclude that she was unwilling to discuss the matter since she felt it was likely to reflect on the financial status of her temporary employer. He thought it distressing, and yet at the same time amusing, perhaps even convenient, that everywhere, nowadays, taste should be written down as indigence. He had glimpsed his cleaner's rooms on one occasion when he had visited her; her son-in-law, an unemployed joiner (curious, Mr Peters had thought, how I am always bumping into unemployed building workers in times like these), had just finished decorating them; the walls were ground-washed with eggshell-blue, and over this there was a heavy stippling of yellow and a colour Mr Peters could only describe as puce. Through the bedroom door, which stood open, Mr Peters could see large golden panel frames painted over an offensive biscuit-coloured wallpaper. The bathroom, of which the door was also ajar, was done out in raspberry wash. Mr Peters was glad to get back to the coolness of his own room.

The only subject on which Mrs Austen would ever talk, apart from details of domestic arrangement, was the fine view from the windows of the room. This comprised a stretch of downland, with hollows and terraced level-lines, which ran away to a broad valley through which a river meandered to the sea in great serpentine loops. Gorse and firs were littered over the slopes.

'You should see it in winter, sir,' said Mrs Austen. 'Just like Switzerland it is. And the boys is up there when it's snowing, sliding down all the day. It's lovely.'

'How nice it will be to sit and watch that,' Mr Peters answered, wishing the conversation would not proceed.

'Yes, sir, and in the spring it's the young couples walking up there, and the summer there's families, and children, comes by car. And the schools, all the schools around, different colour caps and costumes they all have. It's a lovely sight. And you've got the very best view of it, all from your room.'

'It is nice,' Mr Peters said, replacing the occasional table over the patch, which she had uncovered in her dusting; 'nice to think if you were stuck to the room you could always see so much life going on outside.'

'I said just the same, sir,' Mrs Austen smiled, gathering her brushes together; 'I said to George the first time I seen your room, there's everything you can see from the window. It'd be a fine room to be ill in.'

'Yes,' Mr Peters said. 'Good morning, Mrs Austen.'

*

2

The room grew on Mr Peters, and he quickly managed to settle the apparatus of his daily living into its formal pattern. There was the wireless set, for example. Mr Peters was not a devotee of the commercial radio; even the idea of listening to humorous programmes was somehow intolerable to him, for surely there was something indecent in sitting and laughing alone, quite alone, or even with one other person; so that one ended up by being amused inwardly while looking as solemn as if one were in church, and there was something disquieting about that. But still, he liked to keep in touch with the bare facts of the international situation, for although politics was no longer his métier his students kept asking his opinion and he felt he owed it to himself to be able to make reasonable answers. And then there were the sports results and commentaries; Mr Peters did not care to acknowledge his interest in these, for the idea of mechanism in sport was distasteful to him, but he noticed that he always left the wireless on while there were broadcasts of this nature, and that he attached considerable emotional weight to the fortunes of teams and players which had gained his fancy. And yet the sum of it did not warrant a decent radio set. Mr Peters possessed a battered old portable, which he had bought second-hand at the selling out of a bankrupt institute for the blind. It was adequate for his needs, but it was decidedly unlovely. Mr Peters placed it between his favourite armchair and the wall, with the badly battered end hidden. This was all right so long as he did not wish to play it; but he discovered that he only got good reception when the set was rotated to the appropriate angle, and, of all things, the appropriate angle left the broken end exposed to the room and to sight. Reluctantly, Mr Peters moved his armchair so that there was room between it and the wall for the set to rotate completely, and yet remain hidden. His efficiency pleased him. He could let his hand drop over the side of the chair to switch the set on without even having to look at it, and down there in the shadow the jagged end might not have existed.

In the early days of his occupation of the room, Mr Peters found that he could not sit quietly. Whenever he took his favourite place, there would always be some distressing ruck in a chair-cover, or the curtains would be hanging badly, or a piece of the newspaper which he had laid under the carpet to protect it from the still-drying creosote would be peeping out, and then he would have to get up to make the necessary adjustment. And yet, so clear and strict was his idea of the pattern of the room, that he found every readjustment demanding new ones. 'The field,' as he put it, in the words his brother-in-law was so fond of quoting, 'is never quiet.' Yet his persistence, his unwearying application, bore fruit. After a fortnight, and just before the arrival of his wife and child, he had imposed a satisfactory order. On the evening before they arrived he was able to sit, for the second time, during two full hours, doing nothing, but just satisfied by the pattern which he had created. Outside, over the downland, the last birds were moving, and a late mist was rising over the cliffs. The loops of the slow river caught the last light.

His wife and child arrived next day in time for tea. He met them at the station with a taxi. When they reached the house he jumped out quickly, anxious to open the doors and to have the room standing ready for their reception. He was so excited by this intention that he forgot to take his normal share of the paraphernalia which the child had accumulated during the journey, and he was called back by his wife just as he was turning the key in the lock. He pushed the door open and went back. As a result, she entered first, and when he arrived with an armful of torn picture books, his wife was already in the room. She put down her parcels on the sideboard, and began looking over the rest of the house. He played with the child, and awaited her return.

'All right, I've made the tea,' she said, re-entering. He had laid everything ready in the nursery.

'How does it all strike you?' he asked.

'Well, darling, I really haven't had time to look. The kitchen's small.'

'Is it? I thought it wasn't bad. But what about this room?'

'It's very large. Larger than I'd expected.'

'Yes, but look at it.'

'Later, dear. Tea's ready now.'

They went out together for tea. The business of unpacking and seeing to the child kept them both fully occupied for some while afterwards. When they got back to the room, it was getting dark and the child was already in bed.

'Now, dear,' said Mr Peters, as they came through the door. The familiar shape of the room was bathed in the soft light.

'It's nice.'

'Only nice?'

'Well yes, it's nice, pleasant. What else should I say?'

'Nothing. Have you seen the view?'

His wife crossed to the large bay window, and looked down at the river.

'Extraordinary shape, isn't it?'

'Yes.'

'Glacial.'

His wife moved back across the room.

'Oh Christ, I'm tired,' she said, and flopped into a chair. Mr Peters heard the creak of the springs, and winced. But there was another sound, even more disquieting. He switched on the standard lamp, and saw one of the castors of the chair lying out on the polished floor.

'Well that's that,' he said, stooping to retrieve it. 'I knew it would happen soon. It's been loose for some time.'

'You said you'd get it seen to.'

'I hadn't time. I had so much to see to here.'

'Well we can get it done. Leave it now.'

'All right.'

Mr Peters sat down in the opposite chair. He let his hand drop down to the wireless. As the music came, his wife said, 'You won't be able to leave those scissors there, darling. The baby will get them.'

'I hadn't thought.'

He took the scissors from the fire seat. They were a pair he had collected in Sicily. His travelling companion had immediately associated them with the Mafia. They were extraordinarily long, with fine sharp blades of gleaming steel, and wicked cutting points. They were contained in a sheath of leather for safety. Mr Peters had thought them surgeon's scissors, but his friend had pointed to the elaborate pattern on the handles: 'No surgical scissors would have a pattern like that; it would only collect dirt. Much more probably some sort of torture scissors, that men could carry on their belts.' Mr Peters was fascinated by them.

'Oh, well,' he sighed, 'I'll put them up on the mantelpiece. But they're so useful for slitting open letters.'

His wife was lying back with closed eyes. Mr Peters looked at her, dwelling on every detail of her appearance. Her strong resemblance to himself again surprised him. There was the wiry black hair, of the same jetty shine. Then the prominent temples, the wide-set brown eyes, the firm straight nose, the wide mouth with the pendulous lower lip. Very often, by strangers, they were taken for brother and sister rather than man and wife. His wife was amused by their resemblance.

'Have you ever noticed,' she said once, 'how all this talk about people loving their opposites is quite untrue. You look at any married couple. Usually there's a pretty striking physical resemblance. Clearly contrasted physical types hardly ever marry. We're just one pair of many.'

'That raises lots of interesting questions,' he said.

'Narcissus and Narcissa.'

It was now quite dark outside, but Mr Peters did not add to the low light for fear of waking his wife. He distinguished her breathing through the tiny sounds of the evening.

Suddenly there was a scream from the child, who had woken in its dark bedroom. Instantly his wife was awake.

'I'll go on to bed when I've seen to him,' she said.

'I'll come as well.'

'We'll probably have a night full of screaming. Travel upsets him.'

'Can't be helped,' said Mr Peters. He got up from his chair, and put the scissors, which he had continued to hold, back on the fire seat.

'On the mantelpiece, dear.'

'Sorry, stupid of me. I'm not used to having you both here yet.'

'You're coming?'

'Yes.'

3

There were not many houses in their immediate vicinity. It was what is known as an exclusive neighbourhood. The nearest house on the left was large and grey, with unusually steep gables. It was set in a very large garden, which was delineated by walls of grey stone. Mr Peters knew nothing of its occupants. The only persons he saw moving around it were obviously domestic staff. There were several gardeners, who had a busy time keeping the large lawns tidy, the hedges trimmed, and the little groups of trees free of undergrowth. And Mr Peters had seen at least three indoor servants, and also two cars.

'A pretty prosperous household these days,' he remarked. 'Obviously film stars or crooks. Who else could afford it?'

Mr Peters conceived several plans for discovering the identity of the occupants. Perhaps a neighbourly call; but that could look like mere intrusion. Or he could be a commercial traveller, for a seed firm, perhaps. But then they would almost certainly order, and that would be difficult. He even thought of ringing the bell and saying he was from Mass Observation. But he was reduced to watching and speculation. And then, however closely he watched, looking sideways from the bay window, he was curiously unsuccessful. The only living thing he saw apart from domestic servants was a greyhound. It was a small sign, but ever after he felt convinced, in default of further evidence, that the inhabitants were crooks.

On the left there was a rash of plaster villas, two of them with lurid green tiles. Each of these had a neat garden in front, at which Mr Peters mocked. Sometimes, when he took his morning walk for cigarettes, he would stand and gaze at them. One in particular interested him. It was laid out like a mosaic. There were sharp-edged intersecting concrete paths, and sharp-edged perfectly level lawns, and ribbon beds of flowers. At the moment the display was tulips; there were no other flowers visible. When Mr Peters had first arrived, it had been daffodils. They now lay uprooted and discarded in front of the neat concrete garage. The gaudy tulips stood like the banners of a great procession. All tulip colours, Mr Peters convinced himself, were essentially martial. That comprised their suburban appeal.

'Just think,' he said to his wife when he regained the house, 'of the incredibly corrupt sense of power that man must have. His daffodils parade and blossom. He looks, likes, and passes on. The daffodils are thrown aside. Then he calls up his tulip army, a braver, gaudier, display. He stands under his little concrete porch arch, and inspects them. Above him the white arced lambswool rugs – all suburban snuggeries have them – flutter from the bedroom balcony. Flower, my tulips, and fade. Glory and die. Just projecting his will to power on these inanimates. And why?'

His wife knew the answer and began to serve the lunch. Next morning Mr Peters stopped again to survey the tulips. While he was doing so he became aware of a man advancing towards him down the precise path. He was a short figure, with close-cropped hair and moustache. Rimless spectacles. He wore a belted alpaca jacket, close black breeches, grey stockings and wide-strapped shoes. 'Wells,' droned the immediate response in Mr Peters; 'not Wells himself, but the Wells scientist type in every book. Obviously the man's a rationalist and an Independent Socialist.'

'Like it?' the man said.

'I'm quite intrigued,' said Mr Peters.

'Nothing much,' said the man. 'Just a bit of stuff I stuck in.'

'It's most impressive,' said Mr Peters. The man waved a loose hand.

'You're the new fellow? Up the end?'

'Yes, just came.'

'Glad to meet you. Pertwee's the name. Come in, get to know you.'

Mr Peters found himself following the little man up the path. He looked down at the razor-edges of the beds, and into the full breasts of the tulips. The hall was cool and polished, with plants and a brewer's map of the county.

'My study,' said the little man. 'I'm a sociologist.' Mr Peters took in the details of the room. A large black desk, with an array of rubber stamps; labelled drawers; the walls lined with precisely arranged books.

Mr Peters glanced at the top of a pile of pamphlets which stood on the chair to which the little man had waved him. '*Culture, Religion, and the Social Mechanism*, by E. Mortimer Pertwee.' He extended a curious hand.

'Little bit of a thing I wrote,' said the man, coming across. 'Let me move the things. Sit down.'

''Course this town's dead,' said Mr Pertwee. 'In a coma. Stiff with prejudice. I wrote last week to the local paper' (he rolled these last words round his mouth); 'told 'em they were all in a coma. Defined it. Always believed in defining my terms. Too many people going around uttering sloppy ideas. Pin 'em down.'

'Is there much political argument in the local press?'

'My letter wasn't political, you know. No time myself for all these practical politics as they call it. Just ignorance. Ignorance of underlying social mechanisms. Get in a lather before they've half understood the situation. Folly. Just personal arrogance.'

Mr Pertwee took a cigarette from a long silver box.

'Smoke?'

'Thanks,' said Mr Peters, stretching out his hand.

'No, no. Not one of these. Too strong. Roll my own, you know. Smoke all the time. Have another. I've got some ordinary ones somewhere about.' He found a Players' packet and passed it across. Mr Peters opened it, to find it empty.

'Still, I write about all manner of things to them. Let them know where I stand.'

Mr Peters waved the empty packet gently.

'Oh, none there?' said Mr Pertwee. 'My cat must have had them. Got a cat, great friend. Pity you can't have one of mine.'

'What tobacco d'you use?' asked Mr Peters.

'Tom Long or something, they call it. Get four tins a week.'

'But that's not so strong,' said Mr Peters. 'I often use it in my pipe. I'm quite used to it.'

'You wouldn't enjoy these,' said Mr Pertwee. 'Yes, the local press struggles along. Would you like to see some cuttings of mine?'

'Yes, indeed,' Mr Peters assented, feeling unreasonably irritated by the cigarette episode.

From a drawer at his knee Mr Pertwee took a large black book. He turned its pages and handed it open to Mr Peters.

'There's the last I wrote. About the sewage on the beach. Disgraceful.'

Mr Peters read the clipping dispassionately. 'Very good,' he said. 'Can I look back over the others?'

'Yes, yes, any of it. Carry on. I'll just see if I can find you a cigarette. My maid smokes 'em.'

While the little man was gone Mr Peters glanced quickly over the book. It was a large exercise book, with the title on the fly-leaf in large ink letters – 'Controversy Book, E. Mortimer Pertwee.' Mr Peters quickly realized, with surprise, that only Mr Pertwee's letters were included. There were several headed controversies – 'Nationalization' was one. Mr Peters glanced through it. Letter from E. Mortimer Pertwee – 'Nationalization – Plan or Panacea?' Next, of a fortnight's later date – 'Function, Responsibility, or Irresponsibility.' Obviously letters had appeared criticizing Mr Pertwee. These however were not included. Instead appeared a few handwritten lines: 'There followed two replies, from persons I have not heard of. Just the usual stuff. Prejudice. No definition.' And there was a later comment. 'Following my analysis of liberty there appeared a typical piece of sentimental twaddle. I replied as follows.' And so on to the next clipping.

Mr Peters closed the book guiltily as Mr Pertwee re-entered.

'Very interesting,' he said.

'Oh, just a sideline all that,' said Mr Pertwee; 'I couldn't find you any cigarettes.'

'Well, I must be getting on down to buy some,' said Mr Peters, rising.

'Call in again sometime, always here.'

'Thanks, I will.'

They came out into the garden. The sun was warm, and there were vibrations of heat over the brassy tulips. In the next garden a man was working, pouring a powder between the cracks of his crazy paving. Pertwee called to him.

'Hoole, this is Peters. Lives up the end.' Greetings were exchanged.

'Won't shake hands,' said Hoole, a young, bronzed, man. 'Pouring concentrated weedkiller into my crazy paving. Should keep 'em down for a while.'

'Useful stuff,' said Mr Peters. 'Morning.'

4

At his usual shop there were no cigarettes, and Mr Peters was obliged to go farther into the town. He walked along the sprawl of the coast road in a very critical mood. The monstrous houses, white and bulbous, or box-like, strongly impressed him. He knew about this place – scene of a famous building-plots scandal; there were no roads, for the plots had been sold from the map, and no community services had land allotted to them. Among the pretentious houses muddy lanes straggled. Every one who had bought a building plot thought they would be relatively alone above the sea. When the great mass of houses was begun, those farthest from the coast found that their only chance of seeing the water was to build higher than the man in front. The result could be seen in a varied assortment of scaffoldings, towers and galleries, to which the occupants could climb for their vision of the sea.

Mr Peters came back thoughtfully to his own house. At the gate he paused to look at a lilac tree which was beginning to lower. He plucked a stem and pressed the tiny flowers against his face. Above them, his eyes surveyed the rest of the garden. Mr Peters sought for a word to describe it. He was always particular about precision in language, for he knew very well that the act of choosing words is basically the whole moral choice, the recurring crisis of discrimination in perception. 'Dilapidated', then? 'Neglected'? 'Overgrown'? 'Scruffy'? He found decision difficult. 'Wild'? 'Woolly'? 'Grassy'? 'Natural'? The difficulty of settling on a word disquieted him. He suspected that there was some ambiguity in his attitude to the garden. Well, it was rough, untidy, a wilderness of weeds and brambles. Sometimes he could scarcely bear to look at it. He was glad that from the room one's normal angle of vision passed over it and on to the view beyond. But in the sun his eyes would drop sometimes, and there it would be. He knew that in the hot weather he would want to sit outside, and then there would be no escaping it. Out for a lie in the sun. A *lie* in the sun. What about moral discrimination now?

He went to the hedge and peeped through at Hoole's neat garden. He could see the bronzed figure still stooping over the crazy paving, sprinkling the concentrated weedkiller. He smiled. Well, that at any rate makes things clearer, he thought. His eyes rested on the smooth, green lawn. One day he had seen Hoole going over it with a knife, cutting out the daisies. What could be said for a person who subscribed to this artificial division of flowers which are weeds, and flowers which are flowers? On one side the endless toil to produce flowers which were recognized in the catalogues; and on the other, even greater toil to root out and destroy flowers, often as beautiful, but not 'recognized'. The daisy particularly. The daisy was indeed an abiding pleasure, and if gardening meant rooting out daisies, for the sake of toy-soldier tulips, then gardening was not for him.

'The point is,' he said to his wife, 'that these people are really dead. Their daily actions are just like the routine visit-ations of a ghost. Have you ever tried to deflect a ghost from its haunting path? Trying to shift these people is just as killing.

They just clank on regardless, up and down the crazy paving, hoping their tended vegetation will do their living for them.

'Nonsense,' his wife answered. 'They have their habits and their pleasures, just as you do. They're just not your habits, that's all.'

'They've got no contact with living experience, that's the point,' said Mr Peters.

'Oh, experience. That.'

Continuation of the conversation was made impossible by a scream from the child, who had been sleeping in his pram on the sun loggia, shaded by the branches of an elder tree which had taken root under the walls of the house.

'See to him, darling. Rock him in his pram.' Mr Peters walked over wearily. He took the pram handles and began a steady shaking. The child's cries increased. As the pitch of the scream rose higher, Mr Peters's rocking of the pram increased in violence. Soon it was jumping madly up and down, and the child's continued screaming was punctuated by gasps for breath as it shook around inside. Mr Peters noticed that his teeth were set hard. And then, suddenly, the noise ended. Mr Peters lowered the pram gently and crept away. He joined his wife in the room inside.

He picked up a newspaper which his wife had left open on the hearth, and folded it away under a cushion. He emptied the ashtray into the grate, tipping the cigarette ends, which were always a distasteful sight to him, well away from his view. As he drew the ashtray sharply back, he touched the tiles of the fireplace, and the broken tile fell out and clattered below. Mr Peters replaced it with an oath, and then sat back in one movement in his chair. He had become used to the defective springs of his favourite chair, and normally judged the right place to sit without provoking noise from them. But now he sat too far forward and he heard them creak under him, down to the depths.

He looked casually out at the loggia. The pram was moving slightly. The child was obviously awake, and rocking it with its tiny movements. Mr Peters looked back round the room. On the table the vase of lilacs was set in a cloth of tiny flower droppings.

Mr Peters shifted his chair so that his back might be towards this. Again he noticed that his teeth were hard clenched. He relaxed them, consciously, and let the quiet spread through his body.

He watched his wife jump from her chair, and run to the open window on to the loggia. She screamed. Beyond her Mr Peters saw the pram rocking gently towards the open edge of the loggia, towards the drop into the weed-filled garden. Vaguely he realized that he had not secured it in its normal position against the pillar. He watched his wife stretching frantically towards it, and he saw her fingers touch it as it heeled over and fell. Mr Peters closed his eyes.

5

'This is the room I was telling you of,' said the disdainful man.

'Oh, how lovely,' the young woman cried, 'how lovely, Edward.'

'Rather large, isn't it,' said the young man, hanging back at the door.

'Perhaps,' said the disdainful man. 'But I have rarely seen a room with so distinctive an atmosphere. And I, as you know, in the course of my profession, see many, many rooms.'

'And think of the delight of planning to furnish it,' the young woman said.

'Can we see the rest of the house?' asked the young man.

'Certainly, certainly. But I would advise you first to examine the prospect from those windows at the end. It is most striking.'

The young woman ran across to the windows. The young man followed uneasily.

'Oh, how delightful, how delightful.'

They looked down the long river valley, tracing the great bends of water which gleamed under the sun. On the downland the gorse was a blaze of yellow.

'Tell me,' said the young man, 'why did the last people leave?'

The other man dropped his eyes. He put a finger to his lips: 'I think they found the garden too much for them,' he said, and in his voice there was no mistaking the disdain.

B. L. COOMBES

Twenty Tons of Coal

It happened three days ago. Three days have gone – yet my inside trembles now as it did when this thing occurred. Three days during which I have scarcely touched food and two nights when I have been afraid to close my eyes because of the memory that darkness brings and the fear which forces me to open them swiftly so that I shall be assured I am safe at home. Even in that home I cannot be at ease because I know that they notice the twitching of my features and the trembling of my hands.

That was why I forced myself to go along the street the first day after the accident. I wanted to go on with life as it had been before, and I needed the comfort and sympathy of friends. The first I saw was a shopkeeper whom I had known as an intimate for years. He was dressing the window so I went inside to watch him, as I had done many times.

I expect my replies to his talk about poor sales and fine weather were not satisfactory for he turned suddenly and looked at me before he said:

'Mighty quiet, aren't you? Looking rough, too. What's the matter, eh? Got a touch of flu?'

'No! I wish it was the flu,' I answered, 'I could get over that. I've had my mate smashed – right by my elbow.'

'Good Lord!' He is astounded for an instant, then remembers. 'Oh, yes. I heard something about it, up at the Restcwm colliery, wasn't it? That's the way it is, you know. Things are getting pretty bad everywhere. The toll of the road f'rinstance – makes you think, don't it?'

'The roads,' I answer slowly, 'yes, we all use the roads. Can't you realize that this is something different? He was under tons of rock, and everything was pitch dark. No chance to get away; no way of seeing what was coming; no – oh, what's the use? If you've never been there you'll never understand.'

'Don't think about it,' he suggests, 'you'll get over it in time. Best to forget about it.'

Forget! The fool – to think that I can ever forget. I know that I never shall and no man who has been through the same experience ever can.

I went back home; soon afterwards one of my friends called. When he saw me he exclaimed:

'Holy Moses! What the dickens has happened to you?'

He had been with me the evening before that accident but that night had written such a story of fright and fear on my face that he could hardly recognize me.

So I stayed indoors, hoping that time would ease my feelings but jumping with alarm at every sudden word or slam of the door, and dreading the coming of each evening when the darkness of night would remind me of that black tomb which had held my mate but allowed me to escape.

Then again, this morning, after I had heard the clock striking all through the night, I must have surrendered to my exhaustion and slept, for I did not remember anything clearly after four o'clock struck. At five o'clock someone hammered on our front door. In an instant I was wide awake; the bed shook with my trembling. That crash on the door was the roar of falling rock; the darkness of the room was the solid blackness of the mine; and the bedclothes were the stones that held me down. When the knocking was repeated I had discovered that I was safe in bed. In bed – and safe; how can I describe what I felt?

Then I pondered what that knocking could mean. It was obvious that another morning was almost dawning. Griff, that was my mate's name, used to knock me up if he saw no light with us when he was passing to work. Could it be that he was passing: that all else had been a nightmare that this sudden wakening had dispelled? No, I realized it had been no nightmare for I had helped to wash his body – what parts it had been possible to wash without them falling apart.

Then came another thought; could it be that he was still knocking although his body was crushed? I dreaded to look, yet I could not refuse that appeal. I stumbled across the room, lifted the window, then peered down into the darkened street. A workmate was there. He lived some distance away but was on his way to the pit. He had a message for me. He shouted it out so that there should be no doubt of my hearing:

'Clean forgot to tell you last night, so I did. They told me at the office as you was to be sure to be at the Hall before four o'clock today. The inquest, you know. Don't forget, will you?'

Will I – can I – ever forget? Yet so indifferent are we to the sufferings of others that this caller, who is old enough to know better, who is in the same industry and runs the same risks, and who may be in exactly the same position as I am some day, does not realize how he has terrified me by hammering at my door to give that needless message.

Forget it! Is that likely when a policeman called yesterday and, after looking in my face and away again, told me gently that I was asked to be at Restcwm before four o'clock tomorrow – he had to say tomorrow then, of course. Not more than an hour later the sergeant of police clattered up to our door and – very pompously – informed me that I was instructed to present myself at the Workman's Hall, Restcwm, not later than four o'clock on the afternoon of Friday the, etc., etc.

After the caller has gone to his work I get back into bed. I have been careful to put the light on because it will be a while before there is sufficient daylight to defeat my dread of the lonely darkness.

Be there by four – so I must start from here about two o'clock.

Restcwm is a considerable distance away and I have other things to attend to before the inquest. I have to draw the wages for last week's work and I shall have to take Griff's to his house as I have been doing for years. Next week I shall be short of the days I have lost since the accident. I wonder if they will pay us for a full shift on the day that he was killed. I have been at collieries where one sixteenth of a shift was cropped from the men who took an injured man home just before the completion of the working day. I think our firm will not be so drastic as that; they are more humane in many ways than most of the coal-owners.

I lie abed, and think. The inquest will be this afternoon and I shall be the only witness except the fireman. This is the first time I have been a witness or had any connection with legal things and the police. I dread it all. I shall have to tell what happened in pitch darkness about two miles inside the mountain. They will listen to me in the brightness of the daylight and in the safety of ordinary life; and they will think that they understand. They may put their questions in a way that is strange to all my experience and so may muddle me.

I shall have to swear to tell the truth, and nothing but the truth. Nothing but the truth, it sounds so simple. I will try to recall what happened and whisper it to myself in such a way that I shall be question-proof when the time comes.

Griff was there before me that night, as usual, sitting near the lamp-room. He gave me the usual grin at our meeting, then when he had finished the last of that pipeful and had hidden his pipe very carefully under that old coal-tram near the boilers, he took a last look at the moon, then we stepped into the cage and were dropped down.

I remember him saying as he looked upwards before we got under the pit wheels:

'Nice night for a walk ain't it, or a ride through the country. Nice night for anything, like, except going down into the blasted hole.'

Griff is many years older than I am; I expect he is about fifty.

We have worked together for many years. He is well built but quite inoffensive. He has a couple of drinks every Saturday night and chews a lot of tobacco at work because smoking is impossible. He is aware that things are rotten at our job and is convinced that someone could make them a great deal better if they wished to; but who should do it or how it should be done are problems too difficult for Griff to solve. Soon he is going to have one of his rare outings; he is one of a club that has been saving to see Wales play England at Rugby football.

We were two of the earliest at the manhole where the fireman tests our lamps and tells us what work we are to do that night for we are repairers and our place of work is changed frequently. The fireman is impatient and curt, as always.

'Pile of muck down ready for you,' he snaps each word and his teeth clack through the quid of tobacco as he talks, 'there's a fall near the face of the new Deep. Get it clear quick. 'Bout eight trams down now, and you'd best take the hatchet and measuring stick with you because I s'pose as it's squeezing now.'

'Eight trams,' Griff comments as we move away. 'I'll bet it's nearer ten if it's like his usual counting.'

We hurry along the roadway, crouch against the side whilst four horses pass us with their backs scraping against the low roof, then move on after them. As we near the coal workings the sides and roof are not so settled as they were back on the mains. We hear the creak of breaking timber or an occasional snap when the roof above us weakens. The heat increases and our feet disturb the thick flooring of dust.

Where the height is less than six feet timber is placed to hold the roof but where falls have brought greater height steel arches are placed in position. They are like curbed rails, nine feet high to the limit and about the same width. Where they are standing we can walk upright but we must be wary to bend low enough when we reach the roof that is not so high. We have been passing engine-houses as we moved inwards. These are set about four hundred yards apart and become smaller in size as we near the workings. Finally we pass the last one where the driver is crouching under the edge of the arching rock.

The new Deep is the last right-hand turn before we reach the Straight Main. Our tools are handy to our work and we are glad to strip off to our singlets for they are sticking to our backs. We see at once that the official was too optimistic for the fall blocks the roadway and it is difficult to climb to the top of the stones.

'Huh,' Griff is disgusted, 'more like twelve it is. Eight trams indeed. I guessed as much.'

It is squeezing, indeed. Stones that have been walled on the sides are crumbling from the pressure and there sounds a continual crack-crack as timber breaks or stones rip apart. As we stand by, a thick post starts to split down the middle and the splitting goes on while we watch, as if an invisible giant was tearing it in half. Alongside us another post that is quite two foot in diameter snaps in the middle and pieces of the bark fly into our faces. The posts seem no better than matchsticks under the pressure and we feel as if we were standing in a forest – so close together are the posts – and that a solid sky was dropping slowly to crush everything under it.

'Let's stick a couple more posts up,' I suggest, 'because most of these are busted up. Perhaps it'll settle a bit by then.'

We drag some posts along the roadway, measure the height, then cut the extra off with a hatchet that must not be lifted very high or it will touch the roof. When we carry the timber forward we listen after every step, with our heads on one side and our senses alert for the least increase in that crackling. We have measured the posts so that they should be six inches lower than the roof, then the lid can go easily between, but when we have the timber in position we notice that the top has dropped another inch. When we are tightening the lid we are careful not to hold on top for fear that a sudden increase in the pressure may tighten it suddenly and fasten our hands there. Ten minutes after the posts are in position turpentine is running from them – squeezed out by the weight.

The journey rider – this one is called Nat – comes along and we help him to repair the broken signal wires. He knocks on them with a file; there is a bang and rattle as the rope slackens and a tram is lowered to us. It seems that the roof movement is easing a little so I climb on top of the fall to sound the upper top. I have to stretch to my limit to reach it although I am standing quite nine feet above the roadway. The stones above echo hollowly when I tap them with the steel head of a mandrel so we are convinced that they have weakened and may fall at any minute. The awkward part is that we shall have to jump back up the slope and that the tram will be in the way to prevent us getting away quickly.

One of these trams holds about two tons and we had to break most of the stones, so we were busy to get the first tram filled in the first half hour. Nat signalled it to a parting higher up where a haulier was waiting with his horse to draw it along the Level Heading where the labourers would unload it into the 'gobs'. Whilst Nat was lowering another empty tram we noticed the small flame of an oil-lamp coming down the slope.

'Look out, you guys,' Nat warned us when he stopped, 'here's the bombshell coming and he'll want to know why the heck we ain't turned the place inside out in five minutes, you bet he will.'

It is the fireman and he came with a rush, stumbling over a loose piece of coal and almost falling; whereupon Nat turns away, partly as an excuse for not putting out his arm to steady the official and partly to hide the grin that he has started in anticipation of seeing the fireman go sprawling. The fireman recovers, however, and he glares at Nat as if he had read his thoughts. His hurry has caused him to breathe gaspingly; drops of sweat are falling from the end of his nose and the chew of tobacco is being severely punished. He glares at the fall, then back at us as if he thinks we must have thrown more on top of it.

'There's one gone,' I tell him, 'and a good nine left still.'

'Huh!' he grunts, 'don't be long chucking this one in agen. There's colliers below and coal waiting.'

He rushed away to hurry the labourers. We were full again when he returned in twenty minutes' time.

'While the rider's taking these trams up,' he ordered us, 'you roll some of these stones and wall 'em on the sides. Put 'em anywhere out of the way of the rails.'

Griff went to have a drink after we had filled the fourth. The water gurgled down his throat as it would have down a drain.

'Blinkin' stuff's got warm already,' he complained, 'and it was like ice when I brought it into this hole.'

His face is streaked with grey lines where the perspiration has coursed through the thickness of dust; when he wrings the front of his singlet the moisture streams from it. The fireman visited us every few minutes and upset us with his impatience. Even when he did not hurry us with words we could sense that he felt we were taking too long. It was nearly three o'clock in the morning when Nat arrived with the tram that would be sufficient to clear the roadway. It seems that the mountain always becomes uneasy about that hour and small stones had been flaking down like heavy raindrops. We peered out from under the edge of the hole and I said that these falling stones must be coming from the upper edge of the right side. I could see some stones there that had half fallen and become checked in their drop. I got the slender measuring stick – it was about nine feet long – and tried to reach those loose stones but when the stick was to its limit and my arms were outstretched I could not reach the upper top. I climbed upwards on some of the stones that had been walled near the side. When I had scrambled up to about eight feet high it was possible to tap the stones and they fell. It was warm down below but the heat was intense up in the hollow of the fall. The increase of temperature almost stopped my breathing; I noticed the warning smell that is like rotten apples. My head was so giddy that I could not climb down; I slid the last part.

'Phew!' I gasped. 'It's chock full up there. My head's proper spinning.'

'Full? What d'you mean?' the fireman demanded, although he knew.

'Full up of gas,' I replied, 'and there's enough in the hole to put us up to the sky.'

'What are you chirping about?' he snapped back at me, 'there's nothing to hurt up there.'

'Try it and see,' I suggested. 'I notice you haven't tested for any tonight.'

'Get on and clear that fall,' he said, 'there's nothing there.'

'Take your lamp up there,' I insisted, 'it's the only oil-lamp here. I know the smell of gas too well to be sucked in over it.'

Very reluctantly he began to climb but when he was nearly up he jerked his hand and the light was extinguished.

I had expected it, for that was better than showing there was gas present and he was wrong.

'Now just look what you've done,' he complained, 'I'll have to feel me way back to the re-lighter.'

I saved my breath because I knew further comment was useless. The official stayed sitting on the wall like a human crow and watched us while we went on with our filling. We were about half-full when I heard a sound like a stifled sob and a fireman slumped down, then rolled to the bottom quite near to Nat. The rider jumped back as swiftly as a cat, then crouched under the shelter of a steel arch.

'Now, where the devil did that 'un drop from?' Nat demanded. Then he turned to look at what had fallen. 'Good Lord!' he added, 'it ain't a stone – it's him. Out to the blinkin' world, he is. So there was some up there, all right.'

Our lights showed us that the fireman was breathing, although faintly.

'Let's carry him back to the airway,' I suggested, 'there's a current of fresh air there and he'll soon come round.'

'Too blasted soon, likely.' Nat was not sympathetic. 'The only time this bloke is sensible is when he's asleep. And why struggle to carry him when I got me rope as I can put round his neck and the engine as can drag him?'

After we had carried him to the airway we went on with our

job. We had two pairs of steel arches to place in position and bolt together. We were anxious to erect them so that we could cover them with small timber in case any more stones fell. Nat agreed to sit near the official and shout to us if there was any undue delay in his recovering.

'Fan him with me cap.' Nat was angered when I suggested it. 'Why the hell should I waste me energy on him, hey? Let him snuff it if he wants to, I shan't cry.'

He seemed to be looking forward with delight to the time when the fireman would open his eyes and see the sketches that were chalked on the smooth sides of that airway. We had some skilful artists in that district and no one could mistake who was represented as waving that whip behind those three figures who were carrying shovels.

We had the one arch solid and were well on with the second before the fireman recovered enough to stumble up the road towards us. He did not praise us for our speed in erecting; I do not think he was very appreciative of anything just then. He said nothing as he passed but climbed on to one of the tram couplings. Nat warned him to hold tight in a manner that showed that the fireman could fall off under the trams if he liked, then they moved away up the roadway from us.

As soon as we had covered the steel arches we went to have our meal. We moved to where the roof was stronger, covered our shoulders with our shirts and sat on a large stone close to one another. We leant back against the walled sides, partly to ease the ache in our backs, and partly to lessen the target if more stones should fall.

We were supposed to have twenty minutes for eating food but we had finished before that. Griff looked at his watch; it was ten minutes to four. I remember him stating the time and remarking that we had not been disturbed at our food – for a wonder. Hardly had he said that when we saw a light coming towards us. We could tell by the bobbing of the lamp that the one who was carrying it was running.

Whoever is coming it must be a workman because he is carrying an electric lamp. We can hear him panting as he comes and his boots hit the wooden sleepers with a thud.

'Something have happened.' Griff speaks my own thoughts, 'somebody have been hurt bad or –' He does not finish and we wait, tensed, for the message . . . The running man reaches us, pauses, then holds his lamp up to our faces. The shadow behind the lamp becomes more solid and I realize that it is Ted Lewis.

'Puff,' Ted blows his cheeks out, 'all out of wind I am. Been hurrying like old boots to get to you chaps.'

Already we are reassured because if someone was under a fall Ted would have shouted his message at once. After taking a deep breath he explains:

'Old bladder-buster sent me to fetch you chaps to clear a fall he did. Said to come at once and bring your shovels and a sledge.'

'Fall!' We are both annoyed. 'Making all this fuss about a blessed fall.'

'Aye, I know,' Ted insisted, 'but it's on the main and in the way of a journey of coal. He's in a hell of a sweat about it, not 'arf he ain't. Told me to tell you to hurry up – to run along with your tools, he did.'

'Run! Huh!' Griff is disgusted. 'I s'pose as we'd best go, eh? Allus something, there is.'

With our tools under our right arms and our lamps hanging on our belts we hurry after Ted. We are careful to keep our heads down to avoid hitting the low places. Near the top of the third Deep we must meet the fireman, who swings around and walks in front of us. Suddenly he shouts back at us, 'There's ten full trams of coal the other side of this blasted fall and they won't be out afore morning if you don't shape yourselves.'

He is wasting his breath, for his threats and hurryings have lost their effect on us. His forcing is as much part of our working lives as the stones that fall or the timber that will break. Our lives are now a succession of delayed coal and falling roof; besides we are hurrying all we can. The sweat is dropping from our eyebrows; I feel it running over the back of my hand where a stone has sliced the skin away; it smarts as if iodine was smeared over it. The official stops suddenly and gasps:

'Just on by there. Not more'n four trams down and all stones, so it won't take you long. Look lively and get it clear.'

I judge the fall and decide that it is nearer six trams than four. My lamp shows me enough light to see to the top of the hole and to detect the stones that hang, half fallen, around the sides. There is a whitish glint over the shiny smoothness of the upper top. We call that type of roof the Black Pan; it will drop without the least warning.

'What's that smooth up above sounding like?' I ask.

'Not bad,' the fireman answers.

'Have you sounded it?' I ask.

'Course I have,' he answered, and I knew he had not.

'I'm going to do it for myself,' I stated, 'because you can't be too sure.'

I climbed on top of the fall, then tapped the roof with the measuring-stick. Boom – boom – it sounded hollow, as would a tautened drum. I scrambled back down.

'That upper piece is just down,' I said, 'it's ready to fall. Best to put some timber under it?'

'It's right enough,' the fireman insisted, 'and by the time we messes about to get timber here the shift'll be gone and it'll be morning afore we gets that coal by.'

'It would make sure that no more fell to delay us,' I argued, 'and it would be safer then.'

'And if you was to slam in it would be clear quicker,' he snapped; 'it seems as you're bent on wasting time.'

'I'm not,' I replied, 'only I wants to be as safe as I can. It's my body, remember, and a man don't want more than one clout from a stone falling from as high as that.'

'Get hold on the sledge, Griff,' he orders, 'and make a start. This chap have got a lot too much to say.'

Griff looks at the official, then at me. He is hesitant.

'Griff can do what he likes,' I said, 'but I'm not working under that top until it's put safer.'

'You'll do as I tells you or you know what you can do,' the fireman snarls, 'and that's pick up your tools and take 'em out.'

'I'll do that too,' I replied and threw my shovel on the side, 'and what about you, Griff? Are you staying?'

'Don't know what to do, mun,' he mumbles. 'P'raps it'll stay all right until we have cleared this fall. We've done it afore, heaps of times. Let's pitch in and clear away as soon as we can.'

I know that Griff has allowed the thoughts of his wife and family to overcome his judgement.

'Aye that's the idea.' The fireman is suddenly friendly. 'Slam in at it. You won't be long and I'll stand up on the side and keep me eyes on the top. If anything starts to fall I'll shout and you can jump back.'

I know well that before the word of warning could have formed in his throat it would be too late. Griff looks at me in an appealing way. He will not start without me, but I do not want to feel that I am responsible for his losing the job. I decide to risk it with him but to listen and watch most carefully.

We start to work, breaking the big stones and rolling them back one on top of another until we have formed a rough wall that is about a yard from the rail. The roof is quiet for a while and so we work swiftly. The fireman keeps very quiet because he can see we are working to our limit so that we can escape from under that bad piece, and he knows that the quieter he keeps the better we can hear. He sits on the wall, holding his lamp high and looking continually upward.

We had cleared about half of the fall and I had finished breaking a large stone when Griff asked me for the sledgehammer. Our elbows touched when I handed it to him. As he hit with the sledge I lifted a stone on to my knees but it slid down and dropped a couple of feet from the rail. I moved a short pace after it, bent, then began to lift it again. When I was almost straightened up I felt air rushing past my face; something hit me a terrible blow on the back. I heard a sound that seemed to start as a sob but ended in a groan that was checked abruptly. The blow on the back hit me forward. I felt to be flung along the roadway whilst my face ploughed through the small coal on the floor of the heading. I am sure that fire flashed from my eyes, yet I felt at the same time to be ice-cold all over. My legs were dead weights hanging behind me. When I breathed I swallowed the small coal that was inside my mouth. My nose was blocked with dust, so were my eyes. I felt about with my hands before realizing that my face was against the floor, and pushing down my arms to lift myself I whimpered with relief when I found I could use my legs and so my back was not broken.

I could feel something running down my back; obviously it must be blood. Above, below, and around me everything is black with not the slightest sign of light to relieve it. So, whatever has happened the lamps must be smashed and we can have no help from them.

I had just managed to get to my knees and start to collect my thoughts when I heard a scuffle a few yards away. Suddenly a new sound pierced the darkness. It was a sort of half-scream, half-squeal. At first I could not realize what this terrible sound meant; I had never before heard a grown man squeal with fear.

'Quick! Quick! Get me out!' It was the fireman screaming, and he sounded to be quite near to me. It seemed that he had been caught but was still alive. I did not hear the least sound from Griff. I collected my strength and shouted, 'Griff-oh! Are you all right?' I am far more concerned about my mate than the official. Griff was near me when I was hit. He was much more in the open than the fireman, who had chosen a part that was sheltered alongside the stronger side. I had no reply from Griff, but the fireman heard my call and I hear him sobbing with relief at knowing that I am alive and near to him.

'Come here, quick,' he appeals. 'I'm held fast over here. Get me out before more comes. Quick!'

I listen for some seconds, trying to puzzle where Griff was standing. I have lost all sense of direction. Am I nearly on top of my mate or will I press a stone still harder upon him if I move in that direction? While I hesitate the fireman restarts his screaming. Small stones drip around me continually, like the early drops of a shower of solid rain. Probably these are the warning that bigger stones are loosening but I cannot see what is above or which way to crawl and escape. I have lifted one eyelid over the other and the water from that eye has cleared away most of the dust. I can now open both eyes, but I can see no more than I could when my eyes were fast closed. I crawl towards the fireman, guided by his screams. Soon I find myself checked by what feels to be a mass of stone. I climb upwards, scramble over the top, then slide down. I call Griff again, softly, caressingly, as if to coax him to answer, whatever has happened, but no reply comes.

I press my shoulder against the solid side of the roadway so that it shall guide me, then I crawl forward, very slowly. The fireman knows I am nearing him and directs my movements – continually imploring me to hurry. Suddenly I touch something that is softer and warmer than stone. I run my hand along and know it is a human leg. My every nerve seems to grate when I decide it must be Griff's and that he is dead.

'That's the leg.' The fireman's scream relieves me. 'There's a stone on it as is holding me down. Lift it, quick.'

I feel for the stone and set myself to endure the pain of lifting. I might as well have attempted to move the mountain, for three attempts fail to shake the stone. The fireman is speaking near my ear; he is frantic; begs me to hurry; screams at me as would a hysterical woman. I feel about and find a stone that I can move so I push it tightly under the one that holds the leg. This fresh stone will ease some of the weight and will stop any more pressure coming on his foot.

I have realized that I cannot do more until I have help. I must crawl and get others. I tell the fireman so, but he begs me not to go. I know there is no other way, so I turn around and feel my

way over the stones. My fingers touch the cold iron of a tram-
rail, but as there is no sign of a tram on that side I am assured
that this is the right way. I crawl alongside that rail, running my
fingers on it for a guide.

'Don't you be long,' he screams after me, 'for God's sake don't
be long.'

Above, in the darkness, I hear a sound that resembles the
ripping of cloth. It is this noise that stones make when they are
being crushed and broken by the weight that is moving above
them. I must hurry, so that the fireman may be saved and to see
if there is any hope for Griff.

I drag myself along a few yards, rest some seconds to ease the
pain, then drag along again. I must have crawled more than two
hundred yards before I saw a light in the distance. I could not
shout, so I had to crawl close to the repairer who was at work
there. He was some seconds before he understood the message
that I was croaking, then when he did he became so flustered that
he wasted some time hurrying back the way I had come before he
realized it was useless going by himself. I lay in the darkness
while he ran back to call the help that came very quickly. Soon
the roadway was brightened by the lamps of scores of men, who
hurried along and took me with them, and this time we had
plenty of light to see what had happened.

I could see that at least another twenty tons had fallen and the
hole under which we had been at work was now higher than
ever. The place was all alive again, creaking above and around
us. Posts back in the gob were cracking – cracking – as if someone
was firing a pistol at irregular intervals.

The fireman was as I had left him. He had his back against the
side. His right foot was free but the left one was held tightly
under a large stone. We could see no sign of Griff. They lifted a
rail from the roadway, then used it as a lever to ease the stone off
the fireman so that he could be taken back from the danger. He
was only slightly hurt because the weight had only been sufficient
to hold him and the main body of the stone was resting on

others. He would not sit down but wandered amongst the men continually telling them of his own fright and moaning, 'Who would have expected this?' They lost patience at last and someone told him to sit down and not delay the work.

Above the men who strained to clear the fall, huge stones several tons in weight had started to fall, then had pressed against other stones that were moving and each had checked the downward movement of the other. They had locked each other in that position and now remained balancing – partly fallen – but the slightest jar or movement of the upper top would send them crashing down to finish their drop on the gang of men underneath. There was a continual rolling above us like thunder that is distant. Little stones flaked from the larger ones and dropped on the backs of the men as they worked below. Each time a stone dropped all the men leapt back, for a smaller stone is often the warning from a bigger one that is coming behind.

Several of the men stood erect, with their lamps held high and their eyes scanning the moving stones up above. They kept their mouths open, so that the warning shout should issue with no check. The others, busy amongst the fall, tumbling and lifting whilst they searched under the stones, did not hesitate when a warning came – they sprang backwards at once and made sure that no man stood directly behind the other to impede that swift spring.

Men can lift great weights when fear forces their strength. These stood six in a row, then tumbled big stones away until only the largest one in the centre was left. This one needed leverage, so a man knelt alongside to place the end of two rails in position; they had to be careful not to put the end on a man's body. Several men put their shoulders under the rail, then they prised upwards. As the stone was slowly lifted they blocked it up by packing with smaller stones, then started to lift again. When the stone was two feet off the ground they paused; surely it was high enough. There was something to be done now that each man dreaded; then, as if their minds had worked together two men knelt down and reached underneath. Very carefully they drew out what had been Griff.

We retreated with our burden and left the sides to do what crushing, and the roof to do what falling, they wished. The pain of my back had been severe all the while; when the excitement slacked I felt sick and could not stand alone. I leaned against one of my mates for support and he placed his arm around me gently, as if I was a woman.

We all know the verdict well enough, but refuse to admit it. Griff seems to be no more than half his usual size. Someone takes his watch from the waistcoat hanging on the side. They hold the shining back against what they believe is his mouth. Thirty yards away another stone crashes down on top of the others and the broken pieces fly past us whilst dust clouds the air. The seconds tick out loudly through that underground chamber whilst forty men watch another holding a watch; when he turns around someone lifts a lamp near so that they can see. The shining back is not dimmed. We had all known, yet somehow we had dared to hope.

As we are going outwards I notice that the fireman tries to isolate me; he wants to talk. I avoid him and keep in the group. Some distance along I hear a queer sound and look back to see that he has collapsed. His legs have given under him and he cannot stand. He is paralysed with fright. Two of the men place their hands under him and they carry him along behind the stretcher. They have to lean inwards to avoid the sides and bend their heads down because of the top. The fireman senses the hatred that is in all our minds and he sobs continually but no one asks him if he is in pain.

When we reach the main roadway the journey of empty trams is waiting. We place the loaded stretcher across one tram and four men sit alongside it. The fireman is lifted into another tram and the rest of us scramble on.

Suddenly the fireman tries to reassert himself.

'All of you going out,' he complains, 'didn't ought to go, not all of you. That fall have got to be cleared so's to get the coal back first thing.'

It was as if he had not spoken. The rider knocked on the signal wires. We start to move outwards slowly, for the engineer has been warned that it is not coal he is drawing this time. The fireman starts his mumbling again and we realize that he will tell the manager that the men refused to listen to him. Already he has started to cover his tracks.

Outside, it is dark and raining. The lamps on the pit mouth are smeared where the water has trickled through the dust on the globes. There is a paste of oily mud and wet small coal that squelches under our feet. The official limps away to the office. We notice, and comment on the fact, that he walks quickly and with hardly any difficulty. He gets inside the office and we hear him fastening the door before he switches the light on. He intends to be alone when making his report. We hand our lamps in, telling the lamp-men to note the damaged ones and we answer their inquiry as to 'Who is it this time?' They return our checks but put Griff's in a small tin box. A smear of light is brightening the sky but it is raining very heavily when we start on that half-hour's journey to his home. We feel our clothes getting wet on our bodies and the blankets on the stretcher are soaking. Water rushes down the house-pipes and it bubbles and glistens in the light of the few street-lamps.

All the houses near have their downstairs lights on, for news of disaster spreads quickly; besides, it is time for the next shift to prepare. The handles of the stretcher scrape the wall when we take the sharp turn to get through the kitchen door. This is the only downstairs room they have, so we prepare to wash him there. Neighbours have been busy, as they always are in this sort of happening. A large fire is burning, the tub is in, water is steaming on the hob and his clean pants and shirt are on the guard as if he was coming home from an ordinary shift.

I see no sign of Griff's wife. I remember her as small and quiet; a woman who stayed in her own home and was all her time tending to Griff and their five children. I do hear a sound of sobbing from upstairs and conclude that they have made her stop there, very wisely. Sometimes I hear the voices of the children too, but they are soft and subdued, as if they had only partly wakened and had not yet realized the disaster this dawn had brought to them.

I think that is all. I have relived that night fifty, yes, a hundred times since it happened, and each time I have felt that I hated the fireman more. Had that stone hit my back a little harder I would have been compelled to spend the rest of my days in bed with a broken back – and would have to exist on twenty-six shillings a week as compensation. Had I been a yard farther back I would probably be in similar state to Griff – then I would have been worth eighteen pounds, bare funeral expenses, as I would have been counted as having no dependants.

If I appear stupid at the inquiry, as a workman is expected to be, then I will answer the set questions as I am supposed to answer them and 'the usual verdict will be returned'.

Griff was my mate, and nothing I can do will bring him back to life again, but his wife and family are left. He would have wished that I do the best thing possible for them. If I remain quiet, they may be paid about four hundred pounds as compensation – which is the highest estimate of the value of a husband and father, if he is a miner. They will think that one of the usual accidents robbed them of their father, but if they are told he should not have died, it will surely increase their suffering.

If I speak what is true, the insurance company will claim that they are absolved from liability because we should not have worked there. Had we refused we should probably have lost our jobs. The insurance solicitor will be present – ever watching his chance – and will seize on the least flaw in the evidence.

So this afternoon I shall go to the office and draw two pay envelopes that should contain about two pounds sixteen each. One is mine, the other I will take to his house. There five silent children will be waiting whilst their dazed mother is being prepared to go to the Hall and testify that the crushed thing lying in the kitchen was her husband and that he was in good health when she saw him leave the house.

If the verdict is anything except 'Accidental death' that pay packet may hold the last money she will have – unless it is the pension and parish relief.

Later, tonight, I shall have to face another fear; I shall have to go again down that hole and restart work, but at four o'clock I will be at the inquest, shall kiss the Bible, and speak 'The whole truth and nothing but the truth' – perhaps. Would you?

EMYR HUMPHREYS

The Suspect

1

John and Phoebe lived in a large red-brick house at the end of a
tree-lined avenue on the outskirts of a large town in South Wales.
The house, which had been built in 1904 by John's grandfather,
was surrounded by an acre and a half of garden and almost
hidden from the avenue by a fringe of trees which John's grandfather had planted when the house was being built. The long
windows now had double-glazing and the house was kept warm
in winter by oil-fired central heating which John and Phoebe had
installed after the birth of their second child. John was a director
of a construction firm founded by his mother's brother and
Phoebe also worked three days a week as a speech-therapist in a
number of children's clinics. John drove a Volvo estate car mostly
and Phoebe used a small white Mini-Minor.

It was four o'clock on a summer afternoon and in the kitchen
Phoebe was feeding the three children and John stood by the
window and seemed to be contemplating the sundial that stood
in the centre of the lawn that stretched along three sides of the
house. There was the baby in the high chair, the girl with a
picture-book still on her knees, and there was the boy, sullen and
red-haired, with raw patches spreading from his crutch to his
thighs from nightly bed-wetting, watching his mother's every
move, like a private detective prepared to spend a lifetime working on her dossier, even though his mother was smiling at him
gently and spreading his favourite food, a cream and banana
mash, on thin bread and butter and folding it into a sandwich his

small hand could convey easily to his mouth. She wore a transparent pink nylon housecoat over a smart suit. Outside in the
tree-lined avenue, her white mini-car was waiting and her cheeks
were flushed by the effort she was making. Although she was in a
great hurry, she was determined to give the children proper attention. There was an au pair girl from Germany attached to the
household, but this was her day off and in any case Phoebe
preferred to supervise the children's meals herself whenever she
could. If they looked at her as they fed, they saw the smiling face
of a competent, good-looking woman aged twenty-eight who
liked to dress simply but smartly and kept her black hair straight
and short. They saw big eyes and big lips that were always ready
to kiss them.

'I don't think words like "relationship and responsibility" mean
much to little ears,' Phoebe said.

As she spoke she gave her son a special smile and moved closer
to the baby, who was clawing with a sticky hand at her breast, in
order to allow him to feel the softness underneath the covering of
clothes.

'I came home specially,' John said. 'If you'd come upstairs a
minute . . .'

John was tall with fair wavy hair and with more composure
would have been considered exceptionally handsome. As it was
his face twitched nervously and nearly everything his wife said
seemed to hurt him.

'If you put the children first . . .' he began.

'I think I do,' Phoebe said cheerfully, grinning happily at her
daughter who had looked up from her picture-book at the sound
of the word 'children'. 'In fact I know I do. Let's try to communicate on a rational level, John.'

'There's the public aspect of this thing . . .'

With his hands in the pockets of his well-cut business suit he
stared gloomily through the window. The garden was in good
order, the flowerbeds free of weeds, the borders neat and the
grass beautifully cut, but the sight of it did not seem to give him

any pleasure. He was such a gloomy figure that his daughter twisted in her chair to stare at him with open wonder.

'Another piece of cake, Nest?'

Phoebe bent down and gently turned the little girl's head towards her, ready for either cake or a kiss.

'Why should you expect to have everything you want?'

John sounded petulant, about to break out into anger. Phoebe straightened herself and stared at her husband steadily.

'Did you really mean to say that?'

'Come out for a minute,' John said restlessly. 'Just for a minute.'

She looked at each child in turn and then she said:

'Daddy and Mummy are going into the garden for a minute. Call out if you want anything. I'll leave the window open. Mrs Oliver should be here any minute.'

She glanced at her watch.

'She'll be looking after you when you play in the garden. And then she'll be washing you and giving you your supper. And then mummy'll be back and she'll tell you a story in bed if you're still awake.'

In the garden beyond the sundial, John made no further effort to disguise the pain and desperation in his voice.

'Everybody knows about him, Phoebe,' he said.

'Knows what?'

She was sympathetic, calm but smiling slightly.

'With women. His reputation.'

'Well . . .'

Her lips closed. She had decided to make no further comment. As a result she was invested with an aura of tantalizing mystery and John was goaded to further statement.

'He's not qualified,' John said.

This made Phoebe laugh and then put her hand over her mouth when she saw how hurt he looked.

'As an optician. Or as a physiotherapist. I'm pretty sure of it.'

'John.'

She sounded very firm.

'I've told you before. It does no good. Neither you nor I can discuss Max objectively. In that case it is better we don't discuss him at all. We have the children in common. They're yours and they're mine. We run a home together. We still like each other. We're still friends. Let's leave it at that.'

'He's a crook, Phoebe. I'm sure of it. He'll cheat you. He's probably got a whole string of married women.'

'Stop, John.'

'I mean what's all that physiotherapy for? I've heard people joke about it.'

'Stop!'

She was stern now, almost angry. And then again she glanced quickly at her watch. Again he became desperate.

'How much can you expect me to put up with?' he said. 'Do you even think of me? Do you? Think of me?'

She spoke very slowly, certain of the righteousness of her cause.

'We've been married six years,' she said. 'We have three children by accident rather than by design. We're not physically suited. It may be my fault just as much as yours. We were both very immature. Now I've found someone who can satisfy me. Call him my lover if you like. I told you about it from the start. I've been as frank and as honest as I can. I offered you a divorce. You didn't want it. We discussed it fully and we agreed it was necessary to strike a balance between sacrifice and fulfilment. We agreed to carry on for the sake of the children. Nothing has changed. Is there anything else you want to say, because I'm late already?'

'Any other man . . .'

He looked so miserable she was forced to turn away. She walked briskly into the house through the large front door which was open and in the small cloakroom leading off the hall rinsed her hands briskly under the tap. She took off her nylon overall and studied her appearance in the cloakroom mirror. She heard his footsteps on the stone steps first and then swallowed in the expensive softness of the dark blue carpet. Their house was spacious and beautifully ordered and the quality of the furniture and the fittings was the envy of their many friends.

'Phoebe! Phoebe!'

She was running a steel Scandinavian comb through her black hair and she could barely hear his whisper. When she came out into the hall he stared at her with undisguised longing. She smiled at him in the most friendly way as she pulled on her gloves.

'Look after the children,' she said. 'Mrs Oliver will be along any minute. Will you be going to play golf?'

'I don't know.'

He sounded on the verge of tears.

'Phoebe . . .'

'I'm late,' she said.

She hurried down the gravel path, checking to see whether the key of the car was in her handbag. She was rather a small woman, with strong athletic legs, and her quick walk was purposeful and almost defiant, so that if her husband was watching from the drawing-room window he should not imagine she was held back by any sense of guilt; and if, after she had closed the small garden gate behind her, any neighbours were watching her movements they, for their part, should understand she was going about her business with that single-minded intent, characteristic of an able and busy woman who had nothing in the world with which to reproach herself.

2

Resolutely Phoebe rang the bell a third time. Max lived in a flat above his optician's shop in A— Street, which was a shopping centre on the fringe of an old working-class district. At last she heard his steel-tipped heels clattering on the narrow uncarpeted stairs. He opened the door and remained in the shadow against the wall, inviting her to walk up in front of him. There was a smell of stale cooking-fat and in the light of a forty-watt unshaded bulb the wallpaper appeared impregnated with the greasy smoke of many hastily fried meals.

In contrast to his surroundings, Max was very clean. He was a short man with curly hair, merry eyes and unusually broad shoulders. Twice a day he had a shave and a shower and he used an expensive aftershave lotion. His clothes, including his shirts, were specially made for him. Gold cuff-links and a generous display of cuffs drew attention to his hands of which he was very proud. They were broad, soft and beautifully manicured.

'What's the matter, darling? You look worried.'

Phoebe touched his chin with her hand. They were standing in the corridor. She trembled as she waited for him to take her in his arms as he always did when she arrived. A long, breathless, excited embrace that meant that they had found each other at last and that their bodies could communicate endlessly without the use of words. He did indeed kiss her fervently, but it seemed a rather shorter embrace than usual. She suppressed a sigh and reminded herself of the sanctity of his independence and the completely free nature of their relationship. How ironic it would be if a simple greeting should become a fossilized ritual when the whole basis of their relationship was supposed to be free, untrammelled loving.

Max loved music. There was a gramophone in the middle of his living-room floor and long-playing records were littered around it. Phoebe bent down to see what he had been listening to. In the room there was a smell of cigars. A large deep couch stretched the length of one wall. Phoebe walked away from it to look out of the window down on to the street, stepping carefully over the records. It was early closing day and there were few people in the street. Max came to her side and took her hand. He drew her gently towards the couch, looking at her with masterful intensity. Phoebe obeyed him reluctantly. When they were by the couch she took off her suit and kicked off her shoes. Max looked at her appreciatively and with his hands persuaded her to lie own and relax. He stroked her thighs in a way that he knew she usually enjoyed, but in a few moments she sat up and looked at him.

'What's the matter, Max? Has something upset you? Aren't you feeling well?'

He shook his head.

'It's a bit mechanical, darling. Your mind's far away. On other things. I don't mind.'

She picked up his hand and kissed it.

'I know you want to give me what I want and I love you for it. But these things don't just come to order, I should know that. Why the hell should they? You know what I'd like to do? Spring-clean your flat! Shall I do it?'

A look of alarm passed over his face and Phoebe laughed girlishly, tucking her legs under her.

'Shall I cook you a meal? A lovely delicate meal. Shall I?'

Again he shook his head.

'Would you like it if we went to bed or is your bedroom in a hell of a mess? What's the matter, Max? Just tell me.'

'It's nothing really. Nothing you can put your finger on.'

'Is it politics?'

Max was a town councillor. Their first meeting had been in the children's clinic. Max was among a party of councillors who had come to see the clinic in action. The physical attraction had been strong and immediate. As he said afterwards, 'crackling in the air like electricity' between them. They were alone for a few minutes in a school corridor and at once he touched her hand and asked when he could see her again.

'Is your husband friendly with Henbet?'

Phoebe looked as if she were concentrating on what he was saying.

'Which one? The alderman?'

Max nodded impatiently. He wanted an answer.

'There's a business connection. Lloyd, Henbet and Lloyd act for the firm . . .'

'How friendly?'

'Well . . . Henbet is a lot older. It's always difficult to tell wit
John. He's very reserved really.'

'What does he say about me?'

Max was watching her intently.

'You?'

Phoebe hesitated. This kind of discussion had been no part o
the purpose of her visit.

'Well. What would you expect?'

'He's jealous.'

It was a statement, a step towards some conclusion he wante
to establish.

'He still wants you? Come on. Tell me. You can tell, for God'
sake!'

Phoebe looked down modestly.

'All the time,' she said quietly.

Her reaction seemed to distract Max from his line of reason
ing.

'Poor bastard.'

He leaned back into the deep couch, his chin sinking on his chest

'He thinks I've no right to what I'm getting from you. That'
what it amounts to.'

Max looked thoughtful.

'How are the kids?'

Phoebe's face brightened with enthusiasm. This was a subjec
she could always talk about.

'Nest is so intelligent. You should have seen her this morning
Max. She was adorable. She was kneeling on the wall talking t
Mrs Addy's cat, Rupert. A great big grey thing with a bell tie
round its neck. Nest was calling the cat and saying "Would yo
like me to take it off, Ruppy?"'

Carried away with the delight of recollection, Phoebe imitate
her little daughter's voice.

'They're marvellous really,' Phoebe said, 'although I am a bi
worried about John junior.'

'Is there something wrong with me?'

Max threw out both hands dramatically.

'I mustn't go on like a doting mother,' Phoebe said sadly.

'Something suspect?'

'I don't know what you mean, Max.'

'Do they want me to feel guilty because I'm different?'

'Max darling. Who are "they"?'

'"They?" Yes. "They." First sign of a persecution complex, isn't it? There's something going on. Henbet's up to something.'

He became silent as he considered the forces that were silently assembling against him.

'Max . . .'

Phoebe stood up and pulled her petticoat over her head, shaking out her short black hair when she had done so.

'Will you rub my back, darling?'

She lay face downwards on the couch and waited until she felt the pressure of his fingers in the hollow of her back.

'That's wonderful,' she whispered. 'Um . . . marvellous.'

She sighed blissfully and closed her eyes.

'Umm . . . Umm . . .'

She enjoyed the rhythm of the massage, but he gave up just as she was about to turn and put her arms around his neck in the loving way she had done so many times before to show her gratitude for the freedom and frankness he had taught her. Instead, sitting up, she saw his eyes were closed.

'What are you thinking?'

With finger and thumb she lifted one of this eyelids.

'I'm thinking that they're dragging up the past,' Max said. 'And they're doing it deliberately. I can't help brooding over it.'

'"They?"'

'Oh the party, of course. Who else?'

For the first time he sounded irritable and impatient.

'This is a community of over one hundred thousand people. One hundred thousand! But you'd think from some people that the whole lot just existed for their personal convenience. The

Henbets of this world. Just for them to have something to govern. I tell you something. Local government stinks in this part of the world.'

'Tell me,' Phoebe said.

'It all sounds so petty. There are vested interests . . . The thing is there was only one committee I really wanted to be on. What do they do? They keep me off. And then, without consulting me at all, they put me on a secret list that demands the closest scrutiny of my past and my family past. Why did they do that except to dig up every damn secret and start a whispering campaign. Just to reduce me, to break my power. That's the dirty sort of game it is. To break my power and that power is a power for good. They've done it deliberately. My old man, who's dead and buried, mark you, served a prison sentence nearly forty years ago. And they drag that up in a deliberate attempt to discredit me.'

He was on his feet, pacing up and down the room, stepping over his gramophone records, pushing his hands deep down in his trouser pockets.

'Why, Max? Why?'

He looked at her suspiciously, unwilling to have to fumble for phrases to convey truths that should be self-evident.

'Nobody likes a man on his own.'

'But why, politically I mean, why discredit you?'

'Because I'm the most able man there and as far as brains and ability go, I ought to be in the driver's seat.'

Phoebe looked at him, her head hanging to one side.

'I suppose you think I'm being big-headed. A man is entitled to some ambition, isn't he?'

'You look so Jewish,' Phoebe said. 'Like an Old Testament prophet . . .'

'I don't want to be Jewish,' Max cried. 'I just want to be me. That's my whole creed really. Why can't we all just be ourselves?'

'I agree,' Phoebe said, but Max hadn't finished.

'I've got my own moral standards,' Max said, 'and I don't want the whole bloody tribe breathing down my neck from morning till night. I just can't stand it, I never could. I'm a loner really. A loner. Have you heard that expression? You've got to have strength to lead, you know. Real strength. The question is, have I got it?'

'Oh Max, of course you have, darling . . .'

He looked at her sceptically and shook his head.

'You've no idea of the opposition I've had to encounter all my life. My family. Other families. The whole damn world. Here I am now. With a respectable business. Aged forty, living alone in a bachelor's flat. On my tod and the whole bloody world against me.'

Phoebe's head was lowered. He didn't seem to notice her.

'God it's hot in here, I'm sweating like a bull. I think I'd like a shower.'

The bathroom was at the back of the house, beyond the kitchen. It was the cleanest part of the flat, fitted with duck-egg-blue tiles. A shallow bath stretched the width of the room and elaborate chrome shower equipment protruded from the top of each wall. Max seemed to cheer up at the sight of it. Phoebe was in the corridor. He was smiling when he turned to call her.

'You having one too?' he said.

Phoebe clapped her hands childishly. Together they splashed about happily under the water. Max played about with the controls and Phoebe squealed with excitement and pleasure.

She patted his belly with her wet hand:

'You're holding it in,' she shouted. 'Pot-belly!'

'No I'm not.'

Max performed athletic antics under the shower that made them both helpless with laughter. Then they stood still, panting in each other's arms with the water pouring down over them.

'Aren't we like a couple of kids?' Phoebe said. 'Isn't this great? Like the Garden of Eden. You're the only man, Max, and I'm the only woman in the whole wide world.'

'Isn't it marvellous,' Max said, 'to be so clean?'

'Am I? Am I?'

She raised her voice over the noise of the water.

'What?'

'The only woman. I'm not jealous, Max. But I'd like to know. Just tell me if there is. That's all. I won't be cross, honestly.'

'I swear to you, Phoebe . . .'

Max turned off all the taps and wiped the water on his face and on his hairy chest.

'Don't swear, Max. Your word is good enough for me.'

'Since you, Phoebe, it's nobody but you.'

'Just me?' Phoebe looked surprised and delighted.

'Yes.'

'For a whole year!'

'Yes.'

He seemed deeply touched by the effect this had on Phoebe. He took a bath towel and began to dry her face and her body very slowly, kissing her gently as he did so.

'Smooth skin,' he said. 'Just designed to drive a man out of his mind. Big eyes. Big lips. Big breasts.'

The door-bell rang so loudly at the kitchen end of the corridor that they both jumped. Phoebe grabbed the bath towel and wrapped it tightly round herself. She seemed unable to stop herself trembling.

'Are you expecting someone?'

He shook his head.

'Who's there, then?'

He looked suddenly unhappy.

'What's the matter, Max?'

'That damn bell,' he said. 'Suddenly making me feel guilty. As if we had no right to feel free and enjoy ourselves. Anybody would think I was a bloody murderer.'

He opened the bathroom door. The bell rang again and the clanging reverberated urgently in the bare corridor.

'It's the outside world,' he said. 'There was some danger of us enjoying each other. I'll go down and see who it is. Probably only the laundry anyway. The bachelor's friend. Never forgets to call.'

'Max!'

She called after him.

'Where shall I go? Bedroom?'

He nodded and clattered down the narrow stairs. When he opened the door she kneeled down in an attempt to see who was calling. She saw the feet and trousers of two uniformed policemen.

3

'You could say we were *keeping an eye* on him. In that sense, yes . . .'

The lawyer, the elder Mr Henbet, who was an alderman, stressed the phrase in a strangely academic fashion. He sat importantly behind his large desk with his elbows resting on the arms of his high-backed chair and his hands clasped comfortably together. He was handsome still in late middle age, and he smiled at John with professional charm as he peered at him over the gold rims of his half-spectacles. In front of him was an imposing pile of letters and documents, awaiting his signature. The room was large and ornate, but badly lit, as though the dim light added to the traditional solemnity expected in the office of a senior partner.

'I'll be quite frank with you, John. He pretty well thrust himself on us. It happens in politics sometimes even in the best-regulated parties. A man *insinuates* himself in a ward, gathers a bit of support, curries a bit of favour here and there and before you know where you are he's trying to push his way to the top, trying to push his way to the front of the queue for this committee or that, and in no time at all the tail is wagging the dog!'

Mr Henbet's position behind his large desk was unassailable. When he stressed a phrase or a word as he often did, it not only drew his listener's attention to the entire etymology of the word uttered, it also underlined the profound authority of the speaker.

'Politics is a funny game,' Mr Henbet said. 'I wish you were interested. You know, your father was the best mayor this old town ever had.'

'I can't stay,' John said. 'Our daily is looking after the children, but she's not really to be relied on . . .'

Mr Henbet began to finger the documents awaiting his attention.

'You must tell me, John. What is it you would like me to *do*?'

His tone as ever was soft and silky but the stress on the last word was imperious.

John was pulling faces, unable to reduce the complexities of his emotion to recognizable phrases.

'Is he . . . does he . . . has he any power on the council, in the party?'

'Well our majority is only three and one of those is a very sick man. So in that sense he has some power. He's a pretty brazen, pushing sort of chap, in the way these people are sometimes. Although I must say we have two more of them in the party caucus and they can't stand him. We have our ways of keeping him under control. Politics means management, doesn't it, as well as principle?'

Mr Henbet took out a gold-topped fountain-pen from his waistcoat pocket and made it clear he was anxious to start signing his letters. At last John managed to speak.

'He's having an affair with my wife.'

Mr Henbet replaced the pen in his waistcoat pocket.

'Would you like a glass of water?' he said.

'It's been going on for months and I've known about it for months. Condoned it. She told me from the start and I've agreed to everything she's done. What else could I do? I didn't want to lose her. I thought it wouldn't last. Just a phase or something. We were so civilized about it then. I didn't satisfy her physically and she had a right to be satisfied. But we would keep the home together. Put the children first. All her idea really. But I agreed to everything. We would keep the arrangement secret. Tell no one. Be secret. Be discreet. It's been driving me out of my mind.'

'You don't want a divorce?'

The lawyer spoke with judicial care, but John didn't bother to answer.

'If I could get rid of him. Just get rid of him. Anyhow. If I had any guts I'd kill him. Isn't he unqualified? Couldn't he be put out of business? Driven out of his place. Couldn't that be done?'

'That type,' Mr Henbet said, 'they're not so easy to get rid of. They cling and they push and they insinuate themselves into the social structure. I'm not antisemitic or anything like that, but if you study the way some of them claw their way to the seats of power . . .'

'What can I do?'

John's voice was shrill and desperate.

'I want Phoebe back. But he's got control of her. By now, for all I know, her ideas are his. She's mine by right and by law and he's stolen her from me. What can I do?'

The lawyer was thinking deeply.

'I thought you'd found out something about him?' John sounded angry and resentful.

'Not about him. About his father. Which isn't relevant. This isn't an easy case.'

'She's my wife, isn't she?'

'She's *married* to you,' the lawyer said. 'The less we talk of *my* this or *my* that the better.'

'What can I do? He takes money from old women for treatment. That's true, isn't it?'

The lawyer waved aside John's wild accusations and made him keep quiet while he thought more deeply.

'There's just one possibility that occurs to me,' he said.

'Yes,' John said eagerly.

'I could have a talk with her. You could ask her to come and see me. As a friend of the family.'

'Phoebe?'

John was incredulous and suspicious.

'But how could I ask her? I told you this was a secret agreement.

No one was to know about it on any account. I only came to see you because I thought you'd found something out about him, to get rid of him.'

'About his father,' Mr Henbet said.

'I wouldn't have come otherwise. I got carried away. I must ask you to keep this in the strictest confidence.'

It was clear that he had begun to regret having spoken. Perhaps even now the lawyer was thinking of taking advantage of her.

'There are things I could tell her,' Henbet said. 'Calmly and objectively. I know it sounds old-fashioned, but without love and trust any marriage collapses. Now if she could come and see me and I could talk to her . . .'

'I'll see,' John said.

He was on his feet, anxious to get away.

'I would talk to her like a father,' Mr Henbet said. 'A quiet, serious chat. It would make a difference, I think. It's worth a try, don't you think?'

'I'll see,' John said.

He was by the door.

'This is in strictest confidence, of course . . .'

He waited for the lawyer to nod and then he hurried out.

4

Max was kneeling on the floor of his living-room picking up gramophone records. Phoebe had just enough time to collect her clothes as he talked to the policemen at the bottom of the stairs. She left the bedroom door open so that she could hear as much as possible of what was going on while she dressed. The two policemen stood side by side with their hands behind their backs making the room seem small, especially the sergeant who was six foot four. From Max's position near the floor his head seemed tiny on the top of his large body. The sergeant was a very humorous fellow and he usually laughed after every statement he made.

'We're not saying you did it, councillor,' he said, 'but we have to check like, don't we?'

Having stated the humour of the situation, he took his time over his laughter. The constable, on the other hand, young as he was, had a face like a graven image and never smiled at all.

'To cut a long story short,' the sergeant said, keeping his breathing in good order after his bout of laughter, 'all you've got to do, councillor, is to tell us what your movements were between the vital hours of seven and nine-thirty on the night of March 14th and give us a witness or two like, their names and addresses, and we'll be on our way.'

'But for God's sake,' Max said holding out an LP in his right hand, 'that's two months ago. How do you expect me to remember what I was doing two months ago?'

The police sergeant nodded sympathetically.

'It's awful, isn't it?'

His tone was deeply sympathetic, but when he had spoken he laughed just the same.

'It's like this, councillor, you knew the dead girl. That's one thing like, isn't it?'

'I fitted her for a pair of specs. She came here once, twice, perhaps three times. That's all.'

'Not a total stranger, that's one thing, isn't it? You do not deny ever having known her . . .'

'Of course I don't!'

'The next item. You own a black Morris Minor.'

'The world is full of black Morris Minors.'

'Not all with EU as part of the registration number.'

'EU?'

Max's mouth hung open.

'Also,' the policeman said humorously, 'you're dark-haired and you're a bit on the short side. And you told me downstairs you were familiar with Pencoed Wood and that you knew there was a track leading from there to the quarry.'

'Well, for God's sake . . .'

Max was upset. He picked up more records, thinking very hard.

'March 14th,' the sergeant said, ticking off the items gaily on his huge fingers. 'Between seven and nine-thirty. A rather short man driving a black Morris Minor, EU something, and this girl sitting in the passenger-seat. What else can we do except check all the owners of black Morris Minors with EU in the registration like? And especially those who are short, dark and handsome.'

The sergeant laughed heartily at his own joke.

'Isn't it awful?' he said. 'Bothering you like this. Makes you feel guilty from the word go, doesn't it?'

'No!' Max shouted. 'For God's sake, why should it? I was probably at a council meeting that night. What night was it?'

'A Sunday.' The sergeant smiled happily. 'The day of rest.'

'Look here, I keep a diary.' Max got to his feet, dusting the knees of his well-cut narrow trousers. 'I'll get it right away. We'll clear this up in a jiffy.'

'That's right, sir.'

'It's in the bedroom. I won't be a minute.'

As soon as Max was out of the room the young constable turned to look at his superior admiringly. He even ventured to whisper.

'What do you think?'

'Think? What do I think? I think this room could do with a nice clean, that's what I think.'

Again he laughed uproariously. In the bedroom Max shuddered at the sound.

'Just listen to him! He shouldn't laugh like that,' Phoebe whispered indignantly.

'There's no law against laughing.'

Phoebe sat down on the unmade bed. The pale green sheets needed changing. Against the inside wall in wooden cabinets that Max himself had made when he was fifteen there was his collection of birds' eggs. Also in home-made bookcases, which he had never painted, there was his collection of books on the history of local government. The books were very dusty. The doors of his large wardrobe hung open. Most of his suits hung in plastic covers.

'Did you hear? Did you hear, Phoebe?'

There was a profound protest in his whisper. Phoebe nodded sadly.

'There's something behind this, you know. There's something going on. Do you know this sergeant? Ever seen him before?'

'No.'

'The bastards are up to something . . . up to something.'

'Max. Where were you?'

'Me? How should I know?'

'Who was she, Max? Did she come here, into this flat?'

'Some trollope from Trisket Street. Wanted a fancy frame. Green felt and diamanté inlay. She was on the game all right. Good-looking girl too. But crooked. I saw through her all right.'

'Did she come in here?'

'Here? In here?'

Max looked around the room.

'For God's sake, what do you think I am? Where did I put it? My diary. Where is it?'

He rummaged in the drawers marked 'shirts' and 'socks' on the left side of the big wardrobe.

'There's something cooking, I can tell that much.'

He fumbled through his diary. He was upset and frightened.

'Max . . .' Phoebe stood close to him and put her fingertips on his wrists. 'You must keep calm, Max. These are only routine inquiries. Nobody's trying to do you down.'

'Aren't they? Shows how much you know.'

He saw that she was looking at the pages of his diary. She could read the times of council meetings and other engagements. But her attention was taken by a notation of black dots and initials. He closed the diary quickly. It was green and the pages were gilt-edged.

'I'd better hurry back,' he said.

'Max . . .'

'I'll just get rid of them,' he said. 'Quick as I can.'

Back in the living-room, Max closed the door carefully before speaking in a subdued voice that invited the policeman's confidence.

'It's a little embarrassing,' he said. 'I was with a lady. I can account for the whole evening quite easily. There's no problem. No problem at all.'

'That should be all right,' the sergeant said jovially. 'Would you care to give us her name and address, councillor? We'll need to see her of course and she'll need to state she was in your company, like. What you were doing of course is your own affair. We don't go into that!'

His laughter rang out merrily and Max's big eyes rolled upward in despair. This made the sergeant laugh more than ever.

'Name, address and telephone number?'

He was gasping for breath as Max looked in his diary to check the address.

'Take it down, will you, Thomas?'

The straight-faced constable already had his notebook at the ready.

'It's a Mrs Alice Maywell,' Max said. 'M-A-Y-W-E-L-L.'

'That's a nice name,' the sergeant said, shaking with laughter.

'The address . . . The Hermitage, Cliff Road . . . Sergeant! Please!'

With difficulty the sergeant stifled his laughter. He shook his head and wiped his eyes.

'It's all in the day's work,' he said. 'I wish I hadn't got into the habit really.'

'If you could be discreet,' Max said. 'Her husband works at the M— Bank . . . I mean keep it quiet if you can.'

The sergeant put a large finger to his lips.

'Mum's the word,' he said.

As he was shaking with the effort to suppress his laughter, they heard the clattering of high heels as Phoebe raced impetuously down the stairs. They heard the door slam.

'Don't matter how many really,' the sergeant said, laughing again, 'so long as they're not all brides in the bath like, isn't it?'

5

At half-past one in the morning Phoebe heard her little boy whimpering. The door of his room was open and a night-light burned dimly by his bed. She jumped out of bed, hurried in bare feet to pick him up and put him on his pot before he wet the bed. But she was too late. Wearily, her head aching from sleeplessness and too much coffee drunk after supper while she was watching late television, she stripped off his wet trousers and changed his sheets. As she was doing this the boy, wrapped in a blanket, slept soundly on the carpet of his little room. She held him to her breast and kissed him before laying him down gently in the dry bed.

When she returned softly to their own bedroom, John switched on his light. He sat up in bed, his fair hair tousled, his face pale and distressed.

'I can't sleep,' he said.

'I was too late,' she said. 'I had to change the sheets. We've got to do something about it. Without upsetting him of course. But he'll be five in August.'

'Phoebe,' he said. 'Phoebe. I can't stand this any more. I can't. I can't stand it.'

'It's all right. You won't have to any more.'

She pulled her bedclothes up to her chin.

'It's been driving me insane, Phoebe. Killing me . . .'

'I shan't be seeing him again,' Phoebe said. 'The whole thing is over. The course of treatment is complete.'

There was a new note of cynicism in her voice.

'I'd like to go away for a bit,' she said. 'Just a short holiday. Take the children with me. Perhaps when we come back we could try and start again.'

'Phoebe . . . Phoebe.'

She could hear him sobbing into his pillow.

'John.'

He lifted his head.

'You haven't told anyone, John . . .'

'No. No. Of course not.'

'At least you're a man I can trust.'

'Phoebe . . . Phoebe . . .'

'Let's go to sleep now, shall we. I'm so tired. Dead tired.'

They were both silent. The room was filled with moonlight and the shadow of the trees in the garden. John lay on his back, his hands behind his head. She could see the outline of his handsome profile. Then her eyes closed ready for sleep. It was at this point that the little boy started howling.

He called 'Mummy' several times quickly as if he were drowning in his sleep.

'I'll go,' John said. 'Shall I go?'

'No. No.'

Phoebe staggered into her dressing-gown.

'It's me he's calling for.'

ISLWYN FFOWC ELIS

Self-pity

(TRANSLATED BY THE AUTHOR)

It was finished. The last full stop. Big, round, final. The best thing in the book. Ieuan released a heavy sigh, reached for his pipe, got up from his desk and sank, emotionally drained, into the old armchair in front of the old gas fire.

Before he could begin his customary worrying, Esyllt's dark head appeared round the door.

'You've finished the novel?'

Another sigh. 'Yes.'

'Marvellous!'

'It won't be published.'

Esyllt's brow furrowed in puzzlement. 'Don't be silly, Ieuan.'

'I am perfectly sane.'

'But the publishers won't reject it. They've never refused anything by you –'

'I shall refuse to release it.'

'Why?' Esyllt sat opposite, her eyes searching every line and shadow in his face. 'You've been working on it for months!'

'I might just as well have been working in a factory, turning screws.'

'Oh, you're in one of those moods, are you?'

'No, I'm not!' Ieuan got up, exasperated, threw his empty matchbox into the waste-paper basket and fumbled on the mantelpiece for a full one. 'I am certainly not in one of my moods. I'm facing facts. Hard, bitter facts. Facing myself as I am. A writer who has been and is finished.'

'Dear God.' Esyllt's turn to sigh. 'How many times have I heard that lot during the last ten years? Will you have a cup of coffee?'

A pleasant thought.

'Don't bother, Esyllt. Bethan will be home in a minute and you'll be making tea. You might as well start now for that matter. Better for your health than sitting here trying to reason with me.'

Esyllt's large eyes, wondering what to say next.

'I don't like to see you in this humour,' she said.

'You should have got used to me by now. This is how I've been, this is how I am, and this how I always shall be. And I'm sorry. You ought to have married a banker or a farmer: a balanced, phlegmatic man with plenty of money –'

'Oh, stop it. Anyway, you weren't always like this. Years ago, after finishing a book, you seemed to be walking on air. You used to go straight to the piano and start singing at the top of your voice –'

'The happy days of yore . . .' Damn this pipe! A man smoked more matches than tobacco. What Esyllt had just said was mockingly true, although she never mocked him. But the memory hurt terribly. That euphoria that once filled him when a work was completed, all loose ends neatly knotted, a load of creation poured on to a heap of white paper, knowing that it was alive and fascinating and gripping although it would not please everyone. The euphoria that would never return.

'What's wrong with this novel then?' Esyllt still probing.

'It's stone dead.'

'How do you mean?'

Merciful heaven, it was bad enough having to face the catastrophe without having to explain it as well. He would try, however.

'Esyllt. Can you understand what I mean by sixty thousand dead words?'

'No. I can understand a dead man and a dead animal.'

'Listen.' Another match. 'I said a few minutes ago that I might as well have been working for months in a factory turning screws. Well . . . that's what I've been doing really. Screwing sixty thousand leaden words together. If Dr Lewis Edwards or Dr Owen Thomas in the last century had tried to write a novel, this is what it would have been like. Only the words themselves would have been heavier. A good novel ought to be . . . well . . . like a river, if you like, to-ing and fro-ing but sure where it's going, from the mountains to the sea – through heather and rushes, over gravel and stones, between rocks and meadows, but alive all the way. Sprouting suddenly, nimbly in the peat, widening and filling splendidly towards its estuary. And *alive*. That's the main thing. Alive! Dark threats in its depths, words dancing like sun-sparks on its surface . . . Oh, what's the use!'

Esyllt listening, painfully patient, to this analysis, gazing at this strange husband of hers driving his fingers through what remained of his hair.

'This novel's all right, Ieuan –'

'No, it's not!'

'It's you who are saying that.'

'The critics will be saying it. They've been saying it about everything I've written for the past five, six years. And enjoying it. I'm "under a cloud", "over the top", "haven't fulfilled my early promise" – and I'm not yet fifty!'

'Rubbish. What does it matter what they say? You had a lot of popularity too early – you've been saying that yourself – and there's no forgiveness in this world for anyone that's too popular. Not in Wales, certainly. Anyway, how many critics are there? And how many reviews? And who reads them? Not a quarter as many as read one of your books –'

'But what they're saying is important –'

'To whom?'

'Well, to me for one. We have better critics today than we've ever had. They know what's what. I have respect for their judgement –'

'Even if they make an Aunt Sally of you?'

'Well, they have to Aunt Sally someone. They can't praise everybody. They have to be kind to new writers to encourage them – "a brilliant new star" and so on – and they have to be kind to pensioner writers so as not to hurt them in their old age. So what target do they have other than a middle-aged scribbler? He's in the prime of life and ought to be healthy and thick-skinned enough to take a knock. I could die tomorrow, but they don't know it –'

'You mustn't say morbid things like that.' Esyllt rose impatiently and strode to the window. 'Where's that girl, I wonder? Late again. Window-shopping as usual, I suppose.'

Ieuan was sobered. So thoughtless of him to mention sudden death like that. They'd had several shocks during the past two or three years: a dozen or more of the boys who had been with him at college cut down unexpectedly in their forties: ministers of religion mainly. Esyllt was probably thinking of those. Now she turned to him anxiously.

'You're feeling quite well, aren't you?'

'Me?' said Ieuan. 'Oh, I never feel *well*. And I'm getting less "well" year after year. Unfortunately, that's no excuse for writing badly. Some of the world's greatest masterpieces were written in excruciating pain and indescribable agonies.'

'That's right.' Esyllt sat down again. 'You're going to talk now about Tolstoy and Solzhenitsyn and the like. I know you are. "I ought to have gone to the war." "I ought to go to prison." You can't think of anyone who wrote a masterpiece in the midst of a quiet, peaceful life, I suppose?'

'Well . . . I could . . .'

'Come on, then. Name a few, so I can learn.'

'Well . . . some of the women, of course: Jane Austen, George Eliot, the Brontë sisters; Balzac, Flaubert, Stendhal, Zola maybe, Dickens, Hardy, Melville . . . There were some.'

'Some? Quite a few, I'd say –'

'But mind you, nearly every one of them had their tribulations. An unhappy childhood –'

'Like yours.'

'Well . . . yes. Some worn down by a chronic affliction –'

'Like your tight chest.'

'*Touché* again. And of course, personal troubles: political harassment, soured love or an unhappy marriage, depression – very common, that –'

Esyllt looked almost triumphant.

'So the ability or inability to write is a matter of talent and temperament, not what sort of world an author is born into.'

Ieuan sank lower in his armchair.

'You'd like to write as well as Daniel Owen?'

'Any serious Welsh novelist would give his right ear to be able to write as well as Daniel Owen,' he replied morosely.

'Very interesting. A sickly and rather faint-hearted tailor who was acceptable enough to become a town councillor. That's how you described him once. Our greatest novelist, nevertheless. Are you saying now that he would have been an even greater novelist if his leg had been shot away like Robyn the Soldier's, or if he'd broken the law like Twm Nansi?'

'Not like Twm Nansi, woman!'

'Sorry. If he'd broken the law then. Full stop.'

'Wales and the Welsh language were not in so great a crisis then as they are now.'

'I suppose not. Talk about the crisis of Welsh, only yesterday Mrs Williams across the road was asking me when your next book will be out. Read all your books, she said. The occasional Welsh book is all she reads, and that only if it has a good story. That's why she's still able to write the occasional letter in Welsh. And still speaks Welsh to the children. Her eldest will be taking O levels this year and has to read . . . how many . . . half a dozen Welsh books? One of yours among them, anyway.'

'Her whole education ought to be through the medium of Welsh.'

'Of course. Like our Bethan's. Where *is* that girl? But taking the situation at its worst, as it is now – well, it could be worse still – I'm sure there are thousands of people like Mrs Williams all over the country. I've failed completely to persuade her that bilingual road signs and a Welsh TV channel are important, and she wouldn't dream of filling in a cheque or answering the phone in Welsh –'

'Servile through and through –'

'Yes, but where would we be without the likes of her – speaking Welsh and writing the occasional letter in it, the language flowing through her like live water through a dead pipe . . . ? There'd be frightfully few of us if it weren't for people like her. Mind you, I get hopping mad when I hear her say that she borrows your books from the library instead of buying them, when our livelihood as a family depends on the sale of your books among other things. But then I think, "Well, at least she does read the language, and reads your books, and if it's only that thin wire that keeps her and others connected to our culture, cutting that wire would be a calamity. Especially at the eleventh hour like this." You will publish that novel.'

'I've told you: it's too bad –'

'Even for Mrs Williams across the road?'

'Listen.' Ieuan squirming like a tied cat. 'I'm very grateful to Mrs Williams across the road for her kind interest. But there's no future for a literature written for Mrs Williams across the road or for the author that writes it.'

Esyllt shaking her head.

'Well, if that's how you feel today . . . Of course, it would be nice to write . . . what's the word – acceptably enough? – to be awarded an honorary DLitt. by the University –'

'Oh *no*!' Ieuan's right hand fanning wildly. 'We can forget any honour of that sort. Even if I could write "acceptably" enough, as you say, by the time I'm old enough – seventy or more – the University of Wales will be too English to award an honour for a contribution to literature in Welsh. Perhaps someone in the University of Illinois in a century or so will get a doctorate for a thesis on my work. They're rapidly running out of research topics in

the States already. They'll be glad of *anything* in the next century
– if the world survives that long.'

'Oh, dear Father.' Esyllt got up. 'You're right down today, I
see. Beyond comforting. You won't publish your book because
you're afraid of the critics, and you won't publish it for the
common reader, as you call her, even though you want to save
our language. Anyway –'

At that the front door opened and the clatter of satchel and
coat and hockey stick resounded in the hall.

'Heavens, she's come!' cried Esyllt, leaping towards the door.
'And she'll be shouting for her tea –'

'Mam! Is tea ready?'

'In a minute, dear . . .'

Bethan bounced into her father's study, lean, long-legged, her
striking blue eyes almost out of sight in a higgledy-piggledy mass
of hair.

'Hello, Dad! Writing?'

'Have been.'

'How did it go?'

'Rotten.'

'Tough luck.'

'What sort of day did you have in school?'

'Well, what do *you* think, *mon père*? French, physics, maths
. . . Who invented school?'

'As that happened several thousand years ago, I can't name
anyone in particular –'

'Was he – I'm sure it was a *he* – hanged or poisoned or had his
head chopped off . . . anything fascinating like that?'

'It's unlikely.'

'Pity.'

'Look, Bethan. We have to go through unpleasant schooldays
and do our best so that we can have something better when
they're over. I know, I remember, that school was pretty awful,
but –'

'It's a hundred times better today than it was in your time. All right, we'll skip the sermon. Well . . . today wasn't all bad, really.'

'Oh . . . I'm glad to hear it . . .'

'I had ten out of ten from Miss Hughes for my story.'

'Ten out of . . .? What story?'

'The one I wrote last night. Homework.'

'Good girl –!'

'Of course, the old cow had to ask if you'd helped me.'

'A teacher isn't an old cow, Bethan.'

'Oh, isn't she? Well, no, this one doesn't look as if she's ever had a bull –'

'Now, now –'

'Isn't there any sex in your books, Dad?'

The father managed an embarrassed cough.

'Er . . . can I see your story, Bethan?'

'Whatever for?'

'Just interested.'

'Oh, *patres curiosi sunt*! I'll have to hunt through all those books and me wanting my *tea* . . . !'

Nevertheless, she disappeared into the hall. Ieuan heard the prolonged tumult of bag-opening and throwing of book after book . . . Esyllt would be next to shout.

'Tea's ready, Bethan . . . Bethan! All this *mess*!'

'It's Dad. He wants to see some old story . . . !'

'Good grief! Taking a very new interest, isn't he?'

Unfair. Totally unfair. Bethan reappeared holding a red exercise book.

'Here you are, sir. Catch!'

And disappeared. Ieuan, of course, failed to catch the flying book and bent peevishly to pluck it from between his chair and the row of *Encyclopaedia Britannica*. He searched the pages for the story and finally found it.

'*St David's on Fire.*' An arresting title. Shapely handwriting, too, for one so young.

'The Vikings!' Gruffudd shouted at the top of his voice from the hilltop. 'The Vikings are coming!'

One by one the workers in the field raised their heads, and then began to run for their lives, they too shouting, 'The Vikings!'

Yes, indeed. A gripping start to a young story. And this one was beginning to grip Ieuan. This lad Gruffudd wondering how to get his blind father and his mother and younger sisters to safety before the enemy arrived.

Before running to the village, in order to calculate how much time he had, Gruffudd looked once again towards the sea. Already the long low ship under her square striped sail [too many adjectives, but promising] had touched the beach, the dragon's head at the prow as if preparing to blast the cathedral with smoke and fire. The soldiers were not going to waste any time. They were pouring from the ship, the first ones already climbing in a shimmering file up the slope, their big axes and shields and helmets aflame in the morning sun . . .

Well, the Vikings would more likely land and loot under the shades of night, not in broad daylight . . . kindling their own light as they fired the houses . . . But no matter. These, at least, were not leaden words. Ieuan read on like a child in the grip of an adventure story until he reached the very end, criticizing no more.

He closed the red exercise book as devoutly as his grandmother used to close her Bible. He got up slowly, the book still in his hand, and walked to the window. It was a fine evening: an exhilarating spring evening.

Unawares, and without trying, he had nurtured a writer of note. He had no doubts about it. This was not the first time such a thing had occurred. J. S. Bach was an immeasurably greater composer than his musical fathers. Bethan would be an immeasurably greater writer than her literary father. Perhaps she would be the one to write the 'Great Novel' the Welsh literary world had been going on about so long. Ieuan himself was writing quite well when he was thirteen, he knew, but by no means as well as this. The circumstances were different then, of course. For Bethan Welsh was the language of geography and history and biology and several other fields of knowledge, not an island subject as it had been for her father when he was at school. By writing it frequently day after day she had acquired a far greater vocabulary and a more flexible style than would a child of the same age in an English-medium school.

But perhaps Esyllt was right after all when she said that the ability or inability to write was a matter of talent and temperament, not what kind of world an author was born into. And Bethan had the talent, an apparently inexhaustible store of it. The discovery of it this evening had been a shock, an intoxicating astonishment. When she was older and had acquired further experiences – although she had had several already: the drunks she saw fighting one evening, that bloody accident on the street, those youths who had tried to drop a drug into her coke, her classmates of the same age who slept often with boys, so she said – but when she had gathered a heap of experience . . . From now on he would give her every help and encouragement; he would direct her reading and supervise her writing; he would open for her the treasure-houses of the classics –

'Bethan's had her tea.' Esyllt was back. 'We'll have a bite now. The girl's taking Mot for a walk before starting on her homework.'

'Oh . . . fine.' Everything was fine now. 'Bethan!'

She reappeared.

'Did you want something, Dad?'

'Yes.' The girl had changed from her school uniform into a fiery red top and long tight jeans which made her look even more dishevelled. But Ieuan saw the transformation otherwise. She was beautiful, genius incarnate, those blue eyes of hers penetrating the whole world.

'That story's good,' he said.

'What story?' Bethan's brow creased. 'Oh . . . that one . . .'

'I might as well tell you sooner than later. You can write. And there'll come a time when you'll give your whole life to writing, and write better, perhaps, than anyone who's ever written in Welsh before.'

The girl parted her hair to her ears and stared open-mouthed at her obviously disorientated father.

'Write! *Me*!'

'I'm absolutely certain you will.'

A cascade of laughter.

'But, Dad *bach*, there are more important things to do in life than *write*!'

Esyllt throwing a pitying, anxious glance at her husband.

'Well . . .' Ieuan felt the discussion slipping rather awkwardly. 'Perhaps I've told you rather too soon –'

'Dad. Can *I* give a sermon for a change?'

'Well?'

'Firstly. By the time I'll be the same age as you are now, not many people will be able to *read*. Everything will be in signs and symbols and figures, and everyone will have a little radar box on their chest to sense the thoughts of everyone else. There'll be no need even for language –'

'Wherever did you get those mad ideas –?'

'Secondly.' She was merciless. 'Even if people *were* able to read, d'you think *I*'ll be silly enough to shut myself in some dusty old study all day to scribble? And starve for my trouble? I'll do my best in school so that – as you're so fond of telling me – I'll have something better when I finish. But that something won't be writing, not likely. You and Mam haven't had new clothes for years, so you can buy clothes for me. Thank you very much. But *I* won't be so silly. I'll be going abroad for a month every year, not for one week to a caravan about once every two years like you –'

'Well, I worry that you don't have holidays like other children –'

'And I'm going to have a new car every year, not a rusty old crock like that thing that's been in the garage for ages. If there are people who earn tens of thousands a year in a college, in business, as doctors or in the BBC, I can do it as well.'

'But I thought the language was important to you too, Bethan –'

'Oh, I'll do everything I can to preserve The Language – while there's a need for language. I don't mind going to prison; that doesn't frighten me one bit. But I'm not going to starve myself writing and worrying myself sick for the rest of my life to save any language. I've finished. Any other business?'

Without waiting for a reply she whistled for Mot, and the hairy little brown creature raced from the kitchen and sat up panting on his haunches for her to hitch the lead to his collar. Before closing the front door she turned once again, slowly shaking her tousled head.

'Writing. Poor Dad!'

Ieuan and Esyllt heard her laughing all the way to the gate.

ALUN RICHARDS

The Former Miss Merthyr Tydfil

Nothing is more regrettable than the speeches we compose and never make.

'Art be buggered!' Ivy Scuse Lewis would have liked to have said. 'Art, painting, and his bloody gouaches, or whatever he called them. It could take a long walk off a short pier – and the St John's Wood mob who went with it.'

Half of them were queer anyway, she was convinced. Never mind the condescending looks they gave her once they had heard her speak.

'Oh, for a man who simply put his hand up your dress!' she might have said. Well, you knew where you were with plain lust. There was something wholesome about it, like brown bread.

But she said none of these things, smiled her professional, full-lipped, front-of-rostrum smile, and guiltily reflected instead. And more shame on her she thought, considering where she was from and everything.

The truth was that she felt herself threatened by Melville's painting, and also by the new people who had begun to call at their little flat in NW3 since his exhibition. The people were not of her world and defied her understanding. Half of them spoke to her as if she were the maid, she felt. *In service*, to use her mother's dreaded phrase. Them and their Pouilly Fuissé! They were English, of course, people he'd met on these courses of his, and at the gallery, but it wasn't a question of nationality, Ivy knew, it was the art-lark, prattle and paint, all excluding her and everything she stood for, meaning life, being yourself, having an identity of your own.

It was not that they didn't pay her compliments. One of them said she was beautiful. Said it straight out.

'Her dark Celtic good looks,' he emphasized knowledgeably through a mouthful of pâté, standing there against the stereo, six foot of skin and bone in aubergine corduroy, his touched-up, greying sideburns needing a nightly rinse by the look of them.

How could she say she'd turned down the chance of being Miss Merthyr Tydfil years ago? She wasn't from there, but she had her visitor's qualification through her aunt who worked in Hoover's. Then as now, she knew she was fancied and she'd kept her 38–38 at the operational ends, but it was such a wet thing to say, as if she wasn't a person in her own right at all. It seemed they had to pay tribute to her appearance, but that was where it ended. 'Open your legs and close your mouth!' she'd said to herself, her sense of humour always shocking in Melville's eyes. Not that he'd said a word, not so much as a wink coming from his taut little face. If the lights had fused, she wouldn't have been surprised to see them all holding hands in the dark. It was a problem, them, her, and Melville's newly acquired weekend gear, the Breton beret, fisherman's shirt, worn *espadrilles*, and the overall aroma of bare feet and Gauloises which marked the retirement of the primary-school teacher every Friday at 4 p.m. sharp.

But then again, this last she could have laughed at. It was a change from him sitting scowling over his marking. What was more disturbing, was the way he now had of looking through her with the pained expression of a man whose wife had become his burden. At thirty-six, she no longer understood what made him tick.

'Self, self – bloody self!' her mother would have said, in no doubt whatsoever, but then her mother was a tartar who'd remained back home in Aberdarren, ginning up on the corner stool of the bar they called the Two-Foot-Six, making occasional trips to London to see them, and one thing husband and wife continued to have in common, was a sense of relief when Ma returned home. They were always glad to see the back of her. About her ravaged face, outrageous wink and festooned hats was the ever-present whiff of a past that was best left buried. A war widow, she'd gone gay when the Black Yanks hit town; or so the story went. Gossip, riotous nights, slammed doors, vanishing lodgers, the weekly visit of the police court missionary, and a long-departed brother who'd done time, all formed the backdrop of Ivy's crowded memories. She was fond of saying that the street had brought her up. She'd had hearths other than her own to comfort her, and was shrewd enough to discount a good deal of what her mother said. If she'd had any ambition, it was to create in her own life, what had been so clearly lacking in her mother's: order, stability, and some fixity of purpose. It was why she'd married Melville, conscious always of the difference in their backgrounds and ever hopeful that things would be different.

But the melody lingered on, she thought bitterly. She lay now in her black apache outfit, white headband and skin-tight sleep suit on the G-plan divan which Melville had insisted on buying, an extravagance which they could ill afford at the time, but then, when they'd got married, Melville had been more houseproud than arty, and again, she had dutifully fallen in with his wishes. The fact was, she'd tried to be a good sort, and had exhausted herself in the attempt to find some kind of rapport with a man whose face was even more of a mask now than when she'd married him. By arrangement, they'd had no children, then when they'd changed their minds, they hadn't clicked, and the lengthy process of adoption had yielded nothing except Ivy's embarrassment at the social worker's inquiries, and now Melville's painting seemed to dwarf her and everything else.

If she swore at the art-lark, it was as at a rival. His canvases represented his escape from her. Nightly, he was making a world of his own in which she had no part, and the last straw was that he had now adopted a permanent pretence that she was incapable of understanding anything he said.

Their recent row was a clincher and only went to show. It wasn't only the art-lark, it was something else. Although they had lived in London for the ten years of their married life, Melville maintained the Welsh connection in traditional ways. He was a member of the Exiles' groups, attended St David's Day dinners, and frequently spent his Saturdays at the London Welsh rugby ground in whose clubhouse he was inclined to spend a beery Saturday night in the company of like-minded fellows. They frequently had a skinful and Melville would come home hoarse from singing, an aspect of his life that was quite different from his activities with the new people in the art-lark. As it happened, she did not mind a traditional Saturday night out in the least, even went with him on occasions. A man and his beer she could understand. She was no prude, but then again, it was not as simple as that since the very Welshness of the occasion tended to get up her nostrils. Melville spoke Welsh and she did not, and another sign of the times was the way even the London Welsh were quietly separating themselves up into groups so that she tended to be left out and often declined to accompany him as she had done recently. It was an absence she now regretted for it seemed that two worlds had collided when Melville met a prospective buyer who had enthused about his painting. Melville had received, as he said, a certain invitation, but she'd bridled at the very phrase.

'A certain invitation?' she said. What a way for a husband to speak to a wife! His speech was so careful, it might have been carefully thought-out evidence given before a magistrate.

'If you must know, it's Clayton-Hayes.'

'Who?'

'Spencer Clayton-Hayes. He's a millionaire. From Treorchy originally.'

That took her breath away.

'Oh?' she said. If there was one reassuring thing about money, it was that, unlike politics or religion, it contained the possibility of change.

'And he wants me to call up at his flat tomorrow night.'

'Tomorrow night's Christmas Eve.'

'That's why he's so anxious for me to call. He's looking for something to surprise his wife and was delighted he ran into me. He wants me to bring as many things as I have framed.'

'He's heard of you then?'

'He's seen some paintings at the Walter-Thomases.'

'What about Ma? She's coming tomorrow night.'

'I can't possibly meet her now. You'd better get a taxi.'

'On Christmas Eve?'

'You can order it here and go with it to the station.'

'What if the train's late?'

'Then it's late.' Melville's pale green eyes stared at her intensely, his round little face slightly flushed by his irritation. 'I should have thought you'd have been glad for me. If he buys my work, it will be quite a breakthrough. He's a collector, a man of taste and discrimination.'

She bit her lip. That went home.

'Look,' he repeated; 'don't you see? It's such a chance.'

She wouldn't have minded if she could somehow have accompanied him. What was wrong with a wife being an asset to a husband? A millionaire too. She had a vague feeling that money and sex went together. Why couldn't she be a help? She was short on one, but the other was lying fallow.

'Couldn't you fix another night?'

'It's out of the question. I can't dictate to him. Anyway, you'll have to meet your mother.'

They normally spent Christmas in Wales, sharing themselves out between her mother and his people, but this year her mother had expressed a wish to come to London and Melville wanted to use all his spare time for painting. The irony was that he'd completely changed his style since his exhibition. Now he painted Welsh industrial scenes exclusively and his little canvases were all expressions of some aspect of valley life. Pit wheels, ravaged coal tips, cameos of gaunt chapels and back-to-back houses now made neat little patterns whose colours somehow formed an idealized picture of a way of life that was gone. There was something immensely nostalgic about his work, however. It had a prettiness and charm and clearly evoked memories in which people still delighted. It was as if part of experience had been reduced and falsely crystallized into manageable proportions, and although she could not quite express it, Ivy was aware of a parallel with those glass baubles she'd seen as a child. When you shook them, they produced artificial snowstorms, snowflakes swirling down upon some miniature log cabin and showing a little world enclosed with all the properties of a cosy dream.

'I'm going to ask fifty pounds for the larger framed,' Melville said. 'All the Treorchy pieces.'

Ivy was respectfully silent. Money was money.

But that night, she found it difficult to get to sleep. Her anger at her rejection had given way to melancholy. It was not often that she succumbed to self-examination, but when she did, it was usually at these lonely hours of the night, and she had a dismal conviction that, all her life, she had been surrounded by lies. Sex was a lie, marriage was a lie, art was a lie. Living itself was nothing like it was cracked up to be. There came a time in your life when all you could do was look back and then images floated into your mind without rhyme or reason, all combining to make everything that ever happened to you seem disconnected and meaningless. At these hours of the night, there seemed to be an overshadowing greyness to her powers of recall which affected everything like a blight. Take her marriage . . .

Melville's parents, who were ironmongers in a small way, very chapel and self-contained, had raised the earth when they knew who she was. She remembered all the phrases, 'as common as dirt', 'no background to speak of', 'no education', and the most damning of all, 'worked in a factory'. She also 'went to no place of worship' and the very name of the street in which she lived filled them with horror.

Poor old bloody Ruby Street, she thought now. It was in the worst area of Aberdarren, over the tramlines near the canal. Originally, it had received its bad name from the immigrant Irish but the arrival of the Black Yanks had really clinched it. There was a famous incident when the local constable, Ikey Price, had been ordered by his inspector to investigate Number 33, which was suspected of being used as a brothel. Ikey was told to cover the back entrance in anticipation of a raid on the front. Unfortunately, he had climbed over the wall too soon, and upon taking up his station at the lavatory out the back, was at some pains to remain undetected. Fearing discovery, he had crouched down in the lavatory with his cape over his head. ('A very smart disguise in the blackout when you came to think of it!') But two Alabama Joes sauntered out and peed all over him, the inspector's master plot forcing him to be silent all the while. Mind, it was done unwittingly, but in the subsequent raid there were arrests made and Ruby Street was placed out of bounds to US Forces. The irony, as far as Ivy could remember from her mother's account, was that half the blackies were Methodist anyway, and flooded the Sunday schools with chewing-gum and goodies from the PX store. But the damage was done as far as Ruby Street was concerned, and Ikey Price, far from being the hero of the hour, told his story and became the laughing-stock of the district.

The Aberdarren wits came out like flowers after the rain:

'Turned out a bit damp again today, Ikey?'

What a thing to remember, Ivy thought. Her mind was like that. She had an uncanny facility for remembering incidents of that kind which made Melville's short body twist uneasily in his chair when she revealed 'the fur coat and no knickers' side of her nature.

'God bless America!' Ivy always ended up saying when relating the story. It was one up on the police, but Melville did not really share the joke, and at the time of their wedding his mother had actually hinted that she fill in a false address in the registrar's book! She'd been obliged to get married in Melville's chapel, and

the few pews which contained her side of the family were probably disinfected afterwards. The Scuse Lewises had taken care of
everything. He was, after all, their only boy and if ever there was
a case of the groom going to the slaughter, this was it, she
thought.

But that was from the outside. She belittled herself when she
thought of it like that, taking what you might call the street
view of things. The chapel was no different from the street in
that sense. Neither affected your insides or your deepest needs. It
was as if the outside world coated your real self and blanketed
your aspirations, coarsening them in the process. The fact was
she'd had a real sense of Melville's needs and, more than anything,
his need to escape from their cloying respectability and awful
concern for appearances.

He'd told her once that he was eleven before he was allowed to
tie his own shoelaces and the stories of his mother waiting up to
smell drink on his breath would have kept Ruby Street agog if
she'd ever related them. The Welsh Mams in Ivy's book should
have been turned over to the SS and given to the Gestapo for
training. They ate their own young by all she'd heard.

She herself was not that kind of Welsh, but of the earth,
earthy. In the old days, they'd talked about it, and although
they'd lived in London for years, the old ties were still there, and
recently Melville had started to drift back to Welsh haunts. She
had made new friends, learned hairdressing and mixed with everyone, but recently Melville's discovery of the Welsh streets in his
imagination had set his feet moving along ancient trails. There
was not a terrace or a pit shaft that escaped him now, it seemed,
and his best-known study, a group of lads playing dickstones
outside a blacksmith's shop with a haulier and blackened colliers
in attendance, had been bought by a famous London Welshman
who'd described it as 'indicative of the true spirit of our people'.
She'd been there when he said it, as had Melville's mother, but
what relation it had to anything Melville had ever known about,
Ivy could not imagine. If his mother had seen Melville even

talking to a collier in the old days she'd have phoned the police! But there it was, these memories which were now paying off a treat. Everybody was very complimentary, including his mother, whose attitude towards Ivy had softened over the years. Now she spoke of Ivy as one who'd overcome tremendous odds. You'd think she was from Biafra, not Ruby Street, but there, they were all alike in their incapacity to see things as they were.

In Ivy's view. As it was, she could understand the snobbery bit, not wanting your precious to *ychafi* himself, and she also understood their reserve about Ruby Street; but now in addition, there seemed to be this other harassment, the Welshy bit whose lot had miraculously found the guts to get bolshie according to the paper, some of them very nasty with it too. Educated people, mark you. But try as she would, she could only see it as a new madness. Nothing changed, it seemed. First the Revival, then the Band of Hope, now everything in bloody Welsh! Well, fortunately, she was far away now, except that Melville, after years of feathering his nest with the LCC, seemed to have turned the full circle and returned to what he had earlier rejected so conclusively.

'From over by there to by here,' Ivy thought; 'and getting bloody nowhere!' It was the definitive Ruby Street sentence, and having summed the matter up so succinctly, she promptly fell asleep.

But in the morning, there was a telegram which brought her quivering up to the bedroom where Melville had determined on a lie-in.

'It's from Ma. She can't come.'

Melville did not answer. Things had been strained lately and he was inclined to brood over what was said.

'She's broken a bone in her arm: club outing.'

'Oh dear . . . Is there someone looking after her?'

'The people next door, I 'spect. She says she'll phone. She sounds all right. Wishes us all the best.'

'Perhaps we can go down after Christmas?'

She knew he was avoiding what precisely concerned her. The

news meant that she was free to accompany him on his visit to the millionaire.

'Look, cock. You know very well what I'm on about. If you're going to see this fella . . .'

'No,' he said. He understood at once. He stretched out his hand and lit a Gauloise nervously, his round little face tense with the pain of having to tell her. 'It's not what you think,' he began, his concern obvious. 'It's just that, well, with luck, I'll catch him in the right mood.'

'Catch him?' she caught her breath.

'I want him to study my work in, well, silence.'

'What d'you think I'm going to do?'

'It's nothing to do with you,' he said gently by way of explanation.

'Oh, I bloody know that.'

'It's just him and the paintings.'

'Are you going to sit outside on the lav, or something?'

He frowned. He painted the streets but their directness had escaped him.

'It's selling, that's all.'

'Selling?'

'Yes. A certain mood has to be created.' He smiled, as if that were the end of the matter, picked up his reading glasses and put them on. Now the prospective headmaster seemed to look at her, pink-cheeked and reproving. 4C again, she thought; her mark.

She still stood awkwardly in the doorway.

'You won't say, will you?' she bit her lip.

'Look, he's an old man, and he's got memories.'

'Memories?'

'It would be better if there were just the two of us.'

'You sod!'

Now he was aware of the intensity of her feelings, she could see, but she did not wait for him to speak.

'I shan't say anything. Honest. What d'you think I'm going to do? – talk my head off? Well, do you? D'you think I'm going to tell him about Ikey Price or something?'

'He'd probably like that.'

'Well, then?'

'I'd rather you didn't.'

'I'd rather you didn't!' she minced, but while there was still a chance, she kept her cool. 'All right. Look . . . Supposing I was to drop in after? Say I was on my way from shopping?'

'At six-thirty at night?'

'I'll leave it until late, then we can go and have a meal?'

'We can have a meal anyway,' he smiled.

But she wasn't having that.

'You know what I mean, don't you?' It was very simple. She wanted to see the millionaire! And he knew.

'But he's a perfectly ordinary chap.'

'From Treorchy?'

'Originally.'

'Then what's wrong with me calling in on a perfectly ordinary chap from Treorchy originally?' she said breathlessly. 'After you've done your bit of business?'

He took off his reading glasses once more. His eyes were hard and uncompromising and she felt she knew his answer before he spoke.

'You won't say what you mean, will you? I'll let you down, that's it, isn't it?'

'Nonsense.'

'It's not nonsense. Every time we mixes with your sort of people, I can see you wincing. You insult people, you do. Just by looking at them. Me, I mean. Yes, you do.'

'Ivy . . .'

'Look at you, you can't even get out of bed to have a decent row, can you? All right, I'll tell you something else. I don't know why you married me, I don't. At all!'

With that, she flung herself out of the room. God, how she'd tried. Tried and tried. When he'd made no effort at all. From being a petty irritation, a squabble which she could handle in her own way, it now seemed to be much more, as if a match had been struck only to light up greater areas of unhappiness than ever she'd imagined.

In the other room, she heard him get out of bed and begin to dress. She knew that he would attempt an apology, but it made no difference. She'd answered her own question. She was sure that part of the reason why he'd married her was to get away from the dreadful clamminess of his upbringing, but the moment he'd done so and the initial pleasures of conquest had worn off, he'd begun to regret it, as if he too were searching for something and had not found it.

When he came into the room, his face was solemn and his tone of voice indicated that things had gone too far.

'I'm sorry, but it's not personal. It's nothing to do with you at all. It's just that I see this as a chance and I don't want anything to go wrong. That's all.'

She did not reply, kept her thoughts to herself once more and served him breakfast in tight-lipped silence through force of habit. She felt weak and exhausted suddenly. He made her think too much. She did not want to think. She just wanted to be liked. Couldn't he understand that?

Apparently not, but when the time came to leave, he still affected concern.

'I don't like to leave you like this.'

'Why don't you just go?'

'Ivy . . .' he put his hand on her arm.

'Leave me alone.'

'Look . . .'

'It's very common to say "look" all the time. I wonder where you picked that up from?'

'Please . . .'

'Oh, why don't you just go?' she said again.

'Not like this.'

'Listen,' she was already tiring of it and just wanted to be on her own. 'I've got the turkey to stuff.'

And that did it. He was out of the room, off on the art-lark, his suitcase of canvases under his arm like a rep with a foot in the door.

Men, she thought. But she couldn't generalize. It was the Scuse Lewises and their offspring. But the extent of her feeling in the bedroom had startled her. Was she right about her marriage? There were some doors that were frightening to open, but having opened them, you had to decide whether you wanted to follow your inclination and proceed further. So she hesitated. The curious thing was that, despite the intensity of her thoughts, she still felt there was something missing, a key to her understanding of her husband which still eluded her. Why was he like he was? Why did he behave in this way?

She poured herself a large bacardi and coke and put a Frank Sinatra on the stereo.

'Only the Lonely', the record sleeve said.

'You wouldn't bloody nob it!' Ivy said to herself. But it was not like her to sulk for long and she was recovering continuously. To tell the truth, she did not have the energy for a prolonged row. There had been tears in her eyes, and only one thing was certain. Once you got past thirty, you couldn't cry without your eyes giving you away. She felt she looked like the victim of the dentist's apprentice, and for no reason that she could think of, decided to get herself up, doing the best she could with her eye shadow and slipping into a sheath dress, her backless and breathless. She was thus dressed to kill when he returned.

'Well?' she asked. That mask of a face gave nothing away.

But his voice was choking.

'Nothing!' he put down the suitcase and came blunderingly into the room, and she saw his lips quiver as he blinked at her.

'How d'you mean?'

'Nothing,' he said again. 'I didn't sell a picture.'

'Was he in?' She didn't understand.

'Yes, I had difficulty getting to him, but he was in. He . . . he told me to lay out all my canvases on the floor.'

'*The floor?*' she said incredulously.

'Then,' Melville nodded and his face became enraged; 'then he put out all the lights and examined each picture with a pencil torch. It took him twenty minutes. He said he didn't like my brushwork. I didn't get a drink – anything. Not even a cup of tea.'

'But I thought it was practically certain?'

So did Melville. But it was not.

Normally, she would have comforted him with a remark or two, but she was not in the mood. She watched him sit opposite her and loosen his collar, his face still numbed as he stared in front of him.

'It's the end of something,' he said melodramatically.

Lor, what was she going to say? 'What did he look like?' she asked in a low voice.

'Small, bald and mean. But I don't want it mentioned,' he turned his eyes to her.

She shook her head, biting her lip to hide her smile.

'I mean, I don't want anyone to know. Especially your mother.'

She nodded again. She understood that. They sat in an uneasy silence. She had a little picture of the millionaire scrabbling over the floor with the pencil torch and thought it rather a scream, but she did not dwell on it. Evidently, she was required to say as little as possible, but the mention of her mother caused her mind to stray back to Ruby Street once more, and again, she had a vision of that other crouching figure, the suffering uniformed Ikey Price, his peeved face glowering beneath his dampened cape, and then she had a flash of intuition which went to the heart of the matter. The trouble with Melville was that he'd never been peed on before. All his life, he'd been protected in one way or another, all his expectations were ministered to, and despite his attempt at escape, there remained a niceness of conventions, the confident expectation of a style of life and a sameness of manners and language which surrounded him like a comforting mist. She had thought it especially Welsh, this conditioning, but t was merely a dressing and in any case did not affect her. Never been peed on, she thought again. That was it, the trouble with the lot of them, the art mob as well. Her intuition had divined a condition of life that existed irrespective of countries and national boundaries.

'A good job your mother's not coming,' Melville said.

She noticed that he was looking at her anxiously. She was not often silent and she had not stuffed the turkey.

'What have you got yourself done up for?'

She smiled and, for a moment smelt his fear. Whatever she was, she was all he had.

'Nothing,' she said and went presently into the kitchen and put on an apron in preparation for her chore. But for the goodness of her heart, it would have been a right Ruby Street Christmas, she thought: poached egg, flagon and a fag! But that was another dog-end she'd better keep behind her ear for after. As it was, without even seeing the man of mystery, she felt in an awed way that they had both received a salutary lesson in what it took to be a millionaire.

There was a movement behind her in the kitchen doorway and although conscious of Melville's eyes upon her, she did not turn around. Now her strong deft fingers began slowly and confidently to tear the innards out of the turkey.

LESLIE NORRIS

A House Divided

I'm glad I had my boyhood before the war, before the '39 war, that is. I'm glad I knew the world when it was innocent and golden and that I grew up in a tiny country whose borders had been trampled over so often that they had been meaningless for centuries. My home was in a mining town fast growing derelict, in Wales, and the invincible scrawny grass and scrubby birch trees were beginning to cover the industrial rubbish that lay in heaps about us.

It all seemed very beautiful to me, the small, tottering cottages in peeling rows on the hillside, the pyramids of black spoil that lay untidily above them, the rivers thick as velvet where the brown trout were beginning to appear again. But I read in a book that our river had once been famous for its salmon and that the last great silver fish had been caught there in 1880, and I knew that there had been a more complete perfection, a greener Eden.

Further west was such a green country, Carmarthenshire. When I was eleven years old, I was put on a bus for Carmarthen town, there to meet my aunt with whom I was to stay for a whole summer month, and it was then that I entered into my kingdom. My aunt met me at the coach station and we got into a smaller bus, full to its racks with people, parcels, chickens, bundles of newspapers, two sheep dogs. I had never seen grass so ablaze with emerald, nor a river so wide and jocund as the Towy. The bus was full of the quick Welsh language of which I didn't know a word, so I sat warily on the hard edge of my seat, observing from the rims and corners of my eyes. My aunt said nothing to me.

Groaning brokenly, the bus hauled up the hills north of the town, lurching to an occasional amiable halt in the centres of villages, outside the doors of simple inns, at deserted crossroads high on the moors. Through its hot, moving windows I saw small white farmhouses appear, one after the other, each at the heart of an aimless cluster of irregular fields. I knew I would sleep that night in such a house. I had never been away before, not even for one night. I looked at my silent and terrible aunt. She grinned suddenly, dug me ferociously in the ribs, and gave me a round, white peppermint. Comforted, I worked my tongue around the hot sweet. It was going to be all right.

We had reached the flat top of the mountain and the little bus throbbed doggedly along an uncompromisingly straight road. Then we began to drop, running through sweeping shallow bends that took us lower and lower into a valley of unbelievable lushness. As the nose of the bus turned this way and that, I caught glimpses of a superb river, rich and wide, its brilliant surface paler than the sky it reflected. My aunt and I got off at the river bridge. The stone parapets were built in little triangular bays. You could wait in them while traffic passed. My aunt and I did this, and I looked down into the water, relishing its music, its cold clarity dappled over stones.

We had perhaps half a mile to walk, the road turning from the river as it swung south, and then we took a farm track back in the direction of the water. We passed but one house all the time we walked and that was a small, one-storeyed cottage with a low door and three windows set in its front. An old woman sat straight-backed on a wooden settle outside the door. She was shelling peas, placing the pale green ovals as if they were pearls into a china basin held on her lap, letting the empty pods fall into a bucket. She didn't stop doing this all the time she was talking to my aunt. Her long dress, made of some hard material, had been worn and washed to a faded blue. At her throat was a gold brooch which said 'Mother'.

'That's Mrs Lewis,' said my aunt. 'A tough old bird, she is.'

I looked back at Mrs Lewis, upright and purposeful outside her front door in the evening sunlight.

'Is she very old then?' I asked.

'Not so old,' my aunt said. 'Over sixty though, I expect. She used to work the farm next to us until last year. Worked it on her own, she did. Now she lets it to her nephew, Emrys. You'll see him about – his farm is on the river side of this lane and ours down here, on the right.'

My case began to get heavy, so I hoisted it on to my shoulder.

Not long afterwards we turned off the lane and followed a little stream which took us to the house, where my uncle was waiting.

I can't remember what else happened that day, but the pattern of the following days is clear in my mind. Every morning I'd get up reasonably early, wash, and go downstairs to the kitchen. My uncle, a plump, voluble man, would begin talking as soon as he heard my foot on the stairs, and was already launched into some wild tale when I got into the room. He would be stretching up, on the tips of his small feet, to cut rashers from the side of bacon which hung from the beamed ceiling. The knife he used was large, black-handled, and sharp as fright. The bacon, pallid with fat, had two streaks of lean meat running meanly through it, and it swung about as he cut, but years of practice allowed my uncle to carve a slice as uniformly thin as if it had been done by machine. The frying-pan, and the kettle too for that matter, hung from hooks above the enormous fire. My uncle always cooked my breakfast. He would take three of the yellow rashers and place them gently in the iron pan, adding, when the fat had begun to run, a thick slice of bread. Then he'd crack an egg and put that in. It was delicious. The bacon, crisp and dry, broke beneath my knife; the bread, fried brown on the outside, was succulent and full as a sponge with warm fat. Every morning my uncle would put my plate before me with a mild pride. He never stopped talking to me. He stood in front of his fire, his thumbs in his pockets, rocking gently forward and backward on his tiny feet; his eyes opening wide when he reached the climax of some innocent tale. When I'd finished my food he would go off to the fields, there to work with furious, haphazard energy. He had always finished, apart from the evening milking, by early afternoon.

Sometimes I worked with him and he liked this. But more often I would wander away on some inconclusive ploy of my own. Once I tracked the source of the little stream which supplied all our water at the farm, and which had never run dry, they said, even in the hottest summers. It started less than a mile away, in the foothills, a small, round pool filled by three bubbling heads of water. I stayed almost a whole morning, lying on the grass, watching the water burst through a fine white sand, grains of which were carried up and away in an erratic dance. After a time I began to see that there was a kind of regularity in the way the springs gushed up, a kind of pattern. I told my uncle about the springs. He had never been there, but my aunt said she went once a year to clear it of leaves. There were no trees near it. I think she used to go there just to see the sand dancing.

By this time I'd met Emrys Hughes, Mrs Lewis's nephew and our neighbour, so I thought I was entitled to walk over his land, too. The first time I did this I saw Emrys standing beside his dairy. I waved to him, but he didn't wave back. He stood there a moment as if confused, then he turned and dived out of sight. I told my aunt and uncle about this.

'Oh, he's very shy, is Emrys,' my uncle said. 'You needn't worry about that. He don't mind you being on his land, not at all. He'd *like* you to go over.'

My aunt sniffed gently.

'Emrys is very nice,' she said, 'very helpful.'

She thought deeply and then gave her judgement.

'Yes, very nice,' she said delicately, 'but not quite the round penny, if you know what I mean.'

I thought of Emrys, of his long awkward body and innocent, gentle face, of his habit of ducking his head at meaningless moments. I could see what she meant.

'Oh, he's all right,' said my uncle stoutly. 'He's his father all over again, and old Dafydd Hughes never did a mite of harm to anybody.'

So I continued to walk through Emrys's fields and after a while he waved back at me and even spoke to me. He had very little English and our conversation was simple and limited. Mostly we'd stand and beam at each other. His wife was more talkative altogether, and I got into the habit of calling at their house about mid-morning. We used to drink tea, the three of us, out of large Victorian cups, and eat a great many of the round flat cakes full of currants that were baked on a thick iron plate directly above the open fire. I used to read the local paper to Emrys and his wife. It didn't occur to me until much later that they couldn't read. They were both about twenty-three when first I went to stay with my aunt.

Emrys's farm had one great advantage over ours; it was bordered on the west by the miraculous river. What I liked to do was to have my breakfast, do a few jobs about the farm, and then go over to Emrys's. I'd read to them, or we'd hold one of our slow, repetitive conversations, and then, very gently and by a roundabout route so that I would enjoy the going, I'd go down to the river. But, one morning I awoke particularly early, startling my uncle, who was alone in the kitchen, singing and cooking his own breakfast.

'Good God, boy!' he said. 'What's the matter? Can't you sleep?'

We had our food together and I went straight out into the early world. I had never known that such pure light existed and I was suddenly and overwhelmingly filled with a wish to see the river. I ran through Emrys's fields towards the water, and even some distance off I could see the man on the far bank, staggering slightly and hauling away at his fishing rod. When I arrived at the bank, gasping, I could see he'd got into something big, his rod bent in a deep arc from the butt, held in his gripping hands, to the tip which was only inches above the water. I couldn't see the line, even when he heaved sturdily back before winding in. He was not a young man and he wore a clergyman's collar.

'I wish you were over here,' he called. 'I've been half an hour with this one, and I could do with some help.'

I ran for the bridge, over it, and down the other bank, splashing through stony shallows most of the way. But it took me seven or eight minutes and by the time I'd got down to the old boy he'd landed his fish. I'd never seen anything so enormous, nor so beautiful. I spoke for some time to the old man, but apart from the fact that he was on a fishing holiday and that he lived in the Midlands, I can remember nothing of him. I can remember everything about the salmon. I could take you now, at this moment, to the place where I first saw him lying hugely in the grass, his great head up against a clump of dock. I know the gradations of his colour, the position of his every scale. A trickle of blood came over his lower jaw.

'A fresh-run fish,' the old man said.

I didn't know what he meant, but I knew that I soon would. I went home in a daze. I was caught, all right.

It was easier than I had imagined. Both my uncle and aunt thought it entirely natural that I should want to catch salmon.

'Where's that old rod of mine, Marged?' asked my uncle. 'The boy can begin with that. I'll get him a licence when I call into town. Don't forget, boy, the river is dangerous, you'll have to learn it like a book. And have a word with Emrys – he's a marvel with fish, is Emrys.'

He was, too. Boys learn a great deal by imitation, and I learned by imitating Emrys. He knew where every salmon in the river was to be found; he could point out places where legendary fish of the past had been caught by his father or his uncle. I was killing biggish fish right from the beginning, most of them with an old two-piece greenheart that Emrys had used when he was a boy. He had a box full of tied flies, lures of an entirely local pattern that I've never seen anywhere else, although I've caught fish all over the world since. I still have them, the old greenheart and Emrys's box of flies. I've not used either of them since 1948, when I bought the first of my split-cane rods. When my month was up I didn't want to go home.

My uncle jollied me along.

'Time you went,' he said. 'The boys in the Cerys Arms are complaining that there won't be a fish in the river unless we send you home soon.'

He loaded me with gifts, shook hands as if we had been friends for fifty years, and told me to come back at Easter.

'March,' he said. 'That's when the season begins. We'll be waiting for you.'

So year after year I spent my springs and summers in that fertile and timeless place. I'd go into town the day after my arrival. I'd go into Mr Protheroe's shop and buy my river licence. Mr Protheroe would tell me what fish had been caught already and I'd inspect his new stock of tackle. Then it was off to the water. Although Emrys came with me less often than on my early visits, we always had at least five or six long days together. We did some night-fishing, too, after sea trout. The river was unbelievably busy then, its noises louder and more mysterious than in secure daylight, its cool air hawked by bats and soft-flying owls.

The summer of '39 was long and hot, and the river had fallen sadly below fishing level. One Sunday morning Emrys and I were out on the water, fishing for memories mostly. We sat on the bank, throwing a line now and then over runs where we'd caught good fish in other years. The water was warm and stale, and we knew it was no good hoping for anything. The little salmon parr, little fingerlings, sidled lazily in the shallows. We saw my uncle come slowly through the fields, head bowed under the sun.

'Daro!' said Emrys. 'It must be hot to make your uncle walk slow like that.'

But it wasn't the heat. He had come to tell us that war had been declared. We didn't say much about it. We walked back to the house and I packed my case and tackle, mounted the old Rudge Whitworth motorcycle I owned at the time, and rode home. I knew that the world of summer fishing had come to an end. It was time for me to go elsewhere. Within a year I was in the army.

My uncle wrote to me once a fortnight, on Sundays. His careful letters, the narrow, upright script, kept me informed of all his artless news. I learned that old Mrs Lewis had suffered a stroke and was bedridden, that Emrys and his wife had left the farm to live with her. The local lawyer, Lemuel Evans, had found a tenant for the farm until such time as Emrys could return.

Later, Emrys was called up. I couldn't imagine him in the army. He was thirty years old then, and more naïve than most children. In the intervals of keeping myself out of the more senseless military activities, I sometimes thought of Emrys. I needn't have worried. Unable to read, his English an almost unintelligible dialect, he was of little value to the army. He was sent home after serving for three months.

In the spring of 1944 I had some embarkation leave and I spent a week of it at the farm. There was nobody at home when I arrived – it was market day at Cardigan – but the door was never locked in that house. I went inside, dumped my case, got my rod out, and tackled up. I thought I could get half an hour in before my aunt and uncle returned, and I walked through the familiar fields of what had been Emrys's farm, savouring every moment. When I got to the water I unhooked my fly from the cork butt and got some line out ready to cast. The water looked right, a lot of it and a beautiful clear brown, the colour of the peat bogs it came from. I gave my rod a flick or two, just to clear my wrist, then threw a long cast across the pool. Someone shouted behind me, but I took my time, keeping the line nice and tight until I was ready to reel in. Then I looked around.

He was a thickset man, dark and hard, in his late thirties. I smiled at him.

'What do you think you're doing?' he said.

I told him who I was.

'I know who you are,' he said. 'You have no more right to fish my water than anyone else.'

I explained that both Emrys and Mrs Lewis had always allowed me to fish there, but I could see it was useless. I didn't want trouble and he looked strong enough for caution. Holding my rod above my head, I walked out of his farmyard and up the lane. I thought of calling at Mrs Lewis's cottage to complain to her or to Emrys, but there was a little car outside the door when I reached the house, so I walked on. I crossed the bridge over the river, climbed the stile, and moved down the opposite bank. I could see my uncle's surly neighbour standing where I'd left him. I stood with the width of the river between us, and cast in. I've never been a stylish angler; effective, perhaps, but never stylish. But that cast was perfect. I put the fly down as effortlessly as it could be done, the line unrolling smoothly forward on the unblemished surface, the lure falling as naturally as thistledown. It was taken at once, as I knew it would be, and I landed the fish after fifteen minutes. It was the biggest fish I'd ever caught and I still haven't equalled it. Just over eighteen pounds it went, and I cast for it, hooked it, and landed it under the furious, silent gaze of the man on the other side of the river. It was very satisfying. After I'd pulled it out I went lower down and caught two more, both over twelve pounds. I wasn't out more than a couple of hours altogether, and then I waded across downstream, just above an old woollen mill where Emrys and I sometimes fished, and walked back across the fields to my uncle's house. After supper I told my people about their neighbour's boorish behaviour.

'We don't have much to do with him,' said my uncle.

He looked uncomfortable and ashamed.

'He's not a nice man, do you see,' my aunt said, 'not like poor Emrys.'

I could see they didn't want to talk about him, so I said no more. Emrys and his wife came in shortly after. They were pleased and excited. We had a merry evening, but Emrys would say nothing about his three months in the army, however closely I pressed him.

'I didn't like it there,' he said. 'It was terrible in the army.'

'Lemuel Evans came to see the aunt today,' said Mrs Hughes. 'She signed the will. Left everything to Emrys she has, the cottage, the farm, everything. Mr Evans read it out to us, then the aunt signed the will, two copies, then Emrys and me.'

'Why should you sign it?' asked my uncle.

'We are the witnesses,' said Mrs Hughes. 'Emrys has always been able to sign his name, although he's no scholar, of course.'

'Stands to reason I'd have to sign it,' said Emrys. 'All the money comes to me, doesn't it?'

'I'm very glad,' my aunt said. 'Let's hope that Mrs Lewis has many years of happy life in front of her and that when her time comes nothing goes wrong to spoil what is to come to you. You've been very good to her, the two of you.'

When they'd gone I spoke to my uncle about the will. I thought it unlikely that beneficiaries could witness a will they would eventually gain from.

'Say nothing,' said my uncle cautiously. 'Don't get involved in it. We are no match for the lawyers.'

I looked at him and saw with compassion that he had grown old. His talk, that bubbling mixture of innocent wild tales, chuckles, exclamations of surprise and delight, now held long silences also. Sometimes I caught him with a strange look in his eyes, as if he were measuring long distances. He died when I was abroad and my aunt lived only a few years after him.

After the war I didn't go back there. There seemed no reason for it, although I often went down into Pembrokeshire. Last month, though, I took the mid-Wales route and found myself again on that old river bridge. I left the car at the head of the lane and walked down. It seemed unchanged, but Mrs Lewis's cottage was empty and unkempt, its windows covered by an untidy lace of cobwebs and fine dirt. I started to go on to the farm, but couldn't face it now that my people were dead and strangers lived there. I pushed my way through hawthorn and nettle into Mrs Lewis's garden. The apple trees, mossed to the twigs, were covered with the hard red apples I remembered so well. There were greenfinches in the hedge, marvellous birds. I walked around the cottage, remembering. The roof looked sound and dry, the walls sturdy. You can often buy such a cottage for surprisingly little. I could use it for weekends and fish these waters again.

I drove back into town and went into Mr Protheroe's shop, walking into the back room as I'd always done. He was sitting there, white haired and frail, but quite recognizably the man who had sold me so many bits and pieces of my youth. He had a box of flies in front of him. Mallard and claret they were, beautiful flies. I bought a dozen and then I told him who I was. It was heartwarming to be remembered.

'Come down for some fishing?' he asked.

I told him that my interest was rather different, that I had seen old Mrs Lewis's cottage and thought of buying it. He was pleased.

'You ought to come back,' he said. 'There have always been members of your family hereabouts. I went to school with your uncles.'

'We haven't been here for twenty-five years,' I said.

'That's not long when we're talking of families,' he said. 'Old Mrs Lewis's cottage now. It could look very nice with a bit of paint here and there and a good clean-up. Nobody's lived there since she died, or a few months after. Lemuel Evans is the man for you to see. His office is just up the street, next to the Post Office.'

'I expect Emrys Hughes went back to the farm,' I said.

'Well, no,' said old Protheroe. 'There was a big shock over that. When Mrs Lewis died and the will was proved, it turned out that she'd left every mortal thing to Lemuel Evans. The farm, the cottage, every mortal thing. There was a lot of talk, of course.'

He looked out of his window at the orderly garden.

'Nobody could prove anything,' he said.

'What happened to Emrys?' I asked.

'He took it hard,' said Mr Protheroe. 'He let it get on top of him, and he never was, as you know, a man quick to understanding. I see him from time to time, but he's not good for much now. No, not for much. Talks to himself and so on.'

'Not a very nice story,' I said.

'Nothing in this world is perfect,' said the old man. 'Don't let it bother you. Go up now and have a word with Lemuel Evans. Tell him I sent you and let him know who you are.'

I went up to Lemuel Evans's office and was shown into a dirty room, the lower half of its windows covered by screens of rusty gauze the colour of liver. There was dust everywhere. A few box files, sagging and empty, stood on a shelf. Evans was there, a tall old man so dry and sapless he seemed made of tinder. A great plume of white hair swept off his forehead. I asked him about the cottage.

He nodded slowly.

'It's a nice little property,' he said. His voice was astonishingly vigorous. 'A pleasant situation, and very sound. How much would you be thinking of paying for it?'

I told him that there was a lot to be done to the house before anyone could think of living in it and I offered him a silly amount, really silly.

His answer surprised me.

'It will certainly need some renovation,' he said, 'and it will only deteriorate if left empty. I think we can do business at the figure you mention.'

I said I'd think about it and let him know. I couldn't get poor Emrys out of my mind. I thought I might buy the cottage and give it back to Emrys; I thought I ought to ask Evans outright why he had cheated my old friend. I realized I was shaking with anger. I walked out, Lemuel Evans following me to the door.

I went back down the hill towards Protheroe's shop. He was standing outside, waiting for me.

'You won't be buying the house,' he said.

'No,' I said.

'You aren't the first,' he said. 'No, not the first, by a long way.'

I didn't say anything. I was suddenly indifferent to everything.

'Come inside and have some tea,' old Protheroe said.

'I haven't time now,' I said.

I got in the car and drove away. It began to rain as I crossed the river bridge and by the time I'd climbed the hill a persistent soft rain drove in at me. I stopped the car and looked back. The town was hidden by falling rain, its roofs, its bridge, the little outlying cottages, but to the south, the way I was going, the river shone in its valley like an enormous snail track.

DANNIE ABSE

Sorry, Miss Crouch

Whenever my father tucked the violin under his chin and dragged the wavering bow across the strings, his whole countenance would alter. Often with eyes half closed like a lover's, he would lean towards me and play Kreisler's 'Humoresque' with incompetent daring. He was an untutored violinist who, losing patience with himself, would whistle the most difficult bits. I always liked to hear him play the wrong notes and whistle the right ones; and, best of all, I liked his response to my huge, small applause: he would solemnly and elaborately bow. After this surprising theatrical grace he would generally give me an encore.

That August evening he gave me two encores: 'Men of Harlech', and 'Ash Grove'. Afterwards he said, 'You'll be ten next month – wouldn't you like music lessons?'

I was being offered a birthday present. Psss. I wanted a three-spring cricket bat, like the one M. J. Turnbull, the captain of Glamorgan, used; not music lessons. I didn't want to play a violin.

'The piano,' my father said. 'We have a first-class piano in the front room and nobody in the house uses it. Duw, it's like having a Rolls-Royce without an engine. Useless. If your mother wants something for decoration she can have an aspidistra.' He replaced his violin in its case. 'Yes,' he continued. 'You can have lessons. You'd like that, wouldn't you, son?'

'No, don't want any,' I said firmly.

'All right,' he said, 'we'll arrange for Miss Crouch to come and give you piano lessons every Thursday.'

When my mother told me I could have a cricket bat as well, I was somewhat mollified. Besides, secretly I was hoping Miss Crouch would look like a film star. Alas, several Thursdays later I discovered I disliked piano lessons intensely and mild, thin, tut-tutting Miss Crouch did not resemble Myrna Loy or Kay Francis. The summer was almost over and on those long Thursday evenings I wanted to be out and about playing cricket with my friends in the park. So, soon, when Miss Crouch was at the front door, her pianist's hand on the bell, I was doing a swift bunk at the back, my right, cunning cricket hand grasping the top of the wall that separated our garden from the back lane. My running footsteps followed me all the way to Waterloo Gardens with its minnow-smelly brook and the pointless shouts of other children in the cool suggestions of a September evening. In the summer-house my penknife wrote my first poem – I expect it's still there – 'MISS CROUCH IS A SLOUCH'.

My father was uncharacteristically stern about me ditching Miss Crouch. For days he grumbled about my lack of politeness, insensitivity and musical ignorance. 'He's only ten,' my mother defended me. On Sunday, he was so accusatory and touchy that when all the family decided to motor to the seaside I said cleverly, 'Can't come, I have to practise for Miss Crouch on the bloomin' piano.' They laughed, I didn't know why. And now even more annoyed, I resolutely refused to go to Ogmore-by-Sea.

'We'll go to Penarth,' my father said, a little more conciliatory. 'I'll fish from the pier for a change.'

'Got to practise scales,' I said, pushing my luck.

'Right,' my father suddenly snapped. 'The rest of you get ready, that boy's spoilt,' he told my two elder brothers and sister.

My mother, of course, would not hear of them leaving me, the baby of the family, at home on my own. However, I was stubborn and now my father was adamant. Unwilling, my mother, at last, planted a wet kiss on my sulky cheeks and the front door banged with goodbyes and 'We won't be long.' Incredible – hard to believe such malpractice – but they actually took me at my word, left me there in the empty front room, sitting miserably on the piano stool. 'What a rotten lot!' I said out loud and brought my two clenched fists on to the piano keys to make the loudest noise the piano, so far, had ever managed to emit. It seemed minutes before the vibrations fell away, descended, crumbled, into the silence that gathered around the tick of the front-room clock. Then, as I stood up from the piano stool, the front door bell rang and cheerfully I thought, 'They've come back for me. This time I'll let them persuade me to go to Penarth.' I'd settle for special ice-cream, a banana split or a peach melba. Maybe I'd go the whole hog and suggest a knickerbocker glory. Why not? It hadn't been *my* idea to learn the piano as a birthday present. Not only that, *they* had abandoned me, and in their ten minutes of indecision I could have *died*. I could have been *electrocuted* by a faulty plug. I could have fallen down the stairs and broken *both my legs*. It would have served them right.

I opened the front door to see my tall second cousin. Or was Adam Shepherd my third cousin? Anyway, we were related because he called my mother Auntie Katie and he, in turn, was criticized with a gusto only reserved for relatives. Father had indicated he was the best-looking member of the Shepherd family (excluding my mother, of course), and he was girl-mad. 'Girl-mad,' my mother would echo him. 'He needs bromides.'

Standing there, though, he looked pleasantly sane. And, suddenly, I needed to swallow. I would have cried except big boys don't cry. 'What's the matter?' he asked, coming into the hall, breathing in its sweet biscuity smell. I told him about Miss Crouch and my birthday, about piano scales and how I had scaled the wall, about them leaving me behind, the rotters.

'Get your swimming stuff,' Adam interrupted me. 'We'll go for a swim in Cold Knap, it'll be my birthday present to you.'

'Can we go to Ogmore, Adam?' I asked.

Less than a half-hour later in Adam Shepherd's second-hand bull-nosed Morris we had chugged out of Ely and now were in the open country. Adam was really nice for a grown-up. (He was twenty-one.)

'Why do girls drive you crazy?' I asked him.

It was getting late but people were reluctant to leave the beach. There was going to be one of those spectacular Ogmore sunsets. Adam and I had dressed after our swim and we walked to the edge of the sea. There must still have been a hundred people behind us, spread out like a sparse carnival on the rocks and sand. We were standing close to the small waves collapsing at our feet when suddenly a man began singing a hymn in Welsh. Soon a group around him joined in. Now those on the other side of the beach also began to sing. Everybody on the beach, strangers to each other, all sang *together*. When the man who had begun singing sang on his own, the hymn sounded sad. Not now. The music was thrilling and I wished I could play the piano – if only one could play without having to practise.

Adam kept telling me that those on the beach were behaving uncharacteristically. 'Like stage Welshmen,' he said. 'This is like a pathetic English B film. It's as if they've been rehearsed.' But then Adam himself joined in the hymn. In no time at all, somehow, he was next to a pretty girl who was singing like billyo. I had noticed how he'd been glancing at that particular girl even before we went swimming.

'You look like a music teacher,' he said to the girl and he winked at me. Consulting me, he continued, 'She doesn't look like Miss Crouch, I bet?'

'Miss Crouch, who's she?' the girl asked.

Their conversation was daft. I gave up listening and threw pebbles into the waves. I thought about what Adam said – about the singing, like a film. I had been to the cinema many times. I'd seen Al Jolson. And between films, when the organ suddenly rose triumphantly from the pit, it changed its colours just like the sky was slowly doing now – the Odeon sky. Amber, pink, green, mauve. My mother had a yellow chiffon scarf, a very yellow scarf, and she sometimes wore with it an amber necklace from Poland. I don't know why I thought of that. I thought of them anyway, my parents, and soon they would be returning to Penarth. It was getting late. I went back to Adam and to the girl whom he now called Sheila. 'I'm hungry, Adam,' I said. 'We ought to go home.'

Adam gave me money to buy ice-cream and crisps so I left them on the beach and I climbed up on the worn turf between the ferns and an elephant-grey wall. At the top, on the other side of the road, all round Hardee's Café, sheep were pulling audibly at the turf. One lifted its head momentarily and stared at me. I stared it out.

I took the ice-cream and crisps and sat on a green wooden bench conveniently placed outside the café. Down, far below, the sea was all dazzle, black and gold. Nearer, on the road, the cars, beginning to leave Ogmore now, had their side lamps on. Fords, Austin Sevens, Morris Cowleys, Wolseleys, Rovers, Alvises, Rileys, even a Fiat. I was very good at recognizing cars. Then I remembered my parents and felt uneasy. If they returned from Penarth and found me missing, after a while they'd become cross. I'd make it up to them. I'd practise on the piano. I'd tell them about the singing at Ogmore. They'd be interested in that. 'Everybody sang like in a film, honest.'

When I returned to the beach the darkness was coming out of the sea. All the people had quit except Adam and Sheila. It seemed she had lost something because Adam was looking for it in her blouse. They did not seem pleased to see me. Unwillingly they stood up and, for a moment, gazed towards the horizon. A lighthouse explosion became glitteringly visible before being swiftly deleted. It sent no long message to any ship, but another lighthouse, further out at sea, in the distance, nearer the Somerset coast, brightly and briefly replied.

'They'll be worried 'bout me,' I said to Adam.

'They'll be worried about him at home,' Adam told Sheila. She nodded and took Adam's hand. Then my big cousin said in a very odd, gentle voice, 'You go to the car. We'll follow you shortly.'

So I left them and when I looked back it was like the end of a film for they were kissing and any second now the words THE END would appear. I waited inside the car for *hours*. Adam was awful. Earlier he had been nice, driven me to Ogmore, swum with me, messed around, played word games. Ice-cream. Crisps. It was the girl, I thought. Because of the girl he had gone mad again, temporarily. When he did eventually turn up at the car, on his own, pulling at his tie, he never even said, 'Sorry'!

Returning to Cardiff from Ogmore usually was like being part of a convoy. There'd be so many cars going down the A48. And we'd sing in our car – 'Stormy Weather' or 'Mad About the Boy' or 'Can't Give You Anything But Love, Baby'. But it was late and there were hardly any cars at all. Adam didn't even hum. He seemed anxious. 'Your father and mother will bawl me out for keeping you up so late,' he said.

Yes, it was *years* after my bedtime. If I hadn't been such a big boy I would have had trouble keeping my eyes open.

'We'll have to tell them we've been to Ogmore,' said Adam gloomily. 'We'll have to say the car broke down, OK?'

Near Cowbridge, we overtook a car where someone with a hat pulled down to his ears was sitting in the dickey. We followed its red rear light for a mile or two before passing it. Then we followed our own headlights into the darkness. There was only the sound of the tyres and the insects clicking against the fast windscreen.

Adam wished we were on the phone. So did I. Keith Thomas, my friend, was on the phone. So were Uncle Max and Uncle Joe, but they were doctors. You needed a phone if you were a doctor. People had to ring up and say, 'I'm ill, doctor, I've got measles.' I wished we had a phone rather than a piano.

'Have you a good span?' I asked Adam.

'Mmmm?'

'To play an octave?'

At last we arrived in Cardiff, into its mood of emptiness and Sunday night. Shops dark, cinemas and pubs all closed. At

Newport Road we caught up with a late tram, a number 2A, which with its few passengers was bound for the terminus. Blue-white lights sparked from its pulley on the overhead wires. After overtaking it we turned left at the White Wall and passed St Margaret's Church and its graveyard where sometimes Keith Thomas and I would play hide-and-seek.

'Albany Road,' I said.

'Right,' said Adam. 'Don't worry. Don't say too much. I'll come in and explain about us having a puncture.'

'What puncture, Adam?' I asked.

He parked the car, peered at his wristwatch under the poor lamplight. 'Christ, it's twenty to eleven,' he groaned. He needn't worry, I thought. When I told them that from now on I'd practise properly they would let us off with a warning.

When Adam rang the bell the electric quickly went on in the hall to make transparent the coloured glass of the lead lights in the front door. Then the door opened and I saw my mother's face . . . *drastic*. At once she grabbed me to her as if I were about to fall down. 'My poor boy,' she half sobbed.

In our living-room she explained how worried they had all been. They made an especial point of returning early from Penarth and I had . . . 'Gone . . . *gone*,' said my mother melodramatically. Later it seemed they had all searched for me in the streets, the back lanes, the park, and she had even called at Keith Thomas's house to see if I was there.

'You didn't have to run off just because you don't like piano lessons,' my mother said, scolding us.

'I don't like piano lessons,' I said, 'but –'

'He didn't run off,' Adam said, interrupting me. 'We had a puncture, Auntie.'

When my mother told Adam that, as a last resort, they had all gone to the police station, and that's where the others were now, Adam became curiously emotional. He even made an exit from our living-room backwards. 'Gotter get back,' he muttered, 'I'm sorry, Aunt Katie.' Poor Adam, girl-mad.

Before I went to bed my mother gave me bananas and cream and she mashed up the bananas for me like she used to – as if I were a kid again.

'I'll speak to your father about the piano when he comes in,' my mother said masterfully. 'Whatever he says, no more piano lessons for you. So don't fret. No need to run away again.'

I was in bed and asleep before the family returned from the police station. And over breakfast my father, at first, didn't say anything – not until he had drunk his second cup of tea. Then he declared authoritatively, 'I'm not wasting any more good money on any damn music lessons for you. As for the damn piano, it can be sold.' My father said this looking at my mother with rage as if she might contradict him. 'If this dunce, by 'ere,' he continued, 'can't learn the piano from a nice lady, a capable musician like Miss Crouch, well not even Solomon could teach him.'

My mother laughed mockingly. 'Ha ha ha, Solomon! Solomon was wise but he never played the piano. Ha ha ha, Solomon indeed, ha ha ha. Your father, I don't know.'

'Why are you closing your eyes?' I asked my father.

It was time to go to school. I had to kiss Dad on the cheek. As usual, he smelt of tobacco and his chin was sandpaper rough. But he ruffled my hair, signifying that we were friends once more.

'I hate Mondays,' I said.

'Washing day. I loathe them too,' said my mother.

Miss Crouch never came to our house again. And it was almost a week before Dad took down his violin and played 'Humoresque'. I didn't listen properly. I was waiting for him to finish so that I could ask him if, after we had sold the piano, we could have a telephone installed instead – like they had in Keith Thomas's house.

HARRI PRITCHARD JONES

Fool's Paradise

(TRANSLATED BY THE AUTHOR)

'What the bloody hell's wrong with the old bastard: staring like that? I done nothing wrong.' The cop was still hanging about the entrance to the store when she went out, past him, trying to look sure of herself. But her lower lip trembled like a chick held in the hand.

Rita had bought a sliced loaf, a magazine full of pretty pictures, a packet of Mash potato, tea bags and a tin of meat with the picture of a pretty little dog on it to make a stew. She stepped out on to the pavement, to hear the screeching of brakes. Smiling foolishly at the stunned lorry driver, she rushed across the road, fleeing from the eyes of the policeman and the faces in the store window. She hurried home, along Splott Road for a while, then down Aberystwyth Street, along Milford Haven Street, to No. 1A.

The street had long been condemned, but some people refused to leave their homes, and the odd squatter had taken over some of the vacant houses. Bored children had smashed the windows in these and pushed in the doors, forcing Cardiff Corporation to brick them up. By now, there were windows only in the backs of the four abandoned houses at the far end of the street. One reached these – unofficially, that is – over little gates in the back lane, between the rows of decaying garages. But first, you had to run along a dark, narrow entry where the refuse men used to go for the dustbins when there was life and dignity in the street.

It was along this lane John had led her when she was brought here first, after a night in the pub near the crossroads, lending her his greatcoat and embracing her before taking his leave in the early hours. She didn't know how to say no to him, though she was frightened of all sorts of things. At least he'd found her a place to stay, and left her a meat pie, potato crisps and a fag for her breakfast.

No. 1A was three-storey, and dated from just after the First World War, just like the rest of the street. It was solid, with large windows and fireplaces in almost each and every room. Rita had found refuge on the top floor, reaching it by the rusting metal fire-escape. The bottom floor was absolutely dark and difficult to heat, though the occasional drunkard or tramp did sleep there according to Pat. She lived on the first floor, a fair-skinned, red-haired Scot, living with her latest – a lorry driver. But she had others, too, whenever he went on a long journey, especially that smart sailor boy who spoke like a film star, who came by one afternoon just when Rita was going upstairs.

Pat was quite friendly. She'd made her many cups of tea, and asked about where she'd been and what she'd done. She'd promised to help if Rita got into real trouble. Rita thought her a smart piece of goods, standing up throughout every chat, chain-smoking and coughing between every drag. Her hair was like a great mane, combed back in some very difficult way, and she wore slacks in the daytime with a tight green sweater that showed how big her boobs were. She'd given Rita an old pair of shoes, a red raincoat that was only just too big for her, and she'd warned her about men: 'You got a really nice figure, see. Don't want to be looking after a baby up there, do you, love.'

There was a real stove in Pat's place, with a gas cylinder for it, and a log fire in the grate on cold evenings. She got hold of a gas ring for Rita and an old saucepan so she could make tea and warm up her tinned food. One of the men carried a cylinder of gas up the fire-escape to her place. She was still getting little things to give to Pat in return. She went with her to a junk shop to buy a mattress and some rugs, two knives and a fork, plates and mugs and a few underclothes, jumpers and one skirt with a broken zip. The clothes she'd been given when she left the hospital for the hostel were still in fair nick, apart from the shoes. But she'd had to leave behind the greatcoat and the nighties when she'd left there.

Weeks had gone by since she came here. There was now a piece of coconut on the floor, one she'd found on a bin lid one morning, and she'd a poster of Gary Glitter above the fireplace, that was full of cigarette butts and spent matches. John had brought the two canvas chairs, opening them out in front of her astonished eyes, and Pat and one of her friends had found an old deal table in a wash-house out in the back yard. They'd dragged it up to the top floor by rope, and stuffed it into Rita's living-room.

That room was nothing compared with the large dormitory in the hospital, and rather smaller than the one in the hostel. The roof sloped down each side of it, leaving two triangular end walls. It was through a door in one of them she reached her small kitchen and the lavatory, opposite each other, and the fire-escape came up to the window in the other. There were other stairs up to the kitchen end, but they'd been boarded up halfway between the two floors. There was a fair-sized skylight in one of the sloping walls, supposed to open but long sealed by rust. Through it you could see the docks if you stood on top of the table, and see the moon and the stars on a clear night. Rita had spent many hours wrapped up in her rugs on the mattress, staring at the night sky, and trying to gather her few thoughts as she listened to her pretty little transistor.

She'd nicked the radio from the Sunday morning open-air market in Leckwith, but had nearly been caught. There was a smartly dressed chap with a hat staring suspiciously at her as she picked it up and stuffed it into her pocket. He was just about to tell the merchant when a little child ran up to him crying his heart out about something or other. She'd slipped away.

Cigarettes and bread were got the same way, from the stores, and she took a bottle or two of milk off some doorstep or other nearly every day.

The only time Rita wondered whether or not she'd done the right thing, when she ran away from the hostel, was in the middle of a really cold night. About a week or two ago it had snowed. She'd been terribly scared when she heard something slithering down her roof, and nearly ran down to Pat, but was afraid of going outside and of Pat's tongue. She'd warned her not to call after dark unless the place was on fire or the police about. Next day, Pat had explained that it was the snow making the noise, and Rita hadn't got scared since.

But sometimes she'd long for the warmth of her old surroundings, the only ones she really remembered. Now she was on her own, alone; but free. Didn't have to get up at seven-thirty, wash and reach into a pile of underwear for clean ones for herself, and go to breakfast with all the others. All quarrelling because they wanted their food first, and bolting it so no one could pinch it off their plates. She'd had to help spoon-feed one girl when nurses were scarce.

Then everybody would be off to work by nine, packing pencils all day, and having a bit of fun shouting after the boys and flirting on the way back to the wards for lunch – and listening to Peg's transistor. Two more hours after lunch, and a pound or two at the end of the week. 'Let alone your keep, remember: four square meals a day, a comfortable bed and clean clothes. Aren't you lucky.' Television or a film at night, or the occasional dance with the chance of meeting Cliff. But always to bed by half-past nine. Sometimes Marjorie or Barbara would disturb her. She'd give them a kick or a clout or pull their hair. But they'd get their own back by getting her into trouble with the sister or the doctor next day. At one time she'd been friends with Barbara, and Babs would give her little presents on her birthday. But Rita didn't like having her in bed with her, fondling her and playing with her breasts and all that. It was nice being here. Not as much to eat, no television and no heating, but this was her own place, the first she'd ever had. And perhaps John would come again before long with a few biscuits and a cake, and some beer or something.

John did come, some two nights later. He arrived soon after dark, with a little plastic bag in his hand. She heard his footsteps on the stairs and opened the door. As usual, he was out of breath.

'Hello, Rita . . . dear . . . Still here!'

'Hello, John. Long time no see!'

They went into the living-room. He gave her the bag to hold, put his coat to hang on the back of the lavatory door, and his cap and scarf in its pockets. Out of his wonderful bag he drew tins of soup and stewing steak, and two enormous ones of baked beans, and a packet of Jaffa cakes and cream crackers. Then, a complicated tin opener you had to screw on to the wall.

'It's quite easy to use. I've got a screwdriver in my coat. I'll fix it to the wall for you in a minute, by the sink over there, and show you how to use it.'

'I got a tin of meat for you, John, and a loaf I got today.'

She went to get the meat and held it victoriously before his eyes. He stared unbelievingly at it.

'I don't like that particular meat, Rita; sorry. But thank you all the same. If you don't mind, I've got another tin for us tonight – with some baked beans.'

'And I've got some tea!'

'No need for it just yet.'

He went to his bag and brought forth four cans of brown beer.'

'Go and fetch the mugs!'

Between them, the opener was screwed into place and two plates of stewing steak prepared, with hunks of bread and margarine and beer for both. All this without getting through half the food John had brought with him. Then they had a cup of tea and a fag, all to a background of Radio Luxembourg, and with the occasional comment or question by one or the other.

John and Rita were beginning to get to know each other, as

they had had a few such meals by now. He lived with his brother and sister-in-law somewhere in Adamstown, and was a night-watchman starting at half-past eight each night, with one off in every five. Some nights he'd go for a drink with his brother to the pub where Rita and he had met. The others he was beginning to spend with her.

He'd been a collier once, before he lost his wind, and he had a small pension as a result, though he was only forty-seven. He could remember his father and his mother in Tredegar, but they'd gone to heaven a long time ago. He always wore a black greatcoat, a dark blue suit which shone remarkably, a grey flannel shirt and that scarf, and the boots. He'd told her about himself from time to time, and questioned her occasionally. She wasn't a great talker. You'd almost feel she hadn't any parents or relatives. She was from the Homes, from Pembroke originally, and had spent most of her years in institutions of various sorts in Breconshire. And he knew that she didn't like too much talking, police, dealing with money, nor eggs, butter or pork.

Rita had a fine, nubile, animalistic body. That dull look in her eyes was a sign of a passionate nature probably, and John felt a thrill every time he reached out to touch any accessible part of her flesh, a cheek or a hand or any other part. Her main fault was her coarse, dirty and split nails – his little doll. Her head was rather small as well, from her forehead up at least, and all that dandruff spoilt her jet black hair. Perhaps she had some foreign blood. She was of dark complexion, eyes and hair black as utter darkness, and her skin had a lot of blackheads because it was so greasy. But her teeth were large, even and remarkably white. She cared for them diligently.

After supper, when he had thrown the tin and the cans – and the tin of cat food – into a plastic bag and washed the dishes, they started on the rest of the ritual. There was still a saucepan of boiled water on the ring, which John used to wash Rita's hair with the sachet of shampoo he had in his pocket. He dried her shapeless, cropped hair that he'd trimmed on his last visit. Then he put her to sit in front of the fire. Her hair was set in clumsily applied clips, and he started cutting and cleaning the nails of her hands and feet with his pocket scissors and handkerchief. She gladly accepted his attention, sitting passively, listening to her radio with her head and free limbs swaying to the music. Her lips mimed the singer's words, like a fish breathing at the surface of the water.

Then, without any prompting on his part, while John washed his scissors she went to lie on the mattress, in her mini-skirt with safety-pins holding it together where the zip was broken, her green jumper and her short grey socks and black gym-shoes. The multi-stoned ring Cliff had given her in the workshop last Christmas was still on her left ring finger, and the transistor still played away just by her head. John came back, putting out some of the candles, and sat on the bottom of the mattress to shed his boots and his jacket. Then he lay by her side and pulled the rugs over them. He was gentle, and caring of her.

The music played on, dreamily, with a lively rhythm, and the thrilling sound of the brass instrument penetrated through her. Sometimes, the odd note played on the electric guitar would pluck some hidden string in her body, and make her arch her back – fooling poor Johnny. Her heart was with Cliff, and his promise to escape and find her, and live happily ever after. To run away; far, far away. Hitch-hike to Glasgow, as Gloria and Meic had done. She was able to cook fairly well now, with a little help. And perhaps they'd have a pretty little baby for her to look after. She wouldn't have a baby from John; he'd promised. He was nice and kind; at it now playing with her breasts, with his hands under all her clothes. He wasn't in a hurry like Cliff. But Cliff was her man. She spread herself to help John, and felt the weight of his body on her breasts as he rolled on to her. Before long, he was pushing into her, hard and warm, moving in and out to the sound of that drum far away in Luxembourg. She knew how to respond to a beat. She got hold of his ears, and moved her thighs and hips and loins as if she were dancing in the

Recreation Hall to a Gary Glitter disc, or one by the Stones: her belly expanding and drawing back like his, and her being aching for Cliff.

John was finished, but she went on, following the music to its tumescence, floating away on the repeated refrain until it reached its staccato ending – bap . . . bap . . . bap.

By now, John had come out of the lavatory and was boiling another saucepanful of water for their farewell cuppa. She'd drink hers lying down, and leave the radio playing quietly to sing her to sleep when he'd gone. She was glad to have it. What a shame he couldn't come with her to the shops to spend that money he was leaving her now, instead of her having to quarrel with that girl at the desk about the coupons Pat gave her, and having to let her help herself to the right money from Rita's outstretched hand. Wouldn't it be nice to have a fellow to look after her; living with her here, in their little place. Not having to go to Glasgow. She'd get a wardrobe, a television set and plastic flowers, and a table with a picture of forests and lakes on it, and a bead curtain for the opening into the kitchen. She'd get hold of a record-player, an electric light, a cooker and hot water. And plenty of cigarettes. She'd have Cliff, and he'd have a job or the dole. Oh! and lino for the floor.

Should she try and ring him, so far away? And so difficult to contact. It would surely cost a fortune. If she wrote a letter, perhaps they'd read it. But Cliff would find her one day. She'd go to The Prince of Wales's Feathers every Saturday, the place he'd told her he went to when he was free. Please God, he wasn't in that prison round the corner, and that he was thinking of her just now, as she went off to sleep. She threw a kiss to the stars and winked at the moon, before finally closing her eyes for the night.

RON BERRY

November Kill

As if talking to himself, 'More guts than sense in this bitch,' Miskin said. Hunkered over the belly-up Bedlington, he caressed her ribs with his knuckles. Lady wheezed sighs, slaver glistening her teeth inside slack lips. Miskin had three hunting dogs, two rough-coated brindle lurchers, Fay and Mim, and the slaty blue Bedlington.

Beynon's terrier, Ianto, was a long-jawed black and white mongrel.

Miskin's small, clenched mouth accentuated the bumpy profile of his broken nose. He screwed two short vertical furrows up his forehead. 'We'll cover Dunraven Basin this morning.'

'Good,' said Beynon, who had the closed face of a weary spectator. Tall, lean, deliberate in style, he squatted beside Miskin. 'Saw you coming out of the club last night. Any luck?'

'She's solid asbestos,' said Miskin curtly.

'Thought so.'

'Come off it, how would you know?'

'I've tried Glenys.'

'Real kokum you are, Beynon.'

'You were slewed,' Beynon said.

'Same as most Saturday nights,' conceded Miskin.

Beynon levered himself upright. 'Set? Let's go.'

Miskin thwacked his trouser leg with a thin stick. 'Come in, dogs, *in*.' The lurchers fell to heel with the Bedlington.

Beynon clipped a lead on his terrier.

'Train the bloody animal,' jeered Miskin.

Beynon winced mock alarm, 'Ianto's like me, he's uncontrollable.'

'You! There's more temper in a dishrag.'

'I'll frighten the crap out of you one of these days,' said Beynon.

'I'm pooping already!'

'Take it easy, Miskin.'

They grinned, gently grinding shoulders, appreciating a bond without malice.

Eight o'clock Sunday morning, quietness everywhere, two milkmen bypassing each other in whining electric floats, the village main street otherwise deserted. On ahead, Pen Arglwydd mountain jutted up at the November sky, a stillness of dark, bare cliffs intergullied with heathered ledges. Scree slopes gave way to invading bracken. Below the rusting bracken, patches of marshland, mole-tumped pasture, scatters of gnarled oaks, relict oaks older than the village, older than the national anthems of Mighty Albion. Alders lined feeder streams running into Nant Myrddin. Silver birches were spreading eastward, seedspill from a large stand of blackening, dying trees.

The young men followed Nant Myrddin up-river to a sunless, rock-walled gorge. Above the waterfall, half a square mile of sphagnum and rushes. Striding on tussocks, they moved out to dry ground. Now and then, Miskin puled soft repetitive whistling through his pruned lips.

They rested above the craggy amphitheatre of Dunraven Basin. A frizzed silhouette of conifers curved the Basin summit from end to end. Far distant behind them, the flat crown of Pen Arglwydd clung as if suckered to cold blue sky.

Miskin said, 'Lend me your glasses.'

A hidden, grounded raven sounded triple honk calls. Another came peeling over the conifers, swung down, rolled anticlockwise, flapped straight out, hard primaries soughing like bellows, out and out, followed by its honking mate. The big black corvids left the Basin. Down below, acres of glacial bog shone deceptively green.

'See anything?' Beynon said.

Elbows on his knees, binoculars steadied, Miskin breathed

'Naah,' from between his palms. He returned the glasses. 'Take a look at the '83 bury, or maybe it was '84 – remember?

Beynon focused on ancient, fallen rocks underneath a nearside buttress, weathered blocks like collapsed cenotaphs skewed among tons of rubble. At the lower edge of the rockfall, a few hummocks of trampled, peaty soil stippled with posy-size clumps of heather, 'Cubs, Miskin. They're anywhere in Wales by now.'

'Any-bloody-where,' agreed Miskin.

The couchant lurchers were side by side as if on show, like stylized hunting dogs in Egyptian frescos. Lady rattled a snarl at the black and white terrier.

'She's cranky, worse than my mother,' Beynon said.

Miskin flicked his thin stick, lightly rapping the Bedlington's rump. 'Shut it, you nasty sod.' Then he tished a kind of resigned dolour. 'Your mother and mine, Beynon, they're a cowing pair.'

Beynon shrugged.

'Ten years my father slogged his goolies off to give her everything she asked for, the slut.'

Beynon said, 'My father likewise. They're all over though, men with more ballocks than brains.'

'Where's your mother these days?'

Beynon thumbed west towards the conifered skyline. 'Shacked up with some bloke in Swansea. Insurance agent. She's his tax-allowance secretary.'

'Mine's in Spain, running a café with this guy she's supposed to have met on holiday. He's loaded.' Miskin spat aside and scythed the withered tuft of whinberry where it fell with his stick. 'They didn't rear us, Beynon. Me, I saw more dinner-times than cooked dinners.'

'Yeh, true,' said Beynon.

Miskin waggled his fist. 'I was only nine when she decided she'd had enough. After that, nothing, not a word. She vanished. Now, last Christmas, she sends me a poxy card from Spain.'

Hiding his face, Beynon scanned Dunraven Basin through the binoculars. 'I was seven.'

'Why, Beynon?'

'No idea. My father clamps up, he won't talk about her.'

'My father hit the booze. No shape on him till recent. Sits on his arse all day watching television.'

'C'mon, let's move,' said Beynon. 'We're pitying ourselves like two old betsies in a surgery.'

They slanted down from the north corner into Dunraven Basin. Rutted sheep tracks creamed with hard sills of peat, skirted around lichened boulders. Steep pitches of blue-grey shale slurred underfoot.

'Here goes,' said Miskin.

The Bedlington scurried into the fox bury. Soon she surfaced, went sniffing alongside Ianto, watched by Mim and Fay, their tails wagging in slow counterpoise.

Miskin spoke softly, 'Take Mim and your dog. I'll work across from up there.'

Beynon held Mim's scruff. 'Good bitch, Mim. Stay now.' He waited while Miskin climbed to a sheeptrack winding midway around the cirque. Then they kept parallel, rounding inside the vast bowl of Dunraven Basin. The dogs hunted systematically, the lurchers higher, leaping ledges sure-footed as goats, Lady and Ianto nosing holes and crevices.

Miskin came down at the far end.

A buzzard hung like an emblem above the horizon, standing still in the updraught. Harsh *kaark kaark* calls from the two ravens, weaving low over the glacial bog.

Miskin rubbed mucous off his nose. 'I thought we'd raise one this morning.'

'We've seen some good chases this time of year,' Beynon said.

The lone buzzard drifted back over the skyline. A mallard squawked. Beynon spied through the glasses. He saw the drake shooting up from the narrow glittering stream emptying from the bog. The ravens planed and wheeled.

'Something's down there, Miskin.'

'Great. You sorted that out all by yourself.'

'Mouthy bastard,' said Beynon equably. 'Hey, reynard . . . left hand side of the brook, on that stretch of mud.'

'Glasses!' Miskin snatched, he hissed through his teeth, sighting the fox trotting its sidelong gait, front and rear legs inswinging, four pads straight-tracking in the peat-stained silt, then rippling tremors of rushes and tall, fawny grass blades snaked diagonally across the bog. Light-footed over cropped turf and up to scree spillage below a gully, the fox climbed swiftly, skittering over stones like a squirrel.

Miskin pushed the glasses at Beynon.

Beynon said, 'Ta.' He sharpened the focus, thereafter he supplied a commentary: 'Long in the leg, sure to be a dog fox. He's in perfect nick, white tip on his brush, black on his ears, white on his breast. Man-o-man, he's a beaut. What a pelt, aye, wrapped around the neck of a girl by the name of Glenys. Bet you a pint he's heading for the same old bury.'

Miskin gulped, snickering. 'Much too far away to send our dogs after him,' he said.

Beynon said, 'Four hundred yards.'

'More like five.' Staidly polite, Miskin accepted the glasses. 'What's he doing out and about in daylight, ah? There, you're right enough, Beynon, he's just gone to ground.' The dogs milled around Miskin's legs. He flipped neat backhanders. 'Quiet!'

Beynon put Ianto on a lead.

Miskin leashed the Bedlington with a choker. 'Okay, let's bolt the bugger.'

The fox-hole angled down through raked stones. Lady whined, ceaseless shivers quivering her slingy body. They searched for another exit from the bury. Miskin looked worried. 'There's no place for him to bolt. This little bitch, she's on to a pasting.'

'Send Ianto in first,' Benyon said.

'He won't go far, too big around his chest. Fox'll chop his face to ribbons.' Miskin stroked the Bedlington. 'Steady, gel, relax.' Reluctantly, muttering concern, he slipped Lady into the hole.

Ianto bayed like a hound. The brindle lurchers weaved to and fro on tiptoe, wetly black noses twitching, ears full cocked from their sheepdog sire.

They heard the Bedlington barking, a rapid burst followed by growling. 'Christ, she's in deep,' vowed Miskin. Kneeling, he poked his head into the hole. 'Shake him, gel! Meat off him!' He sat back on his heels. 'She's cornered him. It's a block end.'

'Put Ianto in,' said Beynon.

Ianto howled underground for fifteen minutes.

'Call him out, Beynon.'

'Right, he's this side of the bitch, can't get on, and he might make things worse for her.' Beynon shouted at the hole, 'Hee-yaar Ianto! Hee-yaar Ianto!' The terrier came scuttling out, one of his front paws bleeding and a flesh graze on his shoulder. 'Good dog, good dog,' Beynon said.

The November Sunday waned to lifeless evening. Miskin and Beynon shared cheese and ham sandwiches. Without animosity, they argued pros and cons. At dusk they left the Basin, Miskin cursing, effortlessly cursing the Bedlington bitch.

'Take it easy, we'll dig her out,' promised Beynon. 'Hard graft, but we'll do it.'

'She's in deep, man.'

'I know, I know.'

'Listen, Beynon, tomorrow morning: mandrel, round-nosed shovel, hatchet. We'll need a hatchet to make the place safe.'

Beynon said, 'I'll bring a crowbar and a bow-saw. Plenty of timber on top. Those bloody Christmas trees.'

Miskin nodded grunts.

Short-cutting on lower ground, returning to Nant Myrddin, they reached their home village as the first white frost of winter rimed roof slates.

'Half-seven, early start,' said Miskin.

'See you,' agreed Beynon.

*

They felled three sitka spruces, trimmed the six-inch boles and chuted them down grassed gullies to the fox bury. The lurchers pounced, jostling around the hole, kneed and clouted by Miskin. He listened at the cavity. Very faintly, the snarly growling of the Bedlington. 'Beynon, she's in deeper than last night.'

Beynon said, 'Sounds like it.'

Miskin organized the work, his authority from five years at the coal face. Taking turns, they hacked and shovelled surface debris, starting a vertical dig above the trapped fox – Miskin's calculation. By late afternoon they were prising out big stones with the crowbar, from the jumbled bulk of the old rockfall. Interlocked layers of blue pennant sandstone governed the shape and size of their hole. When they were a yard down, a massive, inclined slabstone. Miskin stamped on it. He flung curses.

Mim, Fay and Ianto snoozed, curled on the trampled soil outside the fox bury.

'We'll be here tomorrow,' said Beynon.

'Maybe. Depends on that bastard gravestone.'

'Work around it,' Beynon said.

'No option, man!'

'Anyhow, she's still alright down there.'

'Sheer bloody guts.'

'We'll dig her out, Miskin.'

Evening came, chilling the sweat on their bodies. Their ragged hole was like a shell crater. Props and stayers held the slab of rock. As they trudged home in darkness, Beynon heard Miskin groaning misery. 'Take it easy, butty,' he said quietly.

By Tuesday night they were twelve feet down, hauling up rubble with a bucket and rope. Less often now, Lady's growling sounded hoarse. She responded instantly, feebly, when Miskin yelled at the mouth of the bury.

On Wednesday morning they felled four more sitka spruces. They fixed horizontal timbers across the dig, with props and heavy wedges at each end. Beynon relied on Miskin. He felt safe doing his stints down below, levering his weight on the five-foot crowbar, heaving stones up on the cross timbers.

Mim, Fay and Ianto were thirty yards away, tucked on a wind-trapped mattress of dead molinia at the base of a buttress.

'Weather's changing,' Miskin said. 'Time for some grub. Catch hold.' Gripping wrists, he helped Beynon out of the hole.

Beynon hated failure. And he felt troubled for his mate. 'Miskin, what d'you say we sink a few pints in the Club tonight. Do us good, right?'

'Nuh.'

'We're much closer to the bitch. She's not far below us. To-morrow she'll be ours.'

Miskin argued, 'Listen to me! If it rains the sides of this bloody crib are likely to start slipping!'

'So we shift the bastard muck again!'

Miskin thrust his head into the fox-hole. 'Lay-dee! Lay-dee! Hee-yaar bitch!'

She barked for seconds, then silence.

Miskin chewed a sandwich. 'Weakness, Beynon, she's weakening.'

'But she's safe. We'll get her out.'

'Too bloody true,' said Miskin.

'That's settled then. Tonight we'll have a few pints.'

Hospital charity dance in the social club on Wednesday night. Beynon and Miskin sat in the snooker room. Very soon, as usual, they speculated about their runaway mothers.

Miskin: 'She never felt anything for me when I was a kid. As for my old man, he was on a loser from the start.'

Beynon: 'Before my old lady went off, she treated my sister and me as if we were nuisances in the house. What do they call it, maternal instinct? It's a load of bull.'

Miskin: 'D'you think all women are the same, I mean selfish?'

Beynon: 'Christ knows. They go their own way like cats.'

On and on, the same unforgiving rancour, the same helpless

groping for motive, a reason to shed guilt, absolve themselves and their mothers.

Beynon said, 'My old man's a worrier, he's a clock-watcher taking tablets. Duodenal ulcer according to the quack. Knock it back, Miskin. My turn.' He crossed over to the serving hatch with their empties. Happening to glance above the hooded glare on a snooker table, he saw Miskin brooding, his powerful shoulders humped forward, chin pressed to his chest. Beynon thought, she's been four days without food and water. It'll break Miskin's heart if Lady dies underground in Dunraven Basin. He'll quit. Sell the dogs. No more weekend fox-hunting. By the Jesus, we'll have to dig her out tomorrow.

Miskin raised his full glass. 'Cheers. Before stop tap we'll manage a few more.'

Beynon watched the beer glugging steadily down Miskin's throat. 'Bloody sump you are, comrade.'

They were cheerfully drunk leaving the Club, moodily deter-mined next morning, wading through sodden, crimping bracken. Drapes of mist scudded across towering Pen Arglwydd mountain.

'Showers forecast, dry this afternoon,' said Beynon.

Miskin hooted disgust. 'It'll tamp down all day over in the Basin.'

Beynon said, 'Sure to, butty.'

9 a.m. at the fox bury, Miskin ducking his head into the hole. Silence. 'Lay-dee! Lay-dee!' Far-off husky whining from the Bedlington. Silence again. The lurchers and Ianto cringed away, sensing viciousness. Miskin raged despair.

'Hey man, take it easy,' warned Beynon.

Sheltering from the rain, the lurchers and the long-jawed terrier clumped themselves together on accumulated sheep droppings below a cavernous overhang at the foot of a buttress.

Using the head of his mandrel, Miskin tapped protruding boulders in the sides of the fifteen-foot crater. 'Sounds okay so far. Nothing loose.'

Sweating inside oilskin coats and leggings, they continued hack-ing out stones, rubble and clay. Rising wind lulled the downpour to sheet drizzle driving around the bowl of Dunraven Basin. It was one o'clock. They fed the dogs and themselves. Miskin kept three faggot sandwiches in a canvas bag.

Beynon cooled a pint of tea in his big flask. He said, 'I'll dig for a spell,' clambering down on the cross timbers. He listened, his eyes tightly shut. 'Lady! Hee-yaar bitch!' Then, suddenly, he punched up his arms, shouting. 'She's below us! We're right on top of her!'

Miskin swung down like an ape. He elbowed him away. Beynon spread-eagled himself against the sides of the pit. Balanced on one knee, Miskin placed his ear close to the clay-slimed rubble. Low snoring, like someo е sleeping in another room.

'Lay-dee!'

She yapped briefly. The snoring seemed to come in fading spasms.

'Careful, Miskin!'

'God damn, Beynon, shurrup! I know what I'm doing!'

'All right, all right,' Beynon said.

The wet rubble concealed another tilted stone flat as a table. Scrabbling with his fingers, Miskin clawed down, searching for the edge of the stone. It was a foot thick, lodged in the sides, immovable.

Beynon climbed up the cross timbers. Miskin filled the bucket, Beynon hauled the rope, flung the debris, lowered the bucket. They worked for less than an hour, until Miskin saw clay-water whirlpooling down a cranny below the underside of the big flat stone. Delicately, slowly, Miskin corkscrewed the crowbar at a shallow angle into the fissure. The water swilled away. Like jigsaw trickery, the Bedlington's snuffling, mud-smeared nose appeared. Miskin's yell screamed to castrato. 'She's safe!'

'Thank Christ,' muttered Beynon.

'Those sandwiches!' cried Miskin.

The lurchers and the terrier came bounding down from the overhang. Ianto threw his echoing hound baying. Miskin clubbed Fay when she sprawled into the pit, her hind legs flailing in sliding rubble. 'Get away! Out, gerrout!'

The brindle escaped, curvetting zigzag leaps on the timbers.

But Lady was still trapped under a crack between two stones bed-

ded like concrete lintels. Beynon squeezed the width of four fingers
in the slot. He strained a grin at Miskin, 'Three inches, mate.'

Miskin spoke to the Bedlington while dropping her pieces of
faggot sandwich. 'Good bitch then, good bitch. You're in the
way, Lady. I can't bash these stones if you stay there. Use some
sense now, gel, back off a bit, back off the way you came in.'
Frustrated after several minutes, he stood up, ranting. 'It's like
talking to that bastard shovel!'

'Take it easy,' Beynon said.

'For fuck's sake you've been saying take-it-easy take-it-easy
since last bloody Sunday!'

'Shh't, leave it,' Beynon said, head bowed, not looking at
Miskin. 'You're blowing wind and piss, you're hysterical, like my
old woman, like yours an' all.'

They laughed at each other.

Miskin slid his hand edgewise into the crack. He fingered
Lady's head while Beynon wrenched on the crowbar, creeping
the stones another inch apart. Exhaustion slumped Beynon on his
backside. Miskin had pulled her out. She wriggled. She snorted
ecstasy. Her floppy ears were scagged with cuts, tooth-holes
through her upper lip, clotted blood on her feet, clay matted in
her fur. Miskin mumbled, cradling the Bedlington in his arms,
'You daft bloody thing you, bloody daft, daft . . .'

Beynon let the shakes drain from his limbs. 'She's stinking of
fox,' he said, probing the cavity with the crowbar. 'Aye, he's in
here. Lady killed him.' He picked shreds of fox fur off the chisel
tip of the crowbar. 'Definitely, she finished him.' He slumped
down again. 'I'm knackered.'

Miskin said, 'Thanks, butty.'

They climbed out. Lady lapped the lukewarm tea, then Miskin
carried her all the way home, shovel, mandrel and hatchet roped
across his back. Beynon carried the bow-saw, crowbar and
bucket, a steady plod in cold drizzle, trailed by the brindle lurchers and the long-jawed terrier.

JANE EDWARDS

Waiting for the Rain to Break

(TRANSLATED BY ELIN WILLIAMS)

'Mind that puddle,' said Brend' as we went for a walk along Lôn Fudr in our high heels and peep toes, only to step straight into another puddle. 'Damn,' she says, leaning on the wall to take a look at her shoes, and ask me if I had a hanky she could have to wipe them.

'Only this one,' I say, not wanting to give her the one with the Marquis Tower on it, the pretty silk one I found under the back seat of the double-deck.

'Pretty, smart,' she says, rubbing her shoes with it 'til I was afraid that she'd make a hole in it.

'You've got hairs on your legs,' I said, seeing them shine like a web in the sun.

'Everybody's got hairs, you ninny,' leaning over to peep under my new-look to see mine. 'Not a hair. Safe for a few months more. No hairs, no children.'

'That isn't true.' And I should know, having seen Nain's armpits, when she compared them to an opera singer's.

'Ready,' she says, putting her arm through mine. 'How about looking for two smart lads? Hey, what do you think to those two?' pointing in the direction of the Wern where old Wiliam Jôs and Dic Dalar were in deep discussion. 'Bet you they're arguing about boundaries. At it from morning to night. I don't know why they don't put up a barbed-wire fence like the Germans.'

'Race you to the kissing-gate' – to shut her mouth. I wouldn't like Wiliam Jôs to think we were talking about him, him being such a good man. 'That wasn't fair now,' she says out of breath. Then, whispering: 'Watch it, they're coming after us,' pretending to run away only to break out laughing. 'That scared you then, didn't it? Silly thing. What would two old-timers like that want with pretty young things like us?' And jumped on to the gate to swing back and fro. 'No, it was for your young, inexperienced lads that this was put up. Mind you, at one time, seeing Wil so slow igniting, I thought I'd have to bring him here. Thank goodness I didn't. He would have pulled it off its hinges.' And laughs of course. 'Tell me, what are county-school boys like?'

I pull faces to show that they aren't up to much, which is better than admitting that I'm not interested.

'Swots. Think of nothing but algebra, geometry and physics from morning 'til night. Although, mind you, we learnt a lot in the secondary mod. We weren't altogether stupid. Knew everything about bunsen burners.' And laughs again, that laugh she has when she talks about boys.

Oh, you really need grace. And that's to be had in the strangest and most terrible places, as Mr Thomas the minister would say. 'Grace,' he says, 'is that which purifies and cleanses. Grace is what rids you of the wicked and sinful thoughts of your mind. Grace is purity. Grace is cleanliness. Grace is peace.'

The feeling that comes over me now as I look across the dunes towards Cob Malltraeth where the sun is swaying yellow on the water and throwing strips of red ribbon over Caergybi and far over the horizon to Ireland where the sun sets. And where it will set for ever in my imagination.

'Bloody mites,' says Brend', who had also been studying the sight.

'A sign of fine weather.'

'Fine weather! Fine weather! I'm sick of fine weather. Someone wanting Wil to work in the hay all the time. And he can't say no. I've told him to find work in a factory. And what about you, wouldn't you fancy that? Lots of fun, you know. And a good wage. Doing nothing all day long but sitting on your bum, sewing and listening to Radio Eireann.'

'And making aprons.'

'Making aprons and overalls.'

Radio Eireann, aprons and overalls. No, the stuff my dreams are made of includes aeroplanes, smart clothes and following the sun to all corners of the earth. My dreams make me a snob, according to Alwyn.

'Hey, wake up,' says Brend', giving my arm a nudge. 'Look who's coming across the field.'

No one important, you can be sure. Ifan Jôs Tyn Fawd and Fanny May. Him dressed as farmers do in summer, in an old grey flannel coat and loose trousers, and her in a short dress up to her knees, her hair cut in a straight line under her ears. They both walk past sheepishly enough without raising their heads, she with a silly smile on her face as if she had just won a prize in an eisteddfod. 'He should be neutered,' says Brend' when they were out of earshot. 'Not enough created for some.'

'Perhaps they just bumped into each other,' I say. 'She had a Quaker's Reed in her hand.'

'And a mound of sand and sea grass in her hair. A mother of nine and another on the way, I wouldn't be surprised. Makes you wonder who their father is.'

'Look, they've reached the gate. Do you think they'll kiss?'

'No fear. You don't kiss when you've got a bunsen burner between your legs.' And steps on a puffball 'til her legs are plastered with dust. Then she turns to make a noise like a machine-gun to scare the lapwings that are flying above.

In a while, we come to Lôn Gul and cross the stile into Cae Twysog with its blanket of red poppies swaying in the breeze.

'Pretty,' says Brend', and starts gathering them. 'Come on. What's the matter with you? Have you got bellyache or something?'

'It's unlucky to gather poppies.'

She looks at me in disbelief. Seeing that it was such a lovely evening, I didn't want to talk about Doris. And yet I couldn't stop myself.

Doris was Gwen's friend, and she had been ill in bed for months. Sometimes I'd call to see her, although I never had much to say, as she was two years older than me and in the top class in school and Sunday school. That morning it was Gwen I was looking for. But she wasn't there. And Doris's mother asked if I would mind sitting with her while she popped to the shops to buy some things. And somehow or other, because it was fine perhaps, and the sun shining on the window, we started talking about flowers, leaves and trees. And Doris said that she'd give the world to be able to go to Cae Twysog to see the poppies. 'I know what I'll do,' I said, 'I'll go there this afternoon to gather some for you.'

'Don't say you forgot!' Brend' said, her mouth open wide, ready to chide.

'No . . . No. But by the time I had my lunch and popped to the shops it was late. And when I went over there she . . . she'd left us.'

'Left! Left? Died you mean.' And looked at me as if it was my fault. 'How old did you say she was?'

'Fifteen. Fif-teen.'

'Fifteen! Navy blue! Makes you wonder if there is a God.'

'She believed. Do you know what she'd written before she went? "Rock of ages, cleft for me".' I couldn't say any more because of the lump in my throat.

'Hell of a thing, religion,' says Brend', and bends over to gather more poppies, so that we could pop over to the cemetery to put them on someone's grave.

I wanted to put them on the first grave we saw. But no, Brend' was as fussy as if she had paid for them. Robert Hedd Williams. She didn't like his name. Sounded like a conshi. And everyone knew that a poppy was a soldier's flower.

But before I could retort the most eerie sound came up from

the ground by our feet, like Frankenstein rising from his coffin in the films at 'Reglwys Bach.

'A ghost. I'm going,' says Brend'.

'Going where, you wasters?' says the voice, making us jump into each others' arms like two angels on a tombstone.

'Who's there?' says Brend' sheepishly, in her phone-answering voice.

'Me, of course, who else? Give me a hand, sweetie-pie.' Brend's eyes narrow as she steps to the grave, her arms folded like Dorcas.

'Dic Claddwr, is that you, you rotten thing?' And threatens to kick him back into the grave. 'Look at the sight of you. Look how dirty you are.'

'Did I scare you, girls?' And clucks with laughter as he climbs out. 'Old Modlan Jôs's grave, poor creature. Another year and she'd have had a telegram from the Queen.'

'Be quiet, you stupid thing,' says Brend' turning away and indicating that I should follow her.

'Yes, you go, girls. But it's back that you'll come one of these days, it's back they all come.'

'Well, you can't bury me,' says Brend' haughtily.

'Oh? And where will you be buried then? In chapel with the bigwigs?'

'We're going to be cremated,' says she and turns to me for confirmation.

'Like Gandhi and I. D. Hooson,' I say, getting into the spirit of things.

'Well, you might as well, seeing as that's what's in store for you anyway.'

'Come on,' I say seeing that there was no end to it, 'let's go home.'

But no. Brend' had set her heart on finding a soldier's grave. It was in the very far corner between the stone wall and the rubbish heap that we found it: quite an ordinary-looking stone where the weeds had taken over.

'Listen to this,' Brend' says, honey-voiced, and reads some verse in English. 'That's nice, isn't it?' She starts weeding and orders me to fetch water in a jamjar.

When I came back who was there wrapped up as if it was the middle of winter but Cadi Wilias.

'It's like Piccadilly Circus here,' says Brend' and winks at me.

'I was saying,' said Cadi Wilias, pressing her basket to her breasts, 'how good it is to see the younger generation tending to the graves. You'll never regret it. A lot of comfort to be had in a place like this. And I should know, having been coming here now for near a quarter of a century.'

'Who have you got here? A boyfriend?' says Brend' finding it hard to keep a straight face.

'Someone far dearer, sweet girls. Dear old Mother. Would you like to see her grave? This way. But take care not to step on the graves.'

This was reason enough for Brend' to step on each one, pulling me after her.

'Here we are,' says Cadi in a while, standing in front of a black marble slab, her eyes sparkling behind her thick glasses. 'It's sweet William that I've got for you today, Mother dear,' smiling and how-de-doing no end. 'Your favourite, isn't it?'

'And which is old Father's favourite? Jini flower?' Brend' whispered in my ear, before bending to help Cadi to tend to the grave. 'Look, give me the flowers in the pot. We'll get rid of them for you.'

'Well, thank you very much, young ladies. Thank you very much.'

'And thank you too,' and pushes the petals under my nose. 'Look how pretty they are, none the worse. Would you like to take them home to your mother?'

'She might think I've stolen them.'

'No point in me taking them home. Mam can smell a cemetery miles away. I know what we'll do, let's look for Anti Dol's grave.' Anti Dol, her mother's younger sister. The one with hair like Rita Hayworth and a voice like Vera Lynn, who died of TB.

But although we searched and searched we didn't find the grave of the one with the hair and the voice of a star. And as we didn't know anyone else, and Brend' suspected everyone of being a chapel-goer, a conshi or having voted for Lady Megan, the flowers were thrown on to the rubbish heap.

'Www,' says Brend' as some shivers went through her. 'I won't come here again. It's not a place for young people. And mind that you don't tell anyone that we've been here. Promise?'

'On my honour.'

'Criss cross.'

'Cross my heart and hope to die' – although we were too old for silliness like that in our new-look and our high heels.

'Chip shop next,' she says.

'I've got homework.'

'Huh! Like Cadi Wilias you'll be making eyes at gravestones.'

There were black clouds gathering on the horizon and some dull ache in my belly. And the tide was out in Aber Menai.

'Nice to be young,' says Siani Puw, who was sitting on a Corona box outside her house, wearing her apron and her peaked cap.

'Don't answer her, she's a man,' says Brend'.

'I don't believe it,' although I'd heard it said before.

'You'll see when Dic Claddwr puts her under the clod.'

Mercifully there was nobody much around the chip shop, and we sat on the low wall to eat our chips and to suck the vinegar from the bottom of the bag. And a good feeling came over me 'til Robin Star appeared combing his QP.

'You going to buy me a Vimto, lover boy?' says Brend', kicking her legs in the air to hypnotize him, I suppose.

'Who do you think I am? Rockefeller?'

'How can you refuse, chick?' And leapt at him 'til his legs creaked and his eyes narrowed.

'Hold on, what if that hulk comes back?' collapsing under her weight.

'What hulk?' Sobering.

'God, how should I know? The one on the motor bike with a voice like a thresher.'

'Motor bike!' She turned to me accusingly. 'It was Wil. I tell you that was Wil. Something told me not to go for a walk. Did he leave a message?' she pleaded.

'Nothing that made sense. Said he'd see you when the rain came.'

She took one look at the sky above, and put her arm through Robin's and said that would not be for ages, not for ages.

But that night the rain did come. And listening to its noise beating on the window to the accompaniment of the pain in my belly, I knew that it wasn't only the clouds that had broken. And that, so that you may know, although I didn't have a single hair on my legs.

PENNY WINDSOR

Jennifer's Baby

Richard swore under his breath because he had never really wanted to come. He would have preferred to stay in the flat practising jazz phrases on his trombone. 'Bloody ridiculous', she heard him say as he pushed his way through the crowded corridor.

It was Whitsun Bank Holiday and, since he had been unemployed for months, they couldn't afford much, or go far. The train ride somehow made the day a proper holiday, a ritual, joining in a kind of celebration with the people carrying suitcases and the people parading their children with their buckets and spades down to the beach.

They had caught the midday train, leaving the large, worn pram in the guard's van. Jennifer kept the baby close to her. Kathy waved her small arms as though trying to keep balance on a tightrope, and stared at a woman in a large hat.

'Lovely, sweetheart,' Jennifer said, and kissed the baby's bald head.

She saw Richard looking at her and raised her lips, suddenly embarrassed. 'I'll feed her,' she said and made him help her pour the contents of the vacuum flask into the bottle, pleased to be occupied.

The other passengers watched her curiously and she could feel her face grow red as she bent over Kathy.

A small boy kept tapping his mother's arm. 'A baby. Look, Mam, a baby!' He came to look closer but Kathy was occupied with the milk, sucking frantically.

Jennifer looked past the girl next to her, out of the window. The train travelled along the coast next to the vast sand-flats of the estuary. They shone with puddles of water, were furrowed by the sea. Far out the main stream of water sat, still, in the reaches of sand, moving infinitely slowly to the Atlantic Ocean.

Even though the sun was shining, the feeling was of cold. The sheer force of wide spaces made her glad to be in the train, yet drew her away from her husband and child, and the other people.

It thrust her back into the village in the Swiss Alps, to the walks she took each free day, up the half-frozen river valleys above the forests to the snow. White and hurtful. The lovely, awful monotony of it sent her chasing back to the village again. It threw her back to the German motorways in that very hot summer a few years ago. The road had moved like water, disappeared, reappeared – like the sand-flat waters. She had moved along its edge, small as a fly. And there was no getting away from the sun. Anyway, that summer, she had nowhere in particular to go.

The sand-flats and the snow and the hot motorway, they made her vulnerable. In a world which had no definite places she wandered in circles, lost.

Jennifer realized the baby's bottle was empty and mechanically she took it from Kathy's mouth and watched the amazed blue eyes. 'All gone,' she said, showing Kathy the bottle as though she might understand.

'I'm bringing John to Gary's party next week,' the girl said to her companion, and crossed and recrossed her legs. Jennifer watched Richard watching and was hurt.

After the child's birth they began to go separate ways. She was absorbed utterly in the child, resenting his continuing contact with other people, the outside world. She was content to turn inwards to the child, delighted by her smiles, dismayed and hurt when she cried. It was the baby's dependence, its vulnerability which enchanted her. No longer was she the one to be protected by Richard, woken from nightmares, never left alone when it grew dark in the flat. Now she was strong, and she felt this strength as distinctly as if she were flexing newly developed muscles in her body.

He took up music again, shutting himself away all day practising his trombone and playing records. Sometimes she shouted at him to help her wash the dishes or scrub the floor. And he helped and went back to his music.

She smiled, thinking that now she did not need his love.

The train drew farther inland where the fields sloped in hills and the villages were small market places of not-much-importance. There was a castle ruin high on one hill.

'My brother would like to see that,' Jennifer said absently. But Richard was reading the paper and the remark was only heard by the two girls who stopped talking and smiled at her kindly.

The sun darted over Kathy's face throwing patterns into her eyes. She smiled a magnificent, toothless smile and laughed silently with her mouth wide open. Jennifer smiled back – a conspiracy. She and her daughter formed an exclusive club and outside there were the girls crossing and recrossing their legs, and Richard watching them.

Jennifer didn't know why she had chosen to come to that particular town except that she had never been there before and the fare was cheap. It was a market town set on a hill in a green land.

They stopped outside the station and Richard said, 'Well, what the hell are we going to do now we're here?'

'See the town,' Jennifer said and pushed the pram towards the bridge, refusing to look back to see if he followed.

The river was shallow and wide, looping through the valley fields. She hesitated on the bridge, leaning over the parapet on tiptoe.

'Why don't you wait?' he said, irritated. 'There's no hurry.'

She looked at the water finding ways over the shingle bed.

'What's its name?' she said.

'What?' He was sullen.

'The river.'

'Oh, that.' He shrugged. 'I don't know.'

The main part of the town was on the top of the hill. The streets were quiet except for the noise from the pubs. A man came, drunk, to his home, and the wife half-crying, half-shouting, slammed the door in his face.

'He deserved it,' Jennifer said.

'You don't know,' Richard was pedantic. 'She might have nagged him to drink!'

She told him to shut up.

The baby murmured in her pram at the sound of raised voices, cried once in her sleep. Jennifer bent over her immediately.

'You'll love the baby?' he had asked tenderly when seeing it born. But he hadn't foreseen this mindless devotion. There was something to be pitied in her desperate attempts to communicate with a thing that answered only by crying for food, and small, inarticulate noises.

He had seen his own uselessness that first day in the hospital when she cared only to look at the child, to touch its sleeping face. 'My baby,' she had kept saying. 'My baby – mine.'

He had gone back to an empty flat and played his blues records, unable to reconcile himself to losing Jennifer, losing her to the child.

He went to look in a music shop, admiring one particular trombone, a Conn model which cost a small fortune. He wanted to feel it in his hands and to hear the pure, beautiful sounds he knew he could play on it.

Silently he cursed the boss at the car factory who had been responsible for his redundancy. He had been earning good money. A year or so at that place and he could have bought the instrument.

*

The sun fled over the hills and the sand-flats, and slowly it began to rain. They sheltered in one of the narrow side streets. A hitchhiker sat near them and chewed gum.

'Bastard rain,' he said eventually, and stared at his feet.

'Going far today?' Richard asked.

'Maybe.' He looked at Jennifer. She thought for a moment that he knew her.

'Got anywhere in mind?' Richard persisted.

'Nowhere in particular – just travelling, you know.' He shrugged.

'It's easy enough to get to Ireland from here. There's a ferry leaving every day from just up the coast. Thought of doing that?'

'He said he didn't know where he was going,' Jennifer said.

'No harm in asking.'

Richard pulled up his collar and stuck his hands in his pockets. The summer day had turned cold. 'Back soon,' he mumbled and walked off quickly to the High Street.

The noises of the rain grew louder, more intricate as it hit the roofs, ran along the gutters, down the pipes, a kind of music.

The hitchhiker played a few chords on his guitar, no particular tune. Later he sang, a low moaning song about hobos travelling on the railroads of America.

Jennifer pushed the pram back and forward automatically. Kathy slept, her face very white.

'I used to hitchhike,' Jennifer said, 'before I was married.'

The man didn't acknowledge that he had heard her.

'I saw lots of places – France and Germany mostly. Sometimes I just used to set out with no particular place in mind.' She paused. 'There was this village way up on the cliffs. I've never seen so many colours, red cliffs, blue sea, white houses. There was a hot, dry wind blowing all day and night. And space, so much space . . .' She tailed off and watched the rain flowing down the street, chasing itself into the drains.

Richard came back, his mac clinging to his legs.

'Want some fish and chips?'

'Is there somewhere open?'

'Just down the road. I'll take the pram.'

Jennifer looked back at the man crouched in the alley. 'He's nowhere to go.'

'Silly bugger,' Richard said.

The café was crowded and smelt of fat and wet raincoats. The waitress rushed between tables sullenly taking orders and pushing plates of food and cups of tea in front of the customers.

Women peered in the pram. 'Pretty, isn't she?' they said; 'little girl, isn't it? How old?' Kathy woke and stared at them. 'Ooh, just look at her,' the women cried. 'Sharp little thing. Been in this world before, that's for sure.'

Jennifer was flattered by their attention, as though it was she who was complimented. She rearranged the pram covers, smoothing them with small, fussy movements.

Richard looked from Jennifer's face to the faces of the women. The feeling of being shut out again. He was the father, yet the baby belonged to Jennifer entirely, and perhaps to the other women who, once upon a time, had borne children also.

He turned to the man at the next table and began talking about football. Presently the man left with his wife.

'What were you talking about?' Jennifer asked.

'Ridiculous,' Richard thought. 'Ridiculous to be jealous of a broken conversation with a stranger.'

They tried to think of something else to say. Had they been at home she would have cleared away the dishes and he would have gone to another room to listen to the records.

'It's still raining,' Jennifer said eventually.

'Yes.'

'It's in for the rest of the day.'

'Looks like it.'

She arranged the knives and forks neatly on the plate. Richard tipped up the salt-cellar and watched the salt form a pile on the table.

'When's the next train?'

'Half-past five.'

'Shall we wait here?'

'I suppose so. Kathy will need another feed soon.'

People were beginning to leave, disappearing into the rain. They watched them struggling with umbrellas, cursing the turn in the weather. Soon they were the only people left and it was still an hour before the train went back.

The waitress looked at them sullenly. Jennifer felt very conspicuous.

'We could wait at the station.'

Richard took his paper out again. 'I don't see the point,' he said.

She looked away in disgust. The day was ruined. He had been right, they should have stayed in the flat instead of making this senseless trip, spending money.

'I wish we hadn't come,' she said out loud.

'Your idea!'

'I know. I wanted to go somewhere for a change.'

'Uh huh.'

'Richard, talk to me!'

The rain had no end.

Richard turned a page in the newspaper. He only knew she had spoken. About the rain perhaps, or the baby, about nothing.

'I wonder if the hitchhiker is still out there?' she said.

The back of the paper again. Silence. Only the women gossiped behind the counter. No reply from Richard, no noise from the baby.

Even Kathy had finally let her down. Now she slept, not wanting attention. Jennifer was disappointed, angry. Why had she suffered the long months of pregnancy, the birth pains, the interrupted nights? For what? The baby slept. She was not needed.

'I'm going to the station,' she said.

At the door, Richard called out, 'Aren't you taking Kathy?'

*

The rain tapped on the hood of the pram. Kathy was oblivious. Richard pushed the pram inexpertly, bumping it up and down the kerbs. He stopped outside the music shop in the High Street and once again admired the huge golden bell of the costly trombone. If only he had the money . . . if only he could afford to buy Jennifer a new dress, to buy Kathy a baby chair, to put down a payment on a house. He couldn't do any of these things. Nor did the baby seem to belong to him. At least Jennifer had that, the child. Its birth had somehow diminished him. It had made him terribly aware of his own life. He was forced to rethink, to reassess. He was haunted by his past jobs, his vague musical ambitions, his inability to earn for his wife and child. Everything resolved to this moment – in the rain with Jennifer's baby, looking at a golden instrument he could not possess.

She had given him the baby – a gift, an abdication, a peace present – or none of these things. She didn't know. Running along wet streets, she could not remember why.

She eventually came to the alley where they had sheltered from the rain. The hitchhiker was still there, crouched. She ran from him as one runs from a shadow, knowing there was no getting away. Like him she had nowhere to go, like the Jennifer of three summers ago on the hot motorway. And the town in the rain seemed as long as that motorway, as monotonous as the mountain snow, as unending as the sand-flats of the estuary.

Faced with one wet, grey street after another, she began to wander in circles, lost.

She thought only of the baby. Kathy ran in her blood, screamed in her head. She could taste, smell, see, hear nothing but Kathy. 'I have given her away,' she thought.

She had made herself vulnerable again. The rain wet her clothes and her skin. She had no defence.

Richard sheltered under the collar of his mac, hunched like an old man. The water from the bloated gutters splashed over his shoes and rose slowly. It began to pull at his legs, at the wheels of the pram.

Deeper and deeper he waded into the centre of the rain, still pushing the baby. Turning once he thought he saw Jennifer on the far edge of the rain across a wide, wide space. She waved her hand, it seemed to him, but he was too far away to see if she was beckoning him to come to her or waving him goodbye.

He turned away, pushing the sleeping child farther into the rain.

EIGRA LEWIS ROBERTS

Do You Remember Jamie?

That evening could have ended like any other. They had eaten their meal in customary silence, she picking at the food, he wallowing in it. The last piece of bread had sucked the last few drops of gravy from his plate. Any minute now, he would lick his thick red lips and belch and their evening together would end, there by the table, where it began an hour or so ago. But that evening, as the last morsel left his moist red mouth, he asked, 'Do you remember James?'

'James?' she repeated stupidly, aware, at the same time, of a variety of emotions that could have made her sing and dance, or at least clap her hands, had she been so inclined.

'The Hemmings boy; Steven's friend,' her husband added, impatiently. And he rose and moved away from her.

'Surely you remember James.'

From a distance, she stared at him, the large man who caused the glassware to jingle as he paced the room; a man who made his presence known, even in his silence. He was pacing now, his hands behind his back, his stomach swollen and distorted.

Sometimes she would pretend that, one day, his stomach would burst and all its contents – school lunches, reunion dinners, her wholesome home cooking – would come cascading out of it. And she would take her little brush, her little dustpan, and sweep it all up, wrinkling her nose when she detected cabbage, which she disliked intensely. And if he was good, very good, she would sew him up and button his waistcoat over his new, flat stomach.

Maybe she would touch him. Yes, that would be nice, after all these years.

That night by the table, he would say, 'No potatoes for me, darling' – or just plain 'dear' would do. He would leave some food on his plate, not enough to be wasteful or a slight to her cooking, only a few last mouthfuls that would have caused him to belch, had he taken them.

'Are you coming up?' he would ask, discreetly, not mentioning bed but implying it with a coy glance that befitted his new, flat stomach. 'Leave them,' he would say, as she made to clear the dishes. And with that luxurious thought her imagination always ran dry. For would it not be unthinkable, unforgivable, to go to bed without clearing the dishes? The very thought made her sick with guilt.

'Yes, I remember James,' she admitted, reluctantly. Her husband stopped pacing and eased himself on to a chair.

'I saw him today,' he said, a little breathless from his exertion.

'You saw Jamie?'

Good God, he thought, there she goes again. No, he felt tempted to say, Jesus Christ. But he held his tongue, knowing that the sarcasm would be lost on her. It was fortunate that she was not with him when he met James; fortunate that the boy had not come to this house, as was his intention. It could have been so embarrassing. As it was, it had been pleasant, very pleasant indeed. They had lunched together. The boy had called him 'sir' and had insisted on paying. They had spoken of Steven and his achievements; of James and his hopes for the future.

'Why didn't you bring him home?' she asked.

'Here? Whatever for?'

She carried the dirty dishes through into the kitchen, ignoring the serving hatch. When he had asked her why she didn't use it, seeing it was there and for that purpose, she had explained that it would have been silly to put the dishes down on one side, walk around to the other side, and pick them up again. 'What are hatches for, then?' he had asked. She didn't know. There was very little she did know. But, give her her due, she had been a good mother. James had said that during lunch.

'Your wife was an excellent mother,' he had said.

She paused by his chair. An unpleasant odour of food clung to her. She had spent many hours preparing his meal.

'How did he look?' she asked, shyly.

'About the same.'

'But bigger.'

'Of course.'

'Has he still got his own teeth?'

Good heavens, how should he know? He was not in the habit of asking people he met – 'Excuse me, but have you still got your own teeth?'

'His front tooth was broken. Do you remember? One day at school during football, a boy had kicked him in the mouth. I cleaned him up and made him some custard and he gave me a piece of his tooth. A souvenir, he said.'

There had been so many boys, thousands of boys, with broken teeth and crooked noses. How could he have remembered? He should never have mentioned James. But what did one say to a wife whose capacity of understanding was so hopelessly limited? And he felt obliged to break the silence, to acknowledge her presence. Whatever fault he had, he could not be accused of ignoring even the lowliest of his pupils.

'He was very pleased to hear about Steven.'

'He had such a sweet smile. Sweet, but sad. I used to feel so sad when I saw him smile.'

'He's doing well. Not as successful as Steven, of course, but well, yes, quite well.'

'I was so sorry when the family moved away. I missed him, really missed him. I used to stand by the kitchen window, listening for him. And then, when I realized that he would never come again, I would cry.'

What on earth was she on about now? She looked so stupid,

standing there, her lips pale and limp, talking of tears and sadness. He should never have married her. But he had been young and worried, and she had been gentle and uncomplicated. She had said all the right things, then, that a young man with worries wanted to hear. Everything had been so hard – the bed he slept on, the desk he sat by, the examinations that he had to pass – and she had been so soft, so tenderly, invitingly soft. She had remained so, soft and brainless, a little fluff ball that he had acquired in a time of weakness and lacked the guts to throw away.

He had been terrified that his son would take after her. While she tended to all his bodily needs, he had cultivated the boy's mind. It had grown, flourished, until it was a beautiful thing. Only then had he relinquished his hold. Exhausted, relieved, and completely satisfied, he knew that he had achieved something worth while and was content.

Oh, yes, she had been a good mother. He tried to remember that at all times. He could have found himself a more fitting wife, one who could at least have listened with some measure of understanding, even offer an opinion from time to time, but he doubted whether he could have found a better mother for his son. And it was his son, after all, who was to shape the future.

'I'll retire,' he said.

He had a comfortable bed in his study; one that he could move into, or leave, whenever the mood took him. There, he had everything he needed at arm's length.

She heard the glasses tinkle as he crossed the room, heard him belch as he climbed the stairs. She was standing at the kitchen sink where she used to stand, waiting for her boys to come home. She would leave the window open, even on the coldest day, so that she could hear them from afar, until, at last, she could see them, embrace them with her eyes before they could see her. It was always Jamie who reached her first. He was slight, and moved effortlessly, unlike Steven who was thick and heavy like his father.

Jamie had once told her, in confidence, that he preferred her to his own mother, who was pretty and popular. He had told her too, in Steven's absence, that this room where she now stood, was the Avalon of his life. He had explained, patiently, that an Avalon was a haven, a place that he could escape to. She had asked, she remembered well, what it was that he wished to escape from. He had answered – 'nothing and everything' – and his eyes had become very sad. She could make nothing of his words, but his eyes had haunted her and she had wished that she could keep him there for ever so that he would feel no hurt, no pain. She had loved her son because he was her son but it was of Jamie that she thought, in this kitchen. It was because of him that she willed the sun to break through and the rain to cease. Guiltily, she had often wished that Steven would linger so that this small haven would be hers and Jamie's, alone.

Then, Jamie had moved away and there was only Steven. And there were extra lessons that kept him in school. He would come home with his father, in the car, talking of things that did not concern her and that she would never understand. It was only then that she had realized that there was no purpose in listening any more and that she had closed the window, tightly.

But all that was a long time ago. It must have been, for her to cry. For there were no tears now, only a dry sadness. He had asked her if she remembered James; he, who had always referred to him as the Hemmings boy. 'A bright boy,' he had said. 'Not a patch on Steven, of course, but a bright boy.'

Jamie had cried when he came, alone, to say goodbye. They had spoken of their need for one another, without embarrassment. They had embraced, like two lovers. And she had remembered her husband, a thin, worried young man, who had found comfort in her. She would have liked to tell Jamie about him; make him understand that her husband had not always been like this, fat and pompous, bloated and self-satisfied. She would have liked to tell him not to run, that life was very long and that there was always time to stand by windows; time to wait and listen. But he had gone, and she was still young enough, still warm enough, to be able to cry.

When the knock came, she knew that it must be him, that he would never leave the town without seeing her. She led him into the lounge. It was a dead room, cold and cheerless, a room for those who were not encouraged to linger.

'You can't stay here,' she cried. 'This room is for strangers.'

Outside, in the corridor, he could smell the man and knew that he had recently passed this way. He felt a strange desire to call him so that he would not be left alone with this woman. Resisting the urge, he followed her through the house and into the room that he had been forced to escape from, in memory, so many times.

There was an awkwardness about him, as he sat, that made her feel uncomfortable. He had been so light; he could fit anywhere, so easily. She thought that maybe she should call him James, now, but, undecided, she gave him no name at all.

'I met your husband,' he said.

'Yes.'

'We had a good lunch together.'

'He always lunches well.'

'Is he in?'

'He retired to his study, at nine.'

'He still does a lot of studying?'

'He never stopped. He lives for his work, you know . . . always has.'

She spoke without feeling, as if she was repeating, parrot fashion, something that she had learnt as a child.

'He was a good master. He taught us to respect his subject, to be proud of our heritage.'

Yes, he had taught them respect, and a strange, reluctant admiration, for his subject and for himself. But it was an admiration of dead men, of a stagnant literature. He had lazily followed the monotony of the thick tongue, thinking of other things, the warm, exciting things of life. But later, in this very room, he would, perhaps, remember a line that he caught and would repeat it in his young, childish voice. And she would stare at him and smile, vacantly. There had been so much sadness, even then, in things that were and were to be.

'I understand that Steven is doing well.'

'Yes. His father is very satisfied.'

'I wrote to him once, a long time ago, but he didn't answer.'

'He never writes. He talks to his father, on the phone, about his work. And I go there to say goodbye. There's nothing else to say.'

No, there was nothing else to say. They had been apart for too long. Once, there had been warmth and joy and sharing. Once, he had passed his own home to come to her; he had wished that this woman could have been his mother.

Beyond that door was the man and his house. But this was a place apart; an Avalon; an Innisfree. But he had pretended, with Steven, that it was merely a place where he could make a pig of himself, guzzling home-made apple tart and picking up the crumbs with a moistened finger. There had been a time when Steven had done the same; when he had shouted, 'Race you home, Jamie.' They would fall, exhausted, on the kitchen floor. He would look up and see her standing there and it was as if she had thrown a blanket over them and was lulling them to sleep, there, where the sun had touched the linoleum.

And then, suddenly, he was glad that he had to leave, for he had been aware for some time that the boy, Steven, also belonged to the house and he had felt awkward, picking at the crumbs. But when he came here the last time, he had cried, thinking of all the hardness that lay ahead, of all the dampness that he would have to wade through.

'I should have come back,' he said. 'I wanted to, but there was so little time.'

'You must have had a very full life.'

She spoke as if his life was at an end; as if he had come here to die.

Savagely, he said. 'It's only a beginning. There are so many more mountains to climb, so many more rivers to cross.'

'Are there?' she asked, innocently.

'Oh, yes. Life is such a challenge.'

He knew that he was hurting her; this pathetic little woman; the mother of his friend; the wife of his English master. She was so soft, heart and mind, so easy to crush.

Once, he had met a girl, just like her, and he had gone to her as he had come into this kitchen. And then, as her softness closed in on him, he had remembered Steven's face as he watched him lick the crumbs from his fingers; remembered the gleam of victory in his eyes. And he had pushed her away, so that he could climb, swim, unhindered.

'I met a girl once,' he said. 'She was just like you. I would have liked to marry her, but there was so little time, so many things to do.'

My God, he thought, I'm apologizing to her as if it were her, herself, that I left, sobbing. The stupid little bitch. I only took what she offered, of her own free will.

'Life is very demanding,' he said. 'And so is love. I had to choose. We had our ambitions, Steven and I.'

But, of course, she would never understand what ambition meant. She had moved around this room, waiting, endlessly waiting.

'I'll have to go,' he said, and stood up. The kitchen immediately became smaller and darker. If only I had an apple tart, she thought. He would have recognized the smell, coming through the door, and would have known that he was home. She had waited so long for him to return; had kept the warmth for as long as she could.

There were so many things that she wanted to say and ask. 'Jamie, do you remember? Do you remember . . . ?' How she wanted to know if he remembered as she remembered. Were they memories shared or hers, alone, to brood over, here in her lonely kitchen?

'It was nice to see you again,' he said. He took her hand and shook it, politely. He would have raised it to his lips, but he was afraid that she would mistake his gesture.

'Remember me to Steven,' he said, as he left. 'We had some good times together, Steven and I.'

As he hurried away from the house, he thought – I'll make it. I'll climb, by God I will. I'll wade through all the dampness. Steven my old friend, I'll catch up with you yet.

The dish water was cold and she let it run out. So that was little Jamie, she thought. It was nice to see him again, yes, quite nice.

The next time Steven rang she would say – 'Oh, yes, Jamie called. You remember Jamie. He was asking about you' – only to discover that her husband had already mentioned it and that there was nothing left for her to do but say goodbye.

CLARE MORGAN

Losing

'But what is it like?' she had asked her mother a long time ago, when she was about eight and a half, the middle of the first year in the new school.

'Really. What is it *like*?'

'Oh. It is nothing. It is just a lot of heavy breathing, really. That is all.'

She had been very much older than her years, even then. Distant relatives who came occasionally and went, wondered among themselves if she had ever really been a child.

'Such a dark, serious girl. And a great pity, when you think of it. But there.'

And this one would smooth the multicoloured feather at the side of her felt hat, that one would dust off the brim of his trilby with clean, thin fingers going the same way as the nap, and they would move on to other more important issues, the rising cost of living, the encroachment of socialism, the perils of this (for so they were beginning to think of it) permissive age.

Being very much older than her years even then, she had not made the kind of quick, instinctive reply you might usually get from a child. She waited, saying nothing, watching the nervous movement of her mother's hands straightening and straightening a pair of thick-knitted and unmistakeably male socks.

'These came from Aunt Evelyn,' her mother said irrelevantly. 'I don't think she knows his size.'

How she had watched, after, for him to put on the socks for

the first time, wondering would they fit, watching as he sat down with them in his hand, the lamplight casting the shadow of the kitchen table partly on him as he pulled off his slippers and lined up his boots, troops to pit against the raw morning with ice edging the pond like an ageing eye, and snow clouds massing like great grey packs on the back of Aran Fawddwy.

His bare foot shone in the firelight, bronze and pink mixed in together, like sunset was sometimes, very rarely, towards the end of summer when the dew comes down by about eight o'clock and you take in your things quickly and close your front door against the rising silence. She could see in the firelight the hairs growing below the cuffs of his long-legged winter underpants and down on to his instep, black and wiry as briar. Black and bronze and pink and then the sudden sharp detachment of shadow under the muscly arch.

His foot slipped easily into the thick, knitted sock. First the tensed toes into the precise gap held open by his thumbs. Then quickly over instep and arch, stretched round the hard bulb of his heel, then up over the ankle bones he unrolled the rough knitted stuff until it met the edges of his underpants, engulfed them, drove on smoothly another two inches, and he tidied it with a satisfied pat and drew the trouser bottoms down over it all like a blind.

'What are you staring at?'

She stepped back into the longish shadow which his body cast.

'Nothing.'

'They fit, then,' said her mother from the corner by the stove, peevishly, as if somehow aggrieved.

He put on his coat and went out without answering. Not until nearly an hour later, when it was entirely light, could the kitchen quite rid itself of the cold blast his opening and closing of the door had let enter.

Winter. Spring. Summer. Autumn. Four arcs on a slowly rolling wheel. When you are nine, or ten, or eleven, the length of each is inordinate. The days seemed endless, yet afterwards resemble no more than flakes you could scrape off with the edge of your nail from a healing graze.

When she was nine, she liked winter best. Everything seemed to have stopped. She liked existing in limbo, everything in a state of waiting, with the force of it filling up inside, the growing sense of pressure until things gather, and give.

When she was ten it was spring the young lady (for so her mother began to try to tell her she had become) now favoured. 'I like spring because it is beginning,' she had written for an English composition and been marked down because it was, so Miss Bristow who did English said, bad grammar. She did not understand, Spring *was* beginning – transitive and intransitive, verb, noun, adjective, all of it. '*Spring is beginning.*' She couldn't put it into any other words than those. Any other way she tried to describe it sounded flat and lifeless, or else sounded as if someone else was saying it, not her.

'*Summer is icumen in*' was the start of a verse she learned sometime during the dusty season at the centre of her eleventh year. Rainless days turned into weeks. A fine dry summer developed into something called drought. *Drouth. Drowt.* She tried out the word over and over, balanced it on the tip of her tongue, dribbled it into the succulent parts of her inner gum, slipped the unfamiliar edges of it painlessly past the supple cordings of her throat. *Drouth. Drowt.*

'*Dammit!*'

The shout in the middle of the night, squeezing up through the floorboards as though the parlour were not big enough to contain it. But coming suddenly awake like that, in the middle of the night, with the moon very white on you, it is sometimes difficult to decide whether it was just a dream.

Her mother saying, 'I do pray for rain.' And the sympathetic, superior look of the man who delivered the paraffin as he tilted his head a little to listen and took the funnel out of the ten gallon tank and shook the last few pink drops from it and screwed down the top.

The stream was not a stream any more but a sickly trickle. The stones which the water usually flowed over looked dull and lumpish. You could only just hear the movement of it, a little lurking sound, only just audible at the edge of your head. Everywhere was very dusty. As you walked up the track from the road, your heels kicked up fussy little whorls of dust which hung there for quite a while after you had passed. The ground was hard and began cracking. Every day, cracks you had discovered the previous day widened and deepened. The chickens looked thin and stopped squabbling among themselves over who was to take the first dust bath in the corner of the yard.

At night the downstairs light stayed on a long time.

'*Dammit!*'

The dust settled in the creases that lay like straight drains from both his nostrils to the corners of his mouth. When the dust mixed with his sweat, it pasted his hair together in ugly clumps. His hands were black, the collar of his shirt dirty. He began to resemble in part the carelessly constructed thing she and the others humped from farm to farm at the beginning of each November, to the reedy and discordant chorus.

'A penny for the guy! *Ceiniog. Ceiniog.*'

In her eleventh year, she certainly liked summer best. Short, hot nights. Blurred moons which cast the pointed shadow of the pine across her as she lay in bed. The dusty, acrid smell of the grass. The thin chickens drawing out sore sounds from the backs of their throats like slowly stretched strings.

It was inevitable that when she was twelve, autumn would have its turn as her favourite. She was such a sullen and capricious thing.

'What child can like autumn best?' demanded the departing relatives of themselves, casting the memory of the place firmly over a turned shoulder, shuddering a little as though a sliver of something had insinuated itself at the root of the heart, and was levering it loose.

Autumn was melancholy. That was why she liked it best.

'*I am of a melancholic humour,*' she said to herself, draining

Shakespeare at a sitting, waking to some ancient clash of har-
nesses and kingdoms, falling asleep under the eyeless invigilation
of a Lear, dreaming, perhaps, of Cordelia.

*'I like leaves that are yellow and red, and the frosted pattern of
fern.'*

There was no stillness that could match the stillness of things
when there was absolutely no wind. It was quite different from
the stillness of still life, a book you had just put down on the
table, a chair that nobody was sitting in, an unattended desk. It
was stillness *within which* was movement, like Van Gogh's
Sunflowers, a print she had recently come across in one of her
mother's old books, retrieved from a trunk in the back of the
attic. This movement-within-stillness seemed to her to be at its
peak in the clear days of early autumn, when the sun took longer
and longer to come up and the turning leaves curled round each
other at the edges and dropped like sky divers in a suicide pact to
lie on the ground till the frost got them, and her own feet,
probably, crushed them into brittle bits.

At thirteen and at fourteen no one season seemed better to her
than another. Everything was held together with a sameness, as if
a grey lens had been slipped into her retina, there to interpose
itself between her and the world like the reflection of a grey veil.
Daily, man-made rhythms were of more significance to her than
natural, seasonal ones. What occurred day by day made sense.
The getting up, the half mile walk to the corner, the lift in Mr
Bristow's Landrover which occasionally contained Miss Bristow
and, much less often, Mr Bristow's young and silent wife.

'They keep to themselves,' her mother said, half inquisitive,
half critical, as she handed over the carefully counted brown and
silver coins which went to pay Mr Bristow for his trouble.

These daily events made sense, and the school routine, the bell
every forty minutes, break at eleven-fifteen and whispering among
the rows of gabardine mackintoshes in the empty cloakroom.
Changing for games, stripped of your blue serge bloomers, the
wind hitting your chest through your cellular blouse as though

you had absolutely nothing on. Writing in your pink preparation book lists of things you had no intention of doing. Then waiting on another corner half a mile from the school gates where there was an old wall and a new seat and a carved stone which said 'Grammar School Repaired 1857'. The stone with its carving jarred just a little every time you passed it. The carving was so sharp and clear, as though someone had only yesterday taken his hammer and chisel out of his bag, got down on his knees and manufactured this brief piece of meaning.

She tried to imagine how it had been over a hundred years ago. Vague pictures came to her, insinuations. It was as if she were marooned on a tiny island, straining to decipher across a sea of seasons the faint and blurry shape of the shore. A sense of helplessness overcame her. Once when she felt like that Miss Bristow looked at her, but didn't say anything.

At the beginning of the grey time, towards the end of when she was twelve, she was visited by what her mother said was womanhood.

'But I am b-bleeding,' she said with the first trace of that afterwards characteristic stutter.

'It is nothing. You are hardly losing. Here.'

The strangeness soon faded among the pink and white appliances her mother provided. But the revulsion which she felt, a kind of subdued horror at her own fleshiness, kept with her.

'Be sure you don't have anything to do with boys or men,' said her mother, looking at her carefully over a pile of folded clothes.

After that, she steered clear of anything faintly male. The piano master she went to once a week after school, she became even more restrained with. When he bent over to turn the page of his own score to '*Mae Hen Wlad*' she shrank back into herself and her fingers faltered on the keys. She didn't like the smell of his breath. He said, 'Well, *Cariad*,' and gave her more scales to practise.

'He breathes very heavy,' she said to her mother, who was mending trousers in the uncertain light of the fire.

'No doubt the poor man has asthma,' said her mother without

looking up. 'Don't you think so, Brynmor? That the poor man has asthma?'

He sat with his legs stretched out straight, facing the fire, so his toes seemed in danger of roasting and you could already tell that his thick, knitted socks were yellowing in the heat of it, and the scent of scorching mixed with the heavy, yellowy smell of his sweat.

'Ah,' he said. 'It's likely. That pansy. Playing the pianer.'

She felt his sneer was for her, and she protested.

'But you *said* I should learn. You *said* it was for the best.'

'Now then.' Her mother's voice hovered above the needle plying silvery tracers along the green seam.

'It's a good thing for a girl, the piano. The piano's a good thing for a girl to learn.'

'I hate it. And I hate *him*; and his b-breathin'.'

'O-o-o-oww.'

Miss Bristow was whimpering like a kitten in the corner. Her legs were folded up under her and her face was hidden by her hands and she looked crushed.

Or was it a dream? She tried to decipher some of the little differences which delineate dream from reality. It seemed real enough. She was watching through the window a scene in the Bristows' big kitchen. She had seen Mr Bristow shake his young and silent wife as a cat shakes a rat, until she had run out of the room. She had seen Mr Bristow shake Miss Bristow until she had pleaded and gone limp and whimpered. Miss Bristow had not at first screamed or cried. She had only screamed when Mr Bristow hit her in the stomach. His fist made a soft, thudding sound as it met Miss Bristow's stomach, rather like the sound her mother made, plumping up the pillows when she did the beds.

'Slag!'

Mr Bristow stood over Miss Bristow with his legs apart and his hands hanging down by his sides. He turned to go but as though it were an afterthought, kicked Miss Bristow just where the pelvic girdle hinges with the hard, bony part of the upper thigh. The toe of his boot made a sound like 'slup', but Miss Bristow didn't scream, just twitched like a puppet does when somebody clumsy is trying to manipulate the strings.

She stopped looking in at the window then. She heard a door slam and the sound of his boots as he crossed the yard, a flinty sound, stone against metal stud. She came away from the window as she heard him get nearer, and tried to pretend to herself she had just arrived. His shadow came round the corner before him, flat and black on the stone. Then he appeared like an unnecessary adjunct to the shadow, his very fleshiness somehow unreal, as if you could poke a stick right through it, as if it were matterless.

'Uh?' he said when he saw her.

He seemed the same. Quiet and tidy. You would never have thought there was any harm in him. His hair grew down in a brown wave in front of his ears. She didn't like that. But his hands were clean. He seemed neutral, and his skin, particularly around his mouth and in the middle of his cheeks, was pinkish and neutral. She hadn't really looked at his eyes before, and now that she tried to, they were nondescript.

'Uh?' he said again, but the same as always, nothing friendly or unfriendly.

She held out the packet of twelve bantam's eggs, her mother's offering for something or other, an extra lift.

He said, 'Oh. Ah *Diolch*.' And took them not roughly, as she had supposed, with a great danger of his big thick fingers poking holes through the thin shells, but in his open palms, gently, the effort of gentleness making his fingers quiver, and his arms right up to the elbow as he carried them in.

He gave her a lift back because it was on his way. He didn't say anything as they bumped along, nor did she, just held on to the handle half-way up the door and watched the white light of midday go by them. When you looked outside at the white light and the sky behind it, then inside at Mr Bristow or your feet or the gearstick or the floor, your eyes took time to adjust, and everything seemed black and white like a photograph, but more like a negative, you couldn't really tell who was who, only by outline, and people's hair was white and their faces black and their mouths white so you had to guess their expression.

Mr Bristow's hand looked black. It looked like a black, predatory thing, a giant spider or a great black bat as he moved it around the cab, up to scratch the side of his nose, down to change gear, back on to the steering-wheel which bucked and shuddered as they went over the holes in the road.

She hated his great black hand. The cab got smaller and smaller, the hand bigger still, his nose and his jaw seemed to elongate, his body got squatter, and his deep, even breathing deafened her. When she looked out, the sky and the mountain around her, which rose and fell like a great green sea, hinged and tilted. She thought, 'I must stop this. I must get out,' but could do nothing to accomplish it.

They went on like this for another mile. Just when she could feel something about to give, he yanked on the handbrake and they stopped. He didn't look at her as she climbed down, just muttered something. As soon as she had slammed the door the Landrover began to move, and before she had walked more than a dozen steps it was out of sight.

The smell of half-burned petrol wafted up into her nose and she shied away from it. She could hear the sound of the engine getting fainter as it went down the hill. She crossed the road and walked towards the gate. A buzzard swung into the edge of her vision and hung there like a mobile over a child's cot. She heard it mewing, a high sound, rather like a child. A raven came grunting over the pink tip of Tir Stent and flapped slowly towards the north. A southwest wind made a sucking sound in an old roll of wire. The wind in the grass went wuush, shuush, and rattled the gate in her hand as she opened and closed it. It was a white, high, blowsy, April day. Everything seemed to be running in front of itself, there was no stillness anywhere, her hair whipped and jiggled about her ears and on to her cheekbones. She felt for the first time a sense of herself in relation to everything else, as if she were part of a single system, a fragment of something hurrying towards its own special destiny. She turned and put her hands on the top bar of the gate and looked out over the long horizon, clean and green and very definite at the edges, and felt almost content.

She turned and began walking up the track. Her skirt lifted and billowed in the wind. She felt a sudden cramp in the lower part of her stomach, right at the front and just above the *mons veneris*, whose identity she had looked up in a school biology primer, and which stuck out in trousers. She recognized the symptom and was not surprised when, within a minute, she felt the first tickling in the cotton gusset of her knickers. She fumbled in her pocket and discovered a grubby paper handkerchief which she stuffed in past her knicker elastic under the pretence of bending down to do up her shoe. She felt like crying but didn't, just kept on up the track towards the house which got bigger and bigger, dwarfing the mountain behind and filling up her whole view. She noticed she was clenching and unclenching her hands, first right and then left, rhythmically, in time with her steps to which in turn she controlled and slowed her breathing.

As she neared the house she heard the explosive *phut* of the axe settling its head into a block of wood. Then again *phut* every few seconds as the axe split block after block. *Phut* step step step. *Phut* step step step. She felt like a piece of machine, something self-regulating and contained, and the sound of the axe and her steps and her breathing filled her head until she thought she would never hear anything else ever again.

She entered the yard and walked towards the house. As she approached the kitchen door she saw with unrepeatable clarity its every detail, how the paint was peeling a bit down the one side, little green flakes quivering in the wind, how black and shiny the latch was from a recent cleaning, how bright the hinges looked because they had only been replaced the month before, and just as she saw these things, as they fell into her head as notes do in a musical composition, the door opened and her mother stood back, waiting for her to go in.

DUNCAN BUSH

Hopkins

'Hopkins.'

That was all he said. He's a terse bastard. Never 'Mister Hopkins' (though it's always Mister bleeding Colefax).

Or 'Mel'. (How many years have I been here now?)

Or just plain 'Hello'.

Or 'I'm in a spot of trouble, can you help me?'

Just that, in that short way he got.

'Hopkins.'

With that barest nod, acknowledgement. As if nothing ruffled him ever, or he passed you a dozen times a day like in an office or, more likely, on a bloody parade-ground, so that even using your name, even your last one, was doing you a kind of favour, an extra politeness. Or as if to say. Who else *would* be coming along that particular stretch of narrow road at half twelve on a Tuesday afternoon but me?

I run the window down and looked at it.

'What's happened there?' I said.

He laughed as if it was a silly bloody question. Well, it was. Though he looked pretty silly too, standing there barefoot in the middle of the road with his trousers rolled up and a shoe in each hand with a sock stuffed in it.

I got out and we stood there looking at the Rover.

'I'll tell you one thing,' he said. 'I didn't run out of petrol halfway across.'

It was up to the doors on it. It always have tended to flood on that corner. And there'd been a few parts under water as I'd been getting there, though pretty shallow, just on the one side of the road. But it's low ground just where that stream goes under the road there, and what with all the water along the gutters, it must have been pouring down the hill into it like a sump. It was that orangey yellow floodwater always is. It must have been over knee-deep in the middle. Well, we'd had a week of it, and it had been a hell of a night and morning.

'Must have got water on the leads,' he said. 'I thought I could just plough through it. It didn't look that deep.' Then he looked at me. 'You know a bit about cars, don't you?'

I looked vague, I was wishing I didn't know a damn thing. Now he wants me to slip off my coat and save him a garage bill, I thought. 'Could be the leads, I suppose,' I said.

He looked back at the car and pulled a face. 'I'll have to get Ockwell's to send the breakdown van out,' he said. 'That's all there is to it.' He stuck one of the shoes under his arm, turned his palm up and looked at the sky. 'It's stopped,' he said.

'Aye,' I said. 'For how long? Those clouds are full of it.'

'So, Hopkins,' he said. 'Since you're the first on the scene so to speak, can you give me a lift into the village?' Breezy, businesslike, you know. Aye: his business, my time.

'Jump in,' I said.

'Just hang on a sec,' he said. And he put his ox-blood brogues down on the road and rolled his trousers up a bit farther and paddled out to the car again. He let the bonnet down and got a few things, cigarettes and so on, from the dashboard. Then he locked the onside door and paddled all the way round to the other side to check the offside door as well. Just in case some stranger happened down that little road and took their own shoes and socks off and paddled out to steal his car radio or the seat covers or something in the ten minutes or so it'd take us to get into the village and for him to get back out there in Ockwell's pick-up.

Then he came back and opened the van door and looked in for

a second at the seat, as if he wasn't sure whether to take off his cavalry twill trousers as well, or just burn them afterwards. In the end he sat in it with his legs outside and started to put his shoes and socks on. Then he stopped and looked at me over his shoulder. 'I think I should go around another way if I were you,' he said.

'I was just thinking that myself,' I said.

'We don't want us both stuck out there, do we?' he said. 'Blocking the thoroughfare for bona fide passers-by completely.'

'I'll go round by Lobb's farm,' I said. 'That's the best way.'

So I waited for him to get his shoes on and get in, and reversed a bit and backed it up to the gate into the field there, just so I could drive him straight back the way I already come from.

'Cigarette?' he said.

'I don't,' I said.

'I forgot,' he said. 'Of course you don't.'

He lit his cigarette and sat there. I didn't say anything, and we went on a bit. There was a big patch of water on the road again, where you turn off towards Lobb's. But I could see it wasn't deep. It went up like a wing on either side, brown, as we went through it.

Then he started humming. Aye. He don't even bother to make polite conversation, I thought. Just sits there humming and looking at the fields and tapping his fingers on his knee to make you feel it's you who ought to open your mouth and say something, just to break the silence. It's like you know your land's his, and now he's got to make you feel awkward, in your own van too. It's a way they got, those people. They probably don't even know they're doing it, half the time. The only thing is to make sure *you* do.

'Everything all right at home?' he said. 'Your good lady and so on?'

'Fine,' I said.

'What about your boy?'

'He's fine,' I said. 'Last I heard he was, anyway. He's in the air force now.'

'So he is,' he said, like he'd forgotten it. 'Enjoying it, is he?'

'As far as I know,' I said.

I hope he is, I thought. I hope he's at least enjoying it, seeing as how it never did me the blindest bit of good. You break your back to bring them up for sixteen years and then, soon as you want some work out of them, they sign on for the next sixteen and go and live in Suffolk.

'I'm just wondering,' I said, 'whether Ockwell's close for dinner.'

'That I don't know,' he said. He looked at his watch. 'If he does,' he said, 'I know where I can find him. Though I agree it might be better to enlist his services before he's in The Bull.'

If anybody knows anything about the bull, I thought, it's you, mate. So we went on for a bit, just watching the road and listening to the wipers. It was just like a drizzle on the glass now. In the end we got into the village. I pulled in outside the garage. I was thankful to see the roller door was up in the service area, so I knew there must be somebody still working there and I could just drop him off there and be done with it. Then Tony Cass came out of the sales office in his overalls.

'Ah,' Colefax said, 'a sign of life.' He got out of the van, then bent down to look in again. 'I'm grateful to you, Hopkins,' he said. 'It was good of you.'

'Don't mention it,' I told him.

I was glad to drive away. I don't know what it is about Colefax, and the others like him, or whether it's being like that that got them where they are or if it's being where they are that makes them act like that. But, it's as if they always got you at a disadvantage, and everything they do, even if it's no more than opening their mouth to say your last name, which is the way they pass the time of day, is just to keep you there. It's like when you pass each other and you see that white Rover up ahead, coming towards you, and you wish you were on another road or you could turn off somewhere quick before you cross or, when you do, get away with pretending you hadn't noticed it was him driving it, just so you didn't have to lift your hand to him or smile and have him give you that quick nod, never smiling, and watch him past while he leans his head back and narrows his eyes to watch the wing of his car just ease between yours and the hedge or bank where, as like as not, since you always seem to meet the bastard in a narrow part, it's you who've pulled in tight to give him space to pass you without stopping while you wait. Like he got precedence by law, as if he was on a roundabout and coming from the right. It's always the same with those people. They get it because they expect it. Like in the army. It's officers and men. They use the same tone, people like him. That same, English voice. And, you can tell, they just love to hear it coming out of their mouths. They know they only got to open their mouths to put you in your place and keep them in theirs.

But that's the trouble with the country. It's not like in a town. You can't avoid people. You're lucky if you can manage to drive the couple of miles into the village without having to take your hand off the wheel for somebody or other coming the other way. Like you can't help knowing every sod coming and going on these roads, and they know you. And, once you get there, you can't park the bloody van and go into a shop without running into somebody who wants to stop and tell you everybody else's business or know yours.

They don't seem to understand that some days you're in a hurry or you got something else on your mind, you haven't got the time or interest to just stop and jaw. If they want to talk to me, they know what pub I drink in in the nights, at least they damn well ought to by now. There's a lot of times I wouldn't mind a bit of conversation then. Particularly on a week night, when it's quiet. Instead of standing by the bar on my own or having to talk to that bloody old George and looking up every time the door opens, expecting somebody to drop in any minute, even if just for a quick one. But no, they're all at home watching bloody telly, then. Or if you *do* see them, they're talking to someone else, so you feel you're a hanger-on. But if you go into the village in the day to do a bit of shopping and you want to get back quick, it's like they been waiting to waylay you since last week.

I don't know how they think they got the time. All that standing and talking never turned a spade or cleaned a hen-shed out or laid an egg in it. It never made a brass farthing.

I don't know. Sometimes you look at them pigs and chickens scratching and rooting around in the yard and you think, Jesus Christ, they'll live off anything. They'll live off dirt. But I bloody can't. I got my work cut out to live off *them*. But it don't mean I want to tell that to everybody else I meet or got the time to stand around and hear their troubles too.

I don't need nothing off nobody, least of all being liked. So I'd be glad enough if I could just come in here the once or twice a week I need to, and walk from the Co-op to the Post Office and back to wherever I parked the van without having to stop and talk to some busybody who got nothing more profitable to do than stand around and try and find out the ins and outs of my affairs or make sure I know his or, come to that, without having to wave a hand at him across the bloody street. It's like the army there, too, living in a place like this. Wherever you go there's someone expecting you to throw one hand up for them. And, I know what they're like, they'll call you all the miserable bastards under the sun if you don't give them that salute on sight.

Bugger them, I say.

So anyway, I thought, I'll pick up a couple of pounds of corn for the chickens while I'm here. And I could do with some of that baler twine, really. I was looking for something to tie down that tarpaulin on the end of the hay yesterday, and do you think I could find a yard of good string anywhere? I rummaged up some old flex in the end and had to go and get the bloody pliers then, to cut it into bits.

So I went into Noah Rees and Griffin's. Chas wasn't in there, it must have been his dinner time. That woman was serving there. I don't know her name, though I suppose I must have heard it used. Betty, is it? You let it go a bit like that, not knowing it, and then you don't like to ask. Mind you, I don't think she knows mine. She never uses it.

'What a day,' she said.

'What a bloody week,' I told her.

'Terrible,' she said.

'The road's under two feet of water out by Rhys's place,' I said. 'By the little bridge there.'

'Is it?' she said. 'I think there's a few roads like that,' she said. 'From what people have been saying.'

'Aye,' I said. 'I just had to give John Colefax a lift in,' I told her. 'You know that white Rover of his? Well, it's conked out right in the middle of it.'

'Is it?' she said. She drew her breath in sharp, and tutted.

'He must have got water on the leads.'

'There's terrible,' she said.

'Well,' I said, 'I'd have thought he'd have the sense to back up and go round the other way, rather than just plough into it. But I expect he was rushing somewhere. You know what he's like. Like you're always the one who got to pull in by the side for him to pass.'

'Have he got it out yet?' she said.

'I just dropped him off at Ockwell's garage,' I told her. 'They'll have to get the pick-up out to it.'

Then of course she started going on about, what a pity, a lovely car like that.

'Nobody's fault but his bloody own,' I told her. 'You could see how deep it was.' I was going to say more. But I thought he must spend more money in this shop than I do, why take the chance that it gets back to him. 'Anyway,' I said, 'the car'll be all right once they tow it out, dry it off a bit. Though I expect he'll need new carpets in it.'

That was it. She started going on nineteen to the dozen about her sister up in Canton when they had the floods there last year and how every foot of carpet, every stick of furniture they had had been a write-off, three feet of water in the living-room and them huddled upstairs with boats going past in the street outside the bedroom windows almost.

'And the stink,' she said, 'when it went down.' She shook her head. 'They had mud this thick in there.' And she stretched her finger and thumb as far apart as they'd go and stared at me as if defying me to disbelieve her or as if the whole damn thing had all been my fault anyway.

'All over the floor,' she said, 'and three feet up the walls. River mud. Can you imagine the stink?'

But it was worse, she said, when it went down. Because then you didn't just have the stink but you could see what it had done as well, the damage and all that. It broke her sister's heart.

Then she carried on about the insurance and the health hazard and how you'd never believe that river water, even from a river like the Taff, and we all know what goes into that, could be so filthy, and how her sister wanted to move now, it had made a nervous wreck of her, she was afraid to live there now, and how she'd loved that little house they had and now it just wasn't the same, the whole place needed all new carpets and repapering and repainting and they only done it out the year before, and they couldn't face doing it out all over again, starting from scratch again, because it had all been ruined for them now, their little home had all been ruined, spoiled.

I had to stand there.

Jesus Christ, I thought. Talk about a house on fire. It was as much as I could do to get a nod in edgeways, let alone get five pounds of corn and a roll of baler twine out of the shop as well.

She carried on. In the end I heard the bell ping on the door, and someone else come in. She didn't stop. She just carried on talking and she never took her eyes for a second off my face, and it must have been a full minute before she not so much brought things to a close as at least paused long enough for me to look away from her and see who it was had just come in the shop or for her to take another breath.

'It was worse than a burglary,' she said (and now of course she's telling *him* as well as me). 'And I know,' she said, 'because we was burgled last December, and I thought that was bad enough. They took the portable radio, the television. Everything.'

Christ, I thought, if she starts on the burglary as well we'll still be here tomorrow, the three of us, as if we're barricaded in. They'll have to throw a smoke bomb in and storm the place to shut her up.

'Look,' I said. I started to back away. 'I better go. I'm parked in a bad spot. I only called in to see Chas.'

'Oh,' she said. 'He won't be back till after two.'

'It doesn't matter,' I told her. 'I can't wait till then. I'm in a rush.' (I'm trying to back out quick, and waiting for her to take her eyes off my face for another second so that I can just get to the door.) 'I'll call in again,' I told her. I nearly knocked a stand of seeds over as I'm turning to try and make the last five yards.

'I'll tell him you dropped in,' she said.

'Okay,' I told her. 'Right.'

I bet you will, I thought. I bet you'll tell him all about your sister being flooded too, and go through the complete list of things the burglars took as well. After you've gone through it one more time just to make sure there's nothing missing from it with that poor sod who made the worst mistake he'll make all day by coming in right in the middle of it.

I got outside. Jesus Christ, I thought. What is it, what's the reason? It's like you can't seem to get a single simple thing done some days. You can't even get from A to B without meeting some bastard who wants you to do them a favour and run them somewhere else. And while you're there you think, well, at least you can pick up a few things you know you need to save you coming in the next time, and can you even manage that? Can you, fuck. You have to run into a woman like that who got nothing to do but have people coming in and out of the shop all day, and she's talking at you like she haven't seen a human being for a year. How the hell do they keep a business going with a woman like that behind the counter? She don't even give you a fifty-fifty chance to get your money out your pocket.

So I'm standing there now wondering what to do, whether to even bother going up to Kenfig Hill or not. I'd been going to run over there to try and see that bloke breaking up them Nissen huts. I thought I might be able to pick up some of that asbestos sheeting off him cheap. What time is it? I thought. It must be getting on for two by now. Christ, by the time I get up to Kenfig Hill and back the bloody afternoon's gone too. I had half a mind to drop into the Tudor. Call the whole damn day a write-off. Like the last damn week.

I don't know, I thought. Why do I let them get me in a state like this? But it's as if there's always something or someone in your way. You got things on your mind to do, but can you do them? The hell you can. You get a week of it pissing it down so you can hardly put your foot out in the yard, and as soon as it looks like stopping for five minutes or even easing off you get roped into something else because some silly sod thinks his car's a landing craft or some other bugger's sister got mud on her carpets in the floods last year.

I crossed the street and went into the toilets by the sports shop.

I couldn't believe it. I bloody couldn't. *He* was in there. Colefax. He was standing pissing at a stall as I come in. This is never-ending, I thought.

I had to stand beside him. He looked up at me for a second and his mouth twitched.

'I think we'll have to stop meeting like this, Hopkins,' he said. 'Or people will be talking.'

'Ha ha,' I said.

We stood there side by side and looked at the white tiles on the wall in front of us and listened to the water trickling away by our toecaps. As he was shaking himself he said they'd towed the car in. An hour, old Ockwell had told him.

'Oh,' I said. 'Good.'

He put himself away. I stood there, finishing mine. I hear him walk to the sink on the wall behind me and rinse his hands and pull a paper towel out and dry them. I heard him stroll towards the door on those metal quarters in his heels.

'All the best to you, Hopkins,' he said.

I stood there looking at the two words someone had written in biro on the wall in front of me, above the tiles. Someone always does. The letters were kind of wavery on the rough surface of the plastering.

'The same to you, Mr Colefax,' I said over my shoulder.

GLENDA BEAGAN

The Last Thrush

Each evening the thrush would come. She would hear its click and thump, that sharp repeated sound, that hammer on the anvil. She could not see it. Lying here, how could she? But it was almost as if she could. See it. Be it. Be which of them though? There are two of them out there. Thrush and snail. And the air is warm and calm as the sound carries. It fills the room.

'Time for your medication, Mrs Shone. Can you manage, dear? Let me help you sit up. That's it . . .'

Her voice is too tired to move in the air that holds the sound of the thrush on the step. There it is again. Across the garden at the far end by the shed. The sound has travelled a long way to climb through the white window. And why should such a sound be comforting? It is a murderous sound. And yet there is a closeness to it. A familiar shape.

CLICK. Click. Click. Click. THUMP.

And the probing bill of the thrush scoops thickly, scoops thinly in the softness inside the shell.

Her own pain is misted but still there somehow. Constantly there in the background. Like water seeping slowly on a stone. Out there in the garden on the step of the shed the thrush declares itself. The Russian vine that half buries the shed shifts lightly like an animal in its sleep and moves its cream-white flowers.

Dr Whittaker called today. She smiled at him and the effort of the smile creased and set on her face. Is this what a death mask is? Is this what it means? How fond of him. She has grown so fond of him over the years. They are the same age. Yes, exactly. He'd just joined old Dr Garnett's practice when she was expecting Stephen. Does he ever think about Stephen? Does he ever wonder what he might have been?

And when he asked her whether she felt she needed more of the painkiller, she found, for once, that her voice could be clean and strong. It was her voice. Her own. And she was proud, not so much of the words, their meaning, though that was important too, but of their clarity, their sureness. She was still here.

'No,' she said, pulling the words up from a cool place she still kept inside her. 'No. Really.' And the smile was stuck on her face though she wanted to move it. 'I don't need any more. I'm floating about as   is. As if I'm not properly here. As it is.'

He had smiled then, touched her lightly on the arm. And he was such a big man, clumsy really, though for all his awkwardness his touch was so *bright*. And she had wanted to thank him for the deep space he made in the room. A space for breathing. How did he feel about this, about her? They had grown old together, hadn't they? Isn't it strange? And yet they were neither of them old. Not *old*. Not really. She was a long way off growing *really* old. But what did growing old have to do with dying? With this?

Dr Whittaker moved softly in the room. She saw him write the prescription. She saw him hand it to the nurse. She heard the click of his bag as it closed. And the click of that bag, so near, was somehow so much farther away than that other click, that thump on the step outside. It was ridiculous. How could she possibly know what it was like, how it felt, to be a snail being slowly eaten by a thrush?

But she did know. She felt it. Perhaps God was like a thrush. Hammering. Pounding. Probing inside the human shell. Did she believe in God? Did she believe there was anything out there? In the end?

The agency nurse is young this time. Her name is Jenny. Not a particularly earnest name, perhaps. Jenny. But she is earnest. She is young and earnest and has large capable hands. Everything she does, every move she makes, is competent, is ordered and controlled. She takes a pride in this. But now, as she moves about the old-fashioned kitchen, and to get a new kitchen to look this old, this *natural* would cost you thousands, her thoughts are neither ordered nor controlled. She is thinking about Mark. What is she going to say to him? She reaches for one of those Greek yoghurts from the fridge. Creamy. Plain. Peels off the foil lid and stirs in a little honey the way Mrs Shone likes it.

Mark, the way I feel at the moment I don't want to go to Switzerland with you. Yes, I know I've always said I wanted to go to Switzerland, and I have, ever since I was a child. And I was looking forward to it. But somehow, now, I just don't want to go.

Mrs Shone never complains. I just wish her son would come to see her more often, that's all. He's been twice in five weeks. Fleeting visits. And now he's in France, covering the run-up to the elections, so I don't suppose he'll be back till that's over. I did think it would be quite something. To be able to say I'm nursing Michael Shone's mother. And he *is* just as good looking in real life as he is on T V. It's costing him of course. All this. But I can't say I like him. And somehow I don't think she likes him either. Not really. In fact I'm sure she doesn't. That's stupid, I suppose. But there's always this awkwardness. I don't know . . .

Mark, I can't explain why I don't want to go on holiday with you. I look round this house and I see it through your eyes. *Distinctive country residence of great character set in mature gardens.*

And I don't want this woman to die.

She lies in her golden world. In the light from the window. She is not awake. She is not asleep. She is floating on a lake. Misty.

'Jenny? Are you there?'

'Yes, Mrs Shone, I'm here.'

'What's the time?' Her lips are very dry. Crusted. Jenny gently dampens them.

'Half-past five. Nearly.'

'Has it come?'

'What? What's that, Mrs Shone? I didn't quite hear you.'

'The thrush.'

'M'mm?'

'Can you hear it? Listen. That click sound. There. I'm sure you heard it then. Did you?'

'I think I heard something. Yes.'

'Go and have a look, would you? It's on the step of the shed. Thrushes have always used that step, you know. And I've lived in this house for forty-three years. How many thrushes is that, do you think? How many snails? Stephen brought me some snail shells one day, small and black with gold bands. Like enamel. I'd never seen any like that before. He was always finding things.'

'Stephen?'

Mrs Shone closes her eyes. The lids are papery thin. Transparent.

'You don't know, do you?'

'Know what, Mrs Shone?'

'Just go and look for me, would you, Jenny. On the step of the shed. Please.'

At the side of the house there are two arches. One of roses. One of honeysuckle. The honeysuckle arch has come loose from the wall, the bracket rusted through. As the warm heavy wind rises, it scrapes and rasps against the wall. The kind of noise that strums in your head. Irritating. Repetitive. But this isn't Mrs Shone's sound. It can't be. This is a noise not a sound. And the rest of the garden is hushed and sleepy with late summer and the small shift of branches. So what can it be?

CLICK. Click. Click. Click. THUMP.

Jenny follows this sharp new sound. To the shed. It is bathed in its Russian vine. Its delicacy, its leaves and cream-white flowers, contradict the stationed planks, the square window fixed with chicken wire.

And the thrush is there on the step. Sleek. Purposeful. Hammering then pausing then hammering again. First this way. Then that. Then plunging its bill into the hollow of the shell. Then looking up, its eye shining, a strand of liquid snail flesh glistening on the edge of its bill. And seeing her. Watching closely. But unafraid. Unconcerned. Softly, as she stands there, with hardly a sense that it is about to move at all, it flies, unhurried, as if in slow motion, into the low slightly browning shape of the lilac.

'I'm so sorry, Miss Dawson. I frightened you.'

'No, no. Not at all,' she says, turning, laughing. Then, 'Well, you did a bit, actually, Mr Shone. I didn't know you were there. I didn't expect . . .'

'I've just got a couple of hours. I'll be flying back first thing in the morning. How is she?'

'No change, Mr Shone. It can't be long now. Dr Whittaker called again today. She said she didn't want any more of the medication.'

'She's not in pain?'

'No. I don't think so. But she's brave, you know. Wants to stay alert. It's important to her. And I feel, perhaps I shouldn't say this, I think there's something she wants to tell me but doesn't quite know how.'

'What do you mean?'

'I wondered if you might know who Stephen is? She mentioned him . . . A child I think. Something to do with snail shells.'

In the deep web of the garden with its scents and its quiet hidden murderousness, in the earth, in the bark of the trees, in the golden tent under the damson tree where spiders abseil against the trunk on single threads, there is a strange waiting quietness.

'He was my brother. Hasn't she mentioned him before?'

'I'm so sorry. I shouldn't have . . .'

'No, Miss Dawson. Please. It's hardly your fault, is it? And anyway, it was a long time ago.'

Michael Shone's voice bears the hallmark of urgent action. Incidents accompany it. World events authorize it. War. Famine. Earthquake. That distinctive tone. Does it fit in here? Now?

Jenny tries to turn them round. Turn them back towards the house. He won't let her. Not yet.

'He was drowned. Just a week before his seventh birthday. The pond isn't there any more. All that land went for the bypass years ago.'

'You don't have to tell me. I feel I've intruded.'

'No. I think I should explain. You'll understand then. The distance. Between my mother and me. She never forgave me, you see. She kept everything. His toys. His clothes.' He smiles a strange smile that is both vivid and closed. 'And his snail shells. An ammonite. A piece of amber with a fly in it. Rusty nails. He said they were Roman. That was after some excavations in the fields behind the church. My father was away a lot so it was up to me. It was so morbid. One Christmas, I was ten, I got everything together in boxes and sacks. And I sank them. In the pond. Seemed the best thing to do, but she was so crazy, so, well, demented, when she found out I thought she'd go in after them. It was terrible. She didn't, thank God, but it was what you might call the end of a beautiful friendship. So you see, Miss Dawson, there's usually a simple explanation for these things. Don't you agree?'

Jenny looks up at his face. She looks for the hurt child that must, surely, still be there. She can't find him.

'I think we should go in now, Mr Shone. Your mother actually sent me out to look for the thrush. I don't know what I'm supposed to say to her.'

'I should think you were meant to find something, don't you? Black shells with yellow rings on them? Well, you haven't, have you?'

Upstairs in the steep house Mrs Shone carries on with her dying. Now it's on a higher note. And in a different key. The celestial thrush that is the God she can't believe in is standing by the window. He's blocking out most of the light. He's huge. Glossy. Wiping his great bill on the top of the dressing-table mirror. And now Jenny's come back. Where has she been? And now Michael. Why is he here? How strange it is.

In their nest in the lilac tree a late brood of thrush fledglings thrust their soft bright mouths into the air. On the step of the shed the litter of snail shells gathers. Cinnamon fragments as the light catches them. Mosaic splinters. But mostly plain snail grey.

CATHERINE MERRIMAN

Barbecue

It's Saturday morning and we're headed north out of Beaufort, out of the Valleys, up on to the mountain. Jaz on his Guzzi, Mitch on his Triumph chop, and me on the Z1000, on our way to Crickhowell for a drink. And to get away from our mate Dai, who's panicking back at the field – the others haven't returned from Glastonbury with the bus, and how the hell is he going to lay on a barbecue this evening without the cooking gear?

Not a soul on the mountain but we can't open up the bikes for the hordes of sheep dawdling on the tarmac, bleating and giving us the idiot eye. They've got half a county of moorland to roam across, up here, but as usual they're ignoring it. Mitch reckons it's definite proof of over-civilization, when even the sheep are scared of getting lost.

The other side of the mountain, and we're into Tourist Information Wales. Money and horseboxes and hang-gliders and not a derelict factory in sight. The little town of Crickhowell, nestling snug and smug over the Usk.

We get to the pub and down a swift ale, and we're just explaining to the landlord about the bruises on Jaz's face when the door opens and who should fall through it but the bus crowd. That's Wayne, Pete and the two girls.

'What you doing here?' Mitch bellows across the room at them, making half the bar slop their pints. Short on manners, Mitch is, but the landlord's easygoing. 'Dai's doing his nut, waiting for you.'

The girls duck down the corridor to the Ladies and Pete and Wayne push their way towards us. Pete's got his hair tied back in a dinky plait, instead of loose and ratsy. Wayne's in his he-man rig, bandannaed blond mane over acres of leather-strapped tanned flesh. They stare at the purple lumps on Jaz's face with awe. Sharp little face, Jaz had, when they last saw him. Looks like a plum pudding now. 'Shit man.' Pete looks alarmed. 'How's the Guzzi?'

Jaz tells him, like he was just telling the landlord, that the Guzzi's fine, but that he had a run-in with a couple of lads from Tredegar. Yesterday, it was. He sold them a Suzi, and it blew up before they hit Ebbw Vale. They wanted the Guzzi to make up for it, but he hid it in his mam's back kitchen, and took a thumping on the doorstep instead.

Wayne claps him round the shoulders, making him flinch – thoughtful type, Wayne is – and says he'd have been safer at Glastonbury, where it was all peace and love and a soft landing on mud.

'You there all this time?' I ask. 'Been more than a week.'

'Na,' says Wayne. 'Trouble in Bristol coming back.' He grins wide. 'This publican, he won't serve us 'cos he says we're a coach party. So I backed over his fence, accidental-like, on the way out. The cops had us for criminal damage. Got a conditional discharge.'

Jaz wonders how many hospital visits it takes to cure a conditional discharge, and I tell Wayne how Dai's got it into his head about this barbecue and wants the bus back pronto. The bus is mobile HQ – as well as the cooking gear, everyone's got equipment and spares stashed in it.

'Be back this afternoon,' Wayne promises. 'It's down the lay-by now. Just got to pick up stuff for the girls.'

They disappear after a quick jar. We don't stay long either, because Jaz's getting anxious about leaving the Guzzi in the car park up the road. It's day-tripping weather and the high street's already jumping with valley lads.

Nobody near the bikes though, except a couple of kiddies admiring the puddle of oil under Mitch's chop. Brit bikes need to sweat, Mitch says, he's a patriot. We decide we'll head back and give Dai the good news. We set off up the mountain and at the top I'm in front, revelling in the way the Z1000 powers up the gradients, when I see a dead sheep, lying at the side of the road. Fair-sized corpse, but definitely a lamb, not one of the scrawny ewes.

I flag the others down. There's no one else on the road.

'This fella weren't here when we came across,' I say. 'Did you see him?'

'He weren't here,' says Mitch. 'We'd have noticed.'

Jaz props the Guzzi and squats down to take a dekko. Barbecue, I'm beginning to think.

'How long you reckon he's been dead?' I say.

'How long you been dead?' Jaz asks the lamb, but it stays stum.

'Stick your finger up its arse,' I say. 'See if it's warm.'

'I'm not sticking my finger up any tup's bum,' Jaz says. But Mitch dismounts and says he'll do it, so he can tell his grandchildren about it when he's old, and they refuse to believe he had a wild childhood.

He pokes his finger into the lamb and says it's warm. He looks up and grins. Jaz and I grin back. We're all thinking barbecue now.

We ponder what to do next. We can't cruise into town with a dead tup behind us, even with a jacket on it won't fool anyone.

We decide to dump it in a shallow ditch a few yards from the road and go back to Jaz's place for equipment. His mam's got a smallholding this side of town. They don't keep stock now, but there's any tool you want in the sheds.

When we get there we find Lizzie all a twitter because the two Tredegar lads have been back. Jaz's mam is Lizzie to everyone except Jaz. She says the boys didn't come to the house, but she saw them with another lad in a white van, parked down the track. Jaz takes her into the front room to calm her down, and so she doesn't see us rummaging in the back shed for the axe and knives and a couple of plastic feed bags.

'She all right?' Mitch asks, as Jaz joins us in the hallway on the way out. It's not just politeness, we all got time for Lizzie. 'Cos she's always got time for us, I suppose. Jaz says she's okay now, no need to worry.

We drive like vicars on mopeds out of town with the gear stuffed down our jackets, and pootle out to where we've hid the lamb.

There's a few cars on the road now. Mitch's the largest and ugliest of us so we leave him by the bikes to glare at anyone who looks like stopping, and Jaz and I scramble over the heather to the ditch.

We don't bother to skin the lamb, because Pete used to work in a slaughterhouse and can do it blindfold, we just chop off the head and feet and gut it. I'd have left the gore there for the foxes, but Jaz's fretting about an old ewe bleating at the edge of the ditch and says it's the tup's mam and we can't leave bits of her baby lying around. I say fine – you can't argue with Jaz about mother love – just so long as he deals with dumping it later. We stuff the carcass into one bag and the head and feet and as much of the guts as we can scrape up into the other. The carcass bag straps across the tank of the Z1000, and Jaz ties the other to the grab bar of the Guzzi. Then we drive, nice and sedate, the three miles through town to Dai's.

The bus is down the field already, next to Dai's collection of rotting mechanicals. But it's changed colour since last week. Instead of blue it's sickly green, with what look like white ticks round the windows. Down the field a bit the ticks turn out to be peace doves. We bounce the bikes over the grass to where Dai, Pete and Pete's girlfriend Karin are standing by one of Dai's decomposing JCBs.

'What you done to the bus?' demands Mitch, as we prop the bikes. 'Bleeding hell.'

'You know anyone works in a chippie?' Dai asks, not listening. He still looks fraught, despite the return of the bus. He's tugging at clumps of his beard like he's plucking it. 'Need a sack of taters.'

'We got something better than taters,' Jaz says, beckoning him over to the bikes.

'Who painted the bus?' Mitch roars. 'Looks like a fucking play-bus.'

'It was to get in,' Pete says soothingly. 'They said we could park it by the Green Field if we let the kids paint it.' He tilts his head and nods at it. 'Looks okay, I think.'

Behind his back Karin pulls a face and twists her finger into her temple. Dai's standing over the Z1000. 'Jeez,' he whistles, as Jaz opens the bag, 'where d'you get that?'

'What is it?' asks Pete, coming over to look. He peers inside. 'Shit,' he says, stepping back.

'You got to skin it,' says Jaz. 'We done the rest.'

Pete shakes his head and says no way, he's become a vegetarian. But Karin rips into him and says she's pissed off with him flirting with the hippies at the festival and if he wants to become a fairy that's up to him, but he's not sodding well laying it on us.

'Okay, okay,' says Pete, with a look that suggests this isn't the first bollocking he's had over this, and agrees to skin the lamb as his last carnivorous act. Mitch gives him the axe and knives and he humps the bag up the field towards the outhouses. Karin follows him, still giving him mouth.

'Where's Wayne?' I ask.

'In the bus with Josie,' says Dai. 'Better knock first.'

'My face hurts,' Jaz says, touching his cheek gingerly. 'I need a kip.'

'You got to dump that bag,' I remind him.

'Later,' he says.

I don't press it. He's suddenly looking very weary. He's holding his shoulders funny, and where the side of his helmet's been pressed against his cheek-bone it's made a dent in one of the purple bruises. We walk over to the bus and Mitch kicks the side. Josie sticks her head out of one of the windows, pulling a tee-shirt on over her long straggly hair. 'Oi,' says Mitch. 'Jaz needs to kip.'

Josie says, 'Oh right,' and there's some scuffling and groaning inside. She opens the back door tucking her teeshirt into her jeans. She looks at Jaz's face, and winces. 'Better come inside,' she says, 'I got some aspirin.'

As they climb in Wayne hops out pulling on his boots. We start to move back to the bikes.

'You know the boys who did that?' Wayne gives a last hop and jerks his head back at the bus. He means Jaz's face. 'Any of you there?'

'Nope,' says Mitch. 'Just Jaz and Lizzie.'

'Uhuh,' says Wayne. I know what he's thinking. I'm beginning to think it too. It didn't sound so bad, the way Jaz told it, but who likes to tell it bad? And seeing how stiff the boy is, and the mess they made of his face . . . it's out of order to thump a lad, and want his bike off him as well.

'They been round to his place again this morning,' I say, with my eyes on Wayne. 'They're after the Guzzi. Maybe they'll be back.'

Wayne picks up Jaz's helmet and climbs on to the pillion of the Z1000. He grins, patting the seat in front of him. 'Let's go see,' he says.

Lizzie's pleased to see us, specially when we tell her Jaz's fine, resting in the bus. She says she hasn't seen the Tredegar boys again, and doesn't want to, and would we like some chips? Ta, we say, great; it'll be hours before Dai's cooked the tup, if he ever stops bellyaching and gets on with it. We eat the chips in the front room where we can keep an eye on the track outside. Lizzie guesses why we're watching out and says what we do's our own business, but she doesn't want Jaz getting into no more fights. She looks fierce when she says it, and I think it can't be much fun watching your son get beat up on your own doorstep.

Wayne says we're maybe saving Jaz a fight, if the boys are still after the Guzzi, and Lizzie mutters that no bike's worth getting hurt for and she wishes Jaz had just given it to them. She doesn't mean it though.

We wait an hour or so, and then Mitch says we ought to get back to Dai's to make sure he's got the lamb rigged up proper. As we leave Wayne gives Lizzie a squeeze, making her go pink and call him a wicked boy, and we tell her to lock up tight and not to expect Jaz back, because the barbecue'll go on all night.

As soon as we turn into Dai's field we know something's wrong. The fire's not even lit, Pete and Dai are shouting at each other at the front of the bus, Karin's screaming at Pete, and Jaz's sitting next to Josie on the back step with his boots off and his head in his hands like he just died.

Josie comes running over to us. 'They got the Guzzi! Just walked down while Jaz was asleep and we didn't know who they were.'

'Fucking left the key in it, didn't I?' wails Jaz. 'Drove it straight off.'

'Just as well,' Karin snaps, coming up. 'Carrying lump hammers, they were. Saw them.'

'Then why didn't you say so,' yells Pete. 'Stupid cow.'

'Thought they were a couple of Dai's mates, shithead,' Karin shouts back. 'There's always blokes in and out of here.' She's steaming with rage.

'What I want to know,' says Dai, scratching his beard and looking bewildered, 'is how they knew to come here?'

Nobody bothers to answer him, it's such a stupid question. Jaz's got the only big Guzzi in town, and everyone knows he knows Dai, and where the bus is parked. I'm thinking about what's strapped to the back of the Guzzi. No sign of a feed bag on the grass. Can't decide if it complicates things or not.

'We'll go get it back,' says Mitch, wheeling his bike round.

'I'm coming,' says Jaz, struggling to get his boots on.

Wayne gives him his helmet back and gets a spare from the

bus. I remember what Lizzie said about Jaz staying out of fights, but I reckon it's his bike and if there's four of us no one should get hurt. Wayne gets on behind me, Jaz behind Mitch. I tell Wayne about the feed bag as we bump up the field and he says, 'Uhuh,' like he's got to ponder it too.

We go to Tredegar first, the back mountain way. The way you'd go if you'd nicked a big spiteful bike and needed some easy miles to get used to it. Then up into town, round the clock tower, and cruise the streets a while. See a couple of kids on Yams and ask them if they've seen a big Guzzi with two up, but they say they haven't.

We stop in a lay-by the north end of town to decide where to go next. Jaz nods towards the Heads of the Valleys road up ahead and says they'll go for a thrash, definite, they won't be able to resist it. 'Bet they total it,' he moans.

'Which way d'you reckon?' I say. 'Merthyr or Aber?'

'Merthyr,' says Wayne. Jaz and Mitch nod. Aber way the boys'd be heading back on themselves.

We eat up the miles for five minutes or so. Big bare road, the Heads, flattened spoil heaps either side, no trees, no hedges to hide behind. Then, up at Dowlais Top, just before the road sweeps wide of Merthyr, we get lucky. There's a garage at the roundabout and on the forecourt there it is, the Guzzi, and beside it, two lads in helmets. But it's not as lucky as it could be, because parked in front of the Guzzi there's a cop car, and standing by the lads, two flat-top coppers. And shit, the feed bag's still strapped to the Guzzi.

We slow right down to enter the forecourt, and park the bikes a distance away. The cops have seen us and we don't want them nervous, so after we've propped the bikes we take our helmets off. I lay a hand on Jaz, to stop him rushing over and saying too much. If the cops know the Guzzi's stolen, and the boys tell him why, it could be in a lock-up for months while they argue about it.

Wayne's thinking the same; as we walk over he hisses, 'Don't mouth off about nothing, right?'

The cops wave us to a halt a few yards from the boys. They don't want us mixing with them, till they've sussed us out. I'm trying to see what the lads look like under their helmets, in case we need to find them later.

'What d'you boys want?' one of the coppers asks. He's a big red-haired fella. I recognize him, we've met him before.

'That bike's a friend of ours,' says Wayne, smiling at him easy. 'Just came to see how it's doing.'

The copper stares at us. Not unfriendly-like, just letting his mind tick. I look past him to the feed bag. Feet and head and guts . . . it's been a hot d.y . . .

The copper's eyes settle on Jaz. A moment registering the bruises. Then, 'You,' he says. 'You're Jason Williams, aren't you?'

'Yep,' says Jaz.

'This your bike?' He gestures towards the Guzzi.

'Yep,' says Jaz.

'You give these boys permission to ride it?'

Jaz takes a while to think about this. Then shrugs. 'Maybe.'

'That's what they say. That you said they could take it.'

'We said a spin,' I say quickly, before Jaz can foul things up. 'Not all day.'

'So you want it back, right?' The copper's voice says he doesn't believe us, he knows it's nicked, but he's not going to push it.

'Yeah,' nods Jaz, after catching my eye. 'May as well.'

'Okay,' the copper says, stepping back. 'You take it across to the others. Then you lads go home, right? That's that way.' He points back the way we've come.

We all smile and say 'Sure' and 'Right' like we're not going to cause him any trouble. As Jaz walks over to the Guzzi I call out, 'Give the boys their bag. They'll be wanting that.'

It takes a second for the Tredegar boys to grasp what we're talking about. Then they glance at each other quick. They don't know how to play it. Hope they're as stupid as they look. Jaz unstraps the feed sack from the grab bar.

'Shit,' he says, acting indignant as he lifts it off, 'you've scratched the paintwork, what d'you tie this on here for?'

The red-haired copper narrows his eyes at the lads. He's picked up their confusion, but hasn't read it right. 'What you got in there, boys?' he asks.

Jaz drops the bag on to the concrete. It hits the ground with an interesting squelch.

'It's not ours,' one of the lads says, but it comes out rushed, and even I don't believe him. Jaz says, 'Well it weren't there this morning,' as if it's nothing to him, and dusts his hands off.

As the red-haired copper squats down to the bag his mate stabs a finger at Jaz. 'Now hoppit,' he says.

We don't need telling twice. Reckon we've got about five seconds. We race over to the bikes and start them up quick, to drown out any shouts, and don't look round as we fasten our helmets. Just a peek back as we roar out of the forecourt. The bag's standing upright and open on the concrete. One of the lads has got a hand to his belly, the other's turned away, pinching his nose. The red-haired copper's on walkabout, arm across his mouth. Wish I had a camera.

We have to take it easy back to the field, we're laughing so much. Wayne keeps hitting my shoulder with his helmet. 'Oh shit,' he keeps gasping, almost knocking me off the bike. Jaz is arsing about on the Guzzi, circling all the roundabouts twice, punching the sky like he's taking victory laps. Mitch sheepdogs us at the rear, lights blazing, grinning all over his face.

And when we get back, the bonfire's lit, and Pete's got the tup spitted above it. We can smell roast lamb from the top of the field. Everyone jumps up as they see the Guzzi, and suddenly it's a celebration, not a wake. The start of a magic night: stories to tell, evidence to eat, cops to watch out for, and scores even. Best barbecue for years.

Notes on the Authors

Geraint Goodwin (1903–41) born Newtown, Powys, short-story writer, novelist and journalist. A protégé of Edward Garnett, he died of tuberculosis after leaving Fleet Street to return to the countryside. He once said, 'A Welshman has two sides to his nature. He has a strong urge to step on a platform to seek notice and applause, to hit the headlines. Some of us never conquer that; they go through life stepping on platforms. Then there is the other quality, deeper, more real – a childlike love of simple things, of the earth, of the mountains, of the home.' Goodwin's novels and short stories reflect his love of the countryside around his birthplace.

Kate Roberts (1891–1985) born Rhosgadfan, near Caernarvon, Welsh-language novelist, short-story writer and publisher. Universally regarded as one of the finest Welsh prose writers of the century. English translations of her work include *Feet in Chains* (novel, Corgi Books, 1977) and *The World of Kate Roberts* (translated by Joseph P. Clancy, Temple University Press, Philadelphia, 1991).

Rhys Davies (1900–1978) born Clydach Vale, Rhondda Valley, novelist and short-story writer. A prolific writer with an international reputation, he was long domiciled in London and once wrote: 'Writing in English, one is published in London and one has to battle with the ancient recoil of the English from Welsh life.'

Gwyn Jones (1907–) born Blackwood, Gwent, novelist, short-story writer, editor and scholar. Founder of *The Welsh Review* and co-translator of *The Mabinogion*, he was the first editor of *The Penguin Book of Welsh Short Stories*. His *History of the Vikings* brought him international acclaim.

Gwyn Thomas (1912–81) born Porth, Rhondda Valley, novelist, short-story writer, playwright and commentator. His exuberant personality, vivid language and frequent television appearances made him a unique performer but his early work, which he had difficulty getting published, reveals another side to his complex and compassionate nature.

Dylan Thomas (1914–53) born Swansea, Glamorgan, poet, short-story writer and radio playwright. The most famous of all Welsh writers, his short stories and radio plays reached an immense audience.

Alun Lewis (1915–44) born near Aberdare, Glamorgan, poet and short-story writer. He first came to prominence as an outstanding war poet but also wrote short stories, many of them dealing with army life. He died of a gunshot wound while on active service in India.

Glyn Jones (1905–) born Merthyr Tydfil, Glamorgan, poet, short-story writer, novelist and critic. He has also translated Welsh poetry and produced the first major critical assessment of Welsh writing in English, *The Dragon Has Two Tongues* (1968).

Dic Tryfan (Richard Hughes Williams) (1878–1919) born Rhosgadfan, Caernarvon, Welsh-language journalist and short-story writer. Beginning life as a quarryman, he became a journalist but his health was ruined by work in a munitions factory during the First World War. He was the author of several volumes of short stories which were praised for their economy in narrative and dialogue.

Caradoc Evans (1878–1945) born Pantycroy, Llandysul, Dyfed, novelist, short-story writer, playwright. His volume of short stories, *My People*, brought literary esteem in England, vilification in Wales. Virtually all his writing attacked Welsh nonconformity and the Welsh establishment.

Alun T. Lewis (1905–89) born Llandudno, Gwynedd, Welsh-language short-story writer and teacher. He published five collections of stories which were generally acclaimed.

D. J. Williams (1885–1970) born at Rhydcymerau, Dyfed, short-story writer, autobiographer, one of the founders of the Welsh Nationalist Party. Revered in Welsh life for his writing about 'the square mile' around his birthplace.

Raymond Williams (1921–88) born Pandy, Gwent, cultural historian, critic and novelist. One of the most influential critical voices of his time, he also published seven novels, many of them set against the background of the Welsh border country. He completed the first two novels of a trilogy, 'People of the Black Mountains' (Chatto & Windus, 1989), which attracted widespread praise after his death.

B. L. Coombes (1894–1974) born Madley, Herefordshire, essayist and social commentator. An Englishman, he came to work in the Neath Valley at the age of eighteen, married a Welsh girl and lived there for the rest of his life. His autobiography, *These Poor Hands* (Gollancz, 1939, reprinted 1974), was considered one of the most authentic accounts of mining life ever published.

Emyr Humphreys (1919–   ) born Prestatyn, Clwyd, novelist, poet, short-story writer. A Hawthornden prize winner and recipient of the Somerset Maugham Award for fiction, he is the author of *The Taliesin Tradition*, a cultural history of Wales. *Bonds of Attachment*, the final volume of a sequence of novels dealing with Wales in the twentieth century, received the Welsh Arts Council's Book of the Year award in 1992.

Islwyn Ffowc Elis (1929–) born Wrexham, Clwyd, prolific Welsh-language novelist, short-story writer and playwright. The central concern of all his writing has been the survival of Welsh-language culture.

Alun Richards (1929–) born Pontypridd, Glamorgan, novelist, short-story writer and playwright. He edited the previous edition of *The Penguin Book of Welsh Short Stories* and *The Penguin Book of Sea Stories*. The first volume of his autobiography, *Days of Absence*, was published by Michael Joseph in 1987.

Leslie Norris (1921–) born Merthyr Tydfil, Glamorgan, poet, short-story writer, Humanities Professor of Poetry at Brigham Young University, Utah. His short-story collections have won him several prizes, including the David Higham Award in 1978.

Dannie Abse (1923–) born Cardiff, poet, playwright, novelist and short-story writer. A past President of the Poetry Society, he edited *The Hutchinson Book of Post War Poets*. *There was a Young Man from Cardiff*, a sequel to his novel *Ash on a Young Man's Sleeve*, was published by Hutchinson in 1991.

Harri Pritchard Jones (1933–) born Dudley, Worcestershire, brought up in Llangefni, Anglesey, Welsh-language short-story writer and translator. His volume of short stories *Corner People* was published by Gomer Press in 1991.

Ron Berry (1920–) born Blaenycwm, Rhondda Valley, novelist and short-story writer. A former miner, he has written scripts for TV and radio. His novel *So Long, Hector Bebb* (Macmillan, 1966) is one of the few to deal realistically with boxing and he is also the author of *Peregrine Watching* (Gomer Press, 1986).

Jane Edwards (1938–   ) born Newborough, Anglesey, Welsh-language novelist, short-story writer, playwright and broadcaster. Her most recent collection of stories, *Blind Dêt* (Gomer, 1989), reveals a young girl's wry view of the opposite sex.

Penny Windsor (1946–   ) born in Cornwall, poet and short-story writer, now resident in Swansea. Her anthologies of poetry *Dangerous Women* and *Like Oranges* are published by Honno, the Welsh Women's Press.

Eigra Lewis Roberts (1939–   ) born Blaenau Ffestiniog, Gwynedd, Welsh-language novelist, short-story writer and playwright who occasionally writes in English. Her fourth collection of short stories, *Cymer a Ffynt*, was published by Gomer Press in 1988.

Clare Morgan (1953–   ) born near Monmouth, novelist, short-story writer and critic. She has contributed short stories to *New Writing*, *Planet* and *Prism*. Her novel *A Touch of the Other* was published by Gollancz in 1984.

Duncan Bush (1946–   ) born Cardiff, poet, novelist and short-story writer. His poetry collections include *Salt* and *Aquarium* and he has contributed stories to *Granta* and *The London Magazine*. *The Genre of Silence* (1987) was adapted for radio, and his novel *Glass Shot* was published by Secker & Warburg, 1992.

Glenda Beagan (1948–   ) born Rhuddlan, Clwyd, poet and short-story writer. She has contributed to *Poetry Review*, *Encounter* and *Planet*. Her volume of short stories *The Medlar Tree* was published by Seren Books in 1992.

Catherine Merriman (1949–   ) born London, poet, short-story writer, now resident in Brynmawr, Gwent. Her volume of short stories *Silly Mothers* was published by Honno in 1992 and she has contributed to magazines in England and America.